ROANOKE RAIDERS AND POWDER BOY OF THE MONITOR

Two Full Length Historical Civil War Novels

GORDON D. SHIRREFFS

WOLFPACK
PUBLISHING
— EST 2013 —

Roanoke Raiders and Powder Boy of the Monitor
Paperback Edition
Copyright © 2023 (As Revised) Gordon D. Shirreffs

Wolfpack Publishing
9850 S. Maryland Parkway, Suite A-5 #323
Las Vegas, Nevada 89183

wolfpackpublishing.com

Paperback ISBN 978-1-63977-723-5
eBook ISBN 978-1-63977-724-2

ROANOKE RAIDERS AND POWDER BOY OF THE MONITOR

ROANOKE RAIDERS

To my niece and nephew, Laura and Bruce Keene

CHAPTER ONE

I was a bright December day in North Carolina when David Scott and his father rode up the slope of the rutted road in their heavily laden wagon. The steady, rhythmical cadence of metal striking against metal rang through the woods. Micah Scott halted the mule team at the top of the rise and looked down toward the Roanoke River. "Edwards Ferry, Dave," he said quietly.

Dave looked with interest, and with a little fear, at the great metal-sheathed ship hull that seemed to squat in sinister fashion on the ways that had been set up in a cornfield on the riverbank. He had heard many rumors about the fabulously powerful ram *Albemarle* which Commander James W. Cooke, Confederate States Navy, was constructing on the banks of the Roanoke, but he had never realized just how big it really was.

Micah Scott tugged at his reddish beard. "The stories are true then," he said.

"She's a monster," Dave agreed.

The area about the ram was littered with huge balks of timber, iron plating, kegs of spikes and bolts, and all the other materials and equipment required to build a large vessel. The ground was thick with shavings and sawdust. Men worked about the piles of materials and swarmed over the huge bulk of the ram. Sledges thudded against metal and wood while a portable sawmill began to whine steadily, filling the air with the pungent odor of freshly cut pine.

Two large guns squatted near the hull. It puzzled Dave as to why there were only two guns, for he could see three gun ports cut into the superstructure of the ram: one at the front and two on the portside. He figured there must be a port at the stern and two more on the starboard side, and this meant that the ram would require six guns.

Micah Scott held the reins in his strong right hand, for his empty left coat sleeve was thrust into his pocket. He slapped the reins against the dusty flanks of the two mules and drove down the slope toward the ram. The wagon was laden with scrap iron that Dave and his father had salvaged from the wreck of Micah Scott's own little side-wheeler, the *Alice*.

They had been on the road most of the day, driving from their home near Albemarle Sound, to deliver the scrap iron. Commander Cooke was known as the "Iron-monger Captain," because nothing had stopped him from raiding every possible source in the region for scrap metal with which to finish his beloved ram. It had puzzled Dave as to why his father, a pro-Union man, had volunteered to salvage metal from the *Alice* for the *Albemarle,* but he had realized there must be some reason for his doing so. Micah Scott was a man who used foresight and method in everything he did.

Dave's father, a Marylander by birth, had met Alice Denby, a North Carolinian from the Albemarle Sound country, while he had been in the Navy, engaged in making surveys of the North Carolina coast from Albemarle Sound and Pamlico Sound clear down to Little River Inlet close to the South Carolina line. He had married Alice Denby and shortly thereafter had left the Navy. Dave had been born in Baltimore, and when he was still a small boy, they had moved to the banks of the Chowan River, which flowed into Albemarle Sound, to live in the pretty little house that had been willed to Mrs. Scott by her father.

Micah Scott had come of Yankee stock from Massachusetts, and there was salt water in his blood. A skilled pilot and seaman, he had built the little side-wheeler *Alice* to ply the waters of the North Carolina coast a few years before the Civil War had torn the nation apart. There were few men who knew those waters as well as Micah Scott knew them, and much of his knowledge had rubbed off onto Dave while on his frequent trips with his father.

The war had cost Micah Scott the loss of his wife, his left arm, and his side-wheeler. Shortly after hostilities had started, the *Alice* had been returning to Plymouth, on the Roanoke, with Micah Scott in command and his wife and son aboard. They had been to Nassau, in the Bahamas, a long run for such a small vessel, but a mighty profitable one. An excitable commander of a Confederate coastal battery had opened fire on the *Alice,* and she had gone down. Micah Scott had lost his vessel and his arm, and Alice Scott had never fully recovered from her exposure to the cold water. She had lingered on for two and a half years, and during that time she had exacted a promise from her husband that he would not bear arms against the Confederacy while she was still alive.

It had taken Micah Scott some time to decide what to do after the death of his wife, and he had finally made his decision. He meant to travel north and offer his services to the Union Navy, knowing that with his skill and experience, the lack of an arm would make little difference. But before he and David left the Albemarle Sound country, he had decided he wanted to see the great ram with which the Confederacy hoped to smash the strangling Union blockade that hovered off the coast from Hampton Roads, Virginia, down to Cape Fear, North Carolina.

Micah looked at the ram and then at his son. "You realize, of course, Dave, that if that ram is completed and sent down to Albemarle Sound, there won't be a Union vessel able to stop her from wiping out a great part of the Union North Atlantic Blockading Squadron."

"Yes, but the Union Navy has monitors and ironclads to fight her, hasn't it? "

"It does, but in my opinion, not one of them can cross the bar into the sound because of its excessive draft." Micah Scott shook his head. "Davie, this vessel is far more formidable than the *Merrimac*."

Dave's father halted the team near a great pile of rusted scrap metal. "I'll report in," he said. His calm gray eyes studied David. "You look over that ram. Commit to memory everything you can learn about her. You understand? Boys are curious and won't be looked on as suspiciously as these workmen might view a man who asks too many questions."

Dave nodded. He dropped from the wagon and sauntered over to the huge fighting craft. A lean man crawled from under the hull and brushed dirt and shavings from his clothing. "Howdy, son," he said with a smile. "Come to get a job?"

"No, sir."

The man eyed Dave's solid frame and broad shoulders. "You look hefty enough. I can use a boy to carry rivets and suchlike. How old are you?"

"Fourteen, going on fifteen, but I have to work with my father. We just brought in a load of scrap metal for the ram."

"Now *did* you? We can use all we can get. I suppose you're interested in the ram."

"Yes, sir!"

"Some baby, ain't she? A real pet. We'll clear them Yankees from our coast with her all right."

Dave looked up at the overhang of the broad hull. She had seemed big enough from a distance, but close up she looked like a gigantic dinosaur of prehistoric times.

"Yes, sir! One hundred and fifty-eight feet long. Forty-five-foot beam. Draws only eight feet of water, though; enough to make her capable of maneuvering in rivers and sounds."

"Is she all metal?"

"Nope. She's framed with solid yellow-pine timbers and sheathed with four-inch yellow pine. That octagonal shield atop the hull is sixty feet long and plated with two layers of iron each two inches thick!"

Dave whistled. "It'll take a lot of power to move a monster like that!"

"Won't be too hard. She's got two engines of two hundred horsepower each," the man said proudly.

"But why do you have only two guns? She has six gun ports."

The man grinned. "Come on aboard! I'll show you why she needs only two guns."

They clambered up a ladder and stood on the wide fore-deck. The man jerked a thumb toward the bow. "Anyways, the guns don't mean suchamuch. They're good Brooke rifles which hurl a one-hundred-pound ball, which ought to cut through them Yankee seagoing teapots, but the ram is the weapon that'll really put the fear of God into 'em."

There was a heavy-looking wooden snout projecting just below the bow overhang. "That's the ram, then?" asked Dave.

"Yep! We plan to plate it with two-inch iron. That ram will go through wood and iron like a hot knife through butter."

Dave followed the talkative foreman through the forward gun port, noting the thick iron gun-port stopper that was fastened to the gun shield in such a way that it rested on the deck when lowered.

The interior of the gun shield was a bedlam of noise and confusion. Sawdust and dust drifted about and swirled through the open gun ports. Tools, nails, bolts, plating, and balks of yellow pine littered the deck.

Dave's guide walked through the clutter, dodging busy workmen. "You see," he said over his shoulder," "them two Brooke rifles will be placed one each at bow and stern of this superstructure. But they can be drawn back and turned quickly to fire from either a port or starboard gun port. You see them curved metal tracks set into the deck? The gun carriage wheels roll on them. Clever, eh?" Dave nodded soberly. He stopped beside the big funnel that came up from the engine room below, passing through the gun shield to protrude above the armored top deck. He had heard plenty of stories about the *Merrimac,* but she had been a clumsy makeshift beside this well-designed fighting craft.

He heard his father calling to him from outside. "I have to go now," he said to his guide. "Maybe we can bring more scrap metal."

"Yep! Like I said: We can use all we can get. Maybe you'd like to sign up as cabin boy. I'll talk to the commander for you if you like."

"No, thanks," said Dave. "I have to help my father with the fishing and farming. He has only one arm."

The man clucked his tongue in sympathy. "Sho? Lost it in the war, eh?"

Dave looked away. "Yes. Good-by."

"Good-by, son. Maybe you'll see us in the sound soon enough, sinking Yankee gunboats by the dozens."

"Yes...*maybe.*"

Dave left the superstructure and clambered down the ladder. He looked up at the huge ram bow and the heavy metal plating of the gun shield as he reached the bottom. It looked as if it could do just what his guide had said: go through wood and iron like a hot knife through butter.

Micah Scott placed a hand on Dave's shoulder. "The

wagon has been unloaded. I want to get away from here as quickly as I can." There was a worried look on his face.

"What's wrong?"

"Don't look just now, but when you can, look toward that shanty near the sawmill."

As they neared the empty wagon, Dave looked back. A tall, gangling man was leaning against the side of the shanty. There was no mistaking the lank black hair and the straggling unkempt beard, the hooked nose and the piercing black eyes. "Cap'n Ranee," said Dave. "What's he doing here?"

"Blest if I know."

"He's coming toward us."

"I knew he would."

Micah Scott got up into the driver's seat. Dave felt a cold chill run down his back as he heard the thud of Captain Ranee's heavy jack boots on the ground.

"Scott!" called out Ranee.

Dave's father took the reins and looked toward Ranee. "Yes?"

Captain Ranee stopped a few feet from Dave and surveyed Dave and his father with suspicious eyes. He wore a battered slouch hat with a bedraggled ostrich feather stuck in the band. His short Confederate shell jacket was stained with grease and dirt, but the Navy Colt that was thrust through his wide leather belt was clean and shiny.

"What yuh doin' here, Scott?" asked Ranee.

"Delivered some scrap iron for the ram. Salvage from the *Alice*."

Ranee grinned, revealing his stained yellow teeth. He shifted his wad of tobacco and spat almost on Dave's boots. "Bootlickin' us Confedrits at last, eh?" he sneered.

Micah Scott looked coolly at the man. "No, and I never will."

"Ain't it about time yuh did? Livin' here in No'th Carolina and making a living off'n us loyal Confedrits.

Too bad yuh got only one wing. I'd admire to see yuh conscripted, Scott."

Micah Scott looked up and down the slouching man. "What *army* are *you* in, Ranee?"

"*Cap'n* Ranee!"

"*Captain* then. You didn't answer me."

"I'm still commanding Captain Sam Ranee's Provisional Partisan Company, Scott."

Dave's father glanced past the man. "You picked a good place to stay away from the Yankees," he said quietly.

Ranee flushed. He placed a hand on the butt of his pistol. "I got my duties here! I'm guardin' this ram from Yankee spies."

Dave's throat went dry. Sam Ranee was well known and much hated in that country. He had served for a time in Virginia, or so he said, fighting with General Lee, but no one had ever seen proof of that fact. He spent his time riding about the country running down runaway slaves, deserters, and men who spoke openly for the Union. He and his ragtag, bobtail company of guerrillas and local scum had a notorious reputation for pig- and chicken-stealing but not for much else.

"Get down off that waggin," said Ranee. "I got questions to ask yuh."

Micah Scott got down. "I'll talk to Commander Cooke," he said quietly, "but not to you, Ranee."

Ranee stepped forward. He cuffed Dave aside. Dave's ears rang as he fell back against the wagon.

Dave's father stepped in close. He jerked the Colt from Ranee's belt and threw it into a pile of shavings. Ranee threw a hard right hook toward Micah's face, but Micah Scott had been known as a first-class rough-and-tumble man in the Navy and in the Chowan River country. Micah blocked the blow with his left shoulder and hit Ranee on the jaw with a short, pile-driving blow that lifted Ranee clean from his feet and dumped him on the ground. He reached for a sheath knife, but Micah Scott moved in close and stamped his left foot on Ranee's wrist, pinning it to the ground. "Now, Sam," he said with a grin, "you wouldn't start a fight with a one-armed man, would you?"

"Fight! Fight!" a workman yelled.

Men dropped their tools and streamed toward the two men. Micah stepped back. Ranee got to his feet, and there was pure hate in his dark eyes.

A dignified-looking man hurried toward tire two antagonists. He wore a naval uniform. It was Commander Cooke. "Gentlemen! Gentlemen!" he called out.

Ranee wiped the blood that trickled from his mouth. Dave reached into the wagon and placed his hand on a short metal bar that had not been taken with the rest of the metal.

Commander Cooke looked at Ranee. "What happened?"

Ranee jerked a thumb at Micah Scott. "This man ain't no loyal Confedrit. He's a Yankee-lover. I only wanted to ask him some questions, and he hit me."

"He's lying!" said Dave.

"Shut up, you!" snapped Ranee.

Commander Cooke looked at Micah. "Is Captain Ranee right?"

"No. The man doesn't like me. He hit my boy. I disarmed him and knocked him down. When he reached for his knife, I stepped on his arm to stop him from drawing it. That's all."

There was a look of dislike on the naval officer's face as he glanced at Ranee. "This man brought metal for the ram. He came here in good faith. You had no right to annoy him, sir."

"I got my duties to do!"

Cooke raised his head. "I have not seen any orders detailing you to duty here, sir. You've done nothing but lounge around and make trouble."

Ranee shook a fist at Micah. "Yeh, but what about him? Taking my gun, knocking me down, stepping on my arm!"

"A one-armed man, *Captain* Ranee?"

The man who had shown Dave about the ram suddenly began to laugh, and in a moment every man in the crowd was roaring with laughter at the incongruous situation. An unarmed man, with but one arm, had taken a pistol away from the swaggering bully and had knocked him down with ease.

Ranee shot angry looks from beneath his brows at the laughing men; then he looked at Micah Scott. "I'm leavin' here. I ain't appreciated for what I been doin' here, and I aim to go back down south. You look out for me, Yankee-lover!" He turned on a heel, retrieved his pistol, and walked toward the shanty.

Cooke waved a hand. "Back to work, men! We can't get the *Albemarle* finished this way!"

The men drifted off, and then Cooke turned to David's father. "I'm sorry, sir. Ranee is a bully and a braggart." Cooke smiled. "Thanks for getting him out of my hair. I have been wondering how I could do it myself."

Dave's father got up into the wagon, followed by Dave. "Thank you, sir," said Micah. He slapped the reins against the mules and drove toward the rise. He looked back as they reached the top of the rise. "She'll be ready before too long," he said quietly. "She's a veritable Goliath. What did you learn about her?"

Dave related the information he had learned from the foreman. Micah Scott smiled. "You should be a Pinkerton agent," he said. "The Union Navy will be interested in your information. What do you think?"

Dave nodded. They'd be interested all right, but what could they do about it? The Union vessels in the sounds were fast and able, carrying heavy guns, but they could not stop that metal behemoth.

Micah Scott tugged at the reins. "Ranee will make

trouble for us soon enough. I want to get out of this country. Is that all right with you?"

"We're Union men, sir."

Dave looked back at the monster as they drove on. It would take not only vessels and guns of iron to stop her, but men of iron as well.

CHAPTER TWO

The sun was low in the west when Dave pulled his little skiff alongside the rickety wharf in front of his home on the banks of the Chowan. A cold January wind swept across the choppy river and thrashed the tree branches. Dave was chilled to the bone. He moored the skiff and heaved the basket of fish up onto the wharf. The yellow light shone through the dusty windows of the house.

He had been out fishing since daylight and had gone right out into the sound. He had seen Union picket boats at a distance, for Plymouth, on the Roanoke, on the south side of the sound, was in Union hands, but there were other local fishermen out on the sound, and if they should see him talking to the Union sailors, they'd make plenty of trouble for the Scotts. Only the fact that the Denbys, Dave's mother's people, had always been well thought of in that area, had saved him and his father from much annoyance by the secessionists.

Dave was lonely; he was always lonely these days. His parents had taken him out of school shortly after the war had started over two and a half years ago. Some of the older boys in the school had called him Yankee-lover and other cutting names, and there had been a few hard-fought fights. His mother and father had taught him themselves and had taught him well, and as a result he had a better education than most of the grown men in that area. He meant to go to sea someday as his father had done, and not before the mast, but as an officer or master's mate.

He opened the kitchen door and placed the fish basket inside it; then he washed himself in the bucket placed just outside the door. He drew the comb through his thick reddish hair and then went inside. His father came into the kitchen. "Davie," he said quietly, "I've sold the house at last."

The cold searching wind moaned about the eaves and rattled the windows. A shutter banged against the side of the house. The oil lamp guttered in the strong draft.

"I had to, Davie," said Micah Scott. "Your mother always seems to be here still. I couldn't have stood it much longer."

Dave nodded. His mother's invisible presence seemed to linger in the old house where she had been born and raised.

"There are only the two of us now, Davie."

"Where shall we go, Father?"

Micah Scott placed a huge wad of crumpled Confederate bills on the table. "This looks like a great deal of money, but it's hardly worth the paper it's printed upon. I gave your mother my word that I would not take up arms against the Confederacy while she was alive, but I think she understood I would go north when she was gone."

Dave looked at his father's empty left sleeve.

Micah nodded as if he understood what Dave was thinking. "I know these coastal waters better than most men. I need only one arm to be a pilot."

"I know that!" said Dave quickly.

"There are blockade-runners leaving Wilmington almost every day, Dave. They always need good seamen, and more than seamen they need good pilots. They pay well — in gold. We need that money. I can't return to the Navy and leave you penniless in some northern city. We can work our way to the Bahamas or perhaps to Halifax, in Nova Scotia, and take ship from there to New York or Boston. What do you say?"

Dave smiled. "I'm a Yankee too, sir!"

———

THERE WAS a slow drizzle of rain descending on Wilmington as Dave Scott walked along the teeming river front while killing time waiting for his father, who was trying to ship aboard a blockade-runner. The river was full of slim-hulled blockade-runners, anchored in the stream or made fast to the sagging wharves. Across the river he could hear the noise of the big steam presses as they formed bales of cotton. The wharves and warehouses were packed with cotton, tobacco, and barrels of turpentine, all prime outward-bound cargoes. Some of the runners were already loaded with bales of cotton covering the decks in several layers, leaving just enough room to enter the cabins, the forecastle, and the engine room. A crew of men was hard at work, using big screw jacks to compress the bales still further for closer packing on the decks and in the holds.

The blockade-runners would slip down the stream to Smithville and wait for the high tide over the bar to start their runs for Nassau in the Bahamas, Bermuda, or Halifax, which were the main cotton-receiving ports for eventual transshipment to the cotton-hungry mills of England.

The South was in dire need of opium, quinine, calomel, and other medicaments. The rebel armies needed rifles, caps, lead, powder, artillery pieces, and other military equipment. They needed uniforms, shoes, blankets, tents, and other impedimenta. Dave had heard it said that two million people in England were on the brink of starvation because of the loss of cotton for the mills. It was a highly profitable trade for the blockade-runners, for such items as quinine could be bought at two dollars and eighty cents an ounce in Nassau and sold in rebel ports for twelve hundred dollars an ounce. Currency could buy, at ten cents a pound, cotton that in Nassau was sold for fifty cents a pound in gold specie.

Dave had also heard it said that the rebel armies marched on English-tanned leather, wore English-made uniforms, and were largely fed on Cincinnati bacon and corned beef shipped to Nassau by Northern speculators and thence carried into rebel ports by the daring blockade-runners. Most of the runners had been built in England, and were skippered by English captains and crewed by English and Scottish packet rats. Indeed, a great many of the runners were owned by British companies, and the greatest of these was Alexander Collie Company of Glasgow.

It was necessary to give two thousand dollars in Confederate money for one dollar of specie in Wilmington. Dave's father had priced wearing apparel the first day they had been in the port and had been aghast at the costs. A pair of man's boots cost five hundred dollars while a suit of shoddy cost six hundred dollars. An overcoat of poor material cost fifteen hundred dollars. A ham cost fifty dollars, a barrel of flour was worth five hundred dollars, and tea and coffee cost one hundred dollars a pound.

But the blockade-running sailors lived high on the hog because they were paid in gold. Most of them were from Bristol, Liverpool, Milford Haven, and Cardiff, with a sprinkling of Scots and Tynesiders. Micah Scott had told Dave that many of the captains and crews were former members of the Royal Navy, some of them on leave with the blessing of the Admiralty, for the British needed cotton to save their economy. Dave had seen many of the sailors swaggering about town, with gold hoops in their ears and expensive silk scarves about their brown necks, throwing money around with prodigal hands.

But the blockade-runners had brought more than supplies and money into Wilmington. In the summer of 1862 they had brought yellow jack, and before the plague was stamped out, more than a third of the six thousand people of Wilmington had died of the disease.

Dave leaned against a bollard on a wharf and watched with curiosity a lean, buff-colored steamer that was moored, with steam up, in the stream. Her decks were piled high with cotton. Dave saw smoke drifting from the hatches and from the ventilators. A British sailor walked past Dave with a seaman's rolling walk. "Is she on fire?" asked Dave.

The seaman turned quickly. "The *Whisper*, lad? No. 'Tis the provost and his crew smoking out the holds."

"To kill rats?"

The man laughed. "No! The provost thinks there is a deserter stowed away below." He eyed Dave. "Ye're new here?"

"Yes."

The sailor lighted a cigar and puffed it into life. "I've made several trips into here. Every return voyage is slowed down by that scum of a provost poking about looking for deserters. Poor lads. They haven't a chance with that smoke filling the holds. Watch, lad, and ye'll see soon enough."

There were armed men on the decks of the *Whisper*, clad in ill-fitting, butternut-colored uniforms, leaning on their rifles. A lean man paced back and forth, peering at the companionways with a hunter's interest. There was something familiar about him. Then Dave saw the bedraggled feather on the man's wet hat and knew it was Cap'n Sam Ranee. "Ranee!" said Dave.

"Ye know him?" asked the sailor.

"Yes."

"Scum! Last voyage I saw him catch a deserter. He picked the man clean before he took him to the jail. Just a boy he was, hardly older than ye. It made me blood boil to see the lad mistreated by that uniformed jackal."

There was a shout from Ranee. A man had appeared at a doorway, gagging and coughing, blackened by smoke. Ranee whipped out his pistol and smashed the heavy barrel against the side of the deserter's head, driving him to the deck. He booted him twice and then jerked his head at his men. He picked up the unconscious prisoner and hurled him over the rail into a waiting boat. Dave looked away.

"Aye, 'tis hard on them," said the sailor.

The boat was pulled toward the wharf. Dave stepped behind a pile of cotton bales. He watched the provost drag the man to the wharf and throw him into a two-wheeled cart. Ranee swaggered about as though he had just taken a Federal gun battery by storm.

Dave turned to slip away, but the sailor gripped him by the arm. "Ye looking for a berth, lad? I'm bosun on the *Wave Queen,* and we can use a bright lad like ye for cabin boy. Pays well."

"I have to go."

"Fifty pounds a month sterling. Ye can hardly overlook that."

Ranee was close to Dave now. Dave wrenched himself free and ran for the street.

"Wait, you!" yelled Cap'n Ranee.

Dave sprinted down the street, dodging wagons and pedestrians.

"That boy's a deserter!" yelled Ranee.

Dave darted into a filthy alleyway and sprinted for all he was worth. He slipped in the greasy mud and went down. Ranee appeared at the end of the alley. Dave got to his feet and raced for the next street. A familiar figure walked toward him. It was his father.

"What's wrong, David?" asked Micah.

"It's Cap'n Ranee!" gasped Dave. "He's provost."

Micah gripped Dave by the arm and ran him toward a warehouse. They jumped inside and ran to the back of it. Boots thudded in the alley.

Micah tried the rear door, but it was locked. He pushed Dave behind some barrels. "Quiet!" he snapped.

Boots grated on the floor of the warehouse. Micah closed his right hand. Ranee appeared, blinking in the semi-darkness. Micah stepped forward and smashed a fist against the provost's jaw, driving him back against a post. Ranee drew his Colt and slammed it against Micah's head. Dave's father went down. Ranee grinned as he cocked the heavy Colt.

Dave snatched up a thick billet of wood. He darted out and threw it at Ranee. "You!" yelled the provost just as the billet caught him flush on the jaw. He went down, rolled over, and lay still.

Micah got to his feet. "Let's go," he said. "I got a berth on the runner *Phantom,* now in the stream down at Smithville, waiting to leave for Halifax. Her pilot died three days ago of yellow jack. I hired a boat to take us down. We have to hurry. They want to catch the eleven o'clock high water."

They hurried out into the street. Three of the provost's men stood at the end of the street looking the other way. Micah and Dave darted into an alley and walked toward the river. A boat was moored to a wharf, and two powerful-looking Negroes rested on the oars. Dave dropped into the boat and his father followed him. "Take the tiller," said Micah to Dave. He felt inside his coat. "Ranee won't keep us here," he said quietly. Micah drew out a pistol. "Cast off," he said. "Row as hard as you can."

"Yes, boss," said one of the Negroes. His eyes were wide in his head as he shoved the boat out into the stream. Dave took the tiller and looked back. There were soldiers walking toward the wharf. He steered the swiftly moving boat close to the gray hull of a runner, out of sight of the provost's men.

Micah Scott felt his bruised head. "Close, that one," he said, smiling. "Thanks, Davie."

The rain came down heavily as they passed the bow of the runner. It was more than twenty miles down the Cape Fear River to Smithville, point of departure for the blockade-runners.

CHAPTER THREE

The blockade-runner *Phantom* tugged uneasily at her anchor chain where she lay in the Cape Fear River just off Smithville. Mists drifted down the wide river, and there was a spit of rain in the cold air.

Dave stood on the deck outside the little cabin that had been assigned to his father. The water lapped against the thin steel hull of the runner. Now and then he could hear the scraping of a stoker's coal scoop on the iron plates of the engine room below as the black gang got up a head of steam.

Micah Scott came along the deck and stopped beside Dave. "It won't be long now," he said. "Excited?"

"Yes!"

"We'll leave in a little while. The picket boats are due back soon, and then we'll know if we can slip past the blockaders. We haven't decided as yet whether to leave by New Inlet or through the Western Bar Channel. We'll probably take the Western Bar Channel."

"Aren't both channels guarded by rebel forts?"

"Yes. Fort Fisher near New Inlet; Fort Caswell just below us here. The blockaders usually stay beyond range of the cannons at the forts. I've heard that Fort Fisher has English Whitworth guns which can throw a shell five miles at angles of twenty-five degrees. They've made quite a few hits on the blockaders."

"They can't see them at night, though."

"No. It's then that the Federals move their ships in close. They put out their lights and anchor just off the inlets. They form a sort of floating box out there, allowing just enough room for a blockade-runner to pass through into the box, and then shoot off Coston flares to light up the runner. Then it's grape, solid shot, and canister coming in from three sides, with the beach on the fourth side. Some captains prefer the beach to surrendering. They tell me the beaches are cluttered with wrecked and burned runners."

Dave swallowed hard.

"Scared?" asked his father.

"No!"

"Well...*I* am," said Micah Scott, dryly.

"The steward told me the Union seamen raid right up the river, sometimes almost as far as Wilmington."

"Yes. They have a young daredevil out there in command of a fast screw steamer named the *Monticello*. Just a short time ago he penetrated this river with a gig and a cutter, manned by only twenty men.

"They got past Fort Caswell all right and Bald Head too, without being seen, until they were northeast of Smithville. They came down-river then, as though they were rebel pickets, and landed right in the town.

"Cushing, that's the name of the *Monticello's* commander, went ashore with four or five men, in an attempt to capture General Hebert and take him out of town by means of a captured steamer, but there weren't any steamers here at the time.

"Cushing had the brassbound nerve to go right to the general's house, past the barracks of the rebel troops, only fifty yards away. But Hebert, by ill fortune, had gone up to Wilmington, and so Cushing captured Captain

Kelly, chief engineer of the port defenses, and then managed to get away.

"They slipped down the river past Fort Caswell again, hearing the drums playing the long roll to alert the troops. They made it safely to their ship.

"Later, Cushing sent a note to Fort Caswell regretting that Hebert wasn't at home when he had called."

Dave grinned. "I'd like to meet that man Cushing."

"With men like him in the blockading fleet, we haven't much to fear about the vaunted boastings of rebel superiority. Even Colonel Jones, commandant of Fort Caswell, was amused by Cushing's daring and impudence. The result of the whole escapade was a strengthening of the river defenses. Cushing received a roving commission in order to cruise out beyond the line of blockading vessels to catch inbound and outbound blockade-runners."

A seaman came down the deck and knuckled his forehead. "Captain Stewart's compliments, sir," he said, "and he'd like to see ye on the bridge. 'Tis almost time to drop down the river, sir."

Micah walked toward the low bridge. Dave walked forward to where he could see the yellow lights of Smithville dimly through the wet mist.

The *Phantom* was a racer, built in Leeds, England, and owned by Alexander Collie Company of Glasgow. She had a slender hull and outsized paddle wheels in huge housings. There was a turtleback covering over her bow, extending almost to the low superstructure. She had two short, raked masts without topmasts or cross yards. She had two slim, raked funnels which could be telescoped to shorten them. Thin wraiths of smoke drifted from them, and the air filled with the tang of Welsh coal.

Dave walked about the decks, threading his way through the aisles left between the stacked bales of cotton. The vessel had been painted completely in light gray and had a minimum of superstructure and long, sweeping lines. Even as she lay at anchor, she gave the impression of the great speed of which she was capable, for she could do fourteen knots with good anthracite feeding her boiler fires. Most of her two-hundred-foot deck was packed with cotton bales.

A hoarse command rang out from the bridge. Seamen wearing slippers or in their bare feet began to rig tarpaulins over fireroom hatches, ventilators, and companionways to exclude lights and noises. The boats had already been lowered to the decks to cut down the dim silhouette of the *Phantom*. The seamen wore white clothing, as dark clothing could be seen too easily against the light paint of the superstructure. Lookouts scurried up the shrouds to take their posts. They were paid a dollar for every sail or thread of smoke they spotted and fined five dollars if a deckman saw it first. Other sharp-eyed lookouts took their posts at the bow, on the bridge, on the paddle-wheel boxes, and on the quarter-deck.

Dave heard the muffled ringing of coal scoops on the fireroom deck plates. The anchor was hove up short, then catted. The current caught the slender hull as the paddle wheels began to turn. Smoke drifted from the two slender funnels. The lights of Smithville came up abeam and then drifted astern.

The great paddle wheels churned the salty waters into foam. There was a rhythmic coughing of steam from the exhausts. The water curled back from the knifelike prow. The *Phantom* was one of many such vessels engaged in a dangerous trade. Such an enterprise was a gamble with immense profits to the gained. They had losses too, those swift, elusive craft. Many lay wrecked off Cape Fear.

Dave had heard the blockade-running seamen laughing at the Federal Navy's "soapbox" blockade, composed of former merchant vessels, ferryboats, tugs, double-enders, and other mongrel craft, few of which could catch a swift runner like the *Phantom*. Still, as the *Phantom* slipped down the channel, Dave looked through the clinging mist and gentle rain, and felt a touch of fear within him. If men like Cushing could penetrate the stout defenses of the Cape Fear River and land in a town where a thousand rebel soldiers were stationed, they would also have enough courage and skill to stop such racers as the *Phantom*. There was no protection against the heavily shotted guns of the blockaders, and even if the runners had been armed, they would be treated like pirates for firing back. They relied solely on speed and their light coloring to escape.

A man hailed the *Phantom* from the darkness of the river and was answered from the bridge. A little steamer drifted past the vessel, and the decks held men in butternut-colored uniforms, carrying brightly polished rifles. The rebel flag flew from the taffrail. In a moment she had been swallowed by the clinging mist.

Dave went up the ladder to the bridge and peered inside. A brawny quartermaster held the wheel, peering into a funnel-like canvas cover that masked the binnacle light. It was the only light aboard beyond that of the fireboxes in the engine room. Micah Scott stood beside the helmsman, his face drawn as he peered through the wet glass before him. Red-faced Captain Donald Stewart stood behind Micah, and there was a worried look about him.

Beyond Cape Fear were the treacherous Frying Pan Shoals, notorious and dangerous, which stretched ten miles out into the Atlantic. In the channel ahead of them was "the Lump," a small sandy knoll three miles off the bar with plenty of deep water on each side of it, but the night was dark enough for even a skilled pilot like Micah Scott to be uncertain as to exactly where he was.

Dave went down to the deck and out forward of the bridge just behind the turtleback. He saw dim blue lights to starboard and figured they must be from Fort Caswell. The *Phantom* was surging and swaying as she met a stronger current. Spindrift flew back from the cleaving bow as the *Phantom* met quick surges of the sea.

They must be close to the bar now, thought Dave. He turned up his collar against the wet searching wind and peered into the darkness.

He seemed to see shadowy shapes beyond the bow. The faint slapping of the paddles and the vibration of the hull mingled with the rushing noise of the bow wash. It seemed as if the pale waters were rougher. The *Phantom* pitched and shook. There was a faint rushing noise from beneath the thin hull, and then the *Phantom* seemed to ring like a dropped tin pan as she surged across the unseen bar. The shore loom to starboard was dimly visible now as the wind shifted to part the mist. The channel mouth was more than a half a mile wide, but Dave thought he heard the faint roaring of the surf against Smith Island to port.

There were freakish tidal flows in those waters, and it was difficult enough to gauge them during daylight. At night, in the mist, it was almost like a game of blind man's bluff.

The hull began to quiver more strongly with the increased thrusting of the paddle wheels. The vessel had a draft of ten or twelve feet with too narrow a hull, and she began to roll sickeningly in the swells. Soon they would have to start the pumps, for such vessels, built as they were, leaked a great deal.

The *frash-frash-frash* of the paddles increased. Dave stared into the murk. He thought he saw something white just ahead of the *Phantom*. It seemed to be a large cutter with a crew of dark-clad men in it. He made out the dim glistening of the wet oars as the men pulled desperately to get out of the path of the speeding blockade-runner. Dave opened his mouth to yell and thought better of it. His voice would be heard for a great distance.

Suddenly the cutter seemed to be right under the knifelike prow. A man yelled from the cutter. There was a crashing noise as the runner sheared off the tough ash oars, hurling men against each other and into the bottom of the heaving boat. Dave stared over the low rail as the cutter swept past. A gun cracked flatly from the boat. Then the boat was astern. A moment later a rocket shot up from it to trace a crazy wavering course against the night sky.

Dave looked up to see dim blue fights in the distance, and he could make out the tall masts of a dark vessel not two hundred yards from the racing *Phantom*. Another rocket sailed up high into the sky. Coston flares burst into light, and Dave saw two more vessels just beyond the first one he had seen. A gun flashed and thundered.

The *Phantom* heeled hard astarboard as the darkness seemed to come alive with soaring rockets and crashing guns. She followed the surf line, just offshore, with the hiss and pound of her engines timed with the thrashing of the huge paddle wheels. The wind seemed to moan through the rigging and about the superstructure.

Dave heard again the hiss and sucking of the sand against the bottom of the hull. The vessel hit hard and rang like a church bell, and then she turned to sea again with a veil of mist between her and the blockaders.

A seaman grinned at Dave as he walked past. "'Tis all over now, me lad, and ye'll be in Halifax before too long. We've given the Yankees the slip again. Heigh-ho!"

Dave began to breathe easier. He had always felt at home while at sea, for he had been born with salt water in his veins, but this type of business was a little too risky to suit him.

He padded aft and entered his cabin. He dropped onto the bunk without undressing and lay there staring up into the darkness, feeling the sickening lift and sway of the fragile hull as the *Phantom* rushed toward the open sea.

CHAPTER FOUR

Dave opened his eyes with a start as the *Phantom* made a particularly vicious pitch followed by a snap roll. The slender hull seemed to spring upward as though propelled from below, and Dave flew out of his bunk like a great ungainly bird and crashed onto the deck. Pale light showed through the porthole. The engines were driving at full speed, and the straining hull was vibrating and throbbing violently. He pulled himself to his feet, thankful for no broken bones.

Above the pounding of the engines he heard a dull thudding noise. He put on his cap and clawed his way up the sloping deck to the door to grip the handle. Even as he gripped it, to open it, the door swung outward as the vessel made its return roll, and he was hurled clear across the deck to end up with a crash against the gunwale. Spray shot over the rail and doused him. He came up spluttering and heard again the dull thudding noise. Then something seemed to whisper over the *Phantom*.

He pulled himself to his feet. A seaman hurried past him. "Yankee blockader!" he yelled. "A fast one too! That last shot was a close one! Did ye hear it whisper of death as it passed between the funnels?"

Dave felt a little sick. That had been the rushing

noise he had heard. He looked to port. Two slender masts showed above a deep trough in the heaving waves, and even as he looked he saw a sharp bowsprit poke up, followed by a lean black hull. There was a flash and puff of smoke from the blockader, followed by a dull explosion. A cannon ball appeared magically and skipped from wave crest to wave crest only to plunge out of sight beneath the water fifty feet from the bow of the runner.

The steward appeared beside Dave. "She's fast, that one," he said in his Scots burr, "and carrying full sail along wi' her steam power, and in this half a gale too."

"Will she catch us?"

"Her? Catch the *Phantom?* Never a chance, laddie. It's thae guns that might mak' the difference. How they can shoot sae well in this broth of a sea and wi' this wind, is beyond me. One ball through a boiler and we'll blow up intae scrap metal!"

The steward wiped the spray from his bearded face. "Another hour o' darkness and we'd hae made it. Now it's a stern chase and it will be a lang one."

The blockader rode low in the water, and she had fast, trim lines. She was brigantine-rigged, with fore-and-aft sails on her mainmast and square sails on her foremast. She had one slender funnel from which streamed dark smoke.

"Aboot seven hundred ton, I'd say," said the steward.

The *Phantom* had the edge on the blockader as far as speed went, but she was making heavy weather of it, plunging into the rough seas while thick water flowed over the turtleback and poured along her decks. The pumps were pounding steadily as she fought to keep the water down in her fragile hull.

A guy wire snapped like a violin string. Water surged knee-deep past Dave and the steward. The blockader fired again as the blockade-runner turned into the eye of the wind to deprive the pursuing vessel the advantage of her sails. Splinters flew and the steward dropped to the deck. Something clanged against one of the funnels. Dave turned to see a gaping hole where his cabin had been. He could see clear through to the starboard deck. He swallowed hard. Much as he wanted the blockader to run down the *Phantom,* he now wished the straining *Phantom* would drain all the speed she could from her racing engines.

The steward stood up and placed his mouth close to Dave's ear. "If she catches us, we'll spend the rest of the war at Fort Lafayette or Fort Warren eating rats and hardtack. They'll never let yere fayther go, lad, because pilots are considered tae be too valuable to exchange."

The *Phantom* seemed to groan in agony as she plunged deeply and then rose sluggishly to meet the next sea.

"Fog bank three miles ahead," said the steward. "Pilot is makin' for it."

Dave had forgotten about his father. Now he clawed his way along the streaming deck until he reached the bridge ladder. The bow dived down, and there was a thundering crash of green water on the turtleback. He looked over his shoulder to see tons of water, flecked with white foam, bearing down on him.

"Davie! Davie! Davie!" yelled his father from the bridge.

It was the last thing he heard as the water picked him up like a chip and carried him aft past the paddle-wheel housing. The water flowed past, and for a moment he saw his father leaning from the bridge door and staring at him with a set, white face. Then another graybeard of a wave picked David up neatly and flowed with him right over the side, past the thrashing steel paddles. He went down deep into the cold water.

He ripped off his shoes and shrugged out of his heavy pea jacket. His breath was going fast, and there was a mortal fear in him that he'd come up beneath the paddles. He swam down and then outward with all his might until he could bear it no longer. He surfaced to see the slim stern of the *Phantom* a good hundred yards ahead of him, and then he went under again.

He slid off his heavy trousers as he surfaced again. He was a strong swimmer, but little good it would do him now. He saw a man hurl something over the stern. It rose high on a wave and flowed toward him. Dave began to swim slowly and steadily toward the object, conserving his strength. He heard the dull thudding of the blockader's guns now and then, but the *Phantom* was too far away from him by now for him to see if she had been hit again.

Dave looked over his shoulder. He was almost right in the course of the blockader, but she was more than a mile from him. The *Phantom* was swifter all right.

He reached the object that had been thrown overboard. It was a wooden grating, hardly enough to keep him afloat, but it was better than swimming. He rested on it. The *Phantom* was almost to the fog bank by now, and she was out of range too. The blockader fired another gun in rage and frustration just as the tattered fog bank seemed to swallow the *Phantom*.

The fog was drifting toward Dave. It might envelop him before the Union ship found him. He was cold enough from the water, but now the cold of fear settled in his body and mind. If the blockader passed him in the fog, there wasn't a chance for him to survive on the lonely tossing waters.

A shower of spray flew back from the bow of the trim Union vessel. She was still making knots toward the fog bank like a bulldog determined to come to grips with her foe. Dave could see the intricate curling design that had been picked out on the bow in gold paint. She was a beauty, low and trim, more like a yacht than a man-of-war.

The wind snapped out her flag, and it gave Dave a thrill, cold as he was, to see the Stars and Stripes once more. He could see men moving about on her wet decks as she pitched and rolled with a bone in her teeth. Her white sails seemed carved from marble, so taut were they.

She was only a few hundred yards from Dave now. He waved an arm and yelled, but all he got for his pains was a dollop of salt water into his mouth and he spluttered into silence.

The dark hull seemed to tower over him, and he yelled again. He paddled frantically to get away from the sharp cutwater. A sailor yelled from the deck, and another raced up the foreshrouds to look at him. He yelled too and pointed down toward Dave. The bow dipped deeply, showering back spray, and Dave saw the name of the vessel amidst the gold curlicues. It was the *Monticello.* He seemed to remember vaguely hearing about that vessel.

A man looked over the rail of the quarter-deck. "It's just a boy!" he yelled. He cupped his hands about his mouth. "Stand by to come about!"

Dave lost his grip on the grating as the wave made by the passage of the fast vessel flowed over him. He went down and then bobbed up again. The man who had given the commands ripped off his officer's cap and long frock coat. With his long hair blowing in the wind, he climbed to the rail and then dived cleanly into the water with hardly a splash.

The head bobbed up a few feet away from David, and he found himself looking into a bony face plastered with wet brown hair. The officer swam to Dave and held him up, treading water easily. His calm eyes studied Dave. "Take it easy," he said. "It's a nice day for a swim."

His voice gave Dave new courage. The *Monticello* had turned into the wind, and the sails were fluttering and slatting about as the powerful screw bit into the water and drove the vessel toward the two swimmers.

"What ship was that you were on?" asked Dave's companion.

"The *Phantom.*"

A wry look passed across the officer's face. "She's well named. Did we get any hits? "

"One through the cabins. There might have been others. I left her in too much of a hurry to notice any more."

"We have first-class gunners aboard the *Monticello*. Getting a hit at that range and in this sea is first-class shooting."

The blockader was close to them now. Seamen were taking in sail as the screw went into reverse and slowed the way of the ship. A heaving line shot out from the deck, and the plaited knot at the end of it struck Dave on the head. He grabbed it and felt himself being pulled toward the craft. A Jacob's ladder was heaved over the side, and he gripped it as the vessel rose on a swell. He reached the rail, and strong hands pulled him to the deck. "There ye be, all shipshape and Bristol fashion," said a hearty voice.

The officer followed Dave to the deck. "Take him to the galley and warm him up inside and outside," he said. "Dry clothing and a hot drink. Jump and make it so, Scrimshaw."

The seaman knuckled his forehead. "Aye, aye, sir!"

Dave eyed the sailor. He saw a broad, good-humored face framed in salt-and-pepper-colored chin whiskers. "Come ye with me, rebel," said Scrimshaw. There was a strong New England accent to his voice.

Seamen and gunners stared at Dave. A young sailor, about Dave's age, with a magnificently freckled face, stuck his hand below his chin and waggled it at Dave. "Fort Lafayette for you, blockade-runner," he said.

"Stow your gab, Steve Raintree," said a gunner. "The lad is chilled to the bone."

The crew were all rugged-looking men with tanned faces, wearing broad, flat hats and loose-fitting blues. The vessel was as neat and trim from a deck view as she had been from a sea view. Dave was hustled to the galley and inside it. He was grateful to get away from the cutting wind.

A huge Negro clucked his tongue in sympathy as he saw Dave shivering. He stirred a huge copper pot. "Pore little man," he said in a deep voice. "Ol' Ginger fix you up. We got good navy beans for breakus."

The pungent odor of the beans made Dave realize he had not eaten since the late afternoon of the day before. Scrimshaw stepped back and squinted at Dave. "I'll raid the slop chest. We'll rig ye out in honest Union blue, rebel."

"I'm not a rebel," said Dave quickly. "My father is as good a Union man as you, sailor."

"So? And ye on a blockade-runner?"

"I can explain that."

Ginger grinned. "I'll jes bet he kin too, Scrimshaw."

Scrimshaw shrugged. "Ye're liable to find anything in this ocean from sea sarpents to mermaids." He left the galley and slid the door shut.

"Git outta them wet drawers, boy," said Ginger, "else you'll get your death of cold."

Dave stripped himself, and Ginger handed him a big apron to cover himself. The cook ladled some beans into a bowl and handed the bowl to Dave. "Dive in, son. You had a close call, little massa. Old Davy Jones nearly got his cold, wet hands on you."

Dave ate the luscious beans and then smiled at Ginger. "Thanks," he said.

"No bother."

Scrimshaw entered the galley with an armload of clothing. "Get into these duds, boy, and jump to it. The skipper wants to see ye aft."

Dave pulled on warm drawers and a pair of floppy pants. He shrugged into the loose middy blouse and placed a flat hat on his head. There were no shoes, and he had noticed that neither Scrimshaw nor Ginger wore any. They weren't much good on a wet, heaving deck.

"Ye have the right cut to yere jib for a seagoing man," said the sailor.

"My father is a seagoing man," said Dave.

Scrimshaw grinned. "Aye, I would have thought so." He took Dave by the arm. "The skipper is waiting."

"Who was that officer who jumped in to help me?"

Ginger waved a hand. "*That* was the skipper, son."

"He left his ship to save me?"

Scrimshaw nodded. "Ye'll know what manner of man he is after ye get to know him better."

"But he's so young to be the skipper of a man-of-war!"

"Aye, he's young in years, 'tis true, but more of a man at twenty-one years of age than many a skipper twice that age."

"Who is he?"

Scrimshaw raised his head proudly. "Lieutenant William Barker Cushing, U.S.N., commanding the U.S.S. *Monticello!*"

Dave remembered the story his father had told him the night before on the *Phantom*. Cushing! The young daredevil who had almost captured General Hebert!

"Jump and show a leg!" said Scrimshaw. "Smartly now!"

They walked aft along the heaving deck which had been holystoned to almost a pure white. The vessel was neat and shipshape, with gleaming brass and taut rigging.

The sailor led the way down a ladder and along a companionway until he reached the last door in a row of doors. He rapped on it, slid it open, and knuckled his forehead. "Captain Cushing, sir, here is the lad."

Cushing was over six feet tall, of slender but wiry build, and weighed about one hundred and fifty pounds. He was drying his long hair with a towel. "You're all right now, lad?" he asked.

"Yes, sir."

"Your name? "

"David Denby Scott, sir."

"Where are you from?"

"I was born in Baltimore, sir, but I've lived most of my life on the Chowan River in North Carolina."

There was the faintest ghost of a smile on Cushing's face. "A rebel?"

"No, sir!"

"He said his father was as good a Union man as myself, sir," said Scrimshaw.

"Then he must be a good Union man indeed! Sit down, David, and tell me all about yourself."

Dave sat down on a chair and told the story of how he had happened to be aboard the *Phantom*.

Cushing paced back and forth. "You say your father wanted to go to Halifax in order to get a ship to take him to New York or Boston so that he might join our Navy?"

"Yes, sir."

The steady eyes held David's. "The war started three years ago. How is it that he did not leave North Carolina before now?"

Dave explained the loss of the *Alice* and how his father had been disabled; then he went on to tell of how his mother's lingering illness had kept his father at home. He watched Cushing as the young officer looked out of a porthole. "If you don't believe that my father and I are Union men, sir, I can tell you what we learned about the rebel ram *Albemarle*."

Cushing whirled and his eyes seemed to light up. "*What do you know about that ram?*"

"I've seen her and have even been aboard her, sir."

"Tell me everything you know about her. *Everything!*"

Both men listened intently as Dave told all he knew about the powerful ram.

Cushing looked at Scrimshaw when Dave had finished his story. "Then the rumors we have heard are true enough."

Scrimshaw nodded. "It'll be our job, sir, to stop her if we can."

Cushing shook his head. "We have no vessel powerful enough to face her in the sounds. It would take a cutting-out expedition to get her."

Scrimshaw grinned widely. "I know what the Captain is thinking about that too."

Cushing smashed his right fist into his left palm. "It should be *my* job! Who else could do it?"

"No one, sir, with the possible exception of Commander Rowan, sir."

Cushing flushed. "Yes ... he ranks me, sure enough."

Scrimshaw tilted his head to one side. "But *will* he do it, Captain? "

"I hope not."

Cushing paced back and forth as if his agile mind was already conceiving a plan to destroy the ram. He stopped and looked at Dave. "You'll have to stay aboard until we go into Beaufort for supplies. I can drop you at Roanoke Island if you like."

Dave stood up. "Begging the Captain's pardon, sir, but I did not run the blockade to sit ashore."

Cushing smiled. "Well said, lad! Scrimshaw, I place this boy in your care. I saved him from the sea and it seems as if it is up to me to take care of him now. Find him a place to swing his hammock. Have him outfitted at my expense."

Dave knuckled his forehead as he had seen Scrimshaw do. "I don't want to sit around, sir. I'm no idler. I've been to sea and can hand, reef, and steer. Can't I do something aboard the *Monticello?* "

Cushing threw back his head and laughed. "Certainly! We need a cabin boy. The last one jumped ship."

"I'll serve, sir."

Scrimshaw opened the door. "I'll take him under my wing, Captain."

They left the cabin and went up on deck. The ship was making heavy weather of it. Scrimshaw looked aloft. "Rough," he said.

"Will we run for shelter? "

"Not on the blockade, lad! We stay at sea in fair or foul weather."

The fog had blown away. There was nothing to see but a vast expanse of heaving, lead-colored water, with not another ship in sight. Dave looked to the northeast. The *Phantom* was gone and so was his father, and he wondered if his father thought of him as having drowned.

A young officer came toward them. "It seems as if we have a new recruit," he said with a smile as he eyed Dave.

"Not yet, Mister Howorth," said Scrimshaw. Scrimshaw waited until the officer passed them, and then he leaned close to Dave. "That's Ensign Howorth, one of Captain Cushing's right-hand men. He's just as keen as Cushing is to get a crack at the *Albemarle*."

Dave looked away. A feeling of utter loneliness had crept over him. He had always been with his father, and more so in the past years because of their pro-Union feeling which had left them pretty much alone in the Chowan River country. He knew his father was safe, so it wasn't so bad for him, but his father would suffer a great deal until he found Dave again.

CHAPTER FIVE

"**D**o you hear the news there, sleepers?" The loud voice of Jimmylegs, the master-at-arms, cut through the veil of sleep about Dave. He opened his eyes and saw the deck beam inches above his head. His hammock swung steadily back and forth with the surging motion of the ship.

Jimmylegs rattled his billy against the side of the ladder. "Larbolins, ahoy! Eight bells there below! Tumble up, my lively hearties! Steamboat alongside waiting for your trunks! Bear a hand there, bear a hand with your trousers! Bear a hand, my sweet and pleasant fellows! Fine shower bath up here on deck! Hurrah! Hurrah!"

Scrimshaw thrust a sleepy face from beneath his blanket. His hammock swung next to Dave's. "You feel sweet, don't you, Jimmylegs?" he growled.

"Arise, you grizzly bears and growlers!" roared the implacable Jimmylegs.

The blockader surged and pitched, making heavy weather of it. It was four in the morning, the beginning of the morning watch. "Growl you may, but go you must!" howled the master-at-arms.

"Who wouldn't sell a farm and go to sea?" asked Scrimshaw bitterly.

Dave dropped to the heaving deck and pulled on his damp uniform. He had been aboard the *Monticello* for two weeks now, standing watch with Scrimshaw and the others of the port watch. This April weather was rough and dirty off the North Carolina coast. In all that time they had not sighted another blockade-runner, but only the distant topsails of other blockaders or an occasional thread of faint smoke raveled by the strong winds.

"Oilskins today," said Frank Richmond. "It's spitting weather again."

Dave snatched up his oilskins and put them on. He hurried toward the companionway and up the ladder to the deck. Cold fingers of rain touched his face and helped awaken him fully. He looked aloft first, as all good sailors do upon reaching the deck. The *Monticello* surged along under reefed topsails, and the canvas looked as hard as marble. Water flowed along the lee rail as the gunboat drank deeply of the gray-green waves.

Scrimshaw poked his head out of the companionway and scowled. He came up on deck followed by the grumbling members of the watch. He looked aloft. "If the Bermudas let you pass," he sang out, "then beware of Hatteras!" He looked to windward. "See ye the stars, lad? See how they flicker against the dark sky? Rain or snow will follow soon."

"It's raining now," said Dave.

"Just a spit. Mark my words, it'll get worse."

"Winds in the morning, sailors take warning," said Taffy Brown as he buttoned his oilskins.

Scrimshaw looked aft. "'Tis getting cold," he said. "Fire will freeze before this day is out. But the old *Monticello* is all a-taunto. The wind's increasing. There's a fresh hand at the bellows."

"Go below the watch!" roared the boatswain.

The off watch streamed past the new watch, eager to seek the slightly comparative warmth of the berth deck.

"Man the pumps!" roared the bosun.

Scrimshaw shrugged. "'Tis ever thus. Lad, get ye to the galley for a mug-up of jamoke."

Dave walked to the galley. He wasn't really a member of the watch, but he worked with them for the experience it gave him. He was known as an idler, or one who, being at work all day, does not keep watch at night. His duties as cabin boy kept him busy enough, but he didn't intend to waste his time at sea serving officers and helping in the galley when he could gain added skill as a seaman.

Ginger was in the galley hovering over the huge pot of coffee. He handed Dave a cup. "Hungry, boy?" he asked.

"I'm always hungry," said Dave.

"They's some cut-and-come-again over there."

Dave helped himself to hard bread and cold beans, known as cut-and-come-again, food left on the table for the convenience of the crew. When he had finished eating, Ginger handed him a jug of coffee. "Jamoke for the skipper, boy," he said.

"He's up?"

"Yup. We ain't sighted a smokejack since we lost the *Phantom,* and he ain't too happy about it."

Dave took the jug and stepped out on deck. The wind caught at him and drove him reeling down the deck. He plunged down the companionway, grateful for shelter from the gale. He rapped on Cushing's door and then slid it open, knuckling his forehead as he stepped in. "Blowing half a gale, sir. The stars are flickering. Rain or snow will follow."

Cushing grinned. "I see you've been learning some of Scrimshaw Appleby's lore." He put on his oilskins and southwester. "Scrimshaw is a sure enough stick-and-string sailor. Born and raised on sailing ships, or so he claims. Whaler, fisherman, packet rat, smuggler, and man-of-warsman. He's been with me on every ship I've served on from the *Wabash* to the *Monticello.*"

Dave poured out coffee for the skipper.

"You seem to take to this life, lad," said Cushing.

"Yes, sir."

"I expected these last two weeks to make you wish you'd swallowed the anchor."

"I'm not a loblolly boy, sir. I served on my father's ship on a voyage to Nassau, and have been up and down the coast from Norfolk to Savannah."

Cushing bowed. "I apologize, Stormalong," he said with an infectious grin.

Dave couldn't help smiling. Will Cushing kept a happy ship. For his years he was more of a man than men twice his age, as Dave had heard more than one of the *Monticello's* crew say. They took pride in the young man who was known throughout the Navy as one of the most daring men of his time.

"I've made up my mind to sign on, sir," Dave said.

"Enlist, you mean? "

"Yes, sir!"

"You'll have to get your father's permission."

"I don't know where he is."

Cushing eyed David. He had grown to feel a strong attachment for this salty young man he had saved from drowning. There were younger lads than Dave serving in the fleet. "All right!" he said suddenly. "I'll sign you up, and glad to have you!"

"The Captain won't regret it. I know the sounds and rivers, sir."

Cushing studied Dave. "Just what do you mean by that?"

"The whole crew knows the Captain wants to cut out the *Albemarle* if he can get the chance. I know Albemarle Sound, Batchelor's Bay, Roanoke River, and Eastmost River like the palms of my hands by day or night, sir."

Cushing nodded. "I've heard that. But you're too young to poke into places like that. The rebels have ten thousand troops in that area thirsting for fresh Yankee blood. If they should capture you, and you being from that country, it would go hard with you, Davie."

"I'm a Union man, sir!"

Cushing grinned. "How well I know that! Stay below. It's a foul day and my weapons need cleaning. I'll talk to you later."

Dave was left alone in the cabin. He drank some of the coffee and took out the gun-cleaning materials. It was a job he loved, for his father had taught him all about guns and he had often cleaned his father's weapons and used them as well for fowling and hunting. He took Cushing's Sharps carbine from its rack. It had a leather-covered barrel to protect it from salt spray. Cushing had carried it on some of his daring forays into the tidal sounds and rivers of the coast. Dave took out the breech-block and cleaned the inside of the barrel until it glistened. He cleaned the breechblock and rubbed linseed oil into the stock. Then he stripped down the heavy Navy Colt and cleaned it. Last of all he took the ornate dress sword and wiped it carefully.

He shut the door and then buckled the gunbelt about his slim waist and slid the Colt into its holster. He hung the sword from its sling and took the carbine in his hands. He could envision himself following Cushing ashore in the dark o' the moon for some daring foray that would make his name as well-known as that of Will Cushing.

After a time, he took off the belt and hung it up, then replaced the carbine in its rack and the sword on its pegs. He was nothing but a substitute cabin boy. Not for him would be the uniform of a midshipman, a "reefer" with gold anchors on his lapels, a double row of bright brass buttons, a visored cap, and a sword.

Will Cushing was just seven years older than Dave, and he commanded a fine ship like the *Monticello,* but strangely enough, although he had attended the Naval Academy at Annapolis, he had left the Academy before his graduation, later being appointed an acting master's mate in the United States Volunteer Navy. He had served on various ships of the Home and Blockading Squadron, seeing some action, and had been appointed a midshipman. Cushing had served aboard the *Cambridge* when the *Merrimac* had attacked Union vessels at Hampton Roads and had been slightly wounded by one of her shells. In 1862 he had been appointed lieutenant and had requested duty with his friend and hero, Lieutenant Commander Flusser, the "fighting man of the North Carolina sounds." He had seen a great deal of hot action with Flusser and had later been given command of his own vessel at the age of nineteen years.

Dave had learned a great deal about Cushing during his weeks aboard the *Monticello:* that he had fought infantry close in shore with his ship; that, although he had never been known to take his own safety into account, he was extremely solicitous of his ships and his crews; that he was a strict disciplinarian and a first-rate seaman with the most loyal crews in the Navy.

Cushing had raided Confederate installations ashore, barely avoiding capture more than once, and was always in the thick of the fight. He had volunteered more than once to serve ashore as a battery commander in the Army.

Cushing had taken command of the fine and fast *Monticello* for distinguished services rendered and had taken her from Philadelphia to duty off the North Carolina coast as part of the North Atlantic Blockading Squadron, which had as its beat the coast line from Chesapeake Bay to Cape Fear.

The door of the cabin was slid open, and Will Cushing came in with dripping oilskins. "We're in for a blow, boy," he said. He eyed his weapons. "You do a good job, Davie."

"Thank you, sir."

The officer hung up his oilskins. "I'm getting bored with offshore blockading duty," he said.

"It might win the war, sir."

"Yes, but it's a rough duty. Do you realize that the entire blockade stretches for thirty-five hundred miles, from Alexandria on the Potomac, along the sweep of the Atlantic Coast to the Florida Capes, then across the Gulf of Mexico to the mouth of the Bio Grande?"

"That's a lot of salt water," said Dave dryly.

"I saw a report on blockading duty when I was in Washington last year. We of the Navy have to patrol a maze of one hundred and eighty-nine bays, inlets, and harbors. Right now we have thirty vessels off Cape Fear alone. The ships of deep draft usually anchor at night to keep in formation with a lee shore astern, shoals, contrary currents, easterly winds always blowing, with a rough cross chop set up when the ebb tide is met. Ground tackle is strained and cables snap; anchors drag and ships go aground."

"But it is successful, isn't it, sir? "

Cushing smiled. "Yes. I think we average capturing or driving ashore about seventy-five per cent of the block-ade-runners."

"But what about the *Albemarle,* Captain?"

There was a worried look on the officer's long, bony face. "The Navy has strengthened the blockading squadron off Plymouth. Torpedoes as well as obstructions have been placed at the mouth of the Roanoke River. But, as yet, we have no vessel capable of beating her in Albemarle Sound."

Every member of the *Monticello's* crew knew the obsession Cushing had of getting a chance to attack the huge ram, and they all knew he would attack it bare-handed if he had the chance.

———

It WAS dusk when a lookout spied the dim topsails of a ship. Dave stood at the rail with Scrimshaw. "A blockade-runner or commerce destroyer?" asked Dave.

"No. She's one of ours. The *Rhode Island,* I think. See! There goes her kerosene signal lantern."

Many of the crew lined the rails. They were always eager for news, as blockading duty, despite its moments of excitement, could also be mighty boring and monotonous. Virile men, such as composed the crew of the *Monticello,* could while away only so much of their time with fancy ropework, making ships in bottles, and doing scrimshaw work, which was fancy-carved work in bone or wood, from which Scrimshaw Appleby had earned his nickname. His sea chest was full of carved fans, nutcrackers, heads of men, and animals and little ships.

The signal lamp blinked out on the other ship, and a moment later the signalman on the quarter-deck of the *Monticello* began to signal a reply. *Clack-click-click* it went on until the reply was finished, and then there was an answer from the other ship. Then both ships sailed on through the darkness.

In a short time, the crew knew what had been sent from the other ship, the *Rhode Island:* the *Monticello* was to sail to Beaufort for further orders.

"Suits me," said Taffy Brown. "I've had enough of moldy sea biscuits, foul coffee, damp berth decks, and no chance of shore leave. When the war is over, I'll place an oar on me shoulder and walk inland until some rube asks me what it is I have on me shoulder, and it is there I will settle down."

Scrimshaw spat to leeward. "Yell never cut your painter loose from the Navy, Taffy."

Dave looked toward the west. The coast was out of sight and had been for days, but he was eager to get ashore to see if he could find news about his father. If

Micah Scott had reached Halifax safely, he would surely return south to learn what had happened to David.

Scrimshaw placed a hand on Dave's shoulder. "Belike ye'll hear news of your father," he said. It was almost as if he had read Dave's mind.

"I know he'll join the Navy again if they'll take him, with one arm and all."

"Aye, lad! From what ye've told me about him he is as good a man with one arm as any man with two arms."

The course of the ship was changed, and the trim *Monticello* began to beat against a strong wind as she started for Cape Lookout and Bogue Sound.

CHAPTER SIX

The U.S.S. *Monticello* lay at anchor off Beaufort. At one time, before the war, the sleepy town had been known for its fishing and cotton-shipping business, but now the streets were filled with Union soldiers and sailors. Supplies for the blockading squadron were piled high on the wharves, and Union vessels were moored to them or lay in the stream at anchor. There was a curious assembly of vessels there, and many of them had never been intended for naval use.

There were broad-beamed ferryboats carrying heavy guns. There were commercial steamers and sailing vessels that had been taken into the Navy. A tugboat from New York was set up on ways at a small shipyard for work to be done on her hull, which had taken a terrible pounding on the trip down from the north. There were swift double-ended side-wheelers of shallow draft, ideal for use in the tidal rivers, for they could go forward or backward with equal ease instead of being forced to turn around in the narrow channels.

Beaufort had been occupied by Union troops for about two years after the capture of New Berne on the Neuse River. David had been there many times on his father's vessel, the *Alice,* and he was eager to get ashore.

Cushing came down from the quarter-deck of the *Monticello*. His gig lay at the side of the ship. He looked at David. "Come ashore with me, David. We'll try to get news of your father."

"Can I enlist here, sir? "

Cushing nodded. "You're sure you want to?"

"Yes, sir!"

Cushing shrugged. They got into the gig and were pulled ashore, with Scrimshaw handling the tiller. Lieutenant Cushing got out of the boat and waited on the wharf for David and Scrimshaw. "You're fifteen now, are you not, David?" asked the officer.

"Yes, sir, just this past week."

Cushing nodded. "You'll be in the Navy within a few hours then."

IT WAS late afternoon when David walked back toward the wharves with Scrimshaw. He had been examined physically and then sworn into the United States Volunteer Navy, with Will Cushing signing his papers for him. Now he could return aboard the *Monticello* as a full-fledged member of her crew. He looked out at the fine ship. The only thing that spoiled his excitement was the fact that he had not been able to get any news of his father.

They pulled out to the *Monticello* and went aboard. Lieutenant Cushing had stayed in town, and all the officers were ashore too, leaving a master's mate in charge of the ship.

Cushing had been free with shore leave, and there was only a skeleton crew aboard the vessel. David reported in to draw his issue of uniforms and equipment, and later he carried it down to the berth deck to mark his clothing with his name.

The berth deck was empty except for Steve Raintree,

another boy, who had been the pet of the crew until David had come along. Steve had a shock of straw-colored hair and a face that seemed to be entirely composed of freckles and from which peered two intensely blue eyes. Steve was a veteran. He had been aboard the U.S.S. *Ellis* with Will Cushing when Cushing had gone up the New River to Jacksonville, the county seat of Onslow County, and raided it. They had captured two small schooners and raised the Stars and Stripes over the courthouse.

The *Ellis* had not been able to get back over the bar, and they had stayed there watching rebel watch fires along the shore. Two artillery pieces had opened up on the *Ellis,* but they had managed to drive the rebels from their position by accurate shooting with their forward eighty-pounder rifle. Later the *Ellis* had gone aground, and in the ensuing action when the *Ellis* had been shelled by rebel shore batteries, Steve had been wounded in the shoulder, but he had stayed on at his post of duty. Later they had been forced to abandon the *Ellis* and had escaped in one of the small schooners they had captured. Since that time Steve Raintree had served with Cushing.

Dave ignored the tough young veteran. He was a little older than David and a little heavier, and more than once he had hazed Dave as a greenhorn. Dave was marking his clothing when he heard the slap of bare feet behind him. Suddenly a foot capsized his ink bottle, and the black ink spread across the deck and soaked swiftly into the holy-stoned wood. Dave was aghast. It would be up to him to clean it up before the bosun saw the stain. He looked up at Steve.

Steve grinned. "Sloppy landsman," he said.

"I'm no landsman," said David. "I've just enlisted."

"We must be losing the war then. Enlisting green-horns and rebels to boot."

Dave stood up. "I've told you more than once that I'm no rebel, Raintree."

The boy raised his head. "Try and stop me," he said.

"I don't want to fight."

"I figured you wouldn't."

"If Jimmylegs catches us, we'll have to go before the mast."

"He ain't aboard, sonny."

They stood there watching each other. Then Steve placed a bare foot on the spilled ink and began to spread it around as much as possible.

It was too much for David. He shoved the boy back against the side of the ship. Raintree grinned again. Suddenly his right first shot out, catching Dave on the jaw and dumping him neatly right on top of the wet ink. Dave got up slowly. Steve had a wallop like a kicking mule. Before Steve could get his hands up, Dave was upon him, battering away with both fists.

Steve was stronger than David, but Dave had the speed on him. Dave circled, throwing punches from all angles, hitting Steve twice for every blow he took in return. They separated. Blood flowed from Steve's nose, but he was still full of fight. He rushed David and drove him full across the deck to the portside of the ship near a square opening that let in the wind and sun. Dave went down, hitting his head against the side of the ship. He slid down onto the deck.

Steve danced about, throwing punches and looking fierce with blood running from his smashed nose. "Get up, *rebel!*" he cried. "I ain't through whipping you yet!"

Dave felt his jaw. "You haven't whipped anybody yet," he said quietly. He stood up and raised his fists.

Steve launched a ferocious attack, and Dave was hit three times before he got the range and shook the boy with a hard right hook. Steve jumped back, shook his head, and then rushed David, with his head down and both fists battering away. Dave hit him once on the side of the head and then stepped aside to avoid being driven helplessly against the side of the ship. Steve plowed on, right through the opening, and yelled in horror as he felt nothing but air beneath his churning feet. He struck the water with a tremendous splash.

Dave couldn't help laughing, battered as he was. He looked down at the water. Steve came up, gulping air. "I can't swim too good!" he yelled, and then he went under again.

Dave peeled off blouse and trousers, poised himself, and then dove cleanly into the water. He went down deep and saw a dim, struggling figure close to him. He reached out and gripped Steve by his shock of yellow hair. He swam upward with one arm and broke the surface, pulling Steve's head out of the water. "Don't struggle," he warned.

A heaving line shot down from the deck, and Dave gripped it. He saw a boat pulling toward them, and in the stern was Jimmylegs, the tough master-at-arms. They were pulled into the boat and climbed dripping to the deck.

"What is this?" roared Jimmylegs.

The two boys looked at each other.

"Get below, you lubbers!"

They went down the ladder to the berth deck, followed by Jimmylegs. He placed his big fists on his hips and bent head forward. "Well?" he demanded. "Who spilled that ink?"

"I did," said Dave quietly.

"Then what happened?"

Steve raised his head. "I..."

Dave stepped forward. "I spilled the ink. Raintree got excited and fell overboard. I went in after him. That's all, master-at-arms."

Jimmylegs looked from one to the other of them. "So? That's the truth, Raintree?"

"I..."

Dave spoke up again. "It's the truth, sir."

"Fine pair of lubbers! What's the Navy coming to?

Spilling ink on the deck! Falling overboard! I should have you up before the mast for this!"

Scrimshaw came down the ladder. "I'll help them clean it up, Jimmylegs."

The master-at-arms nodded. "I want that deck spotless before mess!" he bellowed; then he left the berth deck.

Scrimshaw eyed the two dripping boys. "What happened to your nose, Steve?" he asked.

"Fell up a mast, Scrimshaw," said Steve.

Scrimshaw nodded. "I'll get some cleaning materials." He went aft along the berth deck.

Steve looked ashamed as he eyed Dave. "I'm sorry," he said. He fingered his nose. "You carry a wallop like a hundred-pound columbiad," he said.

Dave grinned. He thrust out a hand. "Shipmates?" he asked.

Steve smiled and held out his hand. "*Shipmates!*"

———

IN THE DAYS that followed Dave's fight with Steve, he was kept too busy to think very much. The rigging of the ship had to be set up tighter. Sails were taken down and mended. He learned the use of sailor's palm and needle under the skilled tutelage of Sails, the sailmaker, who was responsible for much of the training of boys and green hands.

Working on the intricate rigging was quite a chore. Dave learned the uses of fids, serving mallets, toggles, prickers, marlinespikes, palms, and heavers. His hands toughened with the work. Betweentimes, he learned how to serve the guns and keep them bright and clean. He pulled an oar in the big cutter and also spent some of his free time teaching his new shipmate Steve how to swim better.

The days went by swiftly, and one day Steve and Dave

took out the small gig under sail to look at some of the other ships moored off Beaufort.

"There's a double-ender I ain't seen around here," said Steve as he came about and bent his head under the shifting sail.

Dave looked at the vessel that was churning toward them. She was a fast side-wheel steamer, with one tall funnel and two masts, schooner-rigged, and her sharp prow had been fitted with a heavy-looking bronze beak for ramming.

"I see her name," said Steve as he eased the sheet. "The *Sassacus*. I've heard it said she's the fastest double-ender in the fleet."

The *Sassacus* slowed down, and then her paddle wheels went into reverse to help slow her way. She coasted easily toward shore, and then her anchor went down and she swung with the current.

The boys sailed closer to her. "She carries four Dahlgren guns for broadsides and two Parrott rifles," said Dave.

Steve grinned. "My, my, but you sure are the gunner's mate, though."

"What's the news, matey?" yelled Dave to a seaman who stood on the deck of the *Sassacus*.

"Trouble on Albemarle Sound," said the seaman. "The *Albemarle* came down the Roanoke to Plymouth and passed the obstructions. Our shore guns had little effect on her. She met the *Southfield* and the *Miami* in the river."

"What happened then?" asked Steve.

"Our two vessels were lashed together, the idea of Commander Flusser, of the *Miami*, so that he could get the ram in between his two vessels so as to have her at a disadvantage. But the ram eluded them and rammed the *Southfield* and sank her.

"Commander Flusser pulled the lanyard of one of his forward guns, but the nine-inch shot merely bounced back from the plating of the ram and killed him. The crew of the *Miami* tried to board the *Albemarle* but were driven off, and the *Miami* retreated."

Dave looked at Steve. "Flusser dead. What will Captain Cushing think? Flusser was his shipmate and hero."

The seaman spat into the water. "When the fight was over, the rebel general Hoke attacked Plymouth, and with the help of the ram, he captured the town along with sixteen hundred Union men and twenty-five pieces of artillery. The *Albemarle* is queen of the sound now. We have nothing to stop her."

A man came aft to where the seaman was standing. He had only one arm, the right one, and Dave's heart leaped within him. "Father!" he yelled in delight.

Micah Scott rushed to the rail and thrust down his arm. Dave gripped it and was pulled easily up onto the deck. Micah Scott had tears in his eyes as he bear hugged David with his arm. "I never thought I'd see you again," he said softly.

"What are you doing here?"

"I'm master's mate on the *Sassacus,* newly assigned. I got to Halifax, then took ship for New York, and the train to Washington. I was appointed master's mate, and I requested duty in this squadron. They sent me to the *Sassacus* and here I am."

They went to the galley to get coffee, trailed by Steve. Dave told his father everything that had happened, but he hesitated to tell him he had enlisted.

Micah Scott tugged at his beard. "I'll send you up north to Baltimore," he said. "Your aunt will take you in and send you to school."

Steve grinned. "After he gets his discharge," he said.

Micah Scott stared at Dave. "You enlisted?"

"Yes, sir."

"A child like you?"

Steve grinned. "Some baby," he said.

Dave looked up at his father. "How old were you when you went to sea aboard the old *Constellation?*"

"What has that to do with you?"

"How old?" persisted Dave.

"Sixteen!"

Dave shook his head. "You were thirteen, Dad, and you know it."

Micah Scott looked away. "All right ... all right. I knew you'd enlist someday."

"I'm on a good ship, sir. The *Monticello.* Lieutenant Cushing commands her."

"That wild daredevil? He'll get all of you into trouble from what I've heard about him."

Steve touched his left shoulder. "Yeh," he said dryly.

Micah Scott stood up. "I'll have you transferred aboard the *Sassacus,*" he said.

Dave opened his mouth and then shut it. He didn't want to leave the *Monticello,* and his good shipmates Scrimshaw, Steve, Taffy Brown, Frank Richmond, Ginger, and above all, Will Cushing, but he knew his father would have his way.

"Got to keep an eye on you," said Micah.

"Yes, sir."

"Get back aboard your ship. I'll be over to see Mister Cushing later today."

They cast off from the *Sassacus,* and not a word passed between them as they tacked toward their ship. They made the gig fast to the *Monticello* and clambered aboard. Steve looked at Dave. "I'm happy for you, shipmate," he said, "but I hate to see you leave the *Monticello.* This old tub won't be quite the same no more."

CHAPTER SEVEN

The *Sassacus* tugged gently at its anchor with the flow of the tide in Albemarle Sound. Seven Union vessels in all were anchored in the sound. In addition to the *Sassacus* there were three other double-enders, the *Mattabesett,* the *Wyalusing,* and the *Miami.* There was the *Commodore Hull,* a converted ferryboat with heavy armament, and two gunboats, the *Whitehead* and the *Ceres.* All of them formed the little squadron of tough old Captain Melancton Smith, who had been sent to the sound by Admiral Lee to stop, as best he could, the threat of the formidable *Albemarle* should she venture down the sound.

Dave Scott vigorously polished one of the four nine-inch Dahlgren guns of the *Sassacus.* He had been kept busy enough on the double-ender since he had left the *Monticello.* The *Sassacus* was commanded by Lieutenant Commander Francis A. Roe, and that bearded officer and gentleman kept a taut and happy ship.

The squadron lay off Bluff Point almost midway in the stream between the low shores. The May sun was bright and cheerful. The sun glistened from polished gun barrels and the brass fittings of some of the vessels. An officers' meeting had been called, and the commanders and officers of the squadron were all aboard the *Mattabesett*. Their gigs were moored alongside the double-ender, and every seaman and gunner in the unit kept an eye on her. Rumors were rife aboard every one of the vessels. Something was in the wind.

Assistant-Surgeon Holden stopped beside David. "You'll wear that gun barrel clean through, Davie," he said.

Dave stepped back and looked at his handiwork. "Sponge me dry and keep me clean, and I'll fire a shot to Calais Green," he said, patting the thick barrel of the Dahlgren.

Holden grinned. "We may have to use all our guns before too long," he said.

"Sir, do you think we'll go in after the *Albemarle?*"

"More likely *she'll* come out after *us,*" said the surgeon dryly.

"One against seven?"

"Yes, one ironclad, with heavy Brooke rifles and a massive ram against wooden ships."

Gigs were pulling away from the *Mattabesett*. The sun glistened from the wet oars as they dipped and rose steadily.

Holden filled and lighted his meerschaum pipe. "My nose for battle tells me we won't have long to wait to sniff gunpowder."

Dave nodded. The crew of the *Sassacus* were acting busy at their various chores, but their eyes were on the gig carrying the officers of their vessel. Just the week before, on April 29, the *Albemarle* had brought back a steamer that the Confederates had captured on the Alligator River. On her trip to pick up the steamer she had chased off a Union gunboat. The whole affair had stung the Union squadron which had controlled those waters for so long.

The *Albemarle* had picked up the steamer and some corn barges and had returned triumphantly back to

Plymouth, while the Union vessels had stayed miles away near Roanoke Island, unable to do a thing to stop her. She was queen of the sound now, and there wasn't a Union vessel capable of stopping her.

Things had been going from bad to worse for the Navy. They had lost their coal at Plymouth and had requested coal from General Ben Butler, the politician turned soldier. Butler had outlined a plan whereby several small Army gunboats would "run down" the *Albemarle*, but there had been a bitter controversy over whether the Army or the Navy should have jurisdiction over the gunboats. Butler, in a fit of pique, had refused to give the Navy enough coal to keep steam up, and when they had protested, he had told them to go to captured Plymouth and get their coal stores back from the rebels.

Butler had stoked the fire of controversy by blaming the Navy for the loss of Plymouth. Butler had ideas of replacing Abraham Lincoln as the Republican candidate for the fall presidential election and would do anything to build up his reputation.

The gig pulled alongside, and the captain got up onto the deck of the *Sassacus*. "Mister Mayer," he said to the young ensign, "have the crew fall into quarters. I wish to address them."

The bosun's pipe shrilled at a command from Mayer, and the crew fell into line. Dave stood in the rear rank. His father stood between Acting Master Boutelle and Chief Engineer Hobby.

Captain Roe folded his arms across his chest. "Men," he said, "we have news that the *Albemarle* may soon come down from Plymouth. The duty of this squadron is to stop her. Our plan of attack is for the larger vessels to pass as close as possible to the ram without endangering their paddle wheels, deliver their fire, and then round to for a second discharge.

"The smaller vessels are to take care of some thirty armed launches that are expected to accompany the ram.

The *Miami* will carry a torpedo to be exploded under the *Albemarle,* and a strong net, or seine, to foul her propeller.

"You gun captains must watch your chance to get a shot into her ports when they are open. It will take timing and skill, but you can do it.

"We must be careful to avoid being run down as the *Southfield* was. The fore- and after-pivot Parrott rifles must aim for the roof, ports, hull, and smokestack to seek a weak spot.

"We will go into action with each man armed with cutlass and boarding pistols in case we get a chance to close with her. We have a three-ton bronze beak on our prow and the swiftest ship in the squadron, and it is my intention to close with her and sink her."

The crew broke into spontaneous cheers. Dave warmed to them. He had never forgotten his shipmates on the *Monticello,* but now the crew of the saucy *Sassacus* rated just as high with him.

Roe held up his hand. "The plan of battle is for the squadron to advance in two lines. The first line will be led by the *Mattabesett,* followed by the *Sassacus, Wyalusing,* and *Whitehead.* The second line will be led by the *Miami,* followed by the *Ceres* and the *Commodore Hull.* All vessels will carry nets and lines and will to try foul the *Albemarle's* propeller, but the *Miami* is to have first chance at her with her net. Ramming is optional..." Here the officer smiled, and every man on deck knew what he was thinking about; the *Sassacus would* ram, and be the first to do so if at all possible.

The crew was dismissed. Acting Master's Mate Micah Scott beckoned to his son and then walked aft with him. "This will be a dangerous action, Davie. I know better than to try to get you off this vessel. Younger boys than you have fought and died on the decks of the ships of the United States Navy. What is your post?"

"Powder monkey on the forward pivot gun sir." Micah Scott paled a little. "Well, it can't be helped." It was time for noon mess, and they parted. Dave ate with his mess-mates, and there was very little talk among them. Dave had once heard about the patriotic speeches men made to one another on the eve of action, but he heard none of them in the messroom of the *Sassacus*. The only thing he noted was the lack of appetites among his messmates.

———

By THE MIDDLE of the afternoon the *Sassacus* was ready for action. The awnings had been housed and the decks cleared of anything that might splinter and kill or wound men. Boarding nets had been rigged along the rails, leaving gaps where the guns poked their black muzzles over the sides. Shell, solid shot, and canister were placed near the guns. A gunner's mate was busy placing grenades where they would be handy in case of a close-in action.

Dave walked aft and looked at the six other vessels of the squadron. They were all ready. Wisps of steam drifted from their tall smokestacks as engineers got up steam. It was May 5, 1864, and 3:30 in the afternoon.

Dave thought of the many times he had plied those waters in the little and dainty *Alice*. He had poked into many of the sound inlets in his little skiff and knew them well, but he had never imagined in his wildest dreams that he would be serving aboard a Union warship in those waters, waiting for one of the most formidable armored vessels in the world to poke her nose down the sound.

He leaned against the jack staff and thought back on the *Albemarle,* with her solid pine framing and sheathing plated with four inches of iron; of the two powerful Brooke rifles with their hundred-pound projectiles; of the solid wooden ram plated with two-inch iron; and of the two powerful engines that would drive the ram toward her wooden-hulled opponents. "Like a hot knife through butter," he said aloud.

"You talking to me, boy?" asked the gun captain of the port after nine-inch Dahlgren gun.

"No."

The gunner patted the breech of his charge. "Let me at that blasted rebel iron pot," he said.

"She might not come after all."

The gunner looked up the sound. "No?" he said quietly. "Look."

A streamer of smoke was rising to the west, and two other smaller streamers showed behind it.

"Beat to quarters!" called out Lieutenant Commander Roe from the foredeck.

The young drummer of the *Sassacus* ran to the quarterdeck and raised his sticks. Then he began to beat the long roll, steadily and loudly. In a moment the drums aboard the other vessels began to thud and rumble.

Coal scoops rattled in the fireroom of the double-ender. Thick black smoke began to rise from the smokestacks of the Union squadron. A signalman aboard the *Mattabesett* began to wave his flags.

The crew of the *Sassacus* took their stations. The anchor was broken free from the bottom, hauled up, and catted. The paddle wheels began to turn slowly, holding the craft against the strong current.

The *Mattabesett* began to forge ahead, followed by the *Sassacus* and the others. They began to move toward Sandy Point.

"Cast loose and provide!" came the command.

The gun crews prepared their charges for action. Powder bags were rammed into the gaping muzzles followed by the projectiles. Riflemen climbed up into the rigging, carrying bags of grenades.

Dave was at his position near the forward Parrott rifle under the command of Ensign Mayer. He wet his dry lips and fought down a queasiness in his belly. He glanced back to where his father was stationed near the wheel.

Micah Scott knew those waters like the palm of his right hand.

"There they are!" said Ensign Mayer.

The ram looked like a huge, slab-sided turtle, and there wasn't a sign of life aboard her. Black smoke gushed from her stack, and the Confederate flag snapped in the breeze, half obscured by the billowing smoke. Behind the ram were two other vessels, one of them much smaller than the other.

"The big steamer is the *Cotton Plant,*" said a gunner.

"I think the little one is the *Bombshell,*" said Dave.

Lieutenant Commander Roe raised his field glasses. "The *Cotton Plant* is loaded with troops," he said quietly.

The *Mattabesett* edged toward the southern side of the sound. The line followed her, with the frash-frash-frash of the paddle wheels and the puffing of the steam exhausts getting louder and louder as they gained speed. The water was calm, with hardly a ripple, and the prows of the vessels going into the attack cut cleanly through it, casting long foamy wakes behind them, while the *Albemarle,* with its broad heavy hull, seemed to be piling water up ahead of it as it pushed on.

The gunners of the *Sassacus* stared at the immense ram. Loaders, shotmen, tacklemen, and trainers were ready. "Look alive!" roared Ensign Mayer. The ram's forward gun-port stopper had dropped to the deck, and the snout of a Brooke rifle appeared. The puff of smoke showed almost as though by magic, followed by the heavy thud of the gun. The shell smashed close to the pivot rifle of the *Mattabesett,* cutting away rails and spars. Men dropped to the deck as though flung there by an unseen giant hand.

The ram forged on toward the *Mattabesett,* firing steadily. The double-ender skillfully eluded her while opening fire with her guns. The shock and roar of the discharges echoed across the water.

The *Sassacus* was next in line. A broadside from the

nine-inch guns blasted out, and the projectiles clanged against the iron carapace of the *Albemarle* and bounded harmlessly into the air.

"Pivot gun, fire!" commanded Ensign Mayer.

The gun captain jerked the lanyard, and the Parrott roared defiance. Stinking smoke blew back over the gun crew, and the one-hundred-pound solid shot bounced from the sloping roof of the *Albemarle*.

"Run in!" yelled the gun captains of the broadside guns.

Tacklemen sprang into action and heaved until the guns ran back. Sponge-rammers plunged into the smoking throats of the Dahlgrens and pulled clear. Powder bags went in, followed by the projectiles.

"Stand clear!" the gun captains commanded. "Run out! Fire!"

The Dahlgrens spat flame and smoke and then reared back in recoil against their hurters. The veteran crews had no time to look at the monster they were fighting. They were regulars, skilled and disciplined. It was load and fire, run in, reload, run out, and fire again in a hades of foul smoke, roaring guns, and the splintering smash of shells.

Dave darted forward with a powder bag as the pivot rifle blasted off. Again the projectile bounced from the *Albemarle* like a rubber ball. It was uncanny; the hulk of the ram, with not a man in sight, fired steadily from her ports, like a great mechanical monster, while the steady gun crews of the *Sassacus* stood on the open deck with nothing between them and hundred-pound shot but their sweat-glistening skins.

Now the whole Union squadron was engaged at close quarters, with the swift double-enders racing in and then sheering off after firing to avoid hitting one of their mates.

The *Albemarle* plowed astern of the *Sassacus*. The *Sassacus* heeled well over as her helm was swung hard aport. The little *Bombshell* appeared through the drifting smoke, and the *Sassacus* took her under fire, hulling her many times.

The after-pivot rifle of the *Sassacus* had not fired as yet.

The raging gun captain swung up onto the rail and flourished his pistol. "Haul down your flag and surrender, or we'll blow you out of the water!" he roared.

The rebel flag came down swiftly.

"Drop out of action and anchor, *Bombshell*," ordered Lieutenant Commander Roe.

The *Bombshell* drifted astern until she was clear of the battle, and her anchor plunged down into the water.

The *Sassacus* was about four hundred yards from the ram. The *Albemarle* had evaded the *Mattabesett* and now lay broadside to the *Sassacus*.

Lieutenant Commander Roe saw his chance. He turned to Acting Master Routelle. "Lay her course for the junction of the casemate and the hull!"

Four bells rang out in the engine room. The *Sassacus* charged forward, with a plume of thick black smoke streaming from her smokestack. No guns were fired. All eyes were on the ram.

The gap closed, with water purling back from the ram prow of the *Sassacus*. "All hands, lie down!" commanded Roe.

Dave hit the deck, gripping a powder bag. He could see the huge carapace of the ram through an opening in the railing. He wanted to look away, but the sight fascinated him.

Then the *Albemarle* was within a few feet of the racing *Sassacus*. The double-ender struck with a crash that shook her hull like an earthquake. The *Sassacus* careened, and Dave slid down to the port rail and nearly overside, but a brawny gunner gripped him by the arm and pulled him back. "No time for a swim, messmate," he said with a grin.

The *Sassacus* quivered from stem to stern. The swift plashing of the paddles showed that the engines were unharmed. Dave peered at the ram. A port stopper dropped, and a gun was run out. He could see the gun crew inside. The gun blasted off, and the shell crashed through the flimsy hull of the *Sassacus*. Splinters flew like knives through the smoky air.

The ram moved ahead, twisting the shattered prow of the double-ender. One of the ram's guns was run out and discharged ten feet from the side of the crippled *Sassacus*. There was a shattering roar from below, and steam and hot water gushed up on the canted deck of the *Sassacus*. The overcharged boilers released their contents with banshee screeching that drowned out the roaring of the *Sassacus'* well-served guns.

Rifles rattled from the shrouds of the double-ender. Grenades dropped on the top deck of the ram and exploded as harmlessly as so many firecrackers. The *Sassacus* surged heavily to port.

"She's sinking!" a gunner yelled.

Roe cupped his hands about his mouth. "All hands, repel boarders on starboard bow!"

Dave jumped to his feet and jerked his heavy cutlass from its scabbard. Men rushed up from below, armed with cutlasses and pistols. Some of them had been seared by the escaping steam, but they were ready for further battle.

The *Sassacus'* guns flared through the clinging smoke and steam, hammering away at the iron monster. Projectiles bounded up into the air and splashed into the water.

Dave looked back over his shoulder. There was no sign of boarders, and to send men atop the grated deck of the ram would have been madness. He saw the other ships of the squadron in the distance, lying still in the water while the fighting *Sassacus* carried on the unequal battle alone.

The *Miami* closed in but was yawing and veering badly. The *Wyalusing* was signaling that she was sinking.

"Powder!" screamed Ensign Mayer at Dave.

He snatched up a powder bag and thrust it into the hot muzzle of the big pivot rifle. The ram fired, and the blasting hurled the gun captain and Ensign Mayer to the deck.

The Parrott was depressed and aimed right at the hull of the *Albemarle.* Dave snatched the lanyard from the deck and jerked it. The gun leaped back, and the deck was covered with smoke. "Run in!" yelled Dave. "Load!"

Mayer stood up, holding his head. The gun captain lay unconscious.

"Run out!" commanded Dave. "Stand clear!" He jerked the lanyard again. The projectile smashed against the hull of the ram and shattered. Shards of metal flew back onto the deck of the *Sassacus,* and one of them cut across Dave's left thigh. He felt something warm run down his leg.

Ensign Mayer thrust Dave aside. "Good work, boy! I'll take over! *Powder!*"

A seaman carried the signal books to the rail to hurl them overboard. The *Sassacus* would go down; she *had* to go down. Then she drifted astern of the ram, firing incessantly and taking heavy blows in return from the after port of the *Albemarle.*

The other ships opened fire again. The Confederate colors were shot away. "She's struck!" cried Dave.

But the *Albemarle* was still full of fight, and she kept giving back as much as she took. The fire of the Union vessels became more dangerous to each other than to the ram.

The *Albemarle* was moving slowly away. Her smoke-stack was riddled with shot. The *Miami* shot in to explode her torpedo to no avail. She threw over her net, but it did no good. Then slowly and stubbornly the ram moved up the sound, followed by the Union vessels pouring shot and shell at her. Thick smoke billowed from her riddled smokestack. Dusk was falling over the sound as she fled toward Plymouth.

Dave dropped to the deck and ripped back his trouser leg. The thigh was gashed and bleeding profusely, but it wasn't a serious wound.

A seaman came forward. "Davie," he said, "your father wants to see you."

Dave looked up quickly. "Why?"

"He's been wounded."

Then Dave heard the groaning and screaming of wounded and scalded men, and more fear than he had experienced in the battle came over him. The decks were littered with splinters and chunks of wood and metal. The bronze beak at the prow was twisted and almost torn away. Powder-blackened men dropped wearily beside their guns. The smoke drifted off with the wind. But the *Sassacus* was still afloat, though badly damaged. It would be a long time before she was fit for duty again.

Dave hobbled aft. Ensign Mayer gave him a hand. "Boy," he said, "I'll see to it that you get something for your handling of the gun when I was knocked down."

Dave did not answer. His father had suffered enough from the war; it was more than cruel that he should be hurt once more.

CHAPTER EIGHT

The July heat beat down on the wide, dusty streets of Washington. A battery of horse artillery trotted down Pennsylvania Avenue. One of the gunners glanced at Midshipman David Scott as he waited to cross the street. "Hey, sonny!" he yelled. "Ain't you pretty far from salt water?"

"About as far from salt water as you are from the Army of Northern Virginia!" Dave replied.

"A good answer," a quiet voice said behind Dave.

Dave whirled and looked into the smiling face of Will Cushing. "Sir! What are you doing here in Washington? "

Cushing winked. "I'll tell you in private while we have lunch together." He eyed Dave. "A real 'reefer' now? Midshipman Scott, no less. I heard about your part aboard the *Sassacus*. Admiral Lee promoted you for distinguished services rendered, I hear."

Dave flushed. "Every man aboard the *Sassacus* did distinguished service, sir."

Cushing nodded. "How is your father?"

"Not too well. He was struck through the right shoulder by a splinter, and the muscles were damaged. It would have been bad enough for a man with two arms to have been hit so, but he could not use his right arm at all for a time."

"And you, Dave?"

"I was slightly wounded and was sent with my father to the Naval Hospital here. When he was convalescing I was ordered to duty at the Navy Department." Dave shook his head. "I'm still there, running errands, filling out forms, filing papers, and doing other chores that just make me sick."

"Is your father here now? "

"No, he is with his sister in Baltimore."

"I see. Let's go to Willard's Hotel, and I'll tell you why I'm here."

They walked toward the hotel and Dave looked up at his hero. "How's Scrimshaw, and Steve Raintree, and Ginger? What about Ensign Howorth? How's the old *Monticello?* Did you run down any more blockade-runners?"

Cushing laughed and held up a hand. "One at a time. One at a time."

———

WILL CUSHING SHOVED BACK the dishes to clear a space on the tablecloth. He took out a pencil and began to sketch Albemarle Sound and the mouth of the Roanoke River. "Your old friend, the *Albemarle,* is moored at Plymouth, which, as you well know, is eight miles up the Roanoke from the sound. A mile below the ram is the wreck of the *Southfield,* with the hurricane deck still above water and with a guard of rebel soldiers aboard it."

Cushing was sketching in details as he talked. "We still do not have an ironclad with shallow enough draft to be able to cross Hatteras Bar and enter the sound to go in after her. Admiral Lee will risk no more wooden vessels, such as your *Sassacus,* to fight her again. It took us a month of spy work to locate exactly where the ram is moored.

"It was decided there was but one way to go in and get her, and that is, with a small-boat raid to cut her out and capture her or blow her up."

Dave leaned forward. It had always been Cushing's one desire to get at the ram that had killed his friend and hero, Flusser.

"Commander Steve Rowan was asked to undertake the expedition, but he refused, saying he did not think the command was practical. Secretary of the Navy Gideon Welles and Gustavus Fox, Assistant Secretary of the Navy, went down a list of possible commanders for the expedition without picking out a man. Admiral Lee sent for me and asked me if I'd undertake the task."

"Foolish question," grinned Dave.

"I haven't forgotten Charley Flusser," said Cushing grimly.

The officer leaned forward. "I suggested two plans. One was to approach the *Albemarle* through the swamps with a party of about one hundred men. We would carry an India-rubber boat that might be inflated to torpedo the ram. The second idea was to use two very small low-pressure steamers armed with torpedoes and howitzers. One of them could dash in and attack, covered by howitzer fire from the other, which in turn would go in if the first boat failed."

Dave whistled softly.

Cushing ran his pencil across the white cloth, up the sound to the Roanoke, and thence to the place where he had marked the position of the ram. He stabbed the pencil down so hard that he broke the point. "It can be done!" he said.

"And you're here in Washington for that purpose?"

"Yes!"

"And has the plan been OK'd by the Secretary of the Navy?"

Cushing tapped his coat. "I have orders here in my pocket to proceed forthwith to the Brooklyn Navy Yard to purchase suitable vessels for the operation!" Cushing smiled. "Gustavus Fox wasn't too enthusiastic about the operation, but I talked him into it. He thinks he's sending me to my death."

Dave wet his lips. "Sir, I know those waters almost as well as my father does. I'm sick of shore duty, riding convoy on papers and ink bottles. Let me go with you, sir!"

Cushing leaned back in his chair. "You've already seen your share of danger, Davie."

Dave sat up straight. "I'm big enough and old enough to do a man's work. I know small boats and the Albemarle Sound country. Let me go with you, sir, at least back to duty with the North Atlantic Blockading Squadron. You have influence in the Navy Department."

Cushing grinned. He leaned across the table and gripped Dave's shoulder. "All right, Davie! You can go with me to New York as my aide. I can fix it up. We *Monticello* shipmates ought to stick together." He stood up and reached for his officer's cap.

Dave took the stub of pencil and sharpened it. He ran lines through the drawing Cushing had made on the cloth. "Best not to leave this around where anyone might figure out what it is."

Cushing eyed him. He placed his cap on his head. "You know, Davie, I think you're going to be of some use to me on this expedition after all."

Dave wasn't too worried about Will Cushing's being turned down. He had had friends in the Navy Department since before the war, and his splendid record during the war had marked him as a man to be watched. They knew what he was capable of, and they would never have picked him out for the hazardous *Albemarle* expedition if they had not thought he was probably the most suitable choice for it.

———

THE BROOKLYN NAVY YARD was a bedlam of confusion, thought Dave, as he walked through it with Will Cushing. It sent his thoughts back to the December day when he had seen the ram *Albemarle* for the first time. But there was a great deal of difference between the trampled cornfield on the banks of the Roanoke River, where the ram had been built, and the bustling Brooklyn Navy Yard, where things were sparked by Yankee drive and ingenuity.

There were naval vessels of every type at the yard: screw sloops, screw gunboats known as "ninety-day" gunboats because of the rapidity with which they were built, double-enders such as Dave's old ship the *Sassacus,* single-turreted Monitor-type vessels, double-turreted monitors of the *Monadnock* type, propellers, side-wheelers, rams, ironclads, tinclads which were so-called because of their thin armor, frigates and ships of the line of the old sailing-ship navy, mortar-vessels, and the usual small craft necessary for the successful operation of a navy. It was these last in which Will Cushing was interested, and armed with his orders from Gustavus Fox, he was allowed to poke into every part of the yard in his quest.

The yard was a place of organized confusion. It was piled high with guns, spars, sails, anchors, blocks and deadeyes, coils of cable and lines of chains. There were sail lofts, carpenter shops, foundries, gun sheds, paint shops, and shops of many other types.

Will Cushing and Dave spent their time amidst the smaller craft. There were gigs, wherries, cutters, whaleboats, launches, and steam launches, and it was the last of these that narrowed down the search, for Cushing had not been able to find suitable rubber boats for his expedition.

A number of open picket boats were being built, and

Cushing selected two of them. They were built of wood and had copper-sheathed bottoms, forty-five feet long and nine feet six inches in beam, and drew about three and a half feet of water. They had low-pressure boilers and small but powerful engines turning small propellers.

Dave was kept busy running his legs off on errands for Lieutenant Cushing, and he learned the hard way what was meant by a leg man.

Cushing planned to fit each of the launches with a twelve-pound howitzer to be placed in the bows. The torpedo device that was to be used was the invention of Engineer John L. Lay, of the Navy, and had been introduced by Chief Engineer W. W. Wood. It was a rather complicated device, but it was the only one that could possibly be used, and so Cushing accepted it for his expedition.

Dave accompanied Lieutenant Cushing to a secluded place on the Hudson River. They tested several torpedoes. The device had many defects and had to be kept in perfect condition. It could be exploded well enough if one had the leisure to do it —which would be far from the case in an attack on the *Albemarle*.

Dave had a mechanical turn of mind that he had inherited from his father, and he studied with interest the way the torpedo would be carried by the launches and how the device would be fired.

A boom, or spar, fourteen feet in length, was rigged out on the starboard side of each launch, and attached to the bluff of the bow by a gooseneck hinge. A topping lift was attached to the free end of the boom and thence run up to a stanchion placed in the center of the launch forward of the boiler. There was a block or pulley at the top of the stanchion, and the topping-lift line passed through it to a small windlass situated in the bottom of the boat. By this means the boom could be swung out and raised or lowered as required.

The torpedo itself was attached to the free end of the

boom by means of an iron slide or socket. The torpedo could be detached from the slide by means of a lanyard, or heel jigger, which pulled out a pin, allowing the torpedo to float upward from beneath the water, and in the case of the attack on the ram, the idea was to do this under the hull of the vessel.

The torpedo itself was rather complicated. It was pointed conically at the lower end, and more than half the case was filled with powder, with a metal tube running through it, and had an air chamber at the upper end. At the air chamber end of the torpedo was a grapeshot, held in place in the tube by a pin which could be detached by another line or lanyard once the torpedo was in proper position.

When the grapeshot was released, it dropped down through the tube to the tip of the torpedo where a percussion cap was placed on a nipple. The weight of the grape-shot exploded the percussion cap which in turn exploded the powder charge.

When the boom was not in use, it could be swung around by means of a stern line and made fast to the side of the launch. To use the apparatus, the torpedo was put in place, the spar was swung forward and lowered under the water to the desired position, and the pin lanyard was pulled to release the torpedo and allow it to float upward; then the device was fired by drawing steadily on the lanyard which held the grape-shot pin in place.

Cushing himself planned to position and fire the torpedo, and Dave couldn't help wondering how a man could make all the complicated maneuvers of positioning and firing the device while under cannon and musketry fire and exposed in an open boat. For the first time since he had known Will Cushing he began to have grave misgivings.

———

IT WAS a warm September day as Dave stood on the wharf looking down on the two trim launches, fresh in their new paint, and with their engines and boilers unsullied by use.

"Ahoy, reefer!" a familiar voice called from behind Dave.

Dave whirled. Scrimshaw Appleby was walking in his rolling gait toward Dave, carrying his sea bag over his shoulder. He was girt with a thick leather belt, from which hung cutlass and Navy Colt, and he carried a Sharps carbine in his free hand.

Dave gripped the old sailor so hard he gasped for breath. "Easy, matey!" he said.

"What are you doing here?"

Scrimshaw looked down at the two launches. "I talked Mister Howorth into letting me come along to take one of these two smokejacks south."

"An old stick-and-string man like you?"

Scrimshaw dropped his sea bag. "I'm stick and string all right, but I ain't *old,* matey!"

"Who else is coming along?"

Scrimshaw scratched in his beard. "Ensign Howorth is in charge of Picket Boat Number One, and Ensign Andy Stockholm of Number Two. I'm to go in Number One, along with Acting Third Assistant Engineer Bill Stotesbury, First Class Fireman Sam Higgins, Landsman Lorenzo Deming, Landsman Hank Wilkes, Landsman Bob King, and Midshipman Davie Scott."

Dave nearly fell into the filthy water. "*Me?*"

"Yep."

"What about Lieutenant Cushing?"

Scrimshaw shook his head.

"You mean he isn't to command the expedition after all?"

"I didn't say that! I just saw him near the gate. Says to tell you he got a leave en route, and is going home to Fredonia for a spell, while we take the boats down to

Albemarle Sound. He'll join us at Hampton Roads, I think. Last thing he told me was to take care of you."

"How will we go?"

Scrimshaw sat on a bollard and looked down at the two launches. "Smokejacks!" he said in a sour voice. He spat clear over them. "We take the canal route to Chesapeake Bay. First we go through the Delaware and Raritan Canal, then to Baltimore by way of the Chesapeake and Delaware Canal. Stop at Annapolis, I think, and then take off for Hampton Roads."

"Quite a trip, Scrimshaw."

Scrimshaw spat again. "I don't know, Davie. Howorth and Stockholm are brave men and good fellows, but they ain't exactly what I'd call seamen. They ain't even good mud pilots, far's I'm concerned. That's why they sent old Scrimshaw along."

"Yep," said Dave dryly.

Scrimshaw looked up at him with a cold eye. "Just because you tried to sink the *Albemarle* singlehanded and got promoted to 'reefer' don't prove nothing. I mind the time we fished you out of the Atlantic. You wasn't so biggety then, matey."

Dave grinned at his old shipmate. "I can hardly wait to see you sitting beside a launch boiler under a cloud of soot and smoke, trying to look like old Stormalong."

Scrimshaw waved a hand. "I'll suffer," he said gloomily. "I got a message for you from an old shipmate, Davie."

"Who?"

"Acting Midshipman Steven McAllister Raintree."

Dave stared at him. "Steve is a 'reefer' too?"

"Yup. Pretty soon I'll be the only able seaman left in the whole U.S. Navy, the way they're promoting all you wetnoses. Anyways, Steve says I should tell you, if I see you, that he's looking forward to having you on the *Monticello* again. That boy is sure restless. It'll be a rough day for the Navy when you two lubbers get together."

CHAPTER NINE

Midshipman Dave Scott held the tiller of Picket Boat Number One and steered her into the quartering swell of Chesapeake Bay. Now and then a dollop of water flew over the canvas dodger Scrimshaw had rigged over the bow, and splattered the boiler and engine. A skein of smoke rose from the stubby smokestack and drifted to leeward as Sam Higgins stoked the firebox.

Point Lookout lay far behind them, and somewhere in the mistiness about it wallowed Picket Boat Number Two, with a failing engine. Ensign Howorth, in charge of Number One, had decided to press on, thinking too much time had been lost already.

It had been a rugged trip thus far. Both boats had crossed the Lower Bay and had put into New Brunswick, New Jersey, the entrance to the Delaware and Raritan Canal. Here they had stopped for repairs, for Number One had sat on the rocks at Bergen Point while Number Two had been aground nearby on a sandspit. Both launches had been hauled out of the water for repair to their copper bottoms, and for repair to the hole in the bottom and the damaged keel of Number One.

They had taken aboard a pilot at New Brunswick and

had left for the Delaware River, reaching Baltimore via the Chesapeake and Delaware Canal. At Baltimore, Dave had seen his father and his aunt and had assured them he was only returning to blockading duty aboard the *Monticello*, for his new mission was a secret one.

On the way south to Annapolis, Number One's engine had failed, and she had been taken in tow by Number Two. The next day they had set out with Number One still in tow. A strong southeast wind had driven them into a harbor on the Eastern Shore, where Number One's engine had been repaired. From there they had run into a southwest wind which forced them into the West River.

The picket boat plunged and wallowed in the cross chop. Scrimshaw came aft and squatted beside David. "Now, Davie, with a spar and a few yards of canvas I could steady this smokejack. She wallows like a tin pot in a little sea like this. I'm beginning to wonder if we'll ever make Albemarle Sound."

Scrimshaw had been right when he had said that Howorth and Stockholm were not seamen. They were willing enough, fine fellows and brave as lions, but the handling of small boats just wasn't in their line.

"God willing," said Scrimshaw gloomily.

They were all filthy dirty and burned by the sun, and the heat of the boiler and the laboring engine hadn't helped much. But Dave was happy. He liked the sea and he liked small boats. He did much of the steering, for the others, with the exception of Scrimshaw, were pretty lubberly at it. They'd let the boat veer and waver so that she'd wallow in the cross chops. None of them had learned how to meet the motion of the boat with the tiller. Dave was like Scrimshaw in his preference for sail, and someone should have thought of rigging the boats temporarily with a standing lug or perhaps a sliding gunter rig, but it was too late now.

Will Cushing was supposed to meet them at

Hampton Roads after his leave in his home town of Fredonia, New York. Dave wondered if he had told his widowed mother of the hazardous expedition to which he was committed. She had already lost one heroic son at Gettysburg.

Dave looked astern, hoping to see the telltale thread of smoke that would show that Number Two was following them, but there was nothing to see except the drifting mist and the dingy sails of a fishing boat that was wallowing toward the East Shore. Dave began to have his doubts about Cushing's chances of success. One boat was already having more than its share of troubles, and Dave's boat was laboring along toward Fortress Monroe ready to stop working any minute. But Will Cushing was the kind of man who would paddle up to the *Albemarle* in a canoe and throw rocks at it if he thought he could harm it.

———

ENGINEER BILL STOTESBURY wiped the sweat from his grease-smeared face with a wad of waste and looked at Dave. "I think she's all right now, reefer."

Dave nodded. When they had reached Fortress Monroe, they had been challenged by a patrol boat and then had been towed to the wharf. Ensign Howorth had gone ashore to see if Will Cushing had arrived, to report to him about the missing Number Two, while Scrimshaw had gone to draw rations, coal, and water with Landsmen Lorenzo Deming and Henry Wilkes. Landsman Robert King was busy cleaning up the launch, while Fireman Sam Higgins was cleaning out the fire hole. They were all tired, and drugged from loss of sleep, but there wasn't time to sit around and worry about it.

"Here comes Mister Cushing," said King.

Will Cushing looked pale and drawn. Despite his wiry strength, he suffered a great deal from colds, and it wasn't unusual for him to lose ten pounds in weight every winter. He smiled and waved his hand at the little crew of Number One, and then looked out across the dancing waters of Chesapeake Bay. "No sign of Number Two?" he asked quietly.

"None, sir," said Dave. He had been looking in that direction all morning.

Cushing leaned against a piling. "How is the engine, Stotesbury?" he asked.

"Fine, sir!"

"That's good news in any event. I've arranged for quarters for all of you in the fort."

"Why, sir?" asked Dave.

Cushing made an impatient gesture. "Admiral Lee has been relieved as commander of the North Atlantic Blockading Squadron. Admiral David Porter has taken his place."

"So?" asked Stotesbury.

Cushing grinned wryly. "Admiral Porter has no high opinion of me. He has said more than once that I have more luck than ability. I am to leave here within the hour aboard a tug to look for Number Two."

The men looked at each other. They could see that the young officer was worn thin and tired.

Cushing straightened up. "I wanted to go on with one boat, but the admiral refused to let me."

"Let me go out on the tug, sir!" cried Dave.

Cushing shook his head. "*I* am to go. That's specific."

The officer walked a few steps and then turned. "You're ready for sea, Stotesbury?"

"Yes, sir."

"Good. Get some rest."

They watched him walk slowly toward the fort.

"It's a shame," said Stotesbury.

Sam Higgins spat over the side. "The willing horse does all the work."

"What's the matter with Porter anyway?" asked Landsman King.

"Who knows?" asked Stotesbury. "I know one thing: Mister Cushing isn't well. Why don't they let him alone?"

"There's a war on," said Dave quietly.

They all looked at him.

———

LANDSMAN HENRY WILKES held up his hand. "Hold it!" he yelled excitedly.

Stotesbury reversed the engine, and the launch lost way and then began to move backward. Will Cushing stood up from where he sat beside Dave in the stern sheets. "What is it, Wilkes?"

"The canal is blocked, sir!"

The sluggish waters of the Chesapeake and Albemarle Canal lapped gently alongside the launch. Cushing and Dave made their way forward, leaving Scrimshaw at the tiller. They had left that morning, October 20, from Norfolk, via the canal, to make their way to Albemarle Sound.

Rocks and small-boat hulks had been dumped into the canal. Cushing stared at the obstructions. "We can't get over or around that," he said.

Dave shook his head. Cushing's search for the missing Number Two had been fruitless, and Admiral Porter had finally allowed Cushing to proceed toward Albemarle Sound with the one launch. Cushing had a dispatch in his coat pocket from Admiral Porter to W. H. Macomb, commanding the squadron in the North Carolina sounds, to the effect that Cushing be given the additional men he needed to carry out his mission. Porter had added that he had no great confidence in Cushing's success, but he had ordered Macomb to give him all the assistance in his power and to keep boats ready to pick him up if he failed. If Cushing failed, Macomb was ordered to attack the *Albemarle* if and when it appeared and to keep attacking it even if he lost half his vessels.

Will Cushing bit his lip. "We passed a creek two or three miles back that might allow us to circumvent this obstruction. Turn her around, Scrimshaw!"

It was getting warm, and the heat of the boiler made the boat almost impossible to stay in.

Will Cushing drew out his revolver. "Load and prime," he said.

The men picked up their carbines. They checked their Colt revolving pistols and loosened their cutlasses in their sheaths. This was dangerous country, half controlled by roving bands of rebel partisans and militia and half controlled by occasional Union patrol boats.

Wilkes jumped up and thrust up an arm. "Milldam ahead!" he called out.

Dave looked at Cushing. There was no sign of emotion on the young officer's lean face.

Dave looked at the bank. "There's a tidemark, sir," he said. "The water will rise."

Cushing nodded. He slapped Dave on the shoulder. "I'll make a seaman out of you yet," he promised.

The sun glinted from the brass barrel of the howitzer in the bow as Wilkes slewed the weapon to cover the wooded shore.

Cushing looked at the sky. "About an hour until dusk," he said. "We might make it then."

They sat silently in the boat, watching the tide rise slowly, until Cushing stood up and said: "All right, Stotesbury! Davie, take the tiller."

The launch chugged forward, with David steering for a low place he had noted. As they reached the top of the dam, the rest of the crew jumped over the side and gripped the gunwales to force the heavy craft onward. The bottom scraped and dragged and then plunged into the deeper water on the far side.

"So far, so good," said Cushing. "Slow speed, Stotesbury."

They were only half a mile from the dam when the

launch drove hard aground. The weary men went over the side into the knee-deep water and threw their weight and strength into an effort to get the launch afloat again, but it was no use.

Cushing leaned against the side of the launch. "No sense in killing ourselves," he said. "Get some sleep. I'm going ashore to look around. Any volunteers to go along?"

"I'll go, sir," said Dave.

"Count me in too," said Scrimshaw.

They took their carbines and waded ashore. Cushing led the way through the scrub pines.

The wind moaned softly through the woods as they reached a rutted sand road. "Listen!" said Scrimshaw tensely.

They stopped on the road and listened. They could hear a dog barking from the south.

They padded through the timber and brush until they saw a dim yellow light. "Scout around to the west, Davie," said Cushing. "Scrimshaw, you go east. I'll go straight in. If there are soldiers there, retreat and meet me back at the road."

Dave threaded his way through the brush with his carbine at full cock. The odor of wood smoke came to him. The dog was barking louder now.

Dave saw a ramshackle barn. Beyond it he could make out the creek. There was a low house on the creek bank. A man had come out of the back door, with a shotgun in his hand, and was standing with his back toward Dave, looking to the north.

Dave eased forward and placed the muzzle of his Sharps against the man's back. "Stay where you are," he warned. "Who's in the house? "

"No one."

Dave shoved the carbine forward. He let down the hammer to half cock and then cocked it again. "You're sure?"

The man dropped his shotgun and raised his hands. "Yes!"

Dave whistled softly. Cushing and Scrimshaw came toward him. "Take a look in the house, Scrimshaw," he said.

The dog began to howl. "Quiet, Prince!" said the man.

The dog shut up and went into his kennel. Scrimshaw came out of the house. "No one there," he said.

"Do you have a boat?" asked Cushing of the man.

"Yes, a flatboat."

"Good! We'll borrow it."

They walked down to the creek and got into the flatboat. Dave urged the man ahead of him. Scrimshaw cast off and poled the flatboat along the quiet creek.

They reached the launch and began to unload the coal into the flatboat. When they had finished, they horsed the howitzer into the flatboat. "Get some sleep," said Cushing. "King, you take first watch, and guard this man."

Dave awoke at dawn. Wilkes was standing guard. They awoke the others, and they all went over the side, including the sullen farmer, and shoved the launch into deeper water. The sun was up by the time they had transferred the coal and the howitzer back into the launch. They poled the flatboat to the farm and left it and the man. He stood on the bank watching them and then shook his fist. "You'll never make it, Yankees!" he yelled.

Scrimshaw placed his right hand under his bewhiskered chin and waggled it as he shook his carbine with his other hand.

They reached the Chesapeake and Albemarle Canal again, this time well past the obstructions. "Clear sailing now," said Scrimshaw.

———

IT WAS three days after their experiences at the milldam when Stotesbury stood up on the gunwale and stared ahead. "Patrol boat," he said.

The others looked ahead with reddened eyes. They hadn't seen a soul, friendly or otherwise, in two days. A small side-wheeler was puffing toward them. The Stars and Stripes flew from the jack staff.

"Ahoy, there!" yelled Cushing.

The side-wheeler slowed down, thrashed into reverse, and then coasted easily toward the launch. "What boat is that?" hailed an officer from the bridge.

"Picket Boat Number One, Lieutenant William Cushing, commanding!" called out Wilkes.

"We've been expecting you! How did you get here? "

"Through the canal," said Cushing.

"The canal! Are you mad? Thirty miles of that canal are not guarded by Union forces! Every man who lives along it is a Confederate sympathizer, and there are rebel patrols all along there."

Cushing grinned. "I thought that man who *lent* us his flatboat wasn't too happy!"

"Where are you bound?" called out the officer.

"Roanoke Island," said Cushing.

"Heave them a line," said the officer to a seaman. "We'll be more than pleased to tow you, sir."

The heaving line shot out and was taken by Wilkes. He drew it in and with it the fight hawser that had been attached to it. He made it fast around the bitts in the bow of the boat. Stotesbury shut off the hissing, clanking launch engine. "This will be like an excursion up the Hudson to Poughkeepsie," he said with a grin.

The crew dropped into the bottom of the boat as the side-wheeler moved forward, described a wide curve, and started south down the Pasquotank River.

Dave wadded his sea bag under his head and closed his eyes. He was asleep as soon as his head touched the bag.

CHAPTER TEN

Will Cushing came down to the wharf at Roanoke Island, the great Union strong point, toward Picket Boat Number One. Dave shook Scrimshaw by the shoulder. "Here comes the skipper, mate," he said.

Scrimshaw opened his eyes and yawned. "'Bout time," he said.

Cushing dropped into the boat and sat down in the stern sheets. He had a tattered newspaper under his arm, and there was a worried look on his face. "Still no news of Number Two, Davie," he said. He tapped the newspaper. "It seems as if the rebels have heard about our plans, but they haven't learned the correct procedure. Still, they do know we are after her. Someday our government will learn to muzzle the newspapers in regard to military and naval plans. Another thing: There has already been an attempt made to blow up the *Albemarle*."

"*What?*" roared Scrimshaw. He was wide-awake now.

Cushing shoved back his cap. "Early this summer a coal heaver named Charles Baldwin, with four other men, carried two one-hundred-pound torpedoes on stretchers across the swamps behind Plymouth until they reached the bank of the Roanoke River opposite where the ram was moored.

"Baldwin and another man swam across the river upstream of the *Albemarle* and connected the two torpedoes together by a cable. They swam down the river to put the charges on either side of the *Albemarle's* bow so that they could be exploded from the far bank of the river.

"Guards saw Baldwin, and so Baldwin and his men had to get out of there in a hurry under small-arms fire. That means the rebels will have a closer guard than ever about the ram. It doesn't look good for us."

"We're not quitting, are we, sir?" asked Dave.

Cushing shook his head. "We're supposed to be leaving for Beaufort in the morning with two passengers."

"That's a long way from the *Albemarle,* sir," said Scrimshaw.

Cushing grinned. "Sure it is! But I said, 'We're *supposed* to be leaving.' Actually we'll shove off tonight and go up Albemarle Sound to the squadron blockading Plymouth. There may be spies here, and we want them to think we have gone to Beaufort."

"That's sneaky, sir," said Scrimshaw with a wide grin.

"Round up the crew, Davie," said Cushing. "We'll shove off after dark."

Cushing left the boat to report to headquarters. Scrimshaw patted the torpedo boom. "It won't be long now," he said quietly.

———

THE NIGHT WAS dark and misty, with a hint of rain, when Number One cast off from the wharf and steamed out into the choppy waters. The men huddled in their oilskins as the launch pitched and rolled in the chop, with now and then a dash of spray flying over the plunging bow. The engine was working smoothly, for Stotesbury had torn it apart and practically rebuilt it.

They steamed north and then turned west into the sound channel to head toward the squadron. Dave was at the tiller. He knew those waters by day or by night. The only thing that worried him was that Cushing had not said as yet that Dave could go along in the attack on the ram.

There was little talk among the men. Cushing was buried in his thoughts. The only noise was the dashing of the water against the hull, the chuffing of the engine, and the occasional noise as Higgins opened the fire door and shoveled in some coal.

"Lights," said Scrimshaw at long last.

"Union vessels," said Cushing.

A signal lantern shone and began to flick off and on. Cushing took a signal lantern into the bow and signaled back. "It's the *Shamrock*," he said over his shoulder. "Commander Macomb's flagship. We're to make fast to her."

They came alongside and made the launch fast, and Cushing then led the way aboard. The *Shamrock* was the same type of double-ender as the *Sassacus* was but larger.

Dave had heard that Macomb's squadron was composed of the double-enders *Shamrock*, *Otsego*, *Wyalusing*, and *Tacony;* the gunboat *Whitehead;* the tugs *Chicopee*, *Belle*, *Bazley*, and *Valley City;* and the old ferryboat *Commodore Hull.* The squadron was hardly capable of defeating the *Albemarle*, or even of containing it in the Roanoke, but they would try if they had to, and the odds were high against them.

The crew stood on the wet deck while Cushing reported. They could see the dim blue lights of the other vessels through the mist and rain, riding easily at their anchors, with guns shotted and primed, ready to open fire in an instant should the ram appear.

An ensign came out on the deck from the commander's cabin and called for a small boat. "Where away?" asked Ensign Howorth.

The officer turned. "The commander has asked me to go to the other vessels of the squadron to ask for volunteers for an extremely hazardous expedition. I don't know what it's for, do you?"

"Haven't any idea," said Howorth, with his tongue in his cheek.

"There's jamoke in the galley," said the ensign. "You and your men have a mug-up."

It was the next afternoon when Cushing called his crew to the afterdeck. There were six more men with the crew of Number One. Acting Master's Mate John Woodman, of the *Commodore Hull;* Engineer Charles L. Steever, of the *Otsego;* Coal Heaver Richard Hamilton, of the *Shamrock;* Ordinary Seamen William Smith, Bernard Harley, and Edward J. Houghton, all of the *Chicopee.* They had told the crew of Number One that they had all been picked from a much larger number and that some of their mates had offered a month's pay to go along. It was rumored that Will Cushing needed volunteers, and that was enough of an incentive to make almost every man in the squadron want to go along no matter what the expedition was about.

Cushing told them quietly of his plan. He eyed each one of them in turn as he concluded. "You must not expect nor hope to return," he said. "There is nothing but glory, death, or possible promotion to be gained. You will have the satisfaction of getting in a telling blow at the rebels."

Every man stepped forward, with head up.

Cushing nodded in satisfaction. "It would have surprised me to have seen any one of you standing back. We have a day or so to get ready. Mister Howorth will explain the details."

The next morning Cushing beckoned to Dave. Dave got a chance to talk to Cushing alone. They walked forward and stopped by the port paddle-wheel box. "Davie," Cushing said quietly. "I don't want you to go along."

"I volunteered, sir!"

"I know."

"You didn't refuse me then as you should have, sir. Begging the lieutenant's pardon."

Cushing took off his cap and ran a slim hand through his long hair. "Perhaps you're right," he said. He looked out across the river. "I must have more information on that ram and how she is protected. I know of no one who knows this area as well as you do, but I can't let you risk going ashore on a scout. People know you hereabouts. You'd have to go as a civilian. If they catch you, they'll shoot or hang you."

Dave felt his stomach turn over. There was a sour taste at the back of his mouth. He wet his lips. "I'll go, sir."

Cushing rubbed his lean face. "I can't make up my mind, Davie."

Dave leaned forward. "When I enlisted, sir, there were no strings attached to it. I earned my promotion, sir, and I'm hardly younger than the lieutenant was when he joined the Navy as acting master's mate. The lieutenant has no right at all to turn me down if I want to volunteer."

Cushing nodded. "So be it! Now, here's the plan: We leave tonight to go up the river. It's more of a scout and a trial run than the actual attempt. We can drop you off not far from Plymouth. Do you think you can scout the ram and report back no later than tomorrow evening?"

"Yes, sir!"

"I'll send Scrimshaw with you."

Dave shook his head. "With that rolling gait of his and that New England twang to his voice, they'd spot him right away, sir."

"True."

"I'll go in alone."

Cushing looked away. "All right, Davie...but if anything happens to you ..." His voice trailed off and he walked quickly away.

———

THAT NIGHT at sunset there were heavy clouds on the horizon. The crew of Number One tumbled aboard, with Dave wearing a curious assortment of civilian clothing that had been gathered from the crew of the *Shamrock*. He had concealed a clasp knife, gift of Scrimshaw, and a small revolving pistol inside the roundabout jacket he wore. He didn't feel quite so heroic as the launch was cast off and steamed slowly toward the *Otsego,* which was moored closest to the mouth of the Roanoke River. They picked up the volunteers from the double-ender.

A young officer looked over the rail. "Is it worth ten thousand dollars to you, Cushing, to let me go along?"

Cushing laughed. "Certainly! But you haven't got it." He stood up in the launch. "It's Ensign Gay! I can use another madman or two on this expedition."

Gay swung down the ladder. "Acting Ensign Thomas Gay reporting, sir. Without doubt the only ten-thousand-dollar ensign in the United States Navy."

The launch chugged toward the river. Dave shook his head. The tide was ebbing. He was sure they had started too late.

Suddenly it seemed as though a giant invisible hand was placed against the bow of the boat. The propeller raced, and Stotesbury shut off the engine.

"We're aground, sir," said Howorth.

Cushing smashed a hand down on the gunwale. "Over the side," he said. "Break her loose."

Time drifted past as the volunteers struggled with the heavy launch. It was two o'clock in the morning before Number One slid into deeper water.

"What now?" asked Ensign Gay.

Cushing peered through the darkness. "We'd best go on," he said. "We won't be able to stand another day of waiting."

They had moved about five hundred yards when a sharp hail rang out across the dark waters. "Who goes there?"

"The Johnnies!" said Cushing. "They can't possibly be down this far!"

A small tug loomed up in the darkness, and the crew could see a howitzer pointed at the launch. *"Who goes there?"* the hail came again. There was no mistaking the Yankee twang.

Cushing stood up. "Lieutenant Cushing and crew, of the U.S.S. *Monticello!*"

"How do we know that?"

"Come aboard and see!"

The tug drew in closer and then was alongside. Two men jumped into the boat. One of them flashed a bull's-eye lantern on Cushing's face and then on the crew. "Tom Gay!" said the officer.

"It's Lieutenant Wilson, sir," said Gay to Cushing.

Dave felt a strong hand grip his shoulder, and he looked up into the freckled face of Steve Raintree. "Shipmate!" he said. "What are *you* doing here?"

Steve grinned. "I might ask the same thing of you, Davie."

"It's young Raintree, sir," said Howorth to Cushing.

Steve turned to Cushing. "I volunteered for duty with this squadron after you left the *Monticello,* sir."

"That figures out," said Cushing dryly.

"We could hear your engine plainly," said Wilson.

Cushing bit his lip. "I was afraid of that. We'll have to have it boxed in."

Wilson climbed back aboard the picket tug. "Come on, reefer," he said to Steve.

Cushing gripped Steve by the shoulder. "Do you know

of a place where we can drop off a man without running aground?"

"There is a place about a hundred yards from here where the bank is steep-to. The tide scours out the bottom there. It's about five feet deep."

"Good enough. Will you show us? "

Wilson leaned over the rail. "Go ahead, Raintree," he said.

The launch headed for the shore. Dave stood up. Steve looked at him. "Are they dropping *you* off?"

"Yes."

"Why?"

"I'm to scout the ram."

"*Alone?*"

Dave nodded.

"You need a man with you."

"I can make it."

Steve looked back at the dim outline of the tug. Then he guided Cushing close to the shore. The bow nuzzled the bank. Dave made his way forward and was given a hand up to the bank by Scrimshaw. "See you in Liverpool, mate," he said hoarsely.

The launch went into reverse. She was turned slowly. Suddenly a figure was over the side into the dark waters. The man struck out for the shore. Dave stared at him. He could hear the men in the boat calling out in low voices. The man reached the bank, and Dave dropped onto his belly to grip him by the hand and help him up. "Hello, matey," said Steve Raintree in a cheerful voice. "I made a pierhead jump just to keep you from getting lonely."

Dave stood up. "You crazy fool!"

Steve gripped Dave by the arm. "Let's go! Old Man Wilson will give me a taste of the brig if he catches me."

They hurried into the scrub woods. A cold wind crept over them. Steve kept beating his arms about his wet body. "I'll have to flog the booby all night to keep warm," he said.

Dave stopped. "Go back," he said. "They'll pick you up."

"No!"

"I can't use you. I know these woods and swamps. I can talk like these people. That Yankee accent of yours will surely give you away."

"Will it?" Steve grinned. He lapsed into a perfect imitation of North Carolina speech. "You-all from these here pa'ts, boy?"

Dave couldn't help laughing. Steve was always good for a laugh, and Dave knew his freckled friend had more than his share of courage as well.

"What's the game?" asked Steve.

Dave explained the plan to him.

Steve whistled softly. "And I had to jump into the Roanoke River for a mad thing like that."

"You can always go back, mate."

Steve shook his head. He peeled off his wet midshipman's jacket and buried it under some leaves. He had a gay checked shirt on. "At least my shirt isn't navy," he said. "It was the only clean one I had." He scaled his cap into the brush.

"You'd better get rid of that belt too," said Dave.

Steve took his Navy Colt from its holster. "This won't be of any use until I get it fresh loaded, but I'll keep it for a club." He hid the belt and holster in the brush.

"Let's shove off," said Dave. "It won't be long until daylight. Now listen: We're fishermen. Our boat was taken by the Yankees. We're from the Chowan River area. We're thinking of enlisting in the Confederate Navy to get a berth on the *Albemarle*."

"Aye, aye!"

Dave scratched his chin. "We'll have to have a password in case we get separated in the dark."

"We can use the old Marblehead hail."

"What is it?"

"I call out 'Bodgo!' You answer with 'Molly Waldo!' or visey-versey."

"What does it mean?"

Steve shrugged and thrust out his hands, palms upward. "How should I know? Marbleheaders just use that hail and that answer to recognize each other."

"Bodgo!" said Dave.

"Molly Waldo!"

"Fair enough," said Dave. He started off through the dark woods with Steve close behind him.

CHAPTER ELEVEN

There was a light pattering of rain on the leaves of the trees. The surface of the river was dappled with the drops. The false dawn was lightening the eastern sky. The hurricane deck of a small steamer showed above the water, and beyond that was an anchored schooner with an artillery piece visible upon her deck.

Dave lay on his belly amongst the wet leaves, peering under a bush. "That must be the *Southfield*," he whispered. "The ship Commander Flusser died on."

Steve's teeth were chattering. "Yup. It's her all right. I've seen her before."

"We knew she had a picket guard on her, but we didn't know about that schooner being anchored here."

"Now we know. We'd better shove off."

"We're about a mile from town."

They backed away from the riverbank and walked toward the road. "I'm still cold," said Steve.

Dave shucked his roundabout coat and handed it to Steve.

"You keep it," said Steve.

"I'm dry; you're wet. Put it on."

"No!"

Dave stopped and faced Steve. "*Put it on!*"

Steve raised his head. "Don't give me orders, mate," he said.

"I'm a full-fledged midshipman. You're an *acting* midshipman. I'm in command!"

For a moment they faced each other as they had on the berth deck of the *Monticello* many months before.

"You heard me," said Dave quietly.

Steve suddenly grinned. "Crinkum-crankum, *Midshipman* Scott. You win."

Steve put on the jacket, and they plodded along the wet road.

Dave suddenly stopped. "Look!" he said tensely.

The *Albemarle* was moored close to the shore, near a wharf. The dark mountain of iron looked inexpressibly formidable as she lay there with the rain running down her rust-marked sides. The gun-port stoppers were closed.

Steve whistled softly. "First time I ever saw her. She's big enough to give any sailor Cape Horn fever."

"Wait until you see her in action, matey."

"I ain't *that* anxious to be a hero!"

Dave studied the big ram in the graying light. Then he noticed something in the water. It was a semicircle of logs barely afloat, with their rounded tops showing slick and shiny, chained together to form a boom defense about the *Albemarle*. This was something Cushing had not reckoned on. "The launch can't get over that boom," he said quietly.

"Maybe we ought to go back now," suggested Steve.

It was a good idea, thought Dave, and he was all for it, but he might gain further information in Plymouth. They had come that far; they could go farther. "No," he said.

"Let's go then."

"You can go back."

"And leave a shipmate? Bodgo!"

"Molly Waldo!" said Dave. "I'll go ahead. You wait half an hour and then come in. Keep away from me. Even if you see me, don't talk to me. Learn all you can. I'll meet you back here about noontime."

Dave walked down the road. He could see earthworks near the riverbank. A squad of soldiers marched toward one of them. The streets of the town were empty. The rain pattered down on the drab houses. A wraith of smoke hung over the barracks near the river.

Dave walked down to the riverbank and out onto a wharf. He could see the ram plainly. The log boom completely encircled it. There were piles of firewood on the bank, covered by canvas to keep them dry. He knew they would be lighted at night if an attack came against the ram. The ram was moored at the upriver end of the town, so that an attacking force would have to run the gantlet of shore batteries and heavy rifle fire. Sentries paced along the shore, huddled under strips of canvas that they wore over their heads and shoulders.

There were piles of coal near the wharves, and Dave was sure they were part of the stores captured by the rebels when Plymouth had been recaptured by them with the help of the *Albemarle* in April.

He walked along the river front to get a closer look at the ram. A sentry stepped out of a shelter. "Git, sonny!" he said.

Dave bent his shoulders forward and peered half-wittedly at the sentry. "She's a whopper," he said with an ingratiating grin. "Near as big as Grandpa's barn back home."

"Git!"

Dave shuffled off until he reached the end of the wharf area. It was full daylight now. Soldiers walked up and down the muddy streets. They were a poor-looking lot. Thin little men for the most part, with some of them hardly more than boys, and others graybeards. *Conscripts or militia,* thought Dave. They wore threadbare butternut-colored uniforms, and many of them were barefooted.

He saw a familiar-looking thatch of straw-colored hair. It was Steve Raintree, talking to a gaunt-looking sergeant. They walked toward the barracks, with Steve talking volubly. Trust him to find out how many troops were there and where they were situated.

Dave stepped into a doorway and lounged there, whittling at a piece of wood. There were plenty of soldiers there all right, and even if they were second-rate troops, they could pepper an open launch in the river.

Steve was out of sight so Dave wandered off toward the outskirts of the town. There was a fort situated there. It had been Fort Williams when the Union forces had held the town. Cannon peered from the embrasures, and the rebel flag hung soggily in the damp air. The rain had stopped, and the sun was trying to come out.

He knew there was another fort, once named Fort Wessells after the former Union commander of the troops there. So he walked out toward Welch's Creek and saw former Fort Wessells. It seemed to be well garrisoned, but as at the other fort the troops were a seedy-looking, half-disciplined appearing lot.

He headed for the river again to look at the *Albemarle*. Her flag hung from her mast, and sentries stood on the upper deck. Dave had thoughts of waiting until darkness and sending Steve to warn Cushing about the log boom while he, Dave, would wait his chance and swim out to cut the boom loose. He walked back toward the center of town. A platoon of troops marched by in the mud.

Dave looked for Steve, but the freckle-faced middie was not to be seen. An officer came out of a building from which hung a flag. He yawned and looked up and down the street. Then he looked toward Dave. A wave of fear crept over Dave, and his insides seemed to turn to mush. He recognized the filthy shell jacket and the battered slouch hat with the bedraggled feather in it. He started to walk toward the river.

"Hey, you!" yelled Cap'n Ranee.

Dave walked faster, past a group of curious soldiers.

"Stop that boy!" yelled Ranee.

Dave sprinted toward the river, cut around a sagging warehouse, and ran along the riverbank quite near the huge ram.

Ranee rounded the corner. "Halt or I fiah!" he yelled.

Dave ran on, with head down. A pistol cracked, and he heard the hum of the bullet. He looked back.

"Stop that boy!" roared Ranee.

Dave turned in time to see a lean soldier standing right in front of him with his rifle held up, butt toward Dave. He knew he was going to be hit and threw up an arm. The steel-shod butt drove his arm aside and caught Dave full on the forehead, smashing him back against a building. The last thing he remembered was seeing the tobacco-stained teeth of the grinning soldier.

———

WATER SPLASHED OVER DAVE. He opened his eyes to look up into the sneering face of Cap'n Ranee. "Well, well, well," said Ranee. He threw the water bucket into a corner of the cell. "The Yankee-loving chicken has come home to roost!"

Two soldiers lounged behind Ranee, leaning on their rifles. Ranee turned. "Yuh see this scar on my chin? This Yankee puppy done that in Wilmington months ago when he and his Yankee pappy was escaping from conscription."

"Sure don't he'p yore looks any, Cap'n Ranee," said one of the men with a wide grin.

"Shut up!" Ranee turned to look down at Dave. "What yuh doin' here?"

Dave sat up and felt his aching head. "Come to get a job," he said.

"So? Where yuh been all these months?"

"My father was pilot on the *Phantom*. I was washed overboard in the Western Bar Channel and picked up by a picket boat from Fort Caswell."

"Yeh? So where yuh been since then? "

"Working here and there."

"Here and there? *Where?*"

Dave shrugged. "Near Green Swamp and other places."

Ranee took Dave's clasp knife and pistol from his pocket. "What are these fer?"

"I always had that knife. I found the pistol."

Ranee turned the knife. The brass letters U.S.N, had been fastened to one side. "Yeh? A Yankee Navy knife?"

"It was my father's knife. He gave it to me."

Ranee nodded. "Sure, sure ..." He turned the knife over. The letters U.S.S. *Monticello* had been carved into the bone side. "U.S.S. *Monticello*" sneered Ranee. "I happen to know she wasn't in the Navy befo' the wah. I also happen to know she's part of the North Atlantic Blockading Squadron off Cape Feah."

Dave wet his lips. It was Scrimshaw's knife. "Well," he said quickly, "I was wrong. I found the knife, and the pistol was my father's."

Ranee scratched in his unkempt whiskers. "Sho? Now am I supposed to believe that whopper?"

"You can do what you like, Ranee."

The man moved swiftly. A boot toe caught Dave under the left ribs. He grunted in pain. "*Cap'n* Ranee!" snapped the provost.

"*Captain* Ranee," repeated Dave.

"That's bettah! Now we happen to know theah was a Yankee picket tug and a launch foolin' around neah the mouth of the Roanoke last night. Yuh know anything about thet?"

"No."

The boot toe thudded against Dave's side again. "Youah sure?"

"Let the kid alone, Ranee," said one of the men.

"I'm in command heah!"

"Yeh, yeh, but the kid ain't done nothin'."

Ranee eyed Dave suspiciously. "I'm goin' to tell the cunnel about yuh, Yankee. If we think youah a spy, youah goin' to have a drumhead court-martial and get shot, or mebbe hung."

Dave stood up. "I was only looking for a job."

"We-uns will give yuh a job. Yuh kin take a walk up Ladder Lane and down Rope Street, sonny." Ranee tilted his head to one side, raised his left arm, and jerked it upward as though pulling on a rope, while he goggled his little eyes and thrust out his tongue. He grinned as he walked to the door. "I only wish that Yankee pappy of youahs was heah to go along with yuh!"

They closed and locked the door. Dave felt his side and then his head. Of all the luck to have run into Cap'n Ranee again.

———

THE LONG AFTERNOON had dragged by on leaden feet. It was getting dusk. Dave stood at his cell window and looked out toward the huge ram that seemed to squat on the surface of the Roanoke like some prehistoric monster.

A soldier rounded the corner, carrying a long flintlock rifle at right shoulder shift. He wore a threadbare butternut uniform and a tattered slouch hat from which tufts of straw-colored hair protruded like unshocked wheat. Dave stared at the soldier. It was Steve Raintree.

Steve halted near the wooden-barred window of the cell. "Private Steven Treerain," he said. "Captain

Buscombe's Independent Militia Company of Noth Caholina Infantry, suh!"

"Steve, you've gone mad!"

Steve grinned. "Nope. I got all the information on the troops here and was ready to leave when I heard you were in the brig. I signed up right then and there, figuring it would take some time to get me into uniform, but they ain't fooling around. They need the halt, the lame, and the blind in this milishy outfit. So here I am! What do I do?"

"Get out of that rebel suit and get back to Lieutenant Cushing. Tell him all you know."

"Without you, shipmate?"

"*Without me!*"

Steve shook his head. "'A messmate before a ship-mate, a shipmate before a stranger, a stranger before a dog, but a dog before a "sojer."

"Haul out of here, I say!"

"You ain't in any position to give orders to me, reefer." Steve looked up and down the street, and then he handed Dave a bowie knife. "Swiped that from the sergeant. Get to cutting. I'll be back in an hour or so."

Steve vanished down the street.

Dave walked to the door and listened. He could hear the slapping of cards and the laughing of the guards as they played.

He tested the edge of the knife on his thumb and drew blood. The bars were of exceptionally hard wood and set close together. He worked steadily, with sweat greasing his shaking hands. As he cut through each bar, he plastered the cut with mud from the damp floor of the cell. It was dark outside now. It wouldn't be long before Cushing would make his attempt, and if he didn't know what to expect, he would certainly fail and possibly lose his life and the lives of his crew.

He cut through the last bar and turned quickly as he heard boots grating on the filthy floor of the hall outside.

He slid the knife under the thin blanket on the cot, wiped his hands on his shirt, and sat down atop the knife.

The door was unlocked and swung open. Ranee came in. "The cunnel says he'll question yuh."

"Now?"

"In the mawnin'."

Dave felt relief.

Ranee leaned against the wall. He took out his pistol and slapped the heavy barrel against the palm of his left hand. "But I know how yuh Yankees kin lie. I figger I kin warm yuh up a little for the cunnel."

Dave stood up.

Ranee grinned. "Wheah's youah old man?"

"I don't know."

"Wheah did he go on the *Phantom?*"

"To Halifax, I think."

"Close to Yankeeland, eh?"

"I wouldn't know."

The barrel was hitting harder now. Ranee leaned forward. "Come awn now! Just what are yuh doin' heah in Plymouth?"

"Looking for a job."

Ranee swung the heavy pistol, but Dave jumped to one side. He snatched up the empty water bucket and swung it with all his strength. It crashed down on Ranee's head, driving him to the floor. Dave picked up the pistol, jumped up on the cot, and pushed at the bars. Three of them fell out into the street.

"Cap'n Ranee!" called out a guard. "Yuh all right?"

Dave pushed out two more bars and thrust his head and shoulders through the window. He pulled hard with his arms and fell headlong into the street. He looked up to see a pair of sturdy legs clad in butternut-colored cloth. He raised the pistol.

"Take it easy!" said Steve. "Break for the river!"

Dave ran toward the river.

A guard thrust his head from the window. "Hey, you!" he yelled at Steve. "Yuh see that Yankee boy?"

"He ran toward the center of town," said Steve.

The guard vanished. Steve hurled his ancient rifle into a shed, peeled off his coat and hat, and ran after Dave. It was raining lightly again.

They dashed down the riverside. Men yelled from behind them. There was a rickety wharf sagging down toward the water. A leaky skiff was moored to it. Dave jumped into it, and Steve was close behind him. Steve cut the painter loose. "Shove off!" he snapped.

"All gone, sir!" said Dave cheerily as he heaved against a rotting piling. They slipped out into the current. Dave shipped the warped oars and began to pull steadily. A rifle cracked flatly from the bank, and the slug smacked through the side of the skiff.

Then they were out in the center of the river, with the rain suddenly driving down hard. "A real Irish hurricane," said Steve cheerfully.

The lights of the town drifted astern as Dave pulled hard, helped by the current. They would have to pass the *Southfield* and the moored schooner before too long.

Steve looked ahead. "I see a glim," he said.

"The picket boats," said Dave. His head ached, and he had scraped a shoulder coming through the window, but he felt a lot better, despite the precarious situation they were still in.

The rain sheeted down, and they could hardly see the dim shore.

"There they are!" said Steve.

Dave looked over his shoulder. He could see the low hulk of the *Southfield* and the schooner beyond it. He turned the boat toward the far shore, and they shot toward the boats. There was no one on the deck of the sunken Union boat, but a rifleman was watching them from the schooner.

"Who goes there?" he called out.

"Fishermen," said Steve.

"This time of night?"

"Yup," said Steve.

"Yuh won't catch nothin' down theah but a Yankee or two."

"Good, we-uns will bring one back for yuh."

They passed the schooner. "This skiff is taking water fast," said Steve. "Too fast..."

"Man the pumps!"

"It ain't funny."

"Can you swim any better?"

Steve shrugged. "Not much better, but I have a pig tattooed on my foot. Taffy Brown says that'll save you from drowning."

Water lapped over the side of the craft. "Here's your chance to prove whether he's right or not," said Dave. He cast off his shoes and rolled into the water, followed by Steve. They clung to the water-filled skiff. It drifted toward the shore and soon Dave felt the soft bottom under his feet. They crawled ashore on the opposite bank from which they had come.

"Now what?" asked Steve gloomily.

Dave looked over his shoulder at the forbidding swamp behind them. "It's a long way to the river mouth," he said.

"That's cheering."

They squatted on the soaked ground. Dave began to shiver. "Looks like we go upriver again to see if we can find another skiff."

"Why up? We'll have to pass the *Southfield* again."

"Have you any better idea?"

Steve shook his head. "Let's go. I've been wet so many times since I joined you that I think I'm getting webs between my toes."

They plodded up the mushy bank and faded into the woods when they saw the schooner and the *Southfield*. Soon they were up to their knees in a wet wilderness of mud, briers, and scrub trees. They floundered on and on until they could see lights from across the river. "Plymouth," said Steve.

They hunted the riverbank for a boat, and all they found was the rotting hulk of a corn barge. It was getting late. Cushing would soon be coming up the Roanoke to make his attempt. They had to warn him about the log boom.

"Back we go," said Dave.

Steve wiped the muck from his hands. "One thing I like about you, Davie, is that you never quit."

"Bodgo!"

"Molly Waldo!"

They plodded down-river again through the clinging muck and briers.

CHAPTER TWELVE

The great low trees hung over the dark waters of the Roanoke, obscuring the sky and thickening the darkness. A dog howled mournfully from inland. Steve Raintree shivered. "Who wouldn't sell a farm and go to sea?" he asked.

Dave stopped and leaned against a tree. They were both soaked to the skin and torn by briers and brush. Dave wasn't quite sure where they were. Steve had told him there were about four thousand troops in the vicinity of Plymouth, on both sides of the Roanoke, and it would be easy enough to stumble into one of their camps or into a patrol.

"There's the schooner," said Steve suddenly.

Dave stared into the darkness. Now and then a spit of rain touched his face, blown by the light south wind. Then he made out the dim outline of the schooner. There was a faint splash of yellow light from an opened door, and then it was gone as quickly as it had come. But the dim glow had shown Dave the sunken hulk of the *Southfield* beyond the guard schooner.

"How far are we from the river mouth?" asked Steve.

"Maybe six miles."

"What do we do? Go down there or stay here?"

Dave wiped the rain from his face. They were both tired, and they would have to flounder along through the muck, wading the tidal streams and avoiding prowling rebels. Dave thought fast. "If the launch gets past the schooner and the *Southfield,* she'll strike for the ram. If she can't get past them, she'll *have* to go back."

"So?"

"There's no sense in our killing ourselves in this swamp. If Cushing goes back, we'll go back too. Maybe we can hail him and get a ride."

Steve shrugged. "Oh, I'm getting used to walking in water up to my waist, Davie. *I* don't mind walking."

"But if she does get past the schooner, we'll have to get aboard the launch and tell Cushing about the log boom."

"Maybe we ought to tell him before he reaches the schooner."

Dave shook his head. "If the guard sees him, they'll know something is up. The whole river-front garrison will be alert. Besides, you know very well if Cushing gets past the schooner, *nothing* will turn him back, log boom or no, but it's up to us to warn him about it in any case."

"Aye, aye!"

"Then we wait here."

Steve shivered. "I'll scout around, matey. Ain't no use standing in this drizzle until Cushing gets here."

Steve vanished into the brush.

Dave stood under a tree. His body ached where Cap'n Ranee had kicked him. Dave had felled the provost twice now, and Ranee would never let him get away with anything like that again if he got his hands on Dave.

Shortly after, Steve came out of the brush like a dripping otter. "We're in luck," he said hoarsely. "There's a shack back away."

They threaded their way through the darkness until they were fifty yards from the river. A small shack stood in a little clearing. It sagged precariously, and the door hung loose on leather hinges. They went inside and felt their way about. There was a broken-down bunk in one corner filled with cornhusks. A tattered blanket lay atop the husks.

Steve prodded the cornhusks. "A real donkey's breakfast," he said.

Dave could hear Steve's teeth chattering. "Hop in," he said. "I'll stand guard near the river. You can spell me after a time."

Steve handed Dave the blanket. "I'll burrow into the husks," he said. "You take the blanket."

Dave left the shack and draped the musty blanket about his shoulders. It wasn't much protection, but it was better than nothing at all.

———

A HAND SHOOK DAVE AWAKE. He looked into the pale face of Steve. "Show a leg!" said Steve. "Do you hear the news there, sleeper?"

It seemed to Dave that he had hardly fallen to sleep after his cold, wet watch on the river front, but he knew Steve had probably done more than his allotted time of standing out there in the wet woods.

Dave sat up. "Any sign of them?"

"Nary a one."

"Wonder what time it is? "

"I figure they stand two-hour watches on the schooner.

I can tell when they change guards. They changed twice since you went asleep."

Dave jumped to his feet. "It must be well after midnight then!"

"Yup."

Dave took the damp blanket from Steve. "Hit the sack," he said.

"Maybe I'd better watch with you."

"You've done more than your share, mate. I'll let you know if anything happens."

Steve dropped into the bunk and worked his way down into the husks. His head dropped, and he was off to sleep almost at once.

Dave plodded to the riverbank. Maybe Cushing wasn't coming after all.

He peered through the dimness toward the schooner. There wasn't a sign of life aboard her, but the guard was probably composed of North Carolina boys who were born hunters, with keen ears and eyes.

Then Dave seemed to feel, rather than hear, something else in the down-river darkness. He edged his way to the brink of the river.

There was something dark moving in the water, closer and closer to the schooner; then it moved farther away from the schooner and toward the other bank, to pass between the schooner and the *Southfield*. The wind shifted a little, and Dave heard the faint, muffled beating of an engine. *It was Cushing!*

There was no time to alert Steve. The launch was moving steadily upriver. Dave threw the blanket aside and waded into the cold water. He struck out strongly, fighting the current. He was midway across the river when he heard the soft sound of voices aboard the schooner, and then he saw a spurt of flame from a match, momentarily lighting a bearded face.

Dave passed the bow of the schooner and saw two dim shapes ahead of him: two boats, moving slowly against the current. He saw the short smokestack of the lead boat and the thin outline of the torpedo stanchion, and he knew he was back with his shipmates at last.

"Ahoy, Number One!" he called out softly.

The launch slowed down.

"Ahoy!" said Dave desperately. Then he tried the challenge Steve had taught him. "Bodgo!"

"Molly Waldo!" said a familiar voice. It was Scrimshaw.

A hand gripped Dave by the left arm, and willing hands hauled him into the boat. Dave looked up into the lean face of Will Cushing. "You spend a lot of time getting fished out of cold water, reefer," he said dryly.

The *Southfield* was a dim shape astern, and then the launch was around a bend in the river. A rowing cutter was being towed by the launch, and Dave could see that it was filled with armed men.

"There's a log boom about the *Albemarle*," gasped Dave.

"What's that?" demanded Cushing.

Dave explained as quickly as he could. For a moment Cushing stood there in the darkness staring upriver as though he would pierce the veil with his eyes. "We could land at a wharf downstream from the ram," he said, "and then attack the ram from the shore. I've got a load of tough salts with me in the cutter. We're all heavily armed and willing to tackle twice our number. We could board the *Albemarle*, cut her hawsers, and drift downstream, *if* we could get through that boom."

Dave shook his head. "It's lashed and chained, with stout logs forming it. You'd never get away with it, sir. Besides, there are thousands of troops in the town and the forts near it."

"By grab," said Scrimshaw, "if we could get her loose and down the river, we could start her engines and steam out into the bay with the Stars and Stripes flyin' in the morning breeze!"

"We haven't got a flag," said Higgins.

Cushing grinned. "Who says so? We've got one all right!"

The launch moved slowly up the river, with Cushing in the bow. The water gurgled loudly past the cutwater, and the muffled beating of the engine seemed too loud to Dave. Cushing was in his so-called harness. There were five signal lines to be controlled by him. Ensign Gay, who would handle the torpedo boom had a line attached to his wrist, the other end of which was held by Cushing. The boom would be moved forward when the line was pulled.

Another line held by Cushing was tied to Engineer Stotesbury's ankle. A single pull on it meant Stotesbury should increase speed; two pulls meant he should stop the engine. Another line was attached to the brass howitzer that Ensign Howorth would man at the last possible moment, attaching the line to himself to receive his signals.

The three lines were in Cushing's right hand. In his left hand he held the two lines to control the torpedo after it had been lowered from the boom. One line was to detach it from the boom and allow it to float upward beneath the ram; the other line was to release the firing pin and explode the torpedo.

Dave wondered how Cushing would be able to think of which line to pull at which time. It would take a man with nerves of ice to do it, and do it right.

"There's Plymouth," said Dave suddenly as the launch chuffed around a bend.

The ram was dimly visible, a square-looking silhouette in the darkness at the far end of the town.

Cushing gave the wheel a quick turn and headed in for the bank. There was a wharf there. *No,* thought Dave, Cushing would never get the ram past the log boom.

The silence was broken by the sharp barking of a dog near the wharf. "Who goes there?" called out a voice from the great ram.

Cushing sheered off. The time was past for boarding. He gave the engineer's line a hard pull, and instantly the launch surged forward at full speed.

"Who's there? *Who goes there?*" roared the sentry.

"Ahead fast," commanded Cushing. He turned to look astern toward the cutter towed by the launch. "Cast off,

Peterkin!" he yelled. "Go back and take care of those pickets on the schooner!"

The line was cast off and the launch shot forward, relieved of the heavy drag of the cutter. The engine chugged steadily. Then aboard the ram they heard the hard strident noise of a battle rattle as it was sprung, alerting the crew of the huge ram. It sounded as though a giant had run the length of a big picket fence, dragging a stick across the palings.

They raced toward the *Albemarle*. Rifles began to flash in the darkness. "Who goes there? Who goes there?" called out the guards aboard the ram.

"The boom!" called out Dave to Cushing. *"Don't forget the boom!"*

The logs were but twenty yards away when a huge fire sprang up suddenly on the shore. It was the pile of firewood Dave had seen that very day, and it had been soaked with turpentine. Leaping shadows showed up on the hulk of the ram, only to disappear and reappear at another place. The log boom was plainly visible now, and Cushing steered in close, coolly eyed it, then sheered off away from the ram.

"We're not retreating, sir?" demanded Howorth in dismay.

Cushing's answer was typical of the man. "Full speed!" he yelled.

Bullets pocked the water as the launch gained speed. Rifles crackled like popcorn in a gigantic skillet, and there were sounds overhead as though partridges had taken flight as bullets whispered through the air.

Cushing spun the steering wheel, and the heavy launch heeled over as she turned to head directly for the *Albemarle*.

Scrimshaw handed Dave a Sharps carbine. He was actually grinning as he looked at the ram. "Ain't she as big as the old *Courser*, Stormalong's packet!" he said.

They were close now. A guard fired a shotgun, and the

charge whistled past Dave and tore the back out of Cushing's coat. He dropped three of his lines and stood there perfectly calm as they surged toward the slimy log barricade.

Dave fired the carbine and saw a guard drop his rifle and grip his left arm. Scrimshaw spat over the side and fired his carbine.

Men were racing down toward the riverbank, flourishing their rifles. The flames leaped higher and higher, and smoke drifted toward the launch. Then the firing died away for some inexplicable reason. A marksman stood up on the upper deck of the ram and aimed at Cushing. Dave snatched up a carbine, cocked it, and fired it almost in one fluid motion. The slug sang off the barrel of the guard's rifle, and he dropped it.

"Thanks, Davie!" said Cushing cheerily. He was actually smiling.

The launch engine was pounding away with a full head of steam. The crew stared fascinated at the log boom and then at the wet bulk of the ram.

"What boat is that?" yelled a man on the *Albemarle*.

"Cleopatra's Barge!" sang out John Woodman.

Cushing raised his head. "We'll soon let you know what boat this is, Johnny Reb!" called he.

Cushing gave an order to Ensign Gay. Gay swiftly swung the boom around. Cushing leaned over and yanked the firing lanyard of the howitzer. A double dose of canister glanced from the *Albemarle* and smashed into the men standing near the fire on the shore.

The bow struck something hard. There was a ripping, tearing sound as the bow rose and the launch quivered under the driving of the engine. Cushing swayed and stumbled but did not fall. The hiss of escaping steam came from the boiler. There they were and there they would stay.

Dave looked up at the towering black side of the ram, and it seemed bigger and more formidable than ever. His heart thudded against his ribs in time to the laboring engine.

The boom was full forward by now, and the winch in the bottom of the launch began to grind as the boom was lowered. A gun-port stopper dropped and the snout of one of the ram's eight-inch Brooke rifles peered out. Dave shuddered as he looked into the black maw of the big gun. He could see the gun crew behind it. Twenty seconds to fire, estimated Dave. His skin seemed to crawl, and a ball of ice formed in the pit of his stomach.

The torpedo was fully submerged now. Dave glanced at Will Cushing. There was no emotion on the officer's face. Cushing pulled his right-hand line to release the torpedo. "One! Two! Three! Four! *Five!*" he chanted. He jerked as a bullet ripped at his collar and another at his sleeve, while two more flicked through the slack of his coat. It seemed incredible that he should stand there untouched within point-blank range of the guards.

Slowly Cushing pulled the firing-pin line.

There was a muffled roar from beneath the *Albemarle*. Water spouted up the side of the ram at just the same time as the eight-inch gun blasted flame and smoke toward the launch. But the gun could not be depressed low enough, and most of the charge hurtled over the launch and splashed harmlessly into the river. The shock of the explosion and the firing of the gun had formed a huge wave that dashed against the launch and flattened it as though it had been made of wet pasteboard. Now there was no chance to take the launch off the boom.

Dave was hurled back against the boiler and then against the side of the boat.

There was a brooding silence after the gun fired. "Surrender or we'll blow you out of the water!" yelled the guncrew captain.

Rifles began to flash again. Bullets cut into the boat and sang from the metal boiler. Cushing's left hand was bleeding.

"Surrender!"

"Never!" roared Cushing. He took off his sword, revolver, and coat. He coolly sat down and pulled off his shoes as bullets sang past him. "Men!" he yelled. *"Save yourselves!"* He stood up and dived cleanly into the dark waters.

Dave was yanked to his feet by Scrimshaw. "Over with ye, lad!" he cried. He literally threw Dave into the cold Roanoke and then jumped in after him.

Other members of the crew struck the water. The firelight danced on the little waves. Dave struck out to get past the circle of light thrown by the roaring fire. Then he was in semidarkness, with Scrimshaw splashing along behind him and making heavy weather of it.

Dave looked back as he fought against the current. He wasn't sure, but it seemed to him she was listing a little. The launch was afloat, and some of the crew were still in it. Then Dave looked at Scrimshaw. The old salt was gasping for breath. "Can you make it?" asked Dave.

Scrimshaw nodded. "I got a pig tattooed on me left foot and some salt in me pocket. 'Tis to save me from drowning and for good luck, lad."

Dave looked down-river. He thought he saw the rowing cutter, but a sudden dash of rain cut off his view. Then it seemed as though he was again in the cold ocean far off Cape Fear, as he had been when he had been washed overboard from the *Phantom,* for he could see neither shore as the current swept him and Scrimshaw out of sight of the ram.

Scrimshaw groaned. "Go ye on, mate!" he said.

"No!"

Dave gripped Scrimshaw by the loose collar of his blouse and tried to tow him, but the man was too heavy and Dave's clothing was pulling him down.

"Go on!" said Scrimshaw.

It was a temptation. Dave was tiring fast, and he didn't think he could make the shore himself, and then he thought of the old Navy saying: "A messmate before a shipmate, a shipmate before a stranger, a stranger before a dog, but a dog before a 'sojer'." Dave gripped tighter to Scrimshaw's collar and swam with all his remaining strength through the darkness until his feet hit the muddy bottom of the Roanoke.

Scrimshaw gasped. "I'm done," he said weakly.

"Put your big feet down, mate," said Dave.

"I'll drown!"

"*Put your feet down, I said!*"

Scrimshaw sank a little, and then a beautiful smile came across his homely face. "I never thought I'd love land so much, muddy as it is, Davie."

They waded ashore and dropped on the wet ground. Dave felt sick and weak. He dropped his head into the mud and lay still, listening to the pattering of the rain against the leaves of the low trees.

CHAPTER THIRTEEN

The hard hand gripped Dave by the nape of the neck. "Quiet!" snapped Scrimshaw. "Listen!"

Dave opened his eyes. There was a pale watery-looking light in the eastern sky, and he knew then they were on the western shore of the Roanoke.

Scrimshaw jerked his thumb toward a clump of wet brush, and the two of them crawled into its cover. They lay there listening. Something rustled in the brush inland, and there was a soft sucking sound as if someone was walking slowly through the clinging mud.

Scrimshaw closed his right hand on a thick branch that lay beside him.

The brush rustled again, and Dave saw a dim figure coming toward them. Scrimshaw made a pincers with the thumb and forefinger of his left hand. Dave nodded. They would close in on the intruder from both sides. Scrimshaw touched his lips with his left hand and then gripped his throat. They were to prevent any outcry.

The sucking noise came again. Dave bellied away from Scrimshaw and slid under a bush. The man came toward them and was just between them in the dimness when Scrimshaw whistled softly. Dave got to his feet and plunged forward with outstretched arms, catching the stranger about the waist and driving him hard toward Scrimshaw. The old sailor slipped in the mud, and the stranger was driven against Scrimshaw, knocking him against a tree. Scrimshaw raised his club.

"Bodgo!" gasped the intruder.

"Molly Waldo!" said Dave.

It was Steve Raintree. Dave stared at him and laughed. The young midshipman wore a battered straw hat and had the musty blanket, poncho fashion, about his shoulders, with his head through a hole in it. His freckled face was smeared with mud.

Scrimshaw rubbed his middle. "I thought ye was to get *him*, not me, Davie," he said.

"Where'd you go, Davie?" asked Steve.

Dave explained what had happened. Steve nodded. "I calculated that was where you went."

"The only thing we don't know is what happened to Cushing and whether or not the ram was actually sunk," said Dave.

"I haven't seen Mister Cushing or any of the rest of them," said Steve. "I started inland, looking for a road, about an hour ago and ran into an old Negro. He told that there had been a whopping big explosion at Plymouth and that some Yankee sailors had been captured there. He said he didn't know whether or not the *Albemarle* had been sunk."

Dave looked at Scrimshaw. The old sailor scratched in his beard. "Would take a big hole to sink that ram," said Scrimshaw.

"The Negro told me the woods were full of soldiers looking for us. On both sides of the river they're swarming like mad hornets."

Scrimshaw scratched more vigorously. "That's what I figgered. Where are we, Davie?"

"The Middle River is westerly of us. It runs into the Roanoke some miles down-river. We're on a sort of peninsula between both rivers. Down-river, on the other bank, is Eastmost River, which flows into Batchelor's Bay. The Roanoke trends east this side of Eastmost River and then flows into Batchelor's Bay too. It's mostly cypress swamp country, more water than land. Our best bet is to cross the Roanoke if we can, and work down the far bank to the mouth of the Roanoke."

"Just like that," said Steve dryly.

Scrimshaw hitched up his wet trousers. "I'm for it, mates. I don't hanker to sit out the rest of the war in a reb prison."

"Yup," said Steve. "Only that won't be so bad for you, Scrimshaw. If they catch us, they'll shoot us or hang us— Davie for being a spy and me for being a deserter from Cap'n Buscombe's Independent Militia Company of North Carolina Infantry."

"I always thought ye'd join the rebels if ye had the chance, matey."

"Listen!" said Dave.

Behind them, somewhere in the thick woods, they could hear the barking of a dog and the shouting of men.

"Them ain't no Yankees yelling," said Scrimshaw soberly.

The eastern sky was fairly alight with the coming of the false dawn. Dave had once heard bloodhounds baying along the Chowan River, hunting down an escaped slave, and the sound had haunted him for years. Now he knew how the desperate slave must have felt as he plunged through the swamps with very little hope of escaping.

Steve looked toward the river. "That skiff we escaped from Plymouth in is upriver apiece. Maybe we can caulk her up enough to get across the river before the sun comes up.

The three of them forced their way through the clinging briars until they saw the water-filled skiff close to the shore. They horsed the skiff to the shore and shook it from side to side until most of the water was out of it; then they turned it over and emptied the remainder of the water out of it. "Crinkum-crankum," said Steve. "A lobster basket would make a better craft."

"Can we fix it?" asked Dave dubiously.

Scrimshaw spat. "Jack Tar is a handy man, matey." He stripped off his wet undershirt and tore it into long shreds. "Steve, go ye and find some boards to make paddles. Davie, you scout them woods. Old Scrimshaw will make this skiff was all a-taunto in less time than it takes to get a mug-up of jamoke."

"Jamoke, he says," groaned Steve, "and me freezing to death!"

"Shake a leg there, matey!" snapped Scrimshaw.

The two middies walked into the woods while Scrimshaw set to work. Dave headed west through the swamp. He could hear the barking of the dogs, but the sound seemed to be more toward the north.

He came out onto a rutted road, hardly more than a winding trail through the woods. The wind whispered through the wet trees. It brought thoughts of courageous Will Cushing and the equally courageous men who had served as crew aboard Picket Board Number One. Some of them must have been captured, while others must have been killed or drowned in the cold waters of the Roanoke.

Suddenly he heard the doleful howling of a bloodhound from the south. That placed searching parties to north and south. Then the wind shifted, and he heard the faint mumbling of voices to the west. He faded into the underbrush and crouched in the thick muck.

"How many you figger got away, Clay?" a man called out.

"That officer was one, Dan. There was some others got into the watah too. One of them drownded, that we know for sure. They found his body just south of town."

Dave felt his heart beating like a tom-tom. Then two men came out of the brush and stood there looking up and down the road. They wore faded and muddy butternut-colored uniforms and carried long rifles.

"Listen to them hounds," said the taller of the two soldiers.

"Sounds like music to me, Clay. Them Yankees in the swamp must be sweatin' blood 'bout now."

Clay nodded. "Still," he said reflectively, "them Yankee sailors was the bravest men I ever seen. Yuh see that officer standing there in that launch working them lines? He had to explode that torpedo with Minie balls whistling past his ears and cutting through his uniform."

Dan nodded. "Never thought much of Yankees till then. In a way I almost wish they'd git away."

Clay shook his head. "Cap'n Ranee says he aims to git all of them, 'specially thet youngun, the one he says was a spy."

"Yeh, him and his spies!"

"We'd best keep lookin'. Old Ranee ain't in what I'd call a good mood."

"Where's he gone?"

"To git a boat. Says he'll comb thet river till he roots them all out. Let's go git the rest of the boys and head for the river to meet the cap'n."

The two rebels walked south along the road.

Dave hurried back through the woods. Steve had three flat boards in his hands. Scrimshaw was finishing his rough caulking of the boat. He stepped back and shook his head. "Mebbe she'll keep afloat. I don't know for sartain."

"Get a move on," said Dave. "There's a rebel boat coming down the river. I overheard two reb soldiers talking about it, and the boat is skippered by my friend, Cap'n Ranee."

"Getting light," said Steve.

They rolled the flimsy skiff over and ran it into the water. They got into it and began to paddle. The sun was showing itself to the east.

"There's the *Southfield!*" said Steve suddenly.

The river mist was slowly dissipating, and they could see the hurricane deck of the sunken craft. There was no one in sight on the deck.

"Listen!" said Scrimshaw.

The soft muffled beating of a steam engine came to them from upriver.

They paddled steadily, and despite the coolness of the dawn air, sweat began to run down their faces. The current forced them close and closer to the *Southfield,* and Dave momentarily expected to hear sharp challenges and the crashing of rifles.

The beating of the engine was louder now, and they heard a man call out. "We're close to the *Southfield,* Cap'n Ranee!"

Scrimshaw steered the leaky skiff close to the wreck and looked back over his shoulder. "In close," he said quietly, "behind the *Southfield.*"

They drifted alongside the craft. There was seemingly no one aboard her. The beating of the engine became louder, and they could hear the gurgling of water past the bow of the oncoming boat.

"Tie her up to the *Southfield!*" called out Cap'n Ranee.

The picket boat bumped alongside the other side of the wreck, and there was the sound of boots resounding from her decks. "Ain't no one here, Cap'n Ranee!" a man called out.

"Them Yankees must have captured the guard," said Ranee.

"Do we stay here, Cap'n Ranee?"

"Got to block the river, the cunnel says. They's two or three old schooners being brought down."

The swift current tugged at the skiff. Steve let go his hold, and the skiff drifted swiftly down-river and appeared at the end of the wreck. Scrimshaw stabbed a stubby forefinger toward the low shore, and the two boys paddled with all their strength as they heard the engine of the picket boat cough into life and then settle down to a steady throbbing.

They were fifty feet from the shore when Dave felt water creeping up about his legs. The skiff surged in the flow of the river, and water poured over the sides.

"Abandon ship, all hands," said Scrimshaw.

They rolled over the low sides into the cold water and struck out for the shore. Dave's feet sank into the thick mud as the picket boat appeared beyond the *Southfield*.

"Yankees!" roared a man in the picket boat.

The three fugitives splashed ashore just as a rifle spat flame and smoke. The slug struck a cypress a foot away from Dave.

"Head in! Head in!" yelled Ranee hoarsely. "Them's the two Yankees I want! They's a price on their heads!"

The three fugitives plunged into the wet clinging brush and ran like frightened deer through the swamp, splashing through water and mud, careening from trees and fighting breathlessly through the brush.

Rifles popped behind them, and now and then a slug whined its song of death through the air.

Dave knew what was ahead of them: tidal streams, thick and sluggish; cypress trees intertwined with thorny brush; no pathways.

Scrimshaw coughed. He gripped his side. "Go on, mates!" he said thickly.

The two boys grabbed the old sailor by the arms and forced him through the brush as men yelled to each other behind them. They splashed through a shallow muddy stream and dashed into thicker brush. The briars cut like little knives, and their clothing tore into tatters, revealing their bleeding flesh. Dave felt his strength waning. He staggered against a tree and fell heavily. Scrimshaw went down, face foremost, into the stinking mud. Steve leaned against a tree. "I've shot my wad," he said weakly.

Scrimshaw raised his muddy face. "Slip your cables, mates," he said.

The two boys looked at each other. They knew what would happen to them if they were caught, while all that would happen to Scrimshaw would be a term in a rebel prison until the end of the war. But Dave knew Scrimshaw. Prison life would soon kill him, used as he was to the open life of the sea.

"I'm staying, Davie," said Steve.

Dave nodded. He picked up a soggy branch for a weapon and looked back toward the river.

They had stopped firing, but the noise of their progress through the swamp could be heard plainly.

A deer suddenly bounded into the area where the three fugitives were. He reared up on his hind legs and then darted forward right past them, bounding cleanly across the little stream to disappear into the brush, but the noise of his passage could be heard plainly.

"There they go to the southwest, Cap'n Ranee!" a soldier yelled.

The noise of the pursuit died away to the southwest.

Dave looked at Steve. "I'll never hunt a deer again as long as I live," he said.

"Amen to that, mate!"

They pulled Scrimshaw to his feet and plodded through the clinging muck toward the northeast.

CHAPTER FOURTEEN

The sun was up, and the swamp was receiving some of its heat through the thickly intertwining branches of the cypress trees. Now and then a bird twittered from the trees only to fade into silence as the noise of splashing footsteps came through the swamp.

Steve Raintree stopped walking and wiped the sweat from his dirty face. "Where are we, Davie? You got any bearings?"

Dave leaned against a tree. Scrimshaw was making heavy weather through the muck fifty feet behind them. "Close to the Roanoke, I'd say."

"Beats me how you can tell."

Scrimshaw stopped and leaned on his tree-branch staff. He was in bad shape. "I'll need a careening and an overhauling in dry dock," he said.

"I can smell the sound," said Dave.

Steve wrinkled his nose at the fetid smell of the swamp. "Over this? You got a nose like a bloodhound, Davie."

"Don't mention bloodhounds," said Dave.

"Shove off," said Scrimshaw. "I ain't in the mood to

stay here. Once I get a heaving deck under my feet I'll feel like a man again."

They went on through the woods until suddenly they saw the sunlight glinting from open water. They plodded on until they stood on the shore of Batchelor's Bay.

"There's a tug out there!" said Steve.

The little vessel was moving slowly along the shore, trailing a cloud of smoke.

"'Tis the picket tug *Valley City!*" said Scrimshaw.

Steve stripped off his filthy shirt and attached it to Scrimshaw's staff. He stepped up onto a log and began to wave it back and forth.

"Looks like Stevie is pestered by these flies," said Scrimshaw dryly.

"She's slowing down," said Dave.

A plume of steam shot from the escape pipe as the tug lost way. The sun glinted on the glasses of an officer who stood on the foredeck of the tug. He turned and gave a command. Sailors ran to a cutter and lowered her into the water with a splash, tumbling down into her carrying revolvers and cutlasses. They cast loose and drifted away from the tug. The oars were fitted into their rowlocks, poised, and then began to strike the water together, driving the cutter toward the beach, with sun glinting from the wet oars.

The cutter was fifty yards from shore when the command came. "Way enough!" The oars were lifted from the water, allowing the cutter to drift. "Who are you?" called the officer in the stern sheets.

Dave cupped his hands about his mouth. "Midshipman David Scott, Acting Midshipman Steven Raintree, Able-bodied Seaman Josiah Appleby, U.S.S. *Monticello.* We were with Lieutenant Cushing in Picket Boat Number One."

"Cushing? Where is he?"

The three fugitives looked at each other, hardly

daring to say what was in their minds. *Cushing had not returned.*

"We don't know, sir," called out Dave.

The officer sat down. "Stand by to give way," he commanded. "Give way together!"

The cutter surged toward the beach. Fifty feet from the shore the officer stood up again. "Way enough! Hold water! "The cutter lost way and drifted into the shallow water. "Back water all! Way enough! Oars."

The three fugitives splashed out into the water and clambered aboard. "Thank God," said Scrimshaw. He kissed a gunwale. "I'll never go ashore again as long as I live."

"Stand by to give way!" came the command. "Give way together! Hold water port! Pull hard starboard! Give way together!"

The officer looked down at his three passengers. "I'm Acting Master Brooks. We've been looking for men from the expedition. You say you don't know where Cushing is?"

"No," said Dave.

Brooks shook his head. "How did you make out?"

"We reached the ram and exploded the torpedo under her."

"And came out alive?"

"We're here," said Steve.

"Did you sink her? "

Dave shrugged. "She was listing a little the last I saw of her."

"And Cushing?"

Dave looked away. "The last I saw of him he was swimming away from the launch."

They did not speak again until they were in the neat little galley of the tug, drinking steaming coffee and eating beans and soft bread. Scrimshaw emptied his cup and refilled it. "No more gallant seaman ever lived than

Will Cushing," he said. He raised his cup. "Here's to him!"

———

DAVE STOOD by the starboard rail of the *Valley City,* looking out across the calm water, thinking of Will Cushing. Steve and Scrimshaw were asleep below. The night was quiet, with only a slight swell on the dark waters. Stars glinted in the sky, but there was no moon. The *Valley City* swung at her anchor in Batchelor's Bay, not far from the wide mouth of the Roanoke River. Dave had tried to sleep, but he had kept thinking of Will Cushing and finally had dressed and come up on deck.

Brooks had sent a message to the *Shamrock,* telling Commander Macomb that he had picked up three survivors of Picket Boat Number One, but that Cushing was unaccounted for.

A seaman came up beside Dave and grounded his Sharps carbine. "Still waiting?" he asked.

"Yes."

"He's too brave to die."

"He's still alive."

The man shrugged. "From what you told us it doesn't seem possible that anyone could have come through that hail of bullets they fired at you."

"*He's still alive!*"

The man raised his head. "I hope so. Listen!"

There was a splashing noise off the starboard quarter. The seaman ran aft, cocking his carbine as he ran. Dave followed him.

"Ship ahoy!" the faint hail came across the dark waters.

The seaman turned. "Get Mister Brooks," he said.

"That may be one of our men."

"Aye, and it may *not* be one of our men. The rebels might be trying to blow us up."

Dave aroused Brooks. The crew tumbled out on deck, armed with revolvers, cutlasses, and grenades. A gun was primed and run out.

"Ship ahoy!" the hail came again.

Brooks turned. "Slip the cable! Get under way! Have a boat manned and ready to lower! We can take no chances."

The anchor cable was slipped. The tug had steam up, and she soon got under way in the darkness, with the crew peering out toward the place where they had heard the hail. Scrimshaw and Steve came up on deck.

"Ship ahoy!" The hail sounded desperate this time.

"Who goes there?" challenged Brooks.

"Lieutenant Will Cushing!"

Dave's heart leaped.

"He's dead," called out Brooks. "Stay your distance!"

Dave leaned over the rail. "Bodgo!" he hailed.

"Molly Waldo!"

Dave turned to Brooks. "It's him! It's him, I tell you!"

They could see a small, flat-bottomed, square-ended skiff bobbing in the slight swell. Dave peered closely and saw the long brown hair of the man hanging down over his face. "Mister Cushing!" he yelled.

The *Valley City* came alongside the skiff. Dave, with a heaving line in his hand, jumped down into the skiff and made it fast. He helped lift the exhausted officer over the low rail of the tug and helped carry him into Brooks's cabin. Cushing dropped to the bunk and grinned at Dave. "I knew I'd make it," he said weakly.

He was a mess, covered with mud and scratched and torn by briars. His left hand was bound in a filthy rag. Brooks handed him a steaming cup of coffee. "You're lucky you made it, sir," he said. "Too bad you didn't sink the ram, though."

Cushing grinned again. "No? She's sitting on the bottom in eight feet of water, with a hole in her belly big enough to steam through with this tug, sir!"

Dave yelled. Men at the door had heard what was said, and they began to yell too. A rocket hissed upward to burst in a shower of light. It was followed by another and another, and in the distance could be seen the rest of the squadron.

"Ahoy the *Valley City!*" hailed a seaman aboard the *Commodore Hull.* "What's up?"

"The *Albemarle* has been sunk by Cushing!"

Rockets hissed up from the *Commodore Hull,* and the message was passed from vessel to vessel until the sound was lighted by dozens of soaring rockets that burst with faint popping sounds.

"How did you escape, sir?" asked Scrimshaw of Cushing.

"I struck out downstream once I left the launch. I tried to save Woodward, but the poor fellow went down like a stone. I'm sure Higgins drowned too.

"I managed to reach shore on the Plymouth side of the river and lay there exhausted. When I woke it was daylight, and I was close enough to Plymouth to see the town swarming with soldiers. I heard some soldiers talking but couldn't find out if the ram had been sunk. I made my way through a cypress swamp. You have no idea how hard it is to get through that mud and those briars."

"No, sir," said Steve with a straight face.

"I could see a working party of soldiers sinking schooners to obstruct the channel. About noon I ran into an old Negro. I warned him that Abe Lincoln would skin him if he gave me away. I gave him twenty dollars in sodden greenbacks from my wallet and some texts of Scripture I had, in order to get him to go into Plymouth to see if the ram had been sunk. He was back within the hour and told me the *Albemarle* was indeed sunk and that the rebels would surely hang me to the nearest cypress if they caught me.

"I almost ran into a picket party, but managed to steal their boat, the one I reached the *Valley City* in. I paddled hour after hour until daylight was gone, and reached the mouth of the Roanoke. I steered by a star until I saw this vessel. You know the rest."

"Get some sleep now, sir," said Brooks.

Cushing sat up. "*Now?* No, sir! Get me and my men here aboard the *Shamrock!* There is still work to be done!"

A cutter took them to the flagship, where Cushing reported in to Commander Macomb while rockets still soared through the dark air and the sound of continuous cheering could be heard from the vessels of the little squadron.

Cushing came out on deck and walked to Dave, Scrimshaw, and Steve. "We get under way in the morning," he said with a smile.

"Where away, sir?" asked Dave.

Cushing jerked a thumb. "Up the Roanoke again to try to force a passage to Plymouth."

Steve shook his head. "Well, at least the ram is sunk, and we can fight back from a real fighting ship instead of from Scrimshaw's Ark."

Cushing nodded. "I'd like to see the *Albemarle* sitting on the muddy bottom of the Roanoke, but I'm not sure I'll be here."

"Why, sir?" asked Dave.

"Commander Macomb thinks I should carry a personal report of my success to Admiral Porter at Hampton Roads. He has already sent a picket boat with the news to Roanoke Island. I hope it doesn't get back until after we have recaptured Plymouth."

A lone rocket arched through the dark sky and traced its fiery course until it burst in a shower of sparks. Then the squadron was mantled with darkness again, but there would be little sleep aboard any of the ships that night. Cushing's success had routed sleep from the squadron, and, too, there was the prospect of battle again within a matter of hours. There would be much to do.

CHAPTER FIFTEEN

The morning of the thirty-first of October dawned bright and clear. The squadron lay at anchor at the juncture of the Middle River and Roanoke River. They had left Batchelor's Bay on the morning of the twenty-ninth and steamed up the Roanoke to exchange shots with rebel shore batteries, but they had found that the enemy had sunk schooners near the *Southfield*, effectively blocking that passage to Plymouth.

Dave had insisted that the squadron could traverse the Middle River easily enough, as his father's steamer, the *Alice*, drew more draft than any of them and had steamed that way several times before the war. A reconnaissance had proved Dave right.

On the thirtieth the squadron had gone up Middle River, shelling Plymouth across the intervening neck of land, until it had reached the Roanoke. Now, on the morning of the thirty-first, they were to run down the Roanoke River to attack Plymouth. But brave Will Cushing had left the squadron on the thirtieth aboard the *Valley City* en route to Hampton Roads.

The crews of the vessels were getting ready for the attack. The squat ferryboat, the *Commodore Hull*, was to lead the way, as her construction allowed her to fire dead ahead. The *Whitehead,* which had just arrived with stores and munitions for the squadron, was lashed alongside the *Tacony,* while the tugs *Bazley* and *Belle* were lashed to the *Shamrock* and *Otsego* to provide motive power in case of accident to the engines of the double-enders. The *Wyalusing* was to steam in alone.

Decks had been cleared for action. Guns had been shotted and primed and run out. Boarding nets had been rigged. Cutlasses, revolvers, carbines, and grenades had been issued to the crews. Steam was up in all the vessels. Three bells of the forenoon watch had just been struck aboard the *Shamrock* when the signal flags crept up. "Go ahead fast!" was the command on all the vessels.

Smoke gushed up, the exhausts began to labor, and the water purled back from the bows as the squadron steamed down the Roanoke past Warren's Neck. Almost instantly the guns of Fort Gray opened up on them, but the heavy guns of the Union vessels soon drove the rebels from their posts.

Gun and funnel smoke mingled together and hung over the squadron as they approached Welch's Creek and were taken under fire by the guns of the fort built by the Union forces and captured by the Confederates.

Dave was stationed at one of the broadside nine-inch Dahlgren guns of the *Shamrock,* while Steve was stationed at the gun next to Dave's. Scrimshaw was at the wheel of the double-ender.

A shore battery near Plymouth began to spout smoke and flames, and was answered by the crashing broadsides of the *Shamrock.* Smoke blew back on Dave as the gun was run in, loaded, primed, and run out again to be fired, run in, loaded, primed, and run out again, with the precision of a drill team. The double-ender shuddered now and then as shot struck her. Spouts of water spurted up from the river and deluged the gunners, but it didn't faze them a bit as they fought stripped to the waist, dripping with sweat and river water and blackened by powder smoke.

Minie bullets thudded into the superstructure of the *Shamrock* as rebel sharpshooters fired at the laboring gun crews.

Now all the Confederate batteries were roaring in defiance to the crashing broadsides of the vessels. Sharpshooters fired from houses and from behind trees, and here and there a seaman dropped to the deck. Shell, grape, and canister tore and whistled through the smoky air like the rushing of vast coveys of grouse or partridge.

Dave stepped back as the gun roared back into recoil. Something down-river caught his eyes. It was the *Albemarle,* resting on the bottom, with her carapace showing above the water. Not a gun was fired from her. Dave looked back at Steve and grinned. "There she is!" he yelled.

"Look alive there, reefer!" yelled Dave's gun commander. Dave jumped aside as the Dahlgren spat flame and smoke and reared back. The shell struck full into the center of the rebel fort and was followed by a tremendous explosion that hurled dirt and timbers high into the air atop a gush of flame and gas.

"The magazine! The magazine!" roared the gun captain.

Smoke hung low over the battery as the debris settled about it. The rebel guns had stopped firing. Then suddenly the sweating crewmen could see the rebel gunners abandoning the battery and running into the woods behind Plymouth.

There was a little more sporadic firing from the town, and then it died away as shells smashed into the houses.

"Cease firing!" came the command.

The guns were shotted and primed and run out. The echoes died away in the woods, and the smoke drifted off on the wind. The sudden silence almost seemed to hurt Dave's ears.

The squadron steamed slow ahead until they were opposite the smoke-shrouded town. Anchors plunged into the water, and the vessels turned slowly until they were facing upstream.

"Boats away!" came the command.

The landing parties were ready. Boats dropped to the water to the sound of whirring falls and whining blocks, and the landing parties tumbled into them, armed to the teeth. Swiftly the boats converged toward the sagging wharves and came alongside; they were made fast, and the crews clambered out onto the wharves and formed into parties. Then they moved slowly toward the center of the town, flushing rebel stragglers.

Dave stopped on the main street and looked up and down. Smoke drifted from a burning house. A scrawny dog scuttled off with its tail between its legs. The Stars and Stripes was run up into the breeze, and a steady cheering began from the seamen ashore and from those on the vessels.

Dave picked up a trampled Confederate flag and folded it, placing it inside his coat. He heard a man talking rapidly to an officer. Dave whirled. It was Cap'n Ranee, but his filthy shell jacket was gone and so was his bedraggled slouch hat with its disreputable feather. He wore a dented plug hat and a cutaway coat. "Yes, sirree," he was saying. "Couldn't wait until youuns got back here to old Plymouth. I'm a pro-Union man, suh. Glad to hev yuh back."

Steve Raintree stood behind a post watching Ranee, and he was grinning with delight as he saw Dave. He jerked a thumb toward Ranee. "Real Yankee-lover, ain't he?"

Dave moved closer.

Ranee waved his arms. "Them rebels give us Union men a hard time, suh, a hard, hard time. Now I kin help yuh any way yuh like. Know the country like a book. Kin help yuh flush out these secesh people as soon as yuh want me to. 'Course I don't expect nothin', but if you was to see that I was compensated, so to speak, I'd be mortal obliged."

Dave took out the flag. "Cap'n Ranee!" he called out. "Did you drop this flag?"

Ranee whirled. His face dropped. "What do you mean, suh?"

"Why, Cap'n Ranee! Don't you know me?"

Ranee sprinted toward an alleyway. Steve whistled softly as he threw his carbine in between Ranee's churning legs. The man hit the ground hard and Steve sat down on him. "Your prisoner, Davie," he said. "Too bad for the Confederacy. Old Marse Robert E. Lee is sure going to miss his right-hand man...Cap'n Ranee."

The supply steamer *Rhode Island* plunged and wallowed through rough cross seas off Cape Fear, trailing a raveled scarf of smoke. A cold November wind held the sails as hard as marble. Far to the south could be seen the topsails of another vessel which was approaching the *Rhode Island* on a converging course.

Midshipmen Dave Scott and Steve Raintree stood at the weather rail, watching the other vessel. Steve had been appointed a full-fledged midshipman for his part in the destruction of the *Albemarle*.

Boatswain Scrimshaw Appleby swayed down the pitching deck, muffled in his thick peacoat. He stopped beside the two reefers. "Can ye make her out?" he asked.

"No," said Dave.

They stood there in the keening wind, watching the other vessel. "'Tis the *Monticello*!" said Scrimshaw. "I'd know her by the cut of her sails, for I've mended them many a time with palm and needle."

Dave grinned. The three of them had received orders at Roanoke Island to report back to their own ship, the swift *Monticello*.

"Blockading duty again," grumbled Scrimshaw. "Wet

berths, moldy sea biscuit, and hard salt horse. Who wouldn't sell a farm and go to sea?"

Steve winked at Dave. "Maybe you're getting too old, Scrimshaw, to stay at sea with us young fellers."

"Hah, I'll hand, reef, and steer long after ye two reefers are retired as admirals!"

The *Monticello* drew closer. Cushing was in Washington, waiting for orders, but he had sent a letter to the three of them with good news. He had been promoted to lieutenant commander to date as of October 27, 1864, the date of the destruction of the *Albemarle,* and was now the youngest lieutenant commander in the Navy. Prize money of about eighty thousand dollars, which was to be apportioned out to the officers and men who had been with Cushing, had been awarded for the *Albemarle.* But the best news was that Gideon Welles, Secretary of the Navy, had appointed both Dave and Steve to the United States Naval Academy, which they were to enter at the termination of hostilities in order to further their careers in the Navy. Scrimshaw had been promoted to boatswain. All of them were to serve aboard the *Monticello.*

There was still much work for the North Atlantic Blockading Squadron. Fort Fisher, which kept Wilmington open for the blockade-runners, was to be reduced and captured, and the *Monticello* was sure to participate in the action both by sea with its heavy guns, and by land with sailors acting as infantry. The war was not yet over.

The *Monticello* rounded into the wind, and sailors swarmed aloft to heave her to. It was done with precision. The captain of the *Rhode Island* spoke from his quarterdeck. "Smartly done," he said in admiration.

Steve shrugged. "We'll see to it that it's done a little more smartly once we report aboard for duty, eh, mates?"

"Bodgo!" said Scrimshaw.

"Molly Waldo!" said Dave.

SOURCES FOR THIS BOOK

DAVID SCOTT, his father Micah, Steven Raintree, Captain Ranee, and Scrimshaw Appleby are fictitious characters in this story. The blockade-runner *Phantom* is also fictitious. It was not unusual in Civil War times for a boy to do a man's job; nor were older men and partially disabled men like Micah Scott prevented from fighting.

Much of the research material of ROANOKE RAIDERS comes from *Battles and Leaders of the Civil War* (Century, 1887), of which I have the volumes reprinted by Thomas Yoseloff, Inc., in 1957. Volume IV of *Battles and Leaders* furnished material on the construction of the ram *Albemarle* and her armament; the fight between the *Albemarle* and the *Sassacus;* and the destruction of the *Albemarle* by Commander Cushing from his own account.

The United States Navy (From the Revolution to Date) (P. F. Collier & Son, 1917), furnished photographs and drawings of vessels mentioned in the book. A *Sailors Treasury,* by Frank Shay and Edward A. Wilson (W. W. Norton & Company, Inc., 1951), furnished sailor lore and lingo of great value to the author. Detailed information on the blockade-runners was taken from *Blockade,* by Robert Carse (Rinehart & Company, Inc., 1958).

Other sources were the *Official Records of the Union* and

Confederate Navies in the War of the Rebellion; the Los Angeles Public Library; the Chicago Public Library; the Newberry Library of Chicago. Many other books too numerous to mention, have gone into the making of ROANOKE RAIDERS.

William Barker Cushing died a young man, at the age of thirty-two, but he was known throughout the United States Navy as "Albemarle" Cushing. As is customary today in the United States Navy, a destroyer was named after him. In World War Two, at the naval Battle of Guadalcanal during the night action of November 12-13, 1942, the leading destroyer and the first into action was the U.S.S. *Cushing.* She did not survive the battle.

The author first read about Will Cushing about thirty-five years ago as a boy in Chicago whose one dream was to graduate from Annapolis. That dream never came true, but the story of Will Cushing remained with him until this book was written.

POWDER BOY OF THE MONITOR

To my youngest nephew, Ross Alan Keene, who looks as though he would have been a good powder boy on the U.S.S. Monitor.

CHAPTER ONE

The tall-masted frigate U.S.S. Sabine had been warped to a wharf in the New York Navy Yard the day before in a driving snowstorm, and although the storm had let up overnight, the soot and smoke mingled with the snow had made a mess of her holystoned decks, varnish work, and neatly furled sails. Gray water dripped from her spars and rigging and pattered steadily on the spar deck, seeking ways and means of leaking below. The graceful frigate seemed to tug nervously at her mooring and spring lines as though anxious to get to sea again. But she would be disappointed, for she had been on sea duty many months before this January day of 1862, and she was long overdue for a refitting.

Powder Boy Dick Morgan stood near the gangplank of the frigate looking out across the dingy city with its drifting smoke and drizzling rain, and he did not like what he saw. His ship might be there for several months, and there was a war to be fought down south. It might be over before the Sabine, and Dick Morgan got into it again.

"A real Irish hurricane this," said Dick's brother,

Boatswain's Mate Ben Morgan. He shivered a little and hunched deeper into his damp peacoat.

Dick nodded. "How long will we be here, Ben?"

Ben shrugged. "Maybe until April."

"I hate to think of it."

Ben grinned. "You'll get used to it, young'un. Wait until you've been in the Navy as long as I have. You'll accept it as part of the service. You're hardly more than a loblolly boy now."

Dick scowled. His brother was almost right, for Dick had served aboard the Sabine only since early fall of '61, on blockading duty along the South Atlantic Coast. But he had been raised near salt water and had sailed his own catboat off Long Island when he had been only nine years old. Now at fifteen, he had served for almost half a year aboard one of the finest sailing frigates in the United States Navy. There wasn't a finer, smarter, tighter ship in the whole United States Navy, and Dick Morgan would back that statement with his fists or a belaying pin if necessary, for he was an out-and-out Sabine man.

"Where away?" asked a chin-whiskered salt as he looked to windward and then up at the lowering sky.

Ben turned. "Dick and I were thinking of going to Green-point, Lobscouse."

"What fer?" demanded Lobscouse in his twangy State-of-Maine accent.

Ben smiled. "I want to see this new ship they're building for the Navy. John Ericsson's design. The so-called 'Floating Battery,' Lobscouse."

Silas Jones, known to his mates as Lobscouse, spat to leeward. "Floating Battery?" he demanded. "Iron don't float mate, and ye can lay to that. The man is mad! Can ye lay a sheet of iron on the water and expect it to float? All he's got is a tin raft that'll sink like a stone and take good seamen with her!"

Ben shook his head. "You've seen an iron dipper float atop a breaker of water, haven't you, Lobscouse?"

The sailmaker nodded. "Aye, a dipper, mate! But not a hull ship with heavy guns aboard her, and engines, boilers, stores, and crew! It don't make sense."

Ben started for the gangplank. "Well, Dick and I will take a look at her anyway. They're launching her today at Rowland's Continental Iron Works at the foot of Calyer Street."

Lobscouse squinted his washed-out blue eyes. Then he grinned. "Blow me if I don't think I'll jine ye! When that thing sinks to the bottom, I want to see the look on yere face, mate."

As they walked down the wharf, Dick looked back at the Sabine. There was something almost forlorn about her. He could remember her so vividly as she was at sea, with snow-white canvas stretched marble-hard by the wind, her lines drawn ringing hard, and her fine bow parting the waters so smoothly.

"Look at her, young'un's," said Ben quietly. "Her day may be past."

"What do you mean, Ben?"

The young man shook his head. "She belongs to the past; bless her and all her kind."

Lobscouse snorted. "They'll never replace ships like her. What have they got to do it with, mate?"

"Iron, Lobscouse. Armored ships carrying heavy guns that can blow apart ships like the Sabine."

"Avast!" yelled Lobscouse. "Ye talk like a lubber! So help me, Ben, ye talk like a soger!"

Ben flushed. The word "soger" was the worst term of reproach one sailor could call another.

The sailmaker turned suddenly and placed a hand on Ben's shoulder. "I take that back, mate," he said quietly. "It's only when I hear such talk about stinkin', smokin', noisy iron pots replacin' ships like the Sabine, I get all choked up."

"I don't like it in a sense," said Ben, "but we have to face the truth, Lobscouse."

The old fellow spat contemptuously. "We can handle them rebels easy enough with the ships we got. Why, they don't even have a navy, mate!"

They passed through the gate and walked toward the nearest hack station. Dick looked at his brother. "Is that true, Ben? What about those stories we've heard about the *Merrimac*?"

Lobscouse brightened. "Now there is a ship, Dick! No finer frigate was ever built! I was in her first crew when she was commissioned in Boston in '55. We took her to the West Indies and around the Horn to the Pacific, and I think it was done to impress the world with American shipbuilding." Lobscouse smiled reminiscently. "She was a lovely thing afloat. Fast and handy under sail. But she had one fault."

"What was that?" asked Ben.

"She was steam-powered, and that spoiled her. Engines were no good. Chief Engineer Alban Stimers was a good man, but he always claimed the *Merrimac* was underpowered. I heard she was due for a refitting in the Philadelphia Navy Yard. A fine ship, mates, a fine ship."

They got into a hack, and Ben gave the driver directions, then settled back into his seat. "She wasn't refitted at Philadelphia," he said quietly. "She was still in the Gosport Navy Yard near Portsmouth, Virginia, off Hampton Roads, when the war started. When we abandoned the Yard, the *Merrimac* was scuttled and burned."

"No!" said Lobscouse. Then he brightened a little. "Well, anyway, the rebels won't get any use out of her."

"That's just it," continued Ben. "The rebels raised her sometime last year, according to reports from our spies and Union sympathizers in that area. They cut her down to her water line and built a superstructure like a mansard roof on her berth deck, made of thick oak and pine, cased in heavy metal plates. It's said she's heavily armed with ten 10-inch Dahlgren guns and carries a huge cast-iron ram at the bow."

"Rumors, just rumors," scoffed the sailmaker.

Dick looked out through the dirty, wet glass window of the hack. "Ben may be right, Lobscouse," he said. "I heard some of our officers talking about it. They say we have nothing to stop such a monster if she gets loose in Hampton Roads."

"They got some of the most powerful ships in our Navy down there," said Lobscouse. "*Cumberland*, *Minnesota*, St. Lawrence, Roanoke, and *Congress*. Why, the old *Cumberland* has thirty guns, all of them the newest and most powerful design, and her 10-inch pivots can sink any wooden ship afloat!"

"You did say wooden, didn't you, mate?" asked Ben quietly.

Lobscouse opened and then shut his mouth, but his gingery chin whiskers bristled. "Well, if we haven't got a ship that can face this so-called 'monster,' mate, what can we do about it?" he demanded.

Ben's eyes were thoughtful. "Maybe John Ericsson is doing something about it."

"Ye mean the crazy Floating Battery, Ben?"

"Aye."

Lobscouse snorted. "What do they call this thing?"

Ben looked out of a window, but it didn't seem as though he saw the falling rain, the filthy streets, and the hurrying people. "The *Monitor*," he said.

————

THE COLD, drizzling rain had not stopped when the three shipmates reached Rowland's Continental Iron Works at the foot of Calyer Street. They walked into the yard and saw a crowd of wet people — men, women, and children, soldiers, and sailors, shipbuilders, and idlers — staring quietly at the thing that squatted on the ways, ready for a launching.

Dick's heart sank within him as he looked at Ericsson's unorthodox ship if one could call it a ship, for it was like nothing Dick or anyone else standing there had ever seen afloat.

The hull itself, beneath the overhanging flat iron deck, was graceful enough and well designed, almost as though a huge canoe had been placed beneath a raft of iron and bolted to it. A thick wooden overhang ran entirely around the hull, and it was covered with bolted metal plates. Sitting atop the flat deck was a round structure with two great holes cut into it, obviously for guns. Up forward was a low-sited structure looking as though it was composed of iron logs. Abaft the gun turret was a tall smokestack, or funnel, with twin legs in an inverted U shape penetrating the plated deck, and behind the funnel were two pipes standing up from the deck. Stanchions and a chain rail ran around the circumference of the deck, and here and there were cleats, bollards, and pad eyes fastened to deck plating.

"What is it?" breathed Lobscouse.

A man turned. "Ericsson's Folly. A Cheesebox on a Raft."

"A Tin Can on a Shingle," said a grinning soldier.

"She'll sink like a stone," said a woman. "Iron can't float. Anyone but John Ericsson knows that."

Ben worked his way through the crowd. He spoke to Dick out of the side of his mouth. "John Ericsson is a genius," he said. "The man's past record proves that."

"I've heard something about him," admitted Dick. "He's a Swede, isn't he?"

"Yes. There he is now!" Ben indicated a tall, powerfully built man who was standing beside the *Monitor*. "Ericsson knows more about the displacement of ships than most engineers. He is an excellent draftsman, mechanic, and designer. He invented a locomotive in England that did thirty miles an hour; also a new type of steam pump, a steam-engine condenser, a steam-fire engine, a depth finder for use on ships, a machine for cutting files, and he patented the first modern screw propeller. He built the first propeller-driven ship to cross the Atlantic."

"Ye seem to know a lot about him," grumbled Lobscouse. He peered intently at Ben. "Why, may I ask?"

Ben was studying the squat and ugly iron ship. "I think he has something in this design, mate."

"An iron coffin," said the old sailmaker.

Dick eyed his brother. Ben was a serious young man with advanced ideas who loved the sea and ships as all the Morgans did. Their father was skipper of a coastal ship, and their mother came from a long line of seafaring folk.

"No," said Ben firmly. "The man is far ahead of his time!"

"Aye," said Lobscouse sarcastically. "Ye've heard about the Princeton, have ye not?"

The story came back to Dick's mind. Something about a terrible accident on the U.S.S. Princeton, the first screw-driven, metal-hulled ship in the United States Navy. There had been a terrible gun explosion aboard her on her second trial run down the Potomac in 1842, and it had killed Secretary of State Upshur and Secretary of the Navy Gilmer, as well as killing or injuring other distinguished guests. Then Dick remembered that John Ericsson, with Captain Robert Stockton, his associate in shipbuilding, had designed not only the Princeton but also the great gun that had exploded.

"Well," said Lobscouse, "I don't hear ye defendin' yere hero, mate."

Ben was hardly listening to Lobscouse. "Ericsson did design the original gun, but his specifications had not been followed. Stockton had executed the building of the gun without consulting Ericsson, and when it exploded, he loaded all the blame on Ericsson."

"It sure gave Ericsson a black eye in the Navy Department, Ben," said Lobscouse.

"That was twenty years ago, mate. Right now, we need men of vision like John Ericsson."

There was a gangling young man standing near Dick, and as Ben spoke, the young man's head bobbed up and down as if it were spring-mounted. His earnest blue eyes peered through misty spectacles. "True, oh true," he agreed.

He looked like some kind of solemn wading bird that had happened to come ashore to see the launching. He held a number of damp books and rolls of paper under his left arm. Although he looked much older than Dick, he could be no more than sixteen or seventeen at the most. His spectacles and his grave, earnest look gave him the appearance of a man in his early twenties.

"Who be ye?" asked Lobscouse.

The boy smiled. "Spencer Simpson, the Second," he said. He smiled again. "My friends call me Spec. I guess you can tell why?"

"Aye."

"You work here?" asked Ben.

Spec flushed a little. "Well, not exactly, but I've been around ever since the keel of the *Monitor* was laid."

"For nothing?" asked Lobscouse. "Ye ain't too bright, boy."

"Perhaps not, sir. But this ship will revolutionize naval warfare."

"Hear, hear," said Lobscouse sourly.

Ben studied the young man. "You must know a lot about her, then," he said.

"Indeed I do!" He peered at Ben. "I have all the specifications, sir. She is 172 feet long and has a 41-foot beam and a depth of 11% feet. The supporting hull is 124 feet long, and her total displacement is 776 tons. The turret, built by the Novelty Iron Works, is 20 feet in diameter, rises 9 feet above the deck, and is encased in 8 inches of armor plating. The plating was made in Baltimore. I—"

"Take it easy," said Lobscouse in amazement.

Spec bobbed his head. "The engines were built by Dela-meter and Company, one steam-cylinder design; they drive a nine-foot, four-bladed propeller, which is protected from enemy gunfire and ramming by being underneath the deck overhang, the upper part turning in a sort of well. The *Monitor* carries two 11-inch Dahlgren guns in her turret, which is revolved by its own mechanism. I—"

"But they say the rebel ship built on the hull of the old *Merrimac* has ten big guns," said Dick.

The myopic eyes stared at Dick. "You've heard of the Virginia, as they call it?"

"Yes."

Spec looked up at the rain-streaked *Monitor*. "There, my friend, is the answer of John Ericsson and the United States Navy to the Virginia and her ten guns!"

Ben Morgan grinned. "I think you really believe in her, don't you, Spec?"

"Indubitably, sir!"

"Quiet!" hissed Lobscouse. "They're gettin' ready to let her sink now."

Spec peered angrily at Lobscouse, but he did not speak.

Bookmakers were passing through the wet crowd taking bets about whether or not the ship would sink. Business was good. A big, bearded man laughed and shouted out, "If Ericsson ever finds his battery after she is launched, he will have to fish her up from the mud into which her stern will surely plunge."

It was quiet in the shipyard now except for the steady thudding of the sledges as the launchers drove out the wedges that held the heavy hull on the greased ways. John Ericsson stood on the deck with some of his associates. There were a number of naval officers aboard the strange craft, and some of them didn't look too confident. The rain-laden wind fluttered the wet flags that festooned the *Monitor*.

Out on the water were several small boats, pessimistically waiting to rescue the people aboard the *Monitor* after she sank to the bottom.

Then suddenly, the ship began to slide down the ways. Smoke rose from the friction of the heavy metal hull.

"Ericsson's Folly!" jeered the big, bearded man.

"Maybe he figures she can crawl along the bottom like an iron sea elephant!" cried a grinning seaman.

The *Monitor* hit the water and surged down a little, splattering dirty waves high on all sides, coasting easily along until her mooring lines drew her up short, and there she sat, like a clumsy iron duck on the rain-pocked river. The crowd stared, and then suddenly, the big man began to cheer. One after another, the people cheered Ericsson's Folly, for it was quite apparent that the little ship did not have the slightest inclination to sink.

Ben Morgan smiled. "I knew she'd float."

"Aye," said Lobscouse sourly. "But how will she do in a sea?"

Spec peered at him. "Why splendidly!" he said. "As soon as she gets her trials and a crew of stout Navy tars, she'll be sent south to deal with the Virginia and any other rebel contraption."

Lobscouse rolled up his eyes and waggled his whiskers. "Oh, yes," he said. "Stout Navy tars! What stick-and-string sailor would go to sea in an iron pot that's almost awash on a calm river?"

Ben Morgan was standing at the edge of the river studying the *Monitor*. "I wonder," he said quietly. Then he turned and walked toward the gateway of the shipyard.

Dick looked back as he followed Ben. He had a strange premonition that he would know that ugly little ship quite well before too long.

CHAPTER TWO

The boatswain's pipe twittered aboard the U.S.S. Sabine. "All hands lay aft to the quarterdeck!" came the command.

Dick Morgan followed his brother up from the berth deck to the windy spar deck. The raw air made him shiver. The crew were forming in divisions on the deck under the eyes of Captain Cadwalader Ringgold and another officer, who was middle-aged and heavily bearded. He was studying the men of the Sabine as they fell into ranks.

Captain Ringgold came to the break of the quarterdeck. "Men of the Sabine?" he said, "This officer is Lieutenant John L. Worden, commanding officer of the U.S.S. *Monitor*, who will address you on a matter of the utmost importance to the United States Navy."

The pale-faced lieutenant came forward and slowly surveyed the weather-beaten faces of the crew. "Men," he said, "I have been appointed by Commodore Smith to command the new ship *Monitor* now ready for her trials, and I need a crew. No men will be assigned to my ship unless they volunteer for duty aboard her. With that thought in mind, I have come to your ship, the Sabine, because I know the caliber of the men in her crew."

"Here it comes," Lobscouse whispered.

Worden eyed the waiting men. "I want only the best seamen, engineers, and gunners I can get, and every man must want to serve aboard the *Monitor*. Before I call for volunteers, I warn you that you will serve aboard a new and untried ship which will soon be sent South on dangerous duty. I have served in the Navy for well over twenty years and have never commanded a ship, but I have thoroughly inspected my new command and am quite willing to be the agent in testing her capabilities and will readily devote whatever of capacity and energy I have to that subject."

The wind thrummed through the taut rigging, and gulls cried harshly as they hovered over the frigate. Dick Morgan glanced up at the tall masts and their great squared yards, the geometric pattern of standing rigging, the heavy blocks, and tackles of one of the finest sailing ships in the Navy. Compared to that squat monstrosity of a *Monitor*, the Sabine was like a graceful bird waiting to take wind. Dick Morgan would never leave her.

"This ship will ground on the garbage we heave over the side before we see any action in her," said big Jonas Barklew, gunner's mate.

"Aye," said Hank Bascomb, a shotman on the fore pivot gun of the frigate.

"I now call on all volunteers to take two steps forward," said Lieutenant Worden.

"Fools," said Lobscouse as he watched man after man step forward.

Dick nodded. Trading the Sabine for the *Monitor* was a fool's way of doing things. Suddenly he noticed a tall, blond seaman standing with the volunteers. His brother, Ben.

"That will be quite enough," said Worden with a smile. "More than enough, I think."

Dick shook his head, took his courage into his hands, and stepped forward to stand beside his brother.

"Get back, you young idiot," Ben muttered.

"They asked for volunteers," said Dick. "I'm going with you, Ben."

Then he saw something out of the corner of his eye — a face framed by gingery side-whiskers. He turned and was looking into the weather-beaten and scowling face of Lobscouse.

"They don't need sailmakers on that thing," snickered a man from the opposite rank.

"They got to have someone sew their hammocks for shrouds when they go down," said Lobscouse.

"Yup, matie, but what makes you think you won't go down with 'em?"

Lobscouse paled. "Jehosephat! I never thought of that!"

Worden raised his voice. "Get your gear, men. You will report aboard the *Monitor* as quickly as possible. We have trials to get ready for."

———

It was dusk when the draft from the Sabine and a draft from the North Carolina filed aboard their new ship. Dick Morgan looked across the wet flat deck and saw the water lapping right at the edge of it. If she ever shipped a real sea or two, she'd surely sink like a holystone. He hated to go below, but it was cold and damp on the deck.

Lobscouse looked about the wide berth deck, which was bordered by many doors leading into storerooms. "A bloomin' iron coffin," he said bitterly.

"Stow it, Lobscouse!" snapped Ben Morgan. "We're to go on a tour to get acquainted with her."

"Aye," said Lobscouse gloomily. He rolled his eyes and waggled his whiskers. He didn't have to say anything when he did that. It was expressive and meaningful enough.

Practically everything for the operation and maintenance of the *Monitor* was below her flat upper deck upon which rested the heavy turret amidships; the low pilot-house was up forward, a mere three feet ten inches above deck level; also located there were the ungainly two-legged funnel and the twin blower pipes. There was hardly a scrap of wood above-board on the little ship.

The living quarters were all on one deck below the water line. Ventilation was supplied by powerful pumps that drew in air through pipes on the deck. Beneath and astern of the turret was the galley. The officers' quarters and the wardroom were forward, and beyond them was a ladder leading up to the low pilothouse. Forward from this compartment was a circular anchor well, into which the anchor was raised when the ship was under way.

Abaft the turret and the galley were the boiler and engine rooms. The coal was carried in bunkers that lined the sides of the engine and boiler rooms. In the passageway from the berth deck aft to the galley was the machinery for rotating the turret. The machinery was a small steam engine that could be controlled by one man and that operated the turret by means of a double train of cogwheels connected with the vertical axis of the turret.

The turret itself was a massive thing in which squatted two immense bottle-shaped Dahlgren muzzle-loading cannon, with an 11-inch bore that could throw a shell weighing 168 pounds. Gunner's Mate Jonas Barklew shook his head as he looked about the cramped area within the turret. "I should of had my head examined," he said. "How can we work one gun in here, much less two? Why, mates, the concussion alone might kill us all off with never a mark to show for it!"

Dick was a powder boy, and as such, it was his job to supply the powder bags to the loaders in action. Aboard the Sabine, they had been cramped enough on the gun decks, with a roaring gun close beside them on either hand, but within the turret, it didn't seem possible two great guns could be worked at all.

———

THE MEN ATE QUIETLY, often raising their eyes to look at the deck above them, realizing they were below the water line of this strange, new ship. They could hear the waves lapping against the plated sides and knew there was hardly a foot or more of freeboard on the ship.

Later the watches, duties, and stations were assigned, and the quiet crew turned in, slinging their hammocks close beside one another. There were to be trials in the morning. Dick Morgan almost hoped they would be a total failure and that all of them would be sent back to the Sabine. But he remembered the earnest look on his brother's face and the words he had said the day of the launching. "John Ericsson is a genius. . . I think he has something in this design... Ships like the Sabine belong in the past... We need men of vision like John Ericsson..."

Dick Morgan, powder monkey, fell asleep, dreaming of a huge, black iron monster spitting flame and smoke from roaring cannon as she swept through the sailing ships of the United States Navy like a lethal broom, flying the Stars and Bars from her jack staff.

———

THE OFFICERS and crew of the *Monitor* needed faith in their ship. On February 27, she made her trial run and had to be towed back to her mooring. The engine valves had not been properly set, and the steering mechanism had broken down.

On March 3, the mooring lines were cast off in a swirling snowstorm, and the *Monitor* proceeded slowly to sea. There was a need for her. News had come through a mechanic who had worked on the *Merrimac* before he had had a chance to get out of Portsmouth: The *Merrimac* had been launched, her ten-gun battery had been installed, and she had been fitted with a 1,500-pound ram. Her new superstructure sloped at an angle of 35 degrees and was topped by a grating of 2-inch iron bars. She was to have a crew of 350 trained seamen and gunners. A three-inch-wide iron shield encircled her wooden hull below the water line. The superstructure was plated with two layers of iron, each two inches thick. Nothing like this monster had ever been seen before.

Pressure was being applied to Ericsson from all sides. The *Monitor* was needed now.

The crew settled down for their trip south, but two days later, she was back at her moorings once more. The rudder did not work properly, and the vessel could hardly be controlled. News came that the naval officers in the engineering department wanted to lay her up for a month to install a new rudder, but Ericsson would not wait that long. In his pocket was a telegram from Assistant Secretary of the Navy Gustavus Fox:

IT IS VERY IMPORTANT THAT YOU SHOULD SAY... EXACTLY THE DAY MONITOR CAN BE AT HAMPTON ROADS.

Workmen swarmed aboard the *Monitor*, and in four days under Ericsson's driving will, the repairs were made on the old rudder.

The morning of March 6, the *Monitor* put to sea, towed by the tugboat Seth Low and escorted by the gunboats Currituck and Sachem. The weather was mild and pleasant. The *Monitor* was under way, at last, exactly one hundred and fifty-two days after John Ericsson had shown a dusty cardboard model of her to Navy officials, and at that time, no plans of it existed—nothing but the model and an idea in the head of a stubborn Swede by the name of John Ericsson.

There was a full complement of officers and men aboard the *Monitor*. Lieutenant Worden had, as his Executive Officer, Lieutenant Samuel Dana Greene, formerly of the U.S.S. Hartford, and a volunteer like most of the crew. There were Acting Masters Louis N. Stodder and J.N. Webber, Acting Master's Mate George Fredericksen, Acting Surgeon D.C. Logue, Paymaster W.F. Keeler. First Engineer Isaac Newton was in charge of steam machinery, aided by RW. Hands, A.B. Campbell, and M.T. Sunstrom. There were Captain's Clerk Daniel Toffey, Quartermaster Peter Williams, and Boatswain's Mate John Stocking. Chief Engineer Alban C. Stimers, formerly of the *Merrimac*, was along on the voyage as an official observer for the Navy.

Dick Morgan was sweating as he helped carry heavy shot that had been stored under the berth deck to a more forward position to trim the low-lying ship. He stopped to wipe the sweat from his face and looked into a store-room whose door had become unlatched and had swung open in the motion of the seas. The light from a whale-oil lamp seemed to glint from something in the deepest recesses of the storeroom. Dick stared hard. He was almost sure he could see a pale face behind two shining orbs. He leaned forward and peered into the room.

"It's me," said the apparition. "Spec Simpson."

"The Second?"

"Yes."

Dick looked aft. The corridor was empty. He stepped into the room. "How did you get aboard?" he demanded.

Spec swallowed. "I tried to enlist, and they wouldn't take me, so I slipped aboard. What do you think they'll do to me?"

"Keelhaul you, at least. This is a fine mess."

Spec nodded. "What shall I do?"

"Turn yourself in, I guess."

"Now?" asked Spec hollowly.

Dick couldn't help grinning. "Well, think it over. I'll

bring you some mess. Going to be cold in here tonight. Either give yourself up or freeze to death."

"I'm not quite sure which I prefer," said Spencer Simpson, the Second. He placed a hand over his mouth. "This storm is making me a little sick."

Dick laughed. "Storm? It's like a millpond, mate! "

"Morgan!" roared a voice.

"Who's that?" asked Spec in a scared voice.

"Bosun's mate," said Dick. "He figures I'm sogering."

"Morgan!"

"He sure sounds angry. Who does he think he is, anyway?"

Dick grinned. "My brother, that's all."

"And he talks to you like that?"

"That's his job, Spec. If he went easy on me, the rest of the crew would talk, so he makes it a little rougher to be sure they don't talk. If I was in his rating, I'd do the same to him. It's the service way, mate."

"I suppose so."

Dick shook his head. "Wait until they know you're aboard! I'll see if I can get you a blanket. I still think you ought to turn yourself in. We won't make Hampton Roads for a couple of days."

"I am beginning to think I might have made a mistake," Spec said sadly.

"Me too. Stay put, mate, and keep this door shut."

Dick hurried away. There was a great deal of work to do, and he did not have much time to fool around with Spencer Simpson, the Second.

Stores were being listed and checked into their places. The surgeon was busy taking his infirmary gear from cases and checking his medical supplies.

It was quite late before Dick managed to smuggle some cold cut-and-come-again food—usually left on the mess table for the convenience of the crew—a thick blanket and a container of water into the locker where the stowaway lurked.

"How soon do we get there?" asked Spec dolefully.

"We just sighted Barnegat Light bearing south by west. A cold, clear night, mate."

Dick left Spec to his sorrow and cold quarters and hurried to his hammock in the big berth room. Most of the tired men had already turned in and were sound asleep in their swinging canvas beds. There wasn't much room, for Ericsson, on the principle of the old sailing ships of the line where crews were large and space ever at a premium, had allowed but fourteen inches of space for each hammock, on the assumption that half of them would be on duty at one time.

The ship swayed gently in the easy seas. Dick listened to the swashing of the waves along the sides and realized that something was missing—the thrumming of the wind through taut rigging. It was warm, though. A sort of greasy, oily warmth came from the engine and boiler rooms.

Lobscouse turned in his hammock. "I don't like things," he said sourly.

"What's wrong, Lobscouse?" asked Dick.

"I got a feelin' of dirty weather ahead."

"You usually do," said Dick dryly.

Lobscouse shook his head. "We're due for a spell of bad luck, mate."

"How so?"

"Some lubber passed a spare flag through the rungs of a ladder, that's why! And Jimmy Fox lost a swab overboard just at dusk."

Dick laughed.

Lobscouse cleared his throat. "Bad luck. I got a feelin' they's a Jonah on board."

Dick wondered if Lobscouse knew about Spec Simpson. If Spec were caught and he admitted that Dick had helped him, Dick would have to stand before the captain for punishment.

"I saw a big star doggin' the moon," said Lobscouse,

"and another ahead atowin' her. Sure sign of a blow, and I ain't sure we can take a choppy sea, much less a real blow."

"Quiet down there!" roared Ben Morgan.

"Tomorrow is Friday," said Lobscouse sourly. He turned and pulled his blanket high over his head.

Dick knew what Lobscouse meant. Friday was traditionally unlucky for ships and seamen. After long and uneasy tossing, Dick fell asleep.

Several times during the night, he awoke to feel increased motion in the ship. The dimmed oil lamps swung steadily in their gimbals in time with the hammocks. When the *Monitor* rose a little higher and came down steadily and slowly, it seemed to Dick she was taking too long a time to prove her vaunted buoyancy.

CHAPTER THREE

Friday morning broke clear and cold. The wind increased, and the ship began to pitch and roll with vigor. During the long, windy morning, the seas became increasingly rougher. By the middle of the afternoon, the ship was making heavy weather of it. There was a leak in the berth deck hatch, and nothing could be done to stop the water from flowing down inside the hull in a waterfall.

The *Monitor* was pitching like a wild steer, and waves flowed clear over the low pilot house. Several times they hit the little structure with such force that the seas spurted in through the narrow eye slits and knocked the helmsman from the wheel.

Seas broke over the blower pipes and flowed down in such a stream that the belts of the blower engines began to slip. If they stopped altogether, the engines would cease for lack of artificial draft because the fires could not get air for combustion.

The pumps began to throb as they fought to maintain a low water level. The crew kept at their unfamiliar work inside their unfamiliar ship. Lobscouse looked up at the waterfall streaming down inside the ship. "Lubbers!" he cried. "Can't they even build a ship and pay a seam? Look at that! It's like Niagara!"

Ben Morgan wiped the sweat from his face and leaned against a bulkhead, watching the waterfall. "Ericsson knew what he was doing, but the Navy Yard didn't, Lobscouse," he said wearily. "He designed the base of the turret so that it fitted on a precisely machined groove sunk into the deck. He figured a little water might work in, and he provided a small pump to handle it."

"Sure! Sure!" roared Hank Bascomb. "Look at it! We'll all be in Davy Jones's locker afore morning if this keeps up!"

Ben combed back his wet hair with his fingers. "Those Navy Yard fools pried up the base of the turret and packed it with oakum, figuring it would stop any leaks. Well, now the oakum is washing out. If they had let it alone in the first place, we wouldn't have had any trouble."

Another crew member seemed to come aboard as darkness fell — an unwelcome addition, for his name, was Fear. Somewhere out in the darkness, his shipmate and helper, Panic, hovered around, waiting for his chance, for where Fear was, Panic would soon follow.

The *Monitor* slammed up and down on the seas. Suddenly, as the men worked, a horrible groaning sound began. They stopped their work and stared wide-eyed toward the forward part of the ship. Again and again, the terrible tortured sound came to them at regular intervals until the noise reverberated throughout the ship.

"What is it?" asked Jimmy Fox. His face was deathly pale.

"The banshee," said Mike Reilly. "We're doomed, lads. 'Tis the end coming!"

"Stow that!" snapped Ben Morgan. He walked toward the door that led into the area beneath the forward deck. When he opened the door into the officers' wardroom, the racket seemed to intensify. Ben turned. "Lobscouse! Dick! Bear a hand here!"

"I knew he'd ask for us," said Lobscouse gloomily as he hurried up.

They closed the wardroom door and crossed to the door that opened into the room where the pilothouse ladder led up to the hatchway into the pilothouse. As the ship dipped deeply, the noise seemed to rush at them like the cries of a score of demons.

"The Lord protect us!" said Lobscouse.

Dick's heart thudded erratically, and his throat went dry. He wished he were safe aboard the Sabine, under reefed sails, surging easily through the storm.

Captain Worden came down the ladder. "What is it, Morgan?" he asked.

"It's coming from farther forward, sir."

The four of them stood there listening to the wild and eerie sound, then Ben Morgan smiled. "I have it, sir!"

"Yes?"

"It seems as though the sound comes every time the bow slams down. The forward overhang forces air up through the anchor well. It's like air blowing in a big trumpet."

"Some trumpet," said Lobscouse.

Ericsson, with his advanced ideas, had devised a method of lowering the anchor through a well in the overhanging deck by means of a hand-operated mechanical winch set just forward of the pilothouse ladder so that both anchor and the men working it were protected from enemy fire.

Worden smiled. "You'd better go back and tell the rest of the men," he said. "I'll admit it had me a little nervous."

"How does it look, sir?" asked Dick.

Worden's face was pale and drawn in contrast to his dark beard and mustache. "We're holding our own, young man, and if nothing else happens, we'll be all right when the seas abate."

The loud cries of men came to them from aft. Ben opened the door for Worden, and the officer hurried through the wardroom just as a great sea rolled the *Monitor*. A storeroom door became unlatched, and a blanketed bundle seemed to fly out and across the heaving deck, coming to a stop with a crash against the door of an officer's room.

"What's this?" cried the captain.

Dick's heart sank within him as he saw a white face, with spectacles still firmly in place, rise from the folds of the blanket like the head of a sad-looking turtle. "Only me, sir," said Spec. "Spencer Simpson, the Second."

"A stowaway?"

"Yes, sir!"

The noise of yelling men came to them again, and Worden pulled open the door and ran into the berth deck room. Water was slipping back and forth across the deck, splattering some of the crew lying on the metal, too sick to care whether they lived or died.

Worden crossed to the boiler room to be met by Engineer Newton. The engineer wiped the water from his greasy face. "Water pours down on the machinery through the air blowers, and we can't keep the ventilating system going. If it stops completely, we can't keep the boiler fires going, and that means the steam pumps will stop. I doubt if we can keep even with the water we are taking aboard by using the hand pumps, sir."

Dick followed the two officers into the engine room. The stench of the gas that formed as the fires began to die was thick. Water swirled over the greasy deck plating. An engineer staggered across the pitching room and fell heavily.

"Gas," said Newton as he dragged the man to the doorway.

"Morgan!" commanded Worden. "Get that man up

into the turret for fresh air!" He turned to his executive officer. "Mister Greene, you had better see to it that the hand pumps are rigged! We may lose all our steam!"

No sooner had the commanding officer spoken than the steam pumps clattered to an ominous halt as they lost power.

"We'll have to fight to save this ship, sir," said Chief Engineer Stimers.

Worden's face was fierce in the flickering yellow light of the swinging oil lamps. "Mister Stimers," he said harshly, "There is no question about our saving this ship! Our objective is not merely to float but to fight! We will not lose this ship, sir!"

Stimers and Newton plunged through the black, greasy water to work on the pumps while the choking gas thickened in the engine room.

Boatswain's Mate John Stocking came to Worden. "Hand pumps rigged and at work, sir, but we have scarcely enough pressure to throw the water out through the turret, sir. We could bail, sir, but it's not worth the effort, as we'd have to pass the buckets up through the turret."

"Keep pumping, Stocking!"

The little ship pitched and rolled; the waves smashed down on the deck, flowed entirely over the pilothouse, washed up against the turret, and sent a thick sheet of water upon the men below, working the pumps. Deeper and deeper the *Monitor* wallowed, plunging about at the end of her towline. If that hawser snapped . . .

Oily black smoke hung in the engine and boiler rooms and began to drift out into the berth deck. Coughing, choking, blackened gangmen ran from the boiler room.

Engineer Stimers struggled in the sloshing chaos of the engine room, adjusting and working the valves almost by feel, for he alone, of all men aboard, knew about the engines and their workings, perhaps even more than the manufacturers.

The wind howled in fiendish glee down the funnel, forcing gas back into the ship. One man after another was hauled from the engine and boiler rooms to the fresher air of the turret.

The pumps still faltered along with hardly enough steam pressure from the dying fires. The water rose steadily in the bilges, washing back and forth, spurting through openings, flooding the berth deck, wardroom, and officers' quarters, while, over and above the thudding of the seas and the howling of the wind down the stack and blower pipes, came the steady, eerie groaning of the air rushing up the anchor well.

Suddenly, when they were all sure they would have to abandon their ship or go down to death in the cold seas with her, the seas began to abate, and the wind died away little by little until it was nothing but a strong breeze.

Fire doors banged open in the boiler room, and great scoops scraped on metal plating as good anthracite was hurled into the hungry fireboxes. The blower pumps began to hum, and the pumps picked up with a steady thudding. Steam rose in the boilers and began to hiss at the escape valves. Filthy bilge water flowed from the pumps, and the little ship rose lightly to the heaving seas.

It had been a close thing—much too close.

The cooks passed out cold food to the men who could eat it while others lay about on the wet decks. The turret was packed with men who had suffered carbon-monoxide poisoning, and among them was Chief Engineer Stimers, who probably had singlehandedly saved the ship by his devotion to duty.

There was no rest for those men able to stand on their feet. Lashings were passed about items that might shift in heavy seas. Swabs tried to clean up some of the mess. Surgeon Logue had his hands full, taking care of the seasick, the gassed, and the injured men.

Boatswain's Mate Ben Morgan led a party throughout the ship, hunting for leaks and damage. The cooks started fires in the galley to heat caldrons of powerful coffee to fight chill and exhaustion, and Dick Morgan was sent to the pilothouse with a mug of it for Acting Master Webber, who was standing his trick at the wheel.

Dick scuttled up the ladder and looked curiously around the tiny pilothouse, just about three and a half feet long, two feet eight inches wide, and protruding almost four feet above the deck plating. It had been formed with solid blocks of wrought iron bolted together at the corners. Near the top of the structure, eye slits had been left open completely around the sides. The top had been formed of a plate of iron two inches thick, let down into grooves but not bolted down, so that the crew, in case of an accident, could readily shove it off and escape.

"Take the wheel, Morgan," said Acting Master Webber. He studied Dick with tired eyes. "You look well enough, young man."

Dick took the wheel and peered through the narrow eye slit. He could see the thick hawser rising and falling in the sea, while far ahead of them, the Seth Low wallowed steadily along through the lessening seas. Every time a strain came on the hawser, water spurted from it.

"That's a new hawser, Morgan," said Webber wearily, "in case you were wondering about it. I've hardly watched anything else."

Eight bells suddenly rang throughout the little ship. Midnight and it seemed as though the *Monitor* was safe enough. Dick eyed the seas. It seemed to him that they were rougher. "Shoal water ahead," the officer said quietly.

Then she began to pitch and heave again.

Webber sipped his coffee. "I had a feeling our luck wouldn't last," he said. "Let me have the wheel."

"Finish your Java, sir."

"Thanks, son."

The wheel seemed to feel different under Dick's hands. He had learned to steer long ago and had been told he was a natural helmsman, but this wheel had begun to act up. The bow of the ship began to pay off.

"Bring her back!" snapped Webber. "You'll put too much of a strain on that hawser!"

But the wheel was cranky and had begun to bind. The bow swung farther and farther to port until a wave washed high over it and smashed against the pilothouse, spurting cold sea water against Dick's face, half blinding him. "The wheel's jammed, sir!" Dick called out.

The acting master gripped the wheel and tried to turn it back, but it wouldn't budge. "Get the captain on the voice tube," he said tensely as he fought the stubborn wheel.

Dick whistled sharply into the tube. "No answer, sir," he said after a moment.

"Go get him then! Tell him the wheel's jammed, and I can no longer handle the ship!"

Dick gripped the sides of the ladder and slid down the steel rungs, hitting the deck and spinning around to run aft the instant he hit the metal. The ship was smashing back and forth like a mad thing at the end of the hawser. Objects fell from racks and hooks, clattering on the decks and banging against the bulkheads.

Lieutenant Worden met Dick in the area beneath the turret. "What is it, Morgan," he asked.

"Wheel is jammed, sir! She won't answer the helm!" said Dick hoarsely.

Worden's face went taut. "If that hawser breaks, we'll hit a lee shore," he said. He ran forward toward the wardroom, followed by Dick. "Go into my cabin," said the officer over his shoulder. "There is a flare pistol in a cabinet. Report to me when you have it."

"Aye, aye, sir!"

Worden went agilely up the ladder. Dick darted into the officer's cabin and opened the first cabinet at random. It was then that he noticed the shivering humped shape in the captain's bunk. He turned as he found the flare pistol and stared at the strange form. Suddenly a bespectacled face peered at him.

"Don't shoot, Dick," pleaded Spencer Simpson.

Dick's jaw dropped. "What are you doing in here?"

"Well, you see, Dick, it was the quietest place I could find out of the way of the others, so I..."

"Get out of there!" roared Dick. He gripped Spec by a long, thin leg and hauled him out of the bunk. "Get aft, you lubber! That's the skipper's bunk, you lunkhead! Git!"

Spec scuttled from the room like a great, ungainly stork, and Dick couldn't help exploding with laughter as he ran for the pilothouse ladder. He stopped with head and shoulder protruding into the tiny area. "Flare pistol, sir," he reported.

"Acting Master Stodder has the flares, Morgan. Give him the pistol and tell him to stand by for orders to fire. If we break that hawser, we might be lost! Tell Boatswain Stocking to check the wheel ropes and see what's wrong with them."

Dick slid down the ladder and raced aft, reported to Stodder, then found Boatswain Stocking and gave him his orders.

Ben Morgan crawled out of a deck hatch and stood in front of his brother, dripping greasy water on the deck from his soaked uniform. "How goes it, young'un?" he asked wearily.

"All right with me, Ben. How's the hull?"

Ben shrugged. "Strangely enough, she's as tight as a drum! All the water inside seems to have come from the base of the turret. Why's she pitching about like this? I nearly cracked my skull on the side down there."

"Wheel's jammed, Ben. The ship's practically out of control. If the hawser breaks, we'll have had it."

Ben rolled his eyes. "What else can happen aboard this ship?"

Lobscouse hurried past them, dragging a heavy line.

"Yellow fever, smallpox, cholera, and mutiny, after which the old *Merrimac* will come out to meet us and sink us off Cape Henry!" he growled.

Ben grinned. "Cheerful soul!"

There was nothing to grin or joke about in the following hours. The *Monitor* raged and tore at the hawser while Boatswain Stocking and his detail worked to free the wheel ropes. Other men led by Boatswain's Mate Ben Morgan hunted for leaks. The engineers had their hands full, keeping the propeller turning and the pumps thudding.

The storm was in full fury now, keening and howling like a mad thing. Thick, gray-green seas flowed over the *Monitor* until all that showed above the water was the turret and the swaying stack and the blower pipes, while water spurted in through the pilothouse eye slits, soaking the helmsman and the skipper, then flowing down into the lower areas to seek the bilge. And all the time, the anchor well kept up its horrible threnody as though it was the very voice of the ship itself.

There was no sleep aboard her that wild night as once again; she seemed determined to make an iron shroud of herself not only for her officers and crew but for the hopes of the Union as well.

In the watery light of dawn, they all thought the fight was almost over. Captain Worden hailed the Seth Low, but the wind picked up his voice and hurled it off into the storm. Acting Master Stodder fired a flare, and the gunboat Currituck plowed through the seas in response to the distress signal. Her skipper hailed the *Monitor*, and Captain Worden climbed to the top of the turret, voice trumpet in hand. "Can you help tow us into calmer water, Captain Shankland?"

"What's wrong, Captain Worden?"

"Wheel ropes are jammed! She hardly answers her helm! The strain on the towing hawser is very great, sir!"

"I'll come alongside and pass another hawser to you, sir!"

Boatswain Stocking clambered up to Captain Worden. "Wheel ropes have been cleared, sir," he said.

Suddenly the ship seemed to ride easier as the helmsman got control of her.

Worden hailed the Currituck. "We have control now, sir! Please stand by in case we need you."

Just before daybreak, the seas began to calm down, and by the time the sun rose over the heaving Atlantic, the *Monitor* was riding easy, like a huge metal duck on the gray waters. It was all over, and the ship had been saved. Weary men staggered to their hammocks and fell into them, wet clothing and all, while the cooks passed out dry ship's biscuits and started their galley fires to make coffee.

The engines throbbed steadily, and the pumps began to suck dry by the time the sun was fully up, shining over smoother seas, forecasting a mild, pleasant day for the remainder of the trip to Hampton Roads. She would soon round Cape Charles and pass into Chesapeake Bay, with Hampton Roads but twenty miles smooth sailing after that.

Lobscouse sat on the galley deck, with a mug of jamoke in one hand and a hard biscuit in the other. "I knew it," he growled. "There was a Jonah aboard all the time. That long-legged, side meat and bones, four-eyed, gabbin' Spencer Simpson, the Second. Next to a cross-eyed parson, the only thing worse aboard a ship is a cross-eyed Finn, but I'm ginnin' to think that boy is worse than both of them put together, and ye can lay to that!"

One of the cooks wiped his hands on his apron. "Well, Lobscouse," he said cheerfully, "there ain't much more can happen to this tin hooker."

Lobscouse looked up and scowled. He wet the middle finger of his right hand and pressed the finger against the palm of his left hand, then formed a fist with his right hand and smacked it down hard against his left palm. He took off his battered and wet flat hat and spit into it. "Don't ye be too sure, mate," he said darkly. "I got a feelin' in my bones we ain't through with our troubles yet. Ye wait and see. Somethin' big and terrible is goin' to happen to this bucket afore too long! "

Dick grinned at the cook, then left the galley to follow Lobscouse. He reached his hammock and saw a form in it. For a moment, he thought it was someone else's bunk until he saw the long, skinny legs hanging down at one end and the thin arms at the other. He glimpsed a pale, washed-out face, slightly green about the gills, still wearing a pair of misty-looking spectacles.

"What's the use?" said Dick. He saw a folded tarpaulin lying on the deck, dropped atop it, and before the *Monitor* rolled back to another side, he was sound asleep.

CHAPTER FOUR

That bright day of March 8, the sun sparkled on the water and dried the clothing and gear spread out upon the salt-streaked upper deck of the little *Monitor* as she plodded placidly along behind the puffing Seth Low, with a streamer of smoke raveling from her tall funnel.

Cape Charles was astern, and on the portside of the ship was Cape Henry Light at the turning point into quiet Chesapeake Bay, with Hampton Roads, a haven for the *Monitor*, but twenty miles beyond.

Eight bells rang, ending the afternoon watch and signaling the starting of the first dog watch, four o'clock in the afternoon.

Lieutenant Worden came up on deck, with his binoculars slung about his neck. Dick was sitting there, his back against the sun-warmed metal of the turret. Lobscouse was beside him, patiently and skillfully sewing a seam along a pair of Dick's ripped trousers and glowering occasionally at Spec Simpson, now fully recovered, who was prattling on and on to two amused engineers about how he would have handled the pump emergencies of the day before. "But then, Chief Engineer Stimers did a fine job," said Spec affably. "A fine job indeed."

"Almost as good as ye cud have done, eh?" growled Lobscouse, snapping off a thread between his strong teeth.

"Well, now, Lobscouse—"

"Call me Silas, blast ye!" snapped Lobscouse.

"Silas, then. Well, I would have—"

"Mister Silas, ye lubber!"

"Mister Silas, then. I—"

"Silence, fore and aft!" called out Lieutenant Greene as he stopped beside Lieutenant Worden. Both officers were looking to the west. Worden raised his glasses and peered intently through them.

A far-off, thudding noise drifted across the quiet waters of the bay.

"Thunder," said Spec. His face paled. "Not another storm. I—"

"Silence there!" roared Boatswain Stocking.

Dick stared to the west. A thread of smoke was rising in the still air, and it gradually grew into an ominous-looking cloud high above the place where Hampton Roads was situated. The thudding noise seemed to intensify.

"Thunder?" said Jimmy Fox, with a strange look on his wizened face.

Jonas Barklew stood up and wiped his big hands on his blouse. "Thunder?" He shook his head. "Gunfire, mates. Big guns. Navy guns be like."

"Ours?" asked Hank Bascomb.

The water swashed gently against the sides of the little ship as she rolled along behind her hawser.

Lieutenant Worden lowered his glasses and cased them. "Mister Greene," he said quietly, "see that the ship is stripped of her sea rig. Have the turret keyed up? Prepare for action, sir, for unless I miss my guess, the *Merrimac* is loose among our wooden ships in Hampton Roads."

Boatswain Stocking's pipe twittered, and the crew

leaped into action. They stripped half-dried clothing and gear from the upper deck and carried it below. The stanchions and chain railing were taken down and stored. The two lifeboats were lowered into the water and towed astern by long painters, and the davits were removed and stored. The funnel stays were loosened, and the funnel was lowered to the deck.

In an incredibly short time, the tired crew had stripped their ship for action, until nothing showed above the flat upper deck but the squat turret, the tiny pilothouse, the base of the funnel from which smoke poured steadily, and the jack staff from which flew the Stars and Stripes.

Below, the crew kept working, stowing gear, carrying shot and shell, powder bags, gun equipment, and water-filled buckets into the turret while gunners checked the tackles and the gunlocks of the huge 11-inch Dahlgren's, removing the wooden tampions that had plugged the muzzles and running swabs through the bores to make sure there was no water inside the cannon. The surgeon laid out his instruments. Repair parties were still working at damage done by the storm. Reserves of ammunition and trays of 168-pound cast-iron shot had been placed below the turret. Now and then, a man would stagger a little with weariness, but not one man shirked, and even Spencer Simpson did what he could.

Dick wiped the sweat from his face as he and Hank Bascomb came down the turret ladder after hauling powder bags. He looked at Spec. "Well, Spec," he said, "you'll have a chance to leave the ship before we go into action."

The myopic eyes peered at Dick. "No," Spec said firmly. "I'm staying aboard!"

"You can't! You're a civilian!"

Spec raised his head. "I talked to Engineer Newton and told him what I knew about this ship. He said I'd be handy to have around."

Dick leaned against a bulkhead. "You've already been turned down by the Navy, Spec."

The boy winced as though he had been struck by a fist.

Just then, Lieutenant Greene happened to be passing by, and he stopped and looked at Spec. "I have been wondering what we'll do with you, boy," he said.

"I want to stay aboard, sir."

"He's nothin' but a Jonah," said Lobscouse.

Greene eyed the earnest young face with its glasses glinting in the light of the oil lamps. "I'll talk to the captain," he said. "I understand Mister Newton thinks you know quite a bit about the *Monitor*, Simpson."

Spec brightened. "I was in Rowland's Shipyard the day the keel was laid, sir. I ran errands for Mister Ericsson and Mister Stimers. I helped with some of the sketches and did everything I could to help make this ship, sir."

Lobscouse snorted and then subsided as Mister Greene glanced angrily at him.

"A patriot should never be held back from fighting for his country," Greene said, smiling at Spec. "There are so many men who would do anything to keep from defending their country; it is a pleasure to see one who wants to with all his heart. Come with me, Simpson."

Spec hurried forward after Lieutenant Greene.

Lobscouse shoved back his disreputable flat hat. "Well, I'll be mowed!" he sputtered. "Ye don't suppose they'll sign him up?"

"Never can tell," said Dick, shrugging, but in his heart, he wanted that boy to be part of the crew of the ship he had hardly been away from since its keel had been laid.

When dusk came across the waters, the flames from Hampton Roads could be plainly seen as the *Monitor* plowed along behind the Seth Low. Later, as many of the crew stood on the dark deck staring at the fire, Lieutenant Greene came up from below and steadied his glasses on the conflagration. "It's a fine big ship," he said. "A frigate, by the looks of her. The *Congress* or the *Cumberland* perhaps, lads."

There was no sound of gun firing now, nor had there been any for quite some time, but the results were plainly to be seen in the tall column of flame-shot smoke that towered higher and higher above a gallant ship of the United States Navy.

Dick Morgan stood quietly beside his brother on the gently heaving deck of the *Monitor*, watching those flames dancing and posturing, almost obscenely, against the night sky.

The pilot boat came surging out to meet them and dropped the serious-faced pilot aboard the *Monitor*, which had cast loose from the Seth Low and was proceeding under her own power toward Hampton Roads.

"What's the news, Pilot?" asked Boatswain Stocking as he took the man to Lieutenant Greene.

"It couldn't be worse, friend," said the pilot, eager to tell his fateful news. "The *Merrimac* came out into Hampton Roads about one o'clock today. The *Congress* opened fire on her when she was about a mile away. Her shot might have been puffballs for all the good they did. She came on, shooting her Dahlgren's at the *Congress*, but she was really after the *Cumberland*. I guess the rebs knew she had the most powerful guns. The *Cumberland*'s forward guns did good work for a time, that is. But the slaughter began as the *Merrimac* pounded that old wooden ship to death."

"Where was the rest of the fleet?" asked the boatswain.

"Tugs began to tow the *Minnesota*, Roanoke, and St. Lawrence to bring their guns into battle. The *Congress* retreated into shallow water and went aground. Then one after the other the *Minnesota*, Roanoke, and St. Lawrence went aground too. The *Merrimac* finished off the *Cumberland* without being scratched herself. Then she backed off and came on at full speed and rammed the *Cumberland*, making a hole you could have driven a horse and cart through! But her gun crews fought on while the *Merrimac* moved astern to rake her. The rebs called on her to surrender, but Lieutenant Morris of the *Cumberland* refused to strike his colors. That doomed ship fought on until she sank in about fifty feet of water with her flag still flying. A third of her crew were dead, wounded, or missing.

"The *Congress* was next. She didn't have a chance, sitting there in the mud, but she fought on with as much effect as though she was throwing spitballs at the *Merrimac*. The *Merrimac*'s guns did terrible execution. Lieutenant Joseph Smith, the *Congress*' Commander, was killed, and when the ship was nothing but a shambles, her flag was struck. But some of our Army boys on shore fired at the rebel ram, and the ram fired hot shot into the *Congress* to finish her off."

"We saw her burning," said Lieutenant Greene.

"The *Minnesota* was out there too," continued the pilot, "but by that time, the tide had turned, and the *Merrimac* retreated. But she'll be back, for we have nothing to stop her!"

Greene looked toward the blazing *Congress*. "We might have something to say about that, sir."

The pilot laughed without mirth. "With this Cheesebox on a Raft? She'll sink you with one broadside!"

The pilot went below and set a course for the flagship Roanoke, leaving a silent group of men on the deck of the *Monitor*.

Flames leaped and roared from the dying *Congress*, sending up vast showers of sparks. A feeling of dread seemed to drift over the illuminated waters along with the sparks and the smoke.

Lieutenant Worden reported to Captain Marston of the Roanoke, who immediately ordered him to go to the assistance of the helpless *Minnesota*, aground off Newport News. There was no channel pilot available, so Acting Master Samuel Howard of the Roanoke volunteered.

The slow progress of the *Monitor* was lighted by the fires of the *Congress*, and after midnight the little ship was moored at last beside the huge *Minnesota*.

Shortly afterward, the *Congress* reached her end, not all at once, but in a series of successive explosions as her powder tanks blew up one after the other. Beyond the *Congress* could be seen the tall masts of the sunken *Cumberland*, and from her peak still flew the Stars and Stripes.

A sailor aboard the *Minnesota* looked down contemptuously upon the little *Monitor*. "You'd better write out your last wills and testaments, mates," he called out, "if you aim to fight the *Merrimac* tomorrow. God may have mercy on you, but she won't!"

Gunner's Mate Jonas Barklew shook a big fist. "You can just sit there on that wooden tub, mate, and let us do your fighting for you!"

"Hawww! Hawww! You hear that mates?" the *Minnesota* man said over his shoulder. "A Tin Can on a Shingle is going to fight for us!"

"I ain't so sure but what he might be right," Jonas muttered, "But a man has to believe in his ship, Dick, whatever it is."

Dick nodded. "After all, Jonas," he said, "she did come through that storm. Besides, this was supposed to be a trial trip, not a trip into battle."

Lobscouse dumped his blankets on the deck next to the turret. "Too hot below, mates." He looked at Dick. "Trial trip, is it? It'll be a trial, all right! Between us and the *Merrimac*."

Spec Simpson wandered up on deck with his bedding

gear under his arm. "I have always said that this little ship will revolutionize naval warfare, mates."

"Mates is it?" said Lobscouse. "Why ain't you off this ship, Jonah?"

Spec drew himself up. "Because I have been enlisted by Captain Worden, that's why, mate!"

Jonas groaned. He picked up a piece of wood and snapped it between his fingers to make the lucky break and then crossed the first and second fingers of each hand.

"Childish superstitions," said Spec as he placed his bedding beside that of Dick.

"What's your duty?" asked Dick.

"Wiper in the engine room. Mister Newton said he needed technical assistance, and although Captain Worden wanted me to act as assistant to his clerk, I demurred and insisted on serving where my qualifications best suit me. Now I—"

"Stow your jaw tackle," said Jimmy Fox sourly. "If we're to go into battle in the morning, we'll need sleep!"

"We will not," said Spec. "Tomorrow is Sunday."

"That won't stop the *Merrimac*," said Dick.

Lobscouse came forward with his empty pipe clenched between his teeth. "Sunday is a lucky day for seamen and fishermen."

"Don't put your trust in luck," said Spec. "Put it in good Yankee iron and a well-designed ship, eh, mates?"

"Rather, put your faith in God," said a quiet voice from the darkness.

They all looked up to see the serious, bearded face of Captain Worden as he passed by to go to his quarters for the night.

They could get a little sleep that night, for there was still work to be done aboard the ship. The smell of smoke and wet burned wood hung heavily over Hampton Roads. Beneath oil lamps hung in the lower rigging, the crew of the *Minnesota* were hard at work heaving supplies, extra gear, reserve ammunition, and everything else that could be spared over the sides to lighten the ship so she might float free from the viscous mud that held her to the bottom. If the *Monitor* could not hold off the *Merrimac* the following morning, the *Minnesota* would be doomed, and also the Roanoke, the St. Lawrence, and the rest of the ships at Hampton Roads, unless they could escape to sea. But their purpose was to fight the rebel "ram," not to run away from her, and if she sank them, she would sink any other ships in the United States Navy. None could stop her if she got past the *Monitor*.

If the *Merrimac* was victorious over the *Monitor*, she could then possibly break the Federal naval blockade of Confederate ports, and "King Cotton" would rule once more; British and other European mills were hungry for cotton, the "White Gold" of the Confederacy, and in return, they would pour food and military supplies into the South; the Confederacy would receive recognition as an independent nation and the Union cause would suffer irreparably.

It was hard to sleep on the deck of the *Monitor* that night. Tugboats chuffed through the darkness, towing heavily laden military transport and supply ships to sea. Hampton Roads was a major military base for the United States. It was situated at the mouth of the James River, which was a waterway to Richmond, Virginia, and contained an expanse of quiet harbor ten miles wide, fed not only by the James but also by the Nansemond and the two branches of the Elizabeth. Fort Monroe at Old Point Comfort frowned down upon the harbor, but there was little that Fort Monroe could do to stop the *Merrimac* from cutting her swaths of terror and destruction.

The United States needed Hampton Roads for a contemplated Army attack up the Peninsula paralleling the James, a direct route to Richmond, the Confederate capital. Thousands of troops, batteries of artillery, wagons, horses, and mules, supplies of every imaginable type, pontoon bridges, ambulances, and the myriad things an army needs on a major land operation would have to be brought by sea to Hampton Roads and unloaded at Old Point Comfort under the protection of the guns of Fort Monroe. But if the *Merrimac* controlled the Roads, no unarmed transports and supply ships could be brought into the harbor, thus forestalling a Union land attack on Richmond.

Perhaps the huge rebel ram could even be used to attack Washington, the national capital, via the Chesapeake Bay and the Potomac River. It was a chilling thought. She might head for New York and Boston and demand tribute from those big merchant and shipping cities or sink every ship in their great harbors.

Dick Morgan rolled and tossed on his hard bed. The *Monitor* was tiny compared to the huge, armored mass of the *Merrimac*; she had but two guns to the *Merrimac*'s ten; it had been said the *Merrimac* had a crew of about three hundred and fifty men; the *Monitor* had fifty-eight ready for duty.

"David and Goliath," he said softly to the night sky.

CHAPTER FIVE

The rising sun slowly burned away the low mist that hung over Hampton Roads and gave promise of a lovely spring day. The water was calm, with a slight ripple glinting in the rays of the sun. High overhead, the crying gulls swooped and darted, dropping suddenly to snatch at food. There were other things floating upon the water besides food — timbers and shattered pieces of wood, debris from the ships that had been battered to death the day before, bodies of seamen and gunners of the United States Navy who had kept their trust and had died because they had done so.

The crew of the *Monitor* had little time to enjoy the beauties of a fine spring morning. Before dawn, those men who had bunked aboard the grounded *Minnesota* had been ferried back aboard their own ship. The early morning wind freshened, and the little ship rode easily on the slight swells. The crew were quiet as they went about their duties. It was still an unfamiliar ship to them. Aboard the Sabine or the North Carolina, they would have been ready for action in a matter of minutes after Beat to Quarters had sounded. On the *Monitor,* they were dealing with a ship — if that was the proper term — that no one had ever before taken to sea or into action. They had experienced her seagoing qualities and hadn't been impressed. Now and then, the men on the deck would look across the rippling waters of the Roads toward the misty shore at the mouth of the Elizabeth River where the *Merrimac* had retired for the night. Eight miles was a mighty short distance for a steamer to travel.

"Is that smoke among the trees and the mist there?" asked Hank Bascomb from the grated top of the turret.

Jonas Barklew was wiping the sweat from his broad face. "Could be, mate," he said.

Hank looked down between his bare feet at the men working within the confines of the turret. "Well," he commented, "we're probably as ready for them as we'll ever be."

Dick Morgan shivered a little. It was damp and cold inside the turret. His brother, Ben, glanced at him. "I'm to serve on the starboard gun, young'un," he said. "Maybe you'd be better off below if we go into action."

Gunner's Mate Barklew glanced at Dick. "Aye," he said.

Dick shook his head. "I heard they killed a powder boy aboard the *Congress*," he stated quietly. "He was only thirteen. He stayed at his duty. I'm going to stay at mine."

Ben smiled. "I thought you'd say that."

Jonas Barklew came down inside the turret and slapped a hand on the huge Dahlgren gun beside him. "There's one thing bothering me," he said. "We're to use only fifteen pounds of powder per charge."

Hank Bascomb stared at him. "I never heard the like, Jonas. These guns can safely handle thirty pounds per charge. Why only fifteen?"

Jonas shrugged. "They say a full charge would be too much inside this iron can, mate. Concussion or some such foolishness."

"But the blast would be outside the turret," said Dick.

Jonas held out his hands, palms upward. "Sure, we

know that! Ericsson knows it! Captain Worden knows it too. Everyone knows it but old Commodore Smith, a stick-and-string sailor who knows less about a ship like this than a cat does, but he gave the order. Captain Worden has been trying to get permission to use full charges from the higher-ups around here, but you know the Navy. No one will take the responsibility."

"I wish I had my way," said Ben quietly. "I'd give the full charge. With thirty pounds, we'd smash right through their armor plating!"

They were getting up steam aboard the *Monitor*. The men in the turret could hear the ringing and scraping of the coal scoops on the metal deck below them as the fires were fed and the coals were raked with devil's-claw and slice bar. Layer after black layer of anthracite was skillfully hurled into the fire door and spread across the bed of coals to make them roar with heat.

The decks were clear. Engineers checked the propelling engine and the smaller engine used to turn the massive turret. The fire was put out in the galley after coffee had been brewed. Small arms had been readied and placed in racks. Carbines, pistols, cutlasses, axes, and boarding half-pikes were ready at hand in case the anticipated fight turned into a hand-to-hand affair. If the *Merrimac* had three hundred and fifty men aboard her, as rumored, the odds would be high against the fifty-eight bluejackets and officers of the *Monitor*. Six to one. Six yelling, hot-tempered rebels against one Yankee. According to all the Southern newspapers of the day, one Southerner was a match for ten Yankees.

Dick watched Lieutenant Greene marking the deck so that he would know which was fore and which was aft when the turret was turned in battle. It would be easy enough to get confused when the turret whirled about, as it had done in the few practices they had had with it. At least no one had ever convinced the United States Navy that one rebel seaman was a match for ten salty Yankees.

Sand was spread on the turret floor. Dick felt a little green when he saw it being done. It was a custom brought over from the wooden ships. Blood was slippery, and sand afforded better footing for gunners at their hot and deadly work. That was also why bulwarks near the guns were always painted red — so that bloodstains would not show. Dick forced away the chilling thought. There were eight inches of iron between him and the enemy shot and shell — eight layers of one-inch plate bolted together. But Ericsson had originally planned four layers of two-inch plating, substituting the eight layers when it had been impossible to get delivery of the two-inch plating in time. Dick began to wonder if there would be much difference.

They tested the shell hoist, another of Ericsson's innovations. It wasn't easy to get a 168-pound solid shot up from below through the narrow trap door set into the deck of the turret, so the Swedish genius had forthwith designed a shell hoist. But the opening in the turret deck had to correspond exactly with that of the opening into the lower areas, or nothing would get through. And in the hot excitement of battle, supposing they never did get it lined up and the turret ran out of ammunition? It was another lurking, unnerving thought that Dick had to drive from his mind.

Ben glanced at Dick. "One thing I learned," he said quite casually, "is that action and the shooting of the guns usually drives any doubts out of a man's mind. Isn't that so, Jonas?"

"Aye, mate! A man has no time to be afraid, nervous, or panicky when these big boys begin to sing." He ran a hand along the long barrel of the huge Dahlgren. "They won't let you down. It's the men who might let them down if the truth be known." He glared fiercely about at the men in the turret. There would be a score of them confined in that squat iron cylinder, twenty feet across, nine feet high; there would be eight men and a gun captain to each of the two guns, and Lieutenant Greene, who would command the battery, and Acting Master Louis Stodder.

Ben checked the tackles that were used to pull aside the huge port stoppers that closed the ports against enemy fire while the guns were being loaded. The guns were muzzle-loaders and must be run in so that rammers and swabs could do their work.

The sun was already warming the sides of the turret and filtering down through the grating atop it, making strange barred patterns upon men and guns. Lieutenant Greene went below to check on the men who worked in the powder division.

Jimmy Fox leaned against the side of the turret. "I wonder how good a gunnery officer he is," he said, jerking a thumb toward the deck. They all knew what he meant. The officer was new to the ship, as all of them were new themselves. But there was a difference. They were all trained gunners and had been trained aboard two crack ships, the Sabine and the North Carolina, under gunnery officers who knew their business. They might not be sure of the *Monitor*, but they knew Dahlgren's, and they knew one another as a gun crew should. Lieutenant Samuel Dana Greene was the unknown quantity.

Hank Bascomb tied a scarf about his thick dark hair to keep sweat from running into his eyes when in action. "He was on a good ship, the Hartford when the war started," he said.

"Only three years out of the Naval Academy at Annapolis, though," said Jimmy Fox.

"Twenty-two years av age," noted Mike Reilly gloomily.

They all looked at one another.

"Belay that!" snapped Gun Captain Tom Lochrane. "Ye'll be licked before ye open fire if ye keep on thinkin' like that! We're goin' into battle to win! There is no other way to think! We're men-o-war's men aboard the finest ship, in the finest Navy, in the world, and ye keep on thinkin' that way! What are we up against? A rattletrap of a hulk plated with rusty iron and manned by lubbers! I've heard tell they do not have naval gunners aboard, but landsmen to man and fire them! Artillerymen!" He spat through a gun port.

The men began to grin. "Tell 'em, Tommy," said Boatswain's Mate John Stocking, who was gun captain of the other gun.

Ben crooked a finger at Dick. "Get below and bring up a water breaker or two," he said. "It will be hot, thirsty work in this iron tub when the guns get to their work and the sun warms us up a bit."

Dick went down the ladder to the berth deck and saw Gunner's Mate Joseph Crown organizing his powder division. There was a quiet hustle and bustle inside the poorly lighted interior of the ship. She rose and fell a little in the swell, tugging restlessly at her anchor as though impatient to get into motion. He passed the water breakers up into the turret, then hurried aft to the engine room. The engineers were stripped to the waist, checking and rechecking their charge, while the firemen steadily stoked the roaring fires and steam hissed at the escape valves. A gangling, bespectacled figure moved about with a strange grace and agility, wiping down brass and steel with a huge wad of waste and peering myopically at imagined spots on the glistening metal.

"You'll wear that engine out," said Dick dryly, "before we get a chance to use it, Spec."

Spec turned quickly. "What's doing aloft?" he asked.

Dick grinned. "Aloft? We've set topgallants and royals and are making at least ten knots by the log chip."

The boy flushed. "I mean in the turret? Outside?"

Dick shrugged. "Nothing yet. The sun's hardly up."

"You'd never know it down here," said Spec. "I thought it was still dark outside."

Dick wiped the sweat from his face. "We thought we

saw smoke over by the mouth of the Elizabeth. Might have been mist."

"That's where it is?"

Dick nodded.

"I wonder if they know we're here."

"Who knows?" Dick grinned again. "If they come out looking for trouble, they'll surely find out."

"Yes," said Spec a little uneasily.

"You'll be safe enough down here," said Dick. "Stay at your job. You have iron and coal on each side and, outside the hull, a lot of water to stop shells and shot. Unless they can drop one on the deck, which is impossible because they can't angle a shot like that, there isn't much they can do to hurt the engines, propeller, and rudder."

The boy peered at Dick. "I wasn't thinking about my safety. It'll be you and the others in that turret I'll be thinking about."

Engineer Newton stopped beside them. "If every man aboard does his job and doesn't let the crew and the ship down, there'll be nothing to worry about, lads. We'll keep the engine turning over and a full head of steam; the captain will conn her into the fight and handle her; you gunners will sink the *Merrimac*. It's as simple as all that."

"Yes, sir," said Spec. He smiled thinly at Dick, then held out his hand. "Thanks," he said quietly.

Dick stared at him. "For what, Spec?"

"Why, for being my friend! For being aboard the *Monitor*! For everything!"

Dick took the proffered hand and shook it. "I—" he said, and then his voice trailed off, and his emotions almost took control. "See you in Liverpool," he said suddenly, the old seaman's farewell, meaning that old shipmates would always see each other again, sometime, somewhere. He turned on a heel and left the steaming-hot engine room.

Dick scuttled up on deck, where a few crewmen

stood looking across the Roads. There were two fine-looking ships at anchor midway between Old Point Comfort and the southern shore. "Foreign ships," said a seaman. "The British *Rinaldo* and the French *Gassendi*."

"What are they doing here?" asked Dick.

"They're curious about us, I suppose. This fight today may decide the fate of the world's navies, and France and Great Britain will want firsthand reports."

Another seaman nodded. "Aye, and maybe it'll decide which way they will jump, North or South," he said dryly.

Dick looked across the sparkling waters. It was nearing high tide, and the *Merrimac* needed all the water she could get under her bottom, for it was said she drew twenty-two feet of water. There was a suspicion of dark smoke hanging in the mist along the far shore. The sky was pinkish-white and seemed to blend with the soft, woolly mist. Gulls swooped and dived across the smooth water. They would not be there long if gunfire opened again, as it surely would.

"It's smoke for certain," said an engineer who had come up for a breath of fresh air.

"Aye," said a seaman. "And it's not a picnic they're readyin' for either."

"Be like a picnic for us," said Lobscouse as he came up through the hatch like a bearded jack-in-the-box. "Ye'd better get back in the turret, Dick. All men must be at their posts soon enough."

They went down into the berth deck, thence up the ladder into the crowded turret. They were all there now. Lieutenant Greene picked up the voice tube as a faint whistling sound came through it. He listened for a moment. "Aye, aye, sir," he said quietly. He hung up the tube and turned to look at the waiting men. "Cast loose and provide," he commanded.

The trained gun crews moved swiftly. "Run in!" came the commands, and the heavy guns were drawn back from the ports. "Load!" Dick passed a powder bag to the

First Loader, who thrust it into the muzzle of the gun and slammed it home with a heave of the copper-tipped rammer. A wad followed, then the heavy solid shot was heaved up and dropped into the muzzle and seated firmly home atop wad and charge, to be followed by another wad. Gun captains cocked and capped gunlocks, then checked the lock strings or lanyards.

"Run out!" came the command from both gun captains instantaneously.

The twin 11-inch Dahlgren's were heaved forward by their heavy tackles so that the muzzles protruded from the gun ports like vacant-looking black eyes. "Good time," approved Mister Greene. The men grinned self-consciously. Mister Greene might be all right, at that.

The turret had been turned so that the guns were trained forward. Dick glanced along the barrel of his gun, the starboard one, and saw that she bore almost directly in the little pilothouse. That might be a problem, for they could hardly fire over it. The muzzle blast might be too dangerous for the men inside the iron-log structure and if the muzzles of the guns were depressed too low... He shook his head. It wasn't nice to think about.

Lobscouse looked about the turret. "If a shot hits one of them bolts," he said quietly, "it might drive the thing right into a man, might it not, mates?"

"Right through your solid head," growled Jonas Barklew. "Belay that talk, Lobscouse!"

"I was only thinking, Jonas!"

"That's a new thing for you to do, Lobscouse, but don't start it now. It's not the time! Just stay your own unthinking self until after the battle!"

The crewmen were stripping to the waist and binding cloth about their foreheads to keep the forthcoming sweat from dripping down into their eyes. It would be hot in that great iron tub, with two Dahlgren's furnishing the heat.

The *Monitor* was ready. Steam hissed in the valves.

Engineers, stokers, powdermen, gunners, surgeon, captain, and helmsman were all ready. She tugged at her anchor in the rising tide.

"Maybe they're not coming," said Jimmy Fox hopefully. Suddenly the thudding of drums sounded across the waters of Hampton Roads as ship after ship Beat to Quarters.

Lieutenant Greene walked to the starboard gun port and peered through it. For a long moment, he was silent, and then he turned. "Thick smoke," he said. "It is the *Merrimac*, with two other smaller ships escorting her. She's coming for the *Minnesota*, men."

The wind had begun to freshen. Dick shifted a little and peered from the gun port. A thickening layer of smoke hung over the quiet water. The sun flashed from the silvery wings of darting gulls as they swooped through mist and smoke, away from the oncoming mass of metal. A sickening feeling came over Dick as he saw the *Merrimac* for the first time. She was like a huge, floating barn with many doors cut into the sides. Smoke billowed up from her tall funnel. Flags fluttered from her tall jack staffs.

"Is that her?" said Lobscouse breathlessly from just behind Dick.

Dick nodded. She moved like a great sluggish turtle, and no one could be seen aboard her. It was almost as though she moved without the hand of man to direct her —a prehistoric monster that had come down through the eons of history to live again and to fly the Stars and Bars, as though conjured up by some great Confederate Merlin.

Dick stepped back. She was about four times larger than the *Monitor* and had ten guns to two. The crew of the *Monitor* had had little sleep and not much food in the past forty-eight hours. Fear began to play strange tricks with Dick's stomach.

"She's turnin' to port," said Lobscouse. He swallowed. "Headin' for the *Minnesota*."

"And us," said Ben Morgan. "I wonder if they see us."

Suddenly there was a crashing sound, and something hummed through the air. Ben Morgan looked back at Lieutenant Greene. "She has opened fire with her bow gun, sir. It fell away short."

A tremor ran through the frame of the *Monitor*, followed by the steady clicking of the ratchets of the anchor winch as the anchor was drawn up taut, then pulled free of the muddy bottom. In a moment, the little ship began to move slowly through the water toward the smoke-shrouded behemoth that was still coming on, firing steadily with her bow gun at the helpless *Minnesota*.

The engines throbbed steadily, faster, and faster, and the bow ripple of the little ship increased.

Suddenly, above the thudding of the engines came the clear ringing of eight bells in pairs, eight o'clock, Sunday morning, March 9, 1862.

CHAPTER SIX

There was a sharp, whistling sound in the voice tube. "You may commence firing, Mister Greene," came the calm words of Lieutenant Worden from the pilothouse.

Lieutenant Greene peered along the top of the starboard gun, then stepped back, lock string in hand. "Stand clear!" he snapped as he gave the lock string a firm, steady pull. The big Dahlgren coughed and roared, belching flame and smoke. It slammed back hard against the friction recoil device of John Ericsson. "Direct hit!" said Mister Greene. He stepped to the next gun and sighted along the thick barrel.

"Run in! Sponge! Load!" the commands cracked out one after the other as the starboard gun was reloaded just as the port gun blasted flame and smoke.

Suddenly, almost like a terrible echo of the second shot from the *Monitor* came a thundering, crashing noise, and the turret shuddered and rang like a great out-of-tune bell.

The *Merrimac* had let go her Sunday punch, a full broadside, at almost point-blank range. The men in the turret glanced at one another, at the walls of the turret, and began to grin. "They can't hurt this ship!" yelled Mike Reilly.

They could feel the increased throbbing of the engine and the humming of the blowers as they reloaded the port gun.

Lieutenant Greene picked up the voice tube. "Sir," he said exultantly, "We took the best she has! No bolts have flown out! The turret machinery hasn't been damaged!"

Dick stepped back from his gun and saw Acting Master Louis Stodder lying unconscious on the deck. Jonas Barklew picked him up. "He had his knee against the turret wall," said the huge gunner. "The shock of the solid shot hitting the outside threw him to the deck."

"Get him below, Barklew," said Lieutenant Greene.

The turret was stopped in conjunction with the hole in the deck, and they passed the unconscious man down below. After they did this, the turret was swung again. Meanwhile, they could hear the steady hammering of the guns of their opponent, but nothing was hitting the little Union ship.

The port stoppers were heaved up by the sweating men. Greene sighted the starboard gun. "We'll try for her propeller," he said. "Stand clear!" He jerked the lock string and stepped aside as the great gun recoiled with a thunderous blast. Next, he sighted the port gun and fired it.

Almost instantly, as though the blast of the gun had ignited the charges in the broadside of the *Merrimac*, there came a smashing, thundering reply from the huge ironclad. The *Monitor* shook and shuddered beneath the iron hail. A gunner, Pete Trescott, staggered back from his position and collapsed near the turret-revolving machinery, with blood pouring from his mouth, nose, and ears.

"Concussion," said Mister Stimers. "He leaned against the turret wall."

"Let down the port stoppers," commanded Lieutenant Greene. "Load! Get that man below!"

The men strained at the tackles to lower the heavy stoppers while others went through the precise motions of reloading the two guns. The turret was stopped over the hole in the deck, and Trescott was lowered through it.

The gunnery officer's face was pale and taut. "Trice up the ports!" he said.

The sweating men left the guns and hauled on the heavy tackles to raise the massive stoppers.

"This will never do," grunted Jonas Barklew. "We'll be knocked out raising these slabs of metal."

Greene nodded. "Then we'll turn the ship away while we reload."

His words were echoed by the thundering of the *Merrimac*'s broadside, but nothing hit the little ship. Lieutenant Worden had discovered one tactical advantage: the *Monitor* could outspeed and outmaneuver the *Merrimac* like a lightweight fighter facing a heavyweight. But there seemed to be another advantage as well. The heavyweight depended on the power of his punches to floor the lightweight, and the *Monitor*, as well as being faster and more maneuverable, was seemingly safe from the heaviest punches the *Merrimac* could throw!

The gunners could feel the movements of their ship. The voice tube whistled, and Greene answered it. "She bears to starboard?" he asked, then nodded. He turned quickly. "Stand by," he said.

Dick bent down and peered through a port, through the swirling smoke shot with glinting rays of the sun, to where he saw a huge slab of dark metal, scored by brighter streaks and dents, looming up through the thick haze.

"Stand clear!" came the command.

Greene jerked the lock string of the starboard gun, then leaped to the other and fired it also. Smoke poured back into the turret and began to drift slowly through the grating atop it. "Two hits!" yelled Hank Bascomb exultantly.

"Run in! Sponge! Load!"

The turret swung away from the *Merrimac* just as she fired from her stern gun. The guns were reloaded in jig time. The heat was getting intense within the iron tub of a turret, and the thick smoke had begun to blacken every man. Rivulets of sweat cut white channels on their smoke-blackened skin. The whites of their eyes and their teeth made them look like blackface minstrels, but there were no wide grins on those faces, as on those of minstrels; rather, looks of confidence, broken now and then by quiet smiles. They had a trust in their little ship. Let any stick-and-string sailor kid a *Monitor* man now!

The two fighting ships circled each other, the *Monitor* always keeping between the *Merrimac* and its helpless prey, the stranded *Minnesota*. Time and time again, the huge rebel ship would slowly plow toward the sailing ship, only to find the pesty little *Monitor* in the way since it could move more quickly through shallower water.

Every time the *Merrimac* fired, the *Monitor* seemed to shake off the effect of the solid shot, then spin her turret and spit flames, smoke, and two 168-pound solid shot that shook the ironclad to her very bones.

For two hours, time meant nothing to Dick Morgan as he passed powder charges to the rammer of his gun. Sweat trickled over his blackened skin, his feet slipped and slid on the sanded metal of the deck, while powder smoke made his eyes run and his throat dry up into a brassy tube. Fire, run in, sponge, reload, run out, and fire again, the powder boys like grotesquely streaked automatons obeyed the hoarse commands of Lieutenant Greene, seeing nothing but the hot, smoking gun they served.

The heat was terrible within the turret. Lieutenant Greene looked out at the deck and saw that his white markings had long vanished. Now a strange thing happened, for the men within the turret, and above all, Lieutenant Greene, had no idea of which way the turret was facing because of the constant revolving, first one way, then another. The relentless blasting of the guns, the exertions, the thickening smoke, and concentration of heat within the turret made the whole thing seem unreal.

Greene made his way to the voice tube. "How does the *Merrimac* bear, sir?" he called desperately. He nodded. "To port?" He turned quickly, and an odd look came over his face. Which way was port, which starboard, and which fore and aft?

"Shoot on the fly, sir!" called out Jonas Barklew.

Stimers, now in charge of the turret-revolving mechanism, nodded in agreement.

And so it was, for minute after minute of roaring battle. The guns would be reloaded, the turret turned, and when Lieutenant Greene, crouching behind the thick bottle-shaped breeches of one gun or the other, saw the enemy, he would quickly step back and fire, then fire the other gun, even as the turret turned, like a shot-gunner leading a flying bird.

"The *Merrimac*'s stack looks like a bloomin' colander!" cried Mike Reilly.

"That won't sink her!" said Ben Morgan.

"It'll make it hard to keep up a draft on her fires," said Stimers. "I know those engines. They never were any good and could hardly move the old *Merrimac* through the water. With all that iron hung on her and her deep draft, she'll be lucky if she can move at all."

Greene turned to the voice tube and picked it up as the guns were being reloaded. He whistled into it, then spoke, then whistled sharply once more. A puzzled look came over his blackened face. He whistled again and again, but it was no use. "The tube has evidently been broken," he said.

The engineer nodded. "Vibrations, probably. But we can't stop firing, Mister Greene!"

"Run out!" said Greene. He crouched over the breech of the port gun and peered through the narrow port and thence into the shrouding smoke.

———

DICK'S HEART went out to the young officer, but twenty-two years old, hardly a veteran, since it was his first battle. He had not been trained at the Academy or aboard the Hartford for this fighting from a sealed and stifling iron cylinder filled with smoke, cut off from the advice and commands of Lieutenant Worden, and forced to make his own decisions in the newest fighting machine in the world.

Greene did his best, crouching, peering, stepping back, and firing as the turret swept around. He gave his commands in a steady voice and hardly knew the effect of his firing upon the enemy.

There was one thing the men in the turret knew. The Monitor was holding her own out there in the smoke.

There was another problem that had come up. They could not fire directly forward, along the center line of the ship, because of the low, iron-log pilothouse that rose above the deck almost four feet high. If a solid shot fired from a depressed gun hit that pilothouse, there would be nothing left to control the Monitor.

Something struck the side of the Monitor and grated loudly along her metal-sheathed deck. Dick saw a huge wall of metal only a few feet away from the turret, and cut into the wall were several large openings. Even as he watched, he saw the smoking muzzles of heavy guns appear as if by magic in the openings. The Merrimac had come alongside; she had been that close. "Turn!" Dick screamed at Stimers. The turret began to move.

"Drop port stoppers!" yelled Greene.

The stoppers dropped heavily just as the turret began to move, and then the blasting thunder of the Merrimac's guns almost shattered the eardrums of the *Monitor*'s men. Gunners went down on the deck and looked about dazedly.

The turret was still turning. "Trice up ports!" commanded Greene.

The men heaved mightily at the tackles. If they opened those stoppers and the *Merrimac*'s guns were bearing right on them, it would be the end of the *Monitor*, for there was no other gun crew aboard.

"Run out! Stand clear!" Greene jerked both lock strings at the same time, and the big guns slammed back against the tackle ropes and against Ericsson's clever friction devices while thick greasy smoke poured back into the turret.

"Turn! Run in! Sponge and reload!"

On and on until Dick Morgan felt that he had known no other world but this, the powder charges were getting low, and yet it seemed as though the solid shot of the twin 11-inch Dahlgren's had as little effect on the *Merrimac* as her broadsides had on the *Monitor*. Dick remembered then that they were using half charges of fifteen pounds instead of the usual thirty-pound charges. That might have made a difference!

"She's trying to get to the *Minnesota*!" cried out Boatswain's Mate John Stocking.

So she was, plowing sluggishly across the stern of the *Monitor*, trying to get at the wooden ships she could so easily destroy. But the *Monitor* turned, almost as though sensing what the enemy was going to do, and when the *Merrimac* got within good range of the towering *Minnesota*, a little raft with an iron turret on it was in the way. The ports of the turret flamed and roared, and the shot struck solidly against the casemate of the *Merrimac*. She hesitated, then slowly turned to fire her broadside just as the port stoppers on the *Monitor* dropped, and the turret whirled about like a ballerina to take the thumping shot against the rear of the turret.

"Ammunition almost done, sir!" cried out Gun Captain Lochrane.

Greene turned and wiped the black sweat from his face. "We'll have to pull out of the fight," he said. He grinned at the startled looks on the men's clown faces. "Just to replenish, boys! Just to replenish, we're not through with her yet!"

The men cheered. Stimers had the turret stopped over the deck hatch that led down into the ship, and a man raced forward to notify Lieutenant Worden of the necessity for replenishing the ammunition.

"She's coming right at us!" screamed Hank Bascomb as he peered through a port in the turret.

The gunners stood to their posts. Gun Captain Lochrane looked at Lieutenant Greene. "Last shot in the locker, sir," he said.

Stocking saluted. "We are out of ammunition completely, sir!"

Greene nodded. The *Monitor* was moving swiftly through the water, but the *Merrimac* had by some miracle managed to get up enough steam to cut her off. Smoke poured from the shot-pierced funnel of the great ironclad as she bore down on her little adversary, with the water rippling back from the unseen ram she carried at her submerged prow.

There was nothing to do but wait.

Then the ironclad was upon them and slammed hard against the overhang of the *Monitor*'s side. The turret whirled, and the port stopper was raised. The *Merrimac* was grating and grinding alongside the *Monitor* with as little effect as though she were a tugboat shoving a log raft along. The *Monitor* turned away. Greene fired his last shot. "Fair and true!" he called out. "That must have hurt her! I saw bolts fly from her side and a plate rise!"

The *Monitor* sped for the safety of the shallower water near the north shore, where she knew the *Merrimac* could not follow her. The turret was stopped over the hole in the deck, and the sweating men hauled ammunition and charges up into the overheated turret as swiftly as they could. They seemed imbued with superhuman strength and endurance as they worked. Lieutenant Greene reported to Lieutenant Worden and arranged a relay of two messengers to carry orders and information between the pilothouse and the turret. Paymaster Keeler and Captain's Clerk Toffey were assigned those duties. They would have to shout their messages up through the turret hatchway when and if the turret stopped over it. It was less than makeshift, but it was all they could do.

"The *Merrimac* has been aground, but she is free now!"

"What is her course?"

"Right for the *Minnesota*! The *Minnesota* has opened fire on her!"

"And?"

The answer came in a moment as a blasting, roaring discharge rolled across the water and echoed from the shores.

"That's *Minnesota*'s broadside!" There was silence a moment. "That broadside would have blown any timber-built ship in the world out of the water. The *Merrimac*? unharmed. She is firing with her bow rifle on the *Minnesota*. The shot is going right through the *Minnesota*. She hasn't a chance."

The men worked feverishly, passing up charges and ammunition. They were needed out there!

"She has just fired on a tugboat! Blew it up! There's nothing left but junk and smoke where the tugboat was!"

"Back into action!" ordered Worden.

The men in the stifling turret closed up about their guns. The *Monitor* moved back into action to forestall another attack on the *Minnesota*.

They had edged the *Merrimac* almost a mile away from the *Minnesota* when the little ship opened fire once more.

The smoke again filled the turret. They were close aboard now, so close that they could see the side of the *Merrimac* in the short intervals when she bore into view through the narrow turret ports. The turret would spit flame and smoke and then whirl to take her punishment. The slamming of shot against turret was a fearful sound, but the men were sure of their ship now, and they reloaded their guns in 140-degree heat as though at target practice.

"We are going to ram, sir!" called Toffey up through the open hatchway.

They could hear the rapid beating of the engine as the *Monitor* picked up speed. The port stoppers were down, and the guns loaded and ready for firing when the *Monitor* rammed.

Ben glanced at Dick. "This will be the supreme test," he said quietly.

Shot thudded against the turret and shook the little ship, but she kept on, faster and faster.

"What time is it?" asked Jimmy Fox suddenly.

"Almost eight bells," replied Jonas Barklew.

The men stared at each other. They had been in action for almost four hours!

The *Merrimac* was firing steadily now, evidently to stop the doughty little ship trying to ram her. Then suddenly, one of her shot struck the ship somewhere forward, and the whole structure shuddered. There was no sound of impact from the *Monitor*'s striking the *Merrimac*.

"Trice up the ports!" commanded Greene.

The twin openings showed the stern of the *Merrimac* not fifty yards away. Greene fired one gun, and the shot struck true, ripping off some plating and splinters from the wooden backing beneath it.

The turret ground to a halt over the opening in the deck. Captain's Clerk Toffey peered up into the smoky turret. "You had better come forward at once, sir," he said to Lieutenant Greene. "The pilothouse was struck by that last shot."

Greene leaned toward the white-faced man. "How is the captain?" he asked.

Toffey swallowed hard. "The shot smashed directly against the forward sighting slit, sir. I think Lieutenant Worden has been blinded. His face was just behind the slit and caught the full blast. Some of the iron logs have been shifted or cracked, and the top of the pilothouse has been knocked loose."

Greene turned to Stimers. "Take over here, Mister Stimers," he said quietly. "I shall have to take command."

They could feel the ship edging away and turning sharply as she went out of action. How badly was she hurt? How badly had the captain been injured? Would Lieutenant Greene be able to handle the ship? Those questions ran through every man's mind.

Dick went down the ladder to pick up a reserve water breaker. It was then he saw Lieutenant Worden being brought to the surgeon. His face was a mass of blood, and it seemed as though his eyes must have been blasted from their sockets. But there was no time to waste. Dick hurried back up the ladder as Paymaster Keeler ran toward the base of the turret. "Get ready for action!" he yelled. "We are going in again!"

The turret was turned, and the port stoppers opened, ready for action. Stimers crouched over the breech of the starboard gun, then stepped back. "Stand clear! Fire!" he commanded.

The gun roared. Jonas Barklew peered through the smoke. "She's running!" he yelled. "Low at the stern and smoking like a house afire! She's running, boys!"

The *Monitor* was coming from the shallows where she had gone while the command was changed, and the ship inspected for damage.

Stimers smiled as he bent over the port gun. "Stand clear!" he commanded. "We'll give her a parting shot for good luck, men!" He jerked the lock string, and the gun slammed back, roaring in defiance.

Slowly the great rebel craft limped back across the smoke-covered waters, leaking clouds of smoke from the riddled funnel. Her flags were stained and torn by the gunfire, and pieces of plating and timber hung from her sides and stern. She was low by the stern and seemed to be dragging herself away from the iron mite that had fought her shot for shot and had kept her from destroying the helpless *Minnesota*.

The *Monitor* turned slowly too and proceeded to the side of the *Minnesota*. As the tired men in the turret grinned at one another, they heard the engine stop for the first time in hours and then heard the anchor chain rattle out as the ship was moored. Eight bells rang out aboard her. Twelve o'clock noon, Sunday, March 9, 1862.

CHAPTER SEVEN

T he gunners of the *Monitor* descended from the
turret, and they looked as though they had been
carved from ebony, so black from smoke were
they. Their clothing was soaked with sweat and black
clear through to the skin, and some of them shook spasmodically from the intense battering their nervous
system had taken.

The shooting was over, but it seemed to Dick Morgan
that he could still hear it, and his head seemed to be
twice as big as it really was.

"How is the captain?" each man asked as he reached
the bottom of the ladder.

Captain's Clerk Toffey answered them. "It's not so
bad as we feared. The logs of the pilothouse had been
sealed with cement, and it was the cement that was
driven into his eyes."

"Will he ever see again?" asked Dick quietly.

"We don't know, Dick."

The blowers and ventilators were drawing fresh air
into the steaming hull, and as the engine cooled off and
the fires were banked in the furnaces, the heat began to
dissipate.

Dick and most of the men poured up onto the upper

deck of their ship and looked across the sparkling waters to where the slab-sided hulk they had fought was still steaming slowly toward the Elizabeth River.

"We licked her," said Jimmy Fox exultantly.

"Fought her toe to toe," said Mike Reilly, "and we didn't take more than we gave, lads!"

"Ericsson was right," said Ben Morgan with a grin.

"They won't dare call us them names!" said Hank Bascomb. "Tin Can on a Shingle! Cheesebox on a Raft! The Yankee Notion! Ericsson's Folly! We showed 'em! This is the U.S.S. *Monitor*, boys! The finest fighting ship in the entire world!"

"Aye," said Lobscouse gloomily, "But she might come back, mates. We didn't sink her. She might come back, I warn ye!"

They laughed at the gloomy sailmaker. But he had fought with them, gloomy or not, and on this day, everything was all right. Even Lobscouse.

Ben Morgan was walking slowly about the turret, eying it closely. Then he stopped and looked at the gunners. "Come here, mates," he said.

He placed his hand in a rounded dent deep in the plating. "There is a perfect impression of a rebel solid shot," he said. "Two and a half inches deep."

"A real battle scar," said Tom Lochrane. "We won't let them straighten that out, eh, mates?"

Then, like small boys hunting for treasure, they went over their stout little ship foot by foot, looking for more battle scars. She had been struck twenty-one times. Eight times on the side plates, twice on the pilothouse, four times on the deck, seven times on the turret. All with hardly enough effect to talk about.

Later that day, Lieutenant Worden was taken aboard a tug and sent to Washington for medical treatment and for the thanks of *Congress* and the President of the United States.

The *Minnesota* was stripped of much of her gear,

refloated, and then taken close under the heavy guns of Fort Monroe for protection. Other vessels of the United States were taken from their moorings, away from the danger of another attack of the *Merrimac*. One vessel remained quietly at anchor, scarred but seemingly undamaged, and ready to fight the *Merrimac* whenever she was ready for another trial of strength. Now she would answer to only one name, the name she had proudly earned in her first battle. The United States Ship *Monitor*!

In the days that followed the first contest between ironclads, there was no sign of the *Merrimac* in Hampton Roads. Spies brought conflicting reports to Fort Monroe, but when they were all sifted out, the information seemed to be that the *Merrimac* was in dry dock. She was to receive a new ram, a plating of metal across her bows, and new plates at the water line. Heavy metal port covers were to be fitted to the gun ports. Her engines, never the best, would have to be refitted. Her hull had to be recaulked, for many leaks had started from the ramming of the *Cumberland* and the pounding of the *Monitor*'s guns.

There was also news that the Confederates were planning ways to deal with the *Monitor*, exploiting her weaknesses. They planned to stuff wet canvas down her smokestack hole and blower pipes, to cover the low pilothouse with heavy canvas, and to wedge tight the base of the turret, providing, of course, they could board her. The *Monitor* men began to make their own preparations. Steam hoses were rigged to spray boarders. Mechanics came aboard and built a sloping metal shield over solid wood backing to surround the little pilothouse so that shot would glance harmlessly upward from it. Hand grenades were brought aboard from Fort Monroe.

The heavy wooden frigates that had suffered so much from the *Merrimac* were sent away, and lighter craft with greater speeds were brought in, fitted with rams and heavy ordnance to fight the *Merrimac* should she reappear. Ladders were made so that the tallow-greasy sides of the ram might be scaled by boarders who could shoot down through the huge iron grating atop her superstructure.

The days drifted past, but still, there was no sign of the enemy ram. Newspapers that were brought aboard the little *Monitor* told the story of her epic battle with her huge adversary. The crew sat on the deck one moonlit night, eagerly scanning the papers. "They have named a seegar after us," said Lobscouse. "*El Monitor*."

"And a new-style man's hat!" said Dick.

Jimmy Fox looked up. "A household flour too," he said with a grin. "I hope it is good flour."

"It says here they gave Ericsson,' the greatest man living? a solid-gold replica of the *Monitor*, valued at $7,000 and weighing fourteen pounds," said Hank Bascomb. "I wonder why we didn't get one?"

Mike Reilly smirked. "And they have a new dance too, mates! Ericsson's Gallope!"

"They say Ericsson has paid little attention to all this publicity," said Ben Morgan. "He's occupied almost day and night with plans to improve this design. He thinks the Navy will need all this type ship they can get, and in a hurry too before the rebels design more ironclads."

Jonas Barklew nodded. "The *Monitor* type. It sounds good, eh, lads? The monitor-type fighting ship."

Spec Simpson looked up. "It says here a special Act of *Congress* is planned to make Lieutenant Worden a captain. It should be admiral at least."

"I wonder how he is?" asked Mike Reilly.

Ben Morgan shrugged. "They say he won't be totally blinded, for which we can be thankful. It looked worse than it really was."

"Maybe we ought to send him a letter or something," suggested Jimmy Fox quietly.

"Good thought, Jimmy," said Hank Bascomb. "You write it up, and we'll all sign it. Make it good, mate."

In the following days, there was still no sign of the *Merrimac*. But the Navy Department wasn't taking any chances on her getting loose into Chesapeake Bay. Vessel after vessel was ordered south to form a special squadron to deal with her. A beautiful and fast side-wheel steamship, the Vanderbilt, the pride, and joy of Commodore Vanderbilt, was purchased from him for the token sum of one dollar and immediately fitted with a special ram bow for the special purpose of ramming the stern of the *Merrimac* to damage her rudder and propeller. The Vanderbilt was considered so fast and so maneuverable that she would be able to dart in, deliver her attack, and escape harm. Even so, she was armed with a battery of heavy guns to be able to fight back if attacked.

There was news that a new type of ironclad, the U.S.S. *Galena* was being completed up North and would join the squadron as quickly as possible. She was an orthodox type of ship except for her armor, which was of the "rail-and-plate" principle, composed of closely fitted bars, placed edge to edge, and covered with thin metal plating. It was said that the original design had also called for a backing of thick India rubber on the rather odd theory that the elasticity of the rubber would serve to soften the effect of solid shot on the armor. The armor itself was about three inches thick.

The *Monitor* men were skeptical about the "rail-and-plate" principle and with good reason. They had experienced heavy solid shot fired at point-blank range, and if it could put a two-and-a-half-inch dent into eight inches of armor, such as the *Monitor*'s turret had, it might make junk out of the thinner, jointed armor of the *Galena*.

The *Naugatuck*, a small, partially armored vessel with new type long-range guns, was also expected to join the other fighting ships waiting for the emergence of the *Merrimac*.

There was little time for the veteran crew of the *Monitor* to sit around idly. Under their temporary commanding officer, Lieutenant Thomas O. Selfridge, they drilled daily at the big guns and with small arms to get in practice for repelling boarders, for signaling, for firefighting, for damage control, and for all the other drills necessary to make the *Monitor* as efficient and ready for battle as possible.

There were other rumors drifting about Hampton Roads, and some of them were rather disquieting. There was said to be a lot of criticism over the fact that the *Monitor*, and the *Monitor* alone, had stood in the way of the huge enemy ram. Why hadn't someone taken the responsibility of building a fleet of the little fighting ships? The public was incensed about the loss of the *Congress* and the *Cumberland* and about the horrible slaughtering of their crews. Worst of all was the criticism of Lieutenant Greene for not having pursued the *Merrimac* when she had retreated and not having destroyed her completely.

Other ships joined the little squadron in Hampton Roads. The *Ocean Queen*, the *Illinois*, and the *Arago* arrived with all speed. It was said that work was progressing with great haste on the crippled *Merrimac* and that women and children had volunteered to hold lanterns for the workmen. Some of General McClellan's troops were already at Fort Monroe, and others were on the way. The Confederates knew that if enough Union soldiers arrived at Fort Monroe, it would be a matter of days before they lost Norfolk and its Navy Yard. The *Merrimac* could prevent that disaster if it was ready again for battle.

But almost a month had passed in watchful waiting before the ram appeared on the waters of Hampton Roads. At seven A.M. in the morning, April 11, 1862, the drums aboard the *Minnesota* thudded and rolled Beat to

Quarters, alerting the crews of the other ships. The transports and other ships immediately weighed anchor and raised sail or got up steam to clear the Roads. Steam tugs whistled and chuffed about like mother hens worrying about their chicks as they towed strings of vessels out of harm's way.

Dick Morgan stood on the deck of the *Monitor*, watching the excitement. To eastward were the *Minnesota*, Vanderbilt, and several other vessels. Near Newport News, over six miles from Old Point Comfort, were the *Oriole, Arago, Illinois*, and *Ericsson,* with the fast Baltimore once owned by the Charleston Line. The *Rhode Island*, a fast, heavily armed, and handy supply ship was near the *Monitor*.

The British gunboat *Rinaldo* and the French ship *Gassendi* were anchored midway between Fort Monroe and the Rip Raps, a small rocky shoal three and one-half miles off Old Point Comfort, waiting patiently for more trials of strength between the *Merrimac* and the *Monitor*.

The *Monitor* was now commanded by Lieutenant William Jeffers, who had succeeded Lieutenant Selfridge, and he had been given specific instructions to wait on the defensive in case of an attack by the rebel ram. The partially armored *Naugatuck* was to support the *Monitor* in such an eventuality.

There were other vessels with the *Merrimac* as she moved slowly about beyond range of the Union guns. She steamed ponderously toward Fort Monroe as though daring the *Monitor* and the other Union ships to come out and fight, but it was not so simple as all that. The *Monitor* had been ordered to stay on the defensive and protect the Union vessels and keep the *Merrimac* from entering Chesapeake Bay, where she seemed to show no inclination to go; on the other hand, the *Merrimac* effectively kept the Union fighting ships from ascending the James River in an attack toward Richmond.

The *Monitor* got up steam and moved slowly back and

forth while her guns were manned. Ben Morgan peered through a gun port and eyed the distant ram. "It's like a game of chess," he said at last. "Each of us waiting for the other to move. We won't leave the shallow water, and she can't leave the deeper water. President Lincoln doesn't want us lost in battle, and the rebels don't want to lose their queen piece, the *Merrimac*."

But the Confederate squadron was not idle. A gunboat moved swiftly in on a number of Union supply vessels that had been too tardy in getting out of the way. Another rebel ship joined her, and in a short time, they had hoisted the Confederate flag on two brigs, property of the United States Quartermaster's Department, the *Marcus*, and the *Saboah*, as well as a schooner, the Catherine T. Dix. It was a slap in the face to the *Monitor*, but orders were orders, and still, she waited on the defensive.

But the *Merrimac* did not attack. Hour after hour, she steamed slowly back and forth, as though undecided quite what to do. A wraith of smoke lay low over the sparkling waters, and her bright new flags rippled in the fresh breeze as she maneuvered. But she stayed well out of range of the huge guns at Fort Monroe.

The *Monitor*'s crew waited patiently. They had complete faith in their ship now, and perhaps more than before, for they had had a chance to become better acquainted with her and to rectify some of the minor errors in her construction.

The long day dragged past with no shooting until just before sunset when the *Merrimac* fired a shot at Fort Monroe. The gunners of the *Monitor*, who had been waiting on the deck and atop the turret, cheered and ran to their posts. The *Merrimac* was still out of range for their two Dahlgren's. But the *Naugatuck* had on board one of the new long-range guns, and she answered the fire of the ram with a shot that splashed in the water near one of the *Merrimac*'s escorts.

Gun Captain Tom Lochrane whistled softly. "That was a good shot, mates!" he said. "Three miles at least!"

"I make it three and a half," said John Stocking.

Lieutenant Greene nodded. "That's about the range of those new guns."

The sun had gone down, staining the western sky in rose, gold, and pink. The Confederate squadron retired to anchorages off Sewall's Point.

The Union vessels returned to their anchorages, secured their guns, and settled down for the night.

The *Merrimac* did not reappear the next day, nor the day after that. Soon April was almost gone. General McClellan had a vast land force on the Peninsula now and was besieging Yorktown, the first step in his campaign to capture Richmond. The Army was active, and the Navy marked time at Hampton Roads.

The *Monitor* crew lounged on the deck of their ship one pleasant moonlit evening, looking across the silvery waters toward the southern shore, watching and wondering when Jimmy Fox came up on deck and looked about with a self-conscious grin on his face. "Me and some of the boys have written a letter to the captain," he said. "I'll pass it around and see what you think about it."

When it came Dick Morgan's turn, he held the paper so that the moon shone upon it and read it slowly to himself.

Dear Sir:

These few lines is from your own crew of the Monitor, with their kindest love to you their Honored Captain, hoping to God that they will have the pleasure of welcoming you back to us again soon, for we are already able and willing to meet Death or anything else, only give us back our Captain again. Dear Captain, we have got your Pilothouse fixed and all ready for you when you get well again; and we all sincerely hope that soon we will have the pleasure of welcoming you back to it. We are waiting very patiently to

*engage our Antagonist if we could only get a chance to do so.
The last time she came out, we all thought we would have the
Pleasure of sinking her. But we all got disappointed, for we
did not fire one shot and the Norfolk papers says we are
cowards in the Monitor, and all we want is a chance to show
them where it lies. With you, for our Captain, we can teach
them who is cowards. But there is a great deal that we would
like to write to you, but we think you will soon be with us
again yourself. But we all join in with our kindest love to
you, hoping that God will restore you to us again and hoping
that your suffering is at an end now, and we are all so glad to
hear that your eyesight will be spaired to you again. We
would wish to write more to you if we have your kind
Permission to do so, but at present, we all conclude by
tendering to you our kindest Love and affection to our Dear
and Honored Captain.*

We remain until Death your Affectionate Crew
THE MONITOR BOYS

Dick passed the letter to Spec Simpson, who adjusted
his glasses and began to read it with a critical expression
on his face.

"What do you think of it, mates?" asked Jimmy
anxiously.

"Fine," said Ben Morgan.

"Capital!" said Jonas Barklew.

"Top-notch, Jimmy," said Lobscouse.

Spec cleared his throat. "Well, now, James, not to be
critical, but the spelling' and construction..." His voice
died away as Tom Lochrane passed a thick arm about his
skinny throat, and Jonas Barklew clamped a ham of a
hand down on his left thigh.

Jimmy turned suddenly. "What was that, Spec?" he
asked.

Spec swallowed hard. "The spelling and construction
are just fine, James. Just fine indeed!"

"Thanks, Spec. Like I said, I ain't much for writing."

"True, oh, true! The spirit is there, however. Now I—"

"Stow it, Jonah!" snapped Lobscouse.

Ben Morgan took the letter. "I'll see that it is signed by every man aboard," he said, "and we can get it off by the mail boat the first thing in the morning."

At that time, there was not much else to do aboard the *Monitor*. General McClellan was moving at a snail's pace in his campaign to take Yorktown and then advance to Richmond. McClellan and Secretary of War Stanton feared that the *Merrimac* might get past the *Monitor* and attack the Army forces along the York River. So McClellan stalled before Yorktown while the *Merrimac* sulked at Norfolk, and the *Monitor* idled away the soft spring days, waiting for the *Merrimac* to move as much as President Lincoln wanted General McClellan to move. There was a vast and costly stalemate in Virginia.

CHAPTER EIGHT

The tall, gaunt man in the funeral suit and the high black hat walked quietly about the deck of the *Monitor*, eying her battle scars, pausing to place a hand in the deep dent that was the exact shape of the solid shot that marred the stout turret of the ship.

The crew stood stiffly at attention aft of the turret, but their eyes constantly shifted to study this tall man in the black suit. It wasn't every day that the President of the United States, Abraham Lincoln, visited a ship of the Navy. There were others in his party who were almost as well-known as the President—Secretary of War Stanton, Secretary of the Treasury Salmon P. Chase, and General Egbert L. Viele. It was rumored that Stanton had included the general in the inspecting party because he was slated to be military governor of Norfolk—when, and if, it was taken from the enemy.

Dick Morgan looked to the south. There was a thickening smudge of black smoke near Sewall's Point, and across the Roads came a fast picket boat. The boat commander was hailing each Union ship as he passed it. "The *Merrimac* is getting up steam! The *Merrimac* is getting up steam!" As he passed each ship, the drums began to thud and roll Beat to Quarters.

This was no time for the President of the United States to be aboard. No time for anything but to get ready for action. The *Merrimac* was coming out again!

The instant the President and his party left the deck of the *Monitor;* the ship was readied for action. It did not take long, for the ship was always ready for battle those hectic days; neither did it take long for the *Merrimac* to cross that strip of water.

The *Monitor* gunners eyed the enemy through the port openings in the turret. She was moving slowly and majestically toward Craney Island, at the mouth of the Elizabeth not far from the western shores of the river. The *Monitor* had steam up and was moving slowly too but was staying in the shallows, watching and waiting to see what the enemy would do.

The sun was low in the west, and the thick smoke from the ram drifted slowly across the Roads, but she did not move threateningly toward the *Monitor* or any of the other armed Union ships waiting for her. In a short time, she had stopped near the Island. The Union naval officers watched her through their binoculars, but she showed no signs of moving again. After a time, the smoke ceased coming from her funnel, and when darkness fell across Hampton Roads that May day, she was still at anchor.

In the days that followed this last scare of the *Merrimac*, President Lincoln issued his orders now that he was familiar with the tense situation. The new type ironclad, the *Galena*, and two wooden gunboats were sent up the James River to give support to General McClellan's slowly advancing troops. The *Monitor* with the *Naugatuck*, to be followed later by the *Minnesota* and the Vanderbilt, were to close in on the rebel batteries at Sewall's Point and try their strength. The only conclusion arrived at was that the rebels had but seventeen guns emplaced and very few men to defend them against a land attack backed by naval guns.

The next day a rumor came through to the Northerners that the Confederates were planning the evacuation of Norfolk and the Gosport Navy Yard, but nothing was said about the *Merrimac*, which still squatted menacingly beside Craney Island.

The President came personally to the little ship to give his instructions to Lieutenant Jeffers. They were again to lead a gun attack on Sewall's Point while preparations were made for a landing of Army units on the southern shores. The President himself had crossed to the southern shore and had selected a landing place near Willoughby's Point.

The *Monitor*'s guns pounded the southern batteries that day, receiving enemy fire that had no effect. Once again, the *Merrimac* appeared, steaming toward the Union ships, and the sweating men in the *Monitor*'s turret replenished their ammunition supply and waited for her, but she again turned tail and retreated to her berth at Craney Island.

"Cat and mouse!" roared Jonas Barklew as the *Monitor* turned toward the northern shore. "How long can this go on?"

Tommy Lochrane wiped the sweat from his face. "Mayhap for the rest of the war, Jonas. They come out; we wait for them, they go back."

"Like a bloomin' weather gauge," said Mike Reilly.

But that night, the Union naval guns roared and flamed as Union troops landed at Willoughby's Point, under the command of General Wool, and advanced with little opposition toward Norfolk. There were hardly any Confederate troops left in the area, for they had gone to join the troops that were facing General McClellan's advance up the Peninsula. A partially constructed ironclad, the Richmond, had been secretly towed up the James along with two other rebel gunboats, but the *Merrimac* still remained at her post diagonally across the river from Norfolk.

Flames leaped and postured against the night sky as

the Gosport Navy Yard was burned again, as it had been when the Union forces had left it at the start of the war.

The *Monitor* men were on duty all that night, watching and waiting for the *Merrimac*. It was certain that the rebels would attempt to get their big fighting ship out of the Elizabeth and up the James. She could be taken to within forty miles of the city of Richmond, according to loyal Hampton Roads pilots serving with the Union squadron. There wasn't any doubt that the rebels would make the attempt.

Dick Morgan was on anchor watch just before dawn, the morning of May 11, bundled in his pea jacket, and seated beside the glum Lobscouse. "Sunday mornin'," said Lobscouse. "Another one of them quiet days, stewin' in our own juice, awaitin' for that ship to come out."

Dick grinned. "Maybe she will, Lobscouse."

The words had hardly left his mouth when there was a tremendous flash of orange-red light from beside dark Craney Island, followed by a thunderous explosion. In the glare of the blast, they could see dark pieces of material soaring up into the sky.

"What was that?" yelled Lobscouse.

Dick stared toward the Island. The explosion had occurred right at the place where the *Merrimac* had been moored. It was too good to believe that it had been the great ram.

A daring picket boat of the Union squadron sped past the anchored *Monitor* in the direction of Craney Island, while the decks of the Union ships filled with quiet men, looking toward the site of the great explosion. Then the news came to the squadron and spread with the speed of light throughout the Union forces on water and on land. The Confederates had blown up the *Merrimac*!

The men of the *Monitor* cheered when they heard the news, but even so, they all felt that they would rather have fought the rebel ship to a standstill in order to settle the matter for all time as to which was the better ship.

Norfolk was occupied. There was not a Confederate ship on the waters of Hampton Roads to challenge the Union ships. The Gosport Navy Yard, still smoking, would be rebuilt as a Union base. General McClellan was advancing up the Peninsula. From Union defeat, the day the *Merrimac* had destroyed the *Congress* and the *Cumberland*, until the day the *Monitor* and other Union ships moored off Norfolk, it had been just two months, and in those two months, the entire picture of the war had changed.

"What is there for us to do now?" asked Hank Bascomb as the men of the *Monitor* lolled on the sun-warmed deck of their ship, eying Norfolk now in Union hands again.

"We'll probably sit and rust in Hampton Roads," said Jimmy Fox. "I'd almost ruther be in the Army than do that."

Lobscouse sat in the middle of a great circle of canvas, looking like a whiskered ballerina who sat down upon the deck of the ship with widespread skirts. He was sewing a canvas awning that would be stretched across the top of the turret on metal stanchions. The torrid heat of a Virginia summer would soon be upon them, and they would hardly be able to sleep below decks. Metalsmiths were already making fittings so that great awnings could be stretched fore and aft of the turret for shade. He looked up as Jimmy spoke and grunted deep within his throat.

Hank grinned. "What do you think, Lobscouse?" he asked.

The sailmaker looked up again. "Ye think we'll sit here like a tin duck on the water? No, mates, they'll think of something fer us to do. Mark my words. We may be Abraham Lincoln's pet right now, but it won't save us from fightin,' and ye kin lay to that!"

Ben Morgan nodded. "I've read newspapers that say the same thing, mates. Northern editors seem to think we can take Richmond singlehanded and Charleston after that. You wait! You'll see enough action to satisfy you."

"Aye," said Lobscouse darkly. "They ain't through with us yet, mates! And it won't be long; *it won't be long!*"

And the words of Lobscouse came true within a few days after the occupation of Norfolk, for the *Monitor* was ordered up the James River for a test of strength with the rebel batteries that held the river against the passage of Union ships.

With the *Monitor* was the untried *Galena*, a much bigger ship, with the wide and rounded armored sides of the new type ironclad. The little *Naugatuck* went too.

The heat of summer was already in Virginia when the Union ships plowed slowly up the James River channel. The plan was for the stout ironclads to force a passage and bombard Richmond. Meanwhile, General McClellan and his Army forces were moving up the other side of the Peninsula, along the line of the York River, fighting little battles and skirmishes, moving slowly but steadily toward Richmond. There was news, too, that the partially constructed Richmond, saved from Norfolk and sent up the river to the city for which she was named, would soon be ready for battle. She was rumored to be larger, more heavily armored, and fitted with bigger guns than the *Merrimac* had been.

It was a bright, sunny May day, but there was no chance for the men of the *Monitor* to stay on her deck. The engineers and powder division men were at their stations. The gunners stifled in their iron turret and peered through the gun ports, seeing little of the low countryside, for there were rebels who were sharp-shooters still along those tangled shores, and they could slap a Minie ball through those gun ports.

Slowly and steadily, the little squadron forged up the winding James, watching for sharpshooters, masked batteries, torpedoes beneath the rippling waters, and sunken barges laden with stone to bar the shallow channel. Past Days Point, thence northerly toward Hog Island the tip of a great point, which, when rounded, showed the river to be trending westerly. Past Jamestown Island and Swan's Point, ever deeper into enemy territory.

It was stifling hot within the ship and the turret. The engine throbbed steadily, and the steam hissed in the valves while a thick plume of smoke trailed behind the funnel. It was so hot it seemed as though they were ascending a river in the Congo. Everything was metal aboard the *Monitor*; metal heated by the engines and boilers within and the sun without so that the gunners and engineers dripped sweat as they worked and waited. There was nothing else to do but watch and wait. If they could force those rebel batteries, it would save the lives of many Union soldiers now marching up the Peninsula toward the tangled swamps of the Chickahominy.

Past Malvern Hill and Turkey Bend, following the winding river to Dutch Gap, where the river doubled back upon itself. Up ahead, according to Union spies, the Confederates had constructed river batteries, armed with heavy guns, at Drewry's Bluff, and they had also scuttled ships in the channel.

Now the sharpshooters kept up a steady firing upon the slowly moving Union ships until the pattering against the turret of the *Monitor* sounded like hail. The port stoppers had been lowered to keep the bullets out. Slower and slower moved the ships, feeling their way up the winding channel, waiting for the expected sound of heavy guns firing to bar further passage.

"We must be getting close," said Lieutenant Greene.

Boatswain's Mate Stocking nodded. "Drewry's Bluff is about eight miles from Richmond."

"Only eight miles!" said Mike Reilly. "It'll be aisy!"

"Eight miles of rebel sharpshooters, heavy batteries, torpedoes, sunken ships and barges, and the whole rebel army waitin' up there somewhere," said Lobscouse gloomily. "That's all, mates. Aye, it will be aisy!"

The *Galena* moved ahead like a cautious old woman inching her way across an icy street. The land had changed, and now there were looming heights above the river, two hundred or more feet high. Here and there, the water purled over sunken obstructions. There were also cribs of stone placed in such a way that it was difficult for a ship to maneuver in the narrow channel, and to do so would force her to be at the mercy of the great batteries high on the heights. A gun thudded off. "One of theirs," said Greene. Then began a steady roaring of enemy guns. A solid shot struck the water not far from the *Monitor* and sent up a thick wall of spray. Some of it splashed over the grated top of the turret and came down upon the men standing to the guns.

"Cooling at least," said Ben Morgan. "The *Galena* is moving on," called down Hank Bascomb, who had dared a peek through the top of the turret.

The sound of firing reverberated along the river gorge, and thick smoke drifted from the enemy gun batteries.

"The *Naugatuck* has stopped firing," said Hank. "I think she's burst her 100-pounder Parrott rifle!"

"That leaves us and the *Galena*," said Tom Lochrane. He slapped the breech of his gun. "Time for us to speak, mates."

"Raise the port stoppers," said Lieutenant Greene. "Stay away from the ports, men."

They triced up the heavy stoppers and ran out the guns at the command, but they could not fire yet because the *Galena* was ahead of them.

The voice tube whistled sharply, and Lieutenant Greene picked it up. "Yes, sir," he said quietly. He listened for a time, then hung up the tube. He looked at his sweating men. "The *Galena* is taking a terrible beating," he said grimly. "The rebel shot is crashing through her plating and rails like rocks through glass windows. Lieutenant Jeffers says he can see the metal flying in all directions."

"They can't hurt us, sir!" said Mike Reilly. "Why don't they let us take a crack at thim, sir?"

"We're to move up and cover the *Galena* soon," said Lieutenant Greene.

Even as he spoke, something smashed heavily against the turret and seemed to shake the whole ship. But now, none of the gunners touched the sides of the turret when the ship was under fire. They had learned that lesson in the fight with the *Merrimac*. The turret rang like a cracked bell, but nothing happened to it.

The men began to grin. They knew that nothing the rebels could throw could hurt their ship.

They were moving forward now. The guns thundered steadily, and water splashed high from the solid shot hitting the river surface.

"Stand by," said Lieutenant Greene. He crouched over the breech of the starboard Dahlgren. "Elevate," he said. The gun was elevated until she could be raised no farther. The officer shook his head. "We can't reach those enemy batteries," he said angrily. He peered through the port. "The *Galena* can't stand much more of that pounding. Captain Rodgers is holding her there. She's just been struck again! Metal flying about like tenpins! She hasn't a chance! If only we could elevate these guns more!"

The turret shuddered from a direct hit. The little ship moved on upriver, but there was no chance to fire yet. It would have been a waste of powder and shell.

"If the Army had been able to attack from the land side, we might have made it," said Ben Morgan.

"They've got their hands full as it is," said Lieutenant Greene. "I know this: we can't force those batteries, men."

"Can't we fire, sir?" asked Jimmy Fox.

Greene shrugged. "We'll try," he said. "Stand clear!"

He took the lock string of the starboard gun and stepped back after sighting. He jerked it smoothly, and the great gun slammed back roaring and smoking. He sighted and fired the port gun, then shook his head. "Far too short," he said.

The stinking smoke swirled in the turret and began to drift slowly through the top. The discharging of the guns raised the terrible heat in the turret still more until it seemed to Dick Morgan that they had drifted into the nether regions far below the earth's surface.

They fired a number of times, but it was no use. The guns simply could not be elevated high enough to reach the rebel batteries, and the enemy fired as fast as they could, pouring heavy shot down upon the Union ships on the river's surface far below them until the *Galena* had had enough. The signal flag for Cease Firing crept up on the *Galena*'s halyards. The Union ships turned slowly and retreated.

That night as the ships anchored, the news spread through them. The *Galena* was a mistake and a failure. Her armor was worse than useless, for it did not protect her but weighted her down too much. She had been riddled and almost torn to pieces. Eighteen shots had penetrated her armor and the wooden hull behind it, killing thirteen men. On the other hand, the *Monitor* had sustained three direct hits, none of which had harmed her.

But it had been failure. The ships dropped farther down the river to await orders. There was no chance of relief as long as McClellan might need their support upon the James. The summer heat was on them now, and scurvy had broken out in the ships of the James River Flotilla. No one could stay long beneath the deck of the *Monitor*, and at times the heat reached 160 degrees in the galley from the stoves and the boilers against which they were backed. Cooking had to be done on improvised stoves on the deck.

The *Monitor* would never be given relief as long as the threat of the ironclad Richmond hung over the Union vessels. It was watch and wait again through the long, torrid weeks as McClellan's Peninsula Campaign continued. At the end of May, the battle of Fair Oaks was fought, followed by heavy, pounding rains that filled the swamps and raised the rivers and streams. The fighting at Mechanicsville, Gaines' Mill, White Oak Swamp, and Savage's Station filled the countryside with the thundering of guns and the yelling of men in blue and gray as they fought savagely. But the Union forces gradually fell back, changed their supply base, and defeated the yelling rebels at Malvern Hill. When McClellan at last retreated, that retreat was covered by the guns of the James River Flotilla firing throughout the dark night. By early part of July, the Peninsula Campaign was over.

It wasn't until late in September, when a new guardian arrived at Hampton Roads, that the *Monitor* was relieved. The new guardian was the armored *New Ironsides,* a huge ironclad that was heavily armed. In addition, Newport News had been fortified with six great 200-pounder Parrott rifles to hold back the rebel ram Richmond if it should descend the James.

The little *Monitor*, tired from over seven months' active service, with worn-out engines and a weary crew, steamed up Chesapeake Bay to the Potomac and entered the dry dock at the Washington Navy Yard for scraping, painting, improving her ventilator, and blowing system, and a well-earned rest for officers and crew.

CHAPTER NINE

A cold December wind swept across the gray waters of Hampton Roads, whistling through the taut rigging of the sailing ships, making the anchored ships heave and roll at their moorings. Now and then, the salty waters would wash up on the low deck of the *Monitor* as she tugged impatiently at her anchor. She had been back at Hampton Roads since November, but there was really nothing for her to do but wait, and wait, and wait...

There had been a great deal of excitement and pleasure before the *Monitor* had left Washington to steam south to Hampton Roads on active duty once more. Spic-and-span in her fresh paint, and in better condition than when new, she had been honored by a visit from President Lincoln, who had paid a tribute to her officers and men. A new commander, Captain John Pine Bankhead, had reported aboard to take the *Monitor* south.

Rumors were again rife about the *Richmond*. She had been completed; she had steamed down the James; she was ready to attack the James River Flotilla and destroy it. So the *Monitor* was again needed for her watchdog duties at Hampton Roads. It was all right with the men of the *Monitor*. They had tried the strength of the

Merrimac and had found it no more than the strength of the *Monitor*. Now the *Merrimac* was long gone, and the *Monitor* still existed. She would deal with the Richmond as well, and perhaps better than she had dealt with the *Merrimac*, and this time with full thirty-pound charges in the twin 11-inch turret Dahlgren guns with which she was armed.

But they had been waiting again, as they had waited before, for the rebel threat to materialize, and in the waiting, the new commanding officer had requested and had been denied a transfer to more active duty.

More rumors were hatched during the last weeks of 1862. The Confederates had embarked on a mass building program of gigantic ironclads at Richmond, Wilmington, Savannah, and Charleston. The South wanted to break the Northern blockade of Southern ports, most of all at Wilmington, which was now the chief port of the beleaguered Confederacy. Cotton, the "White Gold" of the Confederacy, was run out of Wilmington in fast ships; those same ships, on their return journeys, brought in military supplies, medicines, and food so desperately needed by the South, for, without them, she could not exist much longer.

It was at Wilmington or thereabouts that stories had formed about the building of two huge ironclads designed to smash the Yankee blockade of Wilmington. They would be finished by January of 1863, according to all the latest reports. The sailing ships of the blockade would not be able to face these threatening monsters, and yet the United States Navy had hardly enough big ships to face them either. Hampton Roads had to be held against the threat of the *Richmond*.

"Listen, mates!" said Boatswain's Mate Ben Morgan as he came into the berth deck. "We're to move south!"

"You're joking!" said Jonas Barklew as he looked up from the game of checkers he was playing with Hank Bascomb.

"No, Jonas! They can't part with a lot of ships to face the enemy ironclads down South, so they're sending quality instead of quantity! The *Monitor* is to report at Beaufort, South Carolina, for further instructions!"

Lobscouse shook his head. "We're to go to sea off Hatteras in December? This is madness!"

Ben shoved back his hat. "The *Rhode Island* will tow us, Lobscouse. A fine, big ship. There's a new monitor here now, the Passaic, and she'll be towed by the *State of Georgia*. We won't leave until the weather is fine."

"Aye," said Lobscouse gloomily, "but ye mind how the weather was when we left New York last March? Ye couldn't have asked for a finer day. But ye remember what happened? This time we must pass Hatteras, the Grave-yard of the Atlantic!"

"Belay that!" snapped Ben Morgan.

"Oh, aye, he says belay that, but it will be no picnic off Old Hatteras, mates, and ye can lay to that!"

The prophecy of Lobscouse was forgotten in the excitement about the news that the *Monitor* was leaving Hampton Roads for active duty.

On December 29, 1862, the *Monitor* was towed to sea at the end of two new 12-inch manila hawsers behind the *Rhode Island*, one of the finest ships of her day. She had a top speed of fourteen knots, heavy 8-inch guns, and an iron ram fitted to her bows. She was a supply ship for the North Atlantic Blockading Squadron and was known as "the Friendly Ship" because of the fresh food, newspapers, and letters from home that she brought to the lonely ships of the blockading force.

The *Monitor* plodded obediently along behind the big side-wheeler, like a toy boat on a double string. She had been rigged for sea, and the weather was fine. The moon rose and silvered the gently heaving waters as the crew ate evening mess. The ship was warm inside, a blessing in winter, compared to the way it was when the summer sun beat down upon her plating and turned her into a great stove.

The State of Georgia and the Passaic vanished into the night, leaving the *Rhode Island* and her little charge alone upon the sea.

There had been quite a few changes in the crew of the *Monitor* through sickness and transfers, but many of the old-timers were left. Lieutenant Greene was still executive officer. Many of the men thought that he should have been given command of the ship he had served on since the day of her commissioning, as long as Captain Worden could not return to her. Captain Bankhead was a stick-and-string sailor of the old school who did not believe in these iron contraptions. To the knowledge of the crew, he had applied more than once for transfer from the little ship they had learned to respect and love.

The crew sought their hammocks, and the lights were dimmed as the *Monitor* heaved gently up and down at the end of her hawsers. Dick Morgan lay awake, staring at the deck a few feet above his head. Spec Simpson had been on sick leave, but he had returned shortly before the *Monitor* had sailed, and he was in the hammock next to Dick.

Dick could not sleep. Being aboard the *Monitor* in action on a tidal river was one thing but being aboard her on the open sea was quite another; Dick knew that more than one of the old-timers had requested a transfer before she had left Hampton Roads for the South. They remembered all too well what had happened last March on their trip south to Hampton Roads. It had been a terrifying experience to men who were used to open decks and high-bulwarked ships instead of an iron raft, hardly a foot above the water, plowing along like a submersible boat, ready at any moment to plunge to the bottom like a leaden fishing sinker.

"Dick?" said Spec softly.

"Yes?"

"Can't you sleep either?"

"No."

Spec peered through the dimness. "I wish we were there, mate."

"We'll make it all right. You're the one who has always sworn by the *Monitor*. What's wrong now?"

"Lobscouse says he lost a swab overboard the morning before we left."

"Superstition, Spec."

"Maybe. But the same thing happened last March."

"We got there, didn't we?"

"Yes," Spec said quietly, "but we almost didn't."

"We're in much better shape now than we were at that time."

"But it wasn't Hatteras, Dick. They say that is an awful place, mate."

The *Monitor* bobbed easily up and down. Strange, uncomfortable thoughts raced through Dick's mind. He had been off Hatteras aboard the Sabine when he had first enlisted, and they had passed through a blow that had made the big frigate creak and groan in every timber. They had gotten through with double-reefed lower courses after losing the fore lower topsail and the mizzen lower top gallant sail, and the pumps had been going for ten hours before the well had sucked dry.

More than one fine ship had gone down off Cape Hatteras in the early days of the war, to add to the decaying wooden bones of many other ships lost off Hatteras in its violent and stormy history. The Cape was at the tip of a long chain of sand bars and low islands off the North Carolina coast and was feared because of the storms and heavy seas that formed there. The Gulf Stream flowed about twenty miles east of the Cape, and southbound vessels were often forced too close to the Cape and then driven ashore.

"The Graveyard of the Atlantic," said Spec hollowly.

"Stow that," said Dick.

But he could not sleep. He slid from his hammock and walked aft on the gently sloping deck to the ladder that led up into the turret. Lieutenant Greene was standing up there. "Good evening, sir," he said.

"Good evening, Morgan. What are you doing up here?"

"I wanted a look at the weather, sir."

"You too?" he smiled. "You're the fourth man who has been up here during my watch." He waved a hand to indicate the smooth, moonlit sea. "You can see for yourself. It's as calm as a millpond."

"Yes, sir."

Dick eyed the big *Rhode Island,* and he wished he was aboard her instead of on the low-lying *Monitor.* He had heard she was a fine, well-found ship, fitted elegantly with polished maple and walnut paneling in the cabins, a luxury ship. The *Monitor* was fine on tidal rivers and in quiet roadsteads. At sea, well, she wasn't exactly the type of ship a man had confidence in.

He went below and to his hammock, but still, he could not sleep. "How fast are we being towed, Spec?" he whispered.

"Six knots, mate."

"Is that all?"

"Aye. They don't want to pull us under, I guess. How does it look up there?"

"Quiet. The moon is well up. I guess we'll be all right, Spec."

Dick closed his eyes and finally fell asleep.

The next morning had dawned cold and clear, and the two ships were alone on the heaving waters. But the wind had come up and was starting to make up a sea. The *Monitor* began to pitch and roll steadily, and water creamed across the low deck, but this time it did not come beneath the turret. Still, there were a few leaks, and the pumps were started to clear the bilges of water.

By noon, the wind had started to howl and drive water from the tops of the waves. The *Monitor* would rise to one sea and then burrow through the next one as though she was going to dive straight to the bottom of the ocean, and the little hull trembled and shook at the savage battering of tons of gray, cold sea water. The pumps took up a faster beating. Every so often, a gray-beard of a wave would sweep across the deck and smash against the turret, spouting up high enough to drench the men at the wheel and then pour down inside the turret, thence to the berth deck and down into the bilges.

The *Monitor* tugged and jerked savagely at her towing hawsers, and the strain began to tell on the hull, for water began to seep in through cracks in the hull where it met the flat upper decking.

Hour after hour, the savage battering went on. The men aboard the *Monitor* became very quiet, and the new men worked nervously, looking at the old-timers as though to reassure themselves that everything was all right. But even the old-timers were taut-faced and grim. They had good memories of the stormy passage from New York to Hampton Roads the past March.

The galley fires were put out, and the men were served cold food since it was impossible to keep pots and pans on the surfaces of the stoves. The hull began to make strange creaking, grinding noises, and the thundering of the seas as they slammed down on the deck and raced clear over it became louder and louder as the long hours wore on. Gear broke loose and smashed on the metal berth deck or rolled back and forth in time to the rhythm of the seas. It was almost impossible to stay on one's feet, and several men were injured when they were slammed against bulkheads or onto the deck.

The seas were getting steeper and steeper, and the wind was working up to gale force. The seam between the hull and the deck was beginning to part, something the great guns of the *Merrimac* had not been able to do to the *Monitor*.

Dick looked in at the engine room and saw Spec standing near the bilge pumps. "Will they keep up, Spec?" he asked.

Spec turned his head and peered at Dick. "They're running at full capacity now."

"They're keeping even with the intake of water, but they're not getting ahead of it, Spec."

The young engineer picked up a wad of waste and carefully wiped an engine casing. "Maybe the gale will abate," he said.

"Maybe."

They looked at each other while the deck rose and fell spasmodically beneath their feet, and the engines drove on steadily. The little ship was putting up a good fight, but the peculiar jumbled-up seas off Cape Hatteras were rough enough for a standard type of ship.

Spec glanced up at the deck over their heads. "I sometimes think I should have chosen service on a regular-type ship, Dick. This little ship is the best for what she was intended for, but she wasn't intended for this kind of service."

Dick left the engine room. All the officers were atop the turret now, watching the seas, eying the twin hawsers that held them to the *Rhode Island*, crouching down behind the thin chest-high rifle plating that had been placed about the wheel as great seas smashed across the foredeck of the ship, cascaded aft and struck the turret to spout high in the air and shower down upon the top. A decision had to be made and that soon, or the *Monitor* would never make it to Beaufort.

In the late afternoon, Captain Bankhead began to think that the powerful strain of the towing hawsers was too hard on the hull of his ship. The constant jerking and slamming of the *Monitor* as it fought the waves and the pull of the hawsers might gradually pull the little ship apart where the hull was attached to the upper deck.

But there was no mast on the *Monitor* and no way to hoist signal flags. The only means of communication was a small blackboard upon which chalked messages were supposed to be read by a signal officer aboard the *Rhode Island*, using binoculars to pick out the words. But no one aboard the *Monitor* could see such an officer through the spray and spume, and it was almost a certainty that he could not read the messages.

The sea abated a little, and in time the signal officer read the urgent message chalked on the board. The *Rhode Island* then lay to, but the seas still battered and washed over the *Monitor* as though to founder her. They could not proceed, and they could not stay there, but it was better to get under way and hope for better seas than to stay and wallow to death in the pounding waves.

Once again, the big *Rhode Island* started towing the *Monitor* through the darkness. They were now directly off deadly Cape Hatteras, and the Cape lived up to its evil reputation. The seas roared across the submerged ridges of sand that extended twenty-five miles into the ocean, the dreaded Diamond Shoals.

One man after another became deathly seasick in the wild, eccentric motion of the pitching diving *Monitor*. No effort was made now to keep order within the hull, and gear rolled back and forth on the deck and smashed against the bulkheads.

Dick helped Engineer Lewis to his bunk. The man was helplessly seasick. On his way aft, Dick saw his brother, Ben, and Boatswain's Mate Stocking coming out of one of the storerooms.

"What's wrong, Ben?" asked Dick.

Ben looked about them to see if any other of the crew were within earshot. "That seam is opening wider. Water's beginning to pour in. If it reaches the coal bunkers and soaks the coal, we'll have a hard time trying to keep up steam pressure."

"We're taking water in through the hawsepipe, too," said Stocking.

The news did not get any better as time passed slowly in the darkness and howling of the gale. Water was rising steadily in the bilges and seeping into the coal bunkers. The bilge pumps could not keep up with the new inflow of water, so the Worthington pumps were attached, but it seemed as though that was little help since water had begun to rise level with the engine room floor and wash back and forth with the motion of the ship. Engineer Hands started the new centrifugal pump to help in the unequal battle.

The water was flowing into the coal bunkers in a steady stream from the long split in the hull, and the wet coal could not keep up the required steam pressure of eighty pounds. The pressure-gauge needle kept dropping and dropping as the stokers used devil's claw and slice bar to work the fires before heaving layers of the wet coal atop them. Gas began to form in the engine and boiler rooms, and the blowers had to be started to bring in fresh air. The water was gaining steadily now, and there wasn't any doubt that the *Monitor* was in extreme peril. A red signal light was displayed atop the turret, a signal to the *Rhode Island* that the *Monitor* would have to be abandoned. Dick Morgan was ordered up to the top of the turret to help the helmsman. When he reached his post, he saw the big *Rhode Island* looming up through the rainy murk, much closer than she would have been, had she still been towing the *Monitor*.

Captain Bankhead slowly brought his sinking ship toward the *Rhode Island* and raised his voice trumpet as they came alongside the big side-wheeler. "We are sinking! Send boats!" he yelled.

The bulk of the *Rhode Island* shielded the low-lying *Monitor* from the worst of the crashing seas, but it would not help for long, as the upper deck was almost constantly awash. The side-wheeler was forced to steam slowly to keep the towing hawsers from getting tangled in her paddle wheel.

A messenger came up from below and saluted the captain. "The coal is soaked, sir. We can't keep up steam pressure."

Bankhead wiped the water from his face and gripped the edge of the metal plating that protected helmsman and wheel from the seas. "Tell the chief engineer to slow down. I want all the steam I can get on the pumps," he said at last.

"We'll have to cut those towing lines, sir," said Lieutenant Greene, "or the *Rhode Island* will tow us under."

"I'll go, sir," said James Fenwick, one of the gunners. He took a boarding ax and clambered down the outside ladder of the turret and then made his way slowly across the pitching deck with water surging as high as his waist at times. The *Rhode Island* was close now, and as she heaved in the great seas, the towing lines would straighten out, spewing water. Then they would slacken as the pressure was released on them.

Fenwick was almost at the towing bitts when a graybeard of a wave swept easily over the deck, picked him up, and carried him over the side to be lost forever in the roaring darkness.

Boatswain's Mate John Stocking grabbed another ax and went down the ladder to the flooded deck. He clung to the ladder as a sea swept clear over his head.

They had lowered two boats from the *Rhode Island*, a launch and a cutter, and the oars were driving them slowly toward the foundering *Monitor*.

"The *Rhode Island* has fouled one of the hawsers!" yelled Lieutenant Greene. The thick cable had been wound into the slowly turning paddle wheel. Now she could not maneuver. That hawser had to be cut!

Stocking worked his way forward and stood poised as

though in a tableau. Gaining balance, he struck hard again and again with the ax, and the line parted, but even as it did so, a wave swept the brave man to his death in the sea.

The *Monitor* began to drift swiftly away from the *Rhode Island*. "Let go the anchor!" commanded Captain Bankhead.

By the time the big hook had struck bottom at sixty fathoms, the *Rhode Island* was hardly discernible in the darkness of the raging storm. But the little ship began to ride easier. There might be a chance yet.

Dick Morgan had heard something above the roaring of the wind and the crashing of the seas — an ominous cracking noise from somewhere up forward.

CHAPTER TEN

Dick Morgan climbed down the ladder inside the turret to the turret deck and thence down the ladder to the berth deck. The ship was riding easier, but there wasn't much hope in Dick's heart. If the *Rhode Island* lost them in the storm, the crew of the *Monitor* would be doomed, for she carried no small boats, and no man could live long if he tried to swim in those seas.

Water was pouring along the berth deck, flowing from the doorway that led into the officer's wardroom. Dick hurried forward in time to see Lobscouse fill the doorway. "We're goners," said the old sailmaker. "The anchor cable ripped out the anchor well, packing as it was let out. The hawsehole is pouring water into the ship like Niagara Falls!"

"The fires can no longer give us steam," said Ben Morgan. "The small pumps have drowned, and the main pump has almost stopped from lack of steam pressure. The water is filling the ashpits. The engineers are stopping the engines to give all power to the pumps. If the pumps fail again—"

There was no need for Ben Morgan to speak further. If the pumps failed again, the ship would be lost. Yet, as

Dick looked about, he saw no signs of panic among the men, newcomers and old-timers alike, but they must all know that the odds against the ship were mounting higher and higher.

She was doomed. It was only a matter of time before the fires would die completely, the pumps would stop, and the ship would fill and sink.

"The moon has showed itself," a drenched seaman said as he descended the turret ladder. "You can see the *Rhode Island*. There's a chance she can run down and pick us all up, mates. Her boats are heading for us now. The captain says for those of you who aren't needed down here to get up atop the turret. The deck is still awash most of the time. It won't be easy to get into the boats, but you'll have to risk it."

One man after another ascended the ladder to the interior of the turret, then climbed the next ladder to the top of the turret. The ship still swung up and down in the heaving swells, but the anchor held firm.

Ben Morgan organized a bailing brigade to be ready when the pumps stopped. The water was rolling inches deep over the berth deck.

Dick scuttled up the ladders and stood atop the swaying turret. He looked at Lieutenant Greene. "The *Rhode Island* doesn't seem to be making much headway, sir," he said.

The officer raised his binoculars and studied the side-wheeler. "The hawser is still fouled in her paddle wheel," he said quietly. "She can't maneuver to help us until it's freed from the wheel. She's safe enough, though. I wish I could say the same about us."

In the long minutes that followed, the pumps began to falter. The bucket brigade started their chain of buckets, but the little water they managed to get up through the turret and emptied over the side was hardly worth the effort. But it kept the men busy and their minds off the cold, wet death that waited patiently for them just beyond the iron hull of their little ship.

Even though the *Rhode Island* was not under power, she was drifting swiftly and directly toward the anchored *Monitor* until she was almost alongside, with one of her small boats tossing on the seas. Then the two vessels were close alongside, and the small boat was in danger of being crushed as the *Monitor* ground against her.

Captain Bankhead looked about. "Abandon ship," he said to the men closest to him.

The men looked down at the deck, hardly ever above water now, with the great waves pouring over it. It was not an enticing prospect, but it was now or never. One man after another went down the ladder, grabbed at the life lines, and made his way into the launch that was now high above the side of the ship, then far below it.

The stern of the *Monitor* rose above the waves and almost smashed into the quarter of the *Rhode Island*. The seas had begun to sense victory now, and they battered steadily at the little ship. Word came up to the captain that the steam pressure had fallen to five pounds — and even that would not last long. The small pumps were useless, and even the big pump was hardly working now.

"Morgan," said Lieutenant Greene, "go below and pass the word. Abandon ship! Make it fast now! There isn't much time!"

Dick took his courage into his hands and slid down the ladder into the darkened turret room, scarcely glancing at the two great Dahlgren's as he worked his way past them and let himself down through the scuttle to the second ladder. Some of the men were standing there with bailing buckets in their hands, staring wearily at him.

"Abandon ship!" said Dick.

"We can still save her!" said Jonas Barklew.

"Aye!" said Lobscouse.

"Abandon ship!" said Dick again. "Captain's orders!

Get up on the turret, mates! There's no time to lose!"

The water was almost to his knees as he went aft to the engine room. In the oily-smelling dimness, he saw the engineers struggling to free the small pumps. "Abandon ship!" he cried. "It's no use trying to save her! Abandon ship!"

The interior of the ship was like a cold, wet tomb and almost as dark. Dick made his way forward, expecting the *Monitor* to dive down and keep on going to the bottom at any minute, but he had a duty to perform, and there were still men inside the doomed ship. He heard the sound of crying and saw one of the cabin boys who had joined the ship at Washington. "Get up on deck, Tommy," he said. "Abandon ship!"

The boy's eyes were wide in his head. "What does that mean, Dick?"

"We have to leave her! Get up on the turret!"

"But the sea! It'll wash us off the turret!"

Dick gripped him by his wet blouse. "Listen, lubber," he said harshly, "I haven't time to argue! You stay down here, and you'll have the sea in on your head in five minutes! Now get up on deck! Jump and make it so!" He released the boy and went forward, glancing back in time to see Tommy scuttle into one of the storerooms.

The wardroom was a watery mess, with gear and food sloshing about on the deck. Water poured in from the forward door. Dick could see the flood of water coming through the hawsehole every time the *Monitor* dipped to meet a sea, and every time she dipped, it was a little deeper, and more water poured in.

There was no one in the room beneath the pilot-house, and the pilothouse itself had been abandoned long ago at the start of the doomed voyage.

"Abandon ship!" he yelled.

"Abandon ship...abandon ship...abandon ship..." an echo answered eerily over the washing of the water and the low thunder of the hull striking the seas.

Dick had a horrible feeling of loneliness as he looked about the dimly lighted berth deck with the oil lamps swinging steadily in their gimbals and with the water flowing back and forth like the smooth surface of a rushing creek with gear floating on top of it. Storeroom doors moved back and forth in the surging of the water.

"Abandon ship! Abandon ship! Abandon ship! All hands topside!" he yelled. Then he started for the ladder that led up into the turret and saw a pale face peering at him through thick glasses. "Spec!" he cried. "Get up on top of the turret! You afraid?"

Spec shook his head, but the fear within him etched itself on his face. "I was up there," he croaked.

"Blamed fool! Why didn't you stay?"

Specs swallowed. "Mister Greene said you were down here, Dick. I thought— Well, that is to say—I didn't want to leave the ship without you."

Dick gripped the thin boy about the shoulders. "Thanks, mate," he said. "I think we're about the last down here."

Even as he spoke, two engineers came through the galley door and swung up the ladder without a word.

"Time," said Spec. He jerked a thumb upward toward the last engineer. "When they leave their engine room, there isn't much hope left." He turned and scurried up the ladder.

Dick paused for a fraction of a second and looked forward. The ship lurched heavily, and a ripple of water seemed to rise in the wardroom and race toward him. He clambered up the ladder inches away from the rising water, and he almost felt as though it would rise up past him and cover him before he fell out into the turret and hauled himself to his feet by gripping a gun tackle. He looked up and could see a few men still standing atop the turret. Something was bumping and crashing against the side of the ship.

The faint yelling of men came to him as he gripped

the sides of the ladder and started up, hanging on tightly as the turret swung this way and then the other, almost hurling him from it. He glanced down to look at the two bottle-shaped Dahlgren's for the last time. The guns that had fought the *Merrimac* to a standstill deserved a better fate, but there was no helping it.

The red signal lamp was still lighted when Dick reached the top of the turret, casting a faint glow upon the white-faced men standing there. The moon passed in and out of banked clouds, now silvering the ocean, now plunging it into dimness. The *Rhode Island* was rising and falling in the seas, and in between the side-wheeler and the *Monitor* were two boats. One was the launch being pulled toward the side-wheeler, heavily laden with her oarsmen and the rescued men of the *Monitor*. The other small boat, a cutter, was being rowed slowly toward the *Monitor* to pick up more men.

Dick looked down the side of the turret. The outside ladder had vanished, but there were plenty of lines hanging there.

"Down you go, young'un," said a voice in Dick's ear. He turned to see his brother, Ben. "You've done more than your share, Dick. Down you go!"

Dick gripped a line and slid down to the deck. He saw a seaman out of the corner of his eye, who was wading toward the weather side of the *Monitor*, crying out to the cutter crew. A wave rose swiftly and quietly over the side of the ship and carried off the screaming man.

The same wave seemed to pick Dick up and drag him toward the side, and he gripped the lifeline tightly as the water poured over his head in a deep flood. He came up spluttering, and fear took control for a moment as he saw how low the ship was lying in the water, almost like a totally submerged reef.

The cutter was alongside now, and man after man leaped into it, although two of them missed and were washed swiftly away.

Dick saw a man coming down the side of the turret, clinging to a line, and as he descended, he yelled at Dick. "Get to the cutter, young'un! The ship won't last five minutes!"

Dick let go of his line, staggered across the deck, braced himself, and then leaped, striking the water but managing to grip the gunwale of the cutter with both hands. A pair of seamen grasped his soaked blouse and heaved him over the side and into the bottom of the cutter like a sack of potatoes, and a moment later, a heavy body landed atop him; he looked up into the grim face of his brother, Ben.

Rain was lashing the seas again as the cutter bobbed and plunged about, banging herself against the overhang of the *Monitor*'s deck. "Are there any men left aboard?" yelled the man at the tiller of the cutter.

Dick got to his knees and looked at the ship. She seemed deserted now, with only the red lamp swinging back and forth atop the turret.

"We can't stay alongside much longer!" yelled a huge seaman as he fended off with his oar.

"Anyone left aboard?" screamed man after man into the teeth of the wind and the sweeping rain.

There was no sign of life aboard the little ship.

"Shove off!" commanded the man at the helm.

The cutter swung away, and the gap of water widened rapidly as the *Monitor* began to drift, a lonely sight through the pouring rain and flying spray, with her red lamp winking steadily through the gathering darkness.

Flares soared up from the distant *Rhode Island*. The weary oarsmen in the cutter were aided by the rescued men of the *Monitor*. But it seemed as though the big side-wheeler was getting farther and farther away. The flares soared up into the sky with a faint plopping noise, casting a ghastly light against the clouds and the sheets of rain. They were signaling to the cutter, but the cutter could not close the gap.

"Too many trips this night," said a gasping seaman near Dick as he heaved on his oar. "My arms are like wood; they are."

"Look," said Ben Morgan quietly.

Dick looked back over his shoulder. A dim, low shape was vanishing to leeward, and as he looked, the red lamp flickered and went out. Dick realized the ship had at last foundered. He turned away, and his heart seemed to swell in his throat.

The *Rhode Island* was far away now, getting smaller and smaller. "Oars," said the man in charge of the boat. He stood up in the stern sheets and stared toward the *Rhode Island*, the rain beating on his face. He stood there a long time and then turned to look at the tired men in the boat. "You men of the *Monitor*," he said quietly, "I am Acting Master's, Mate Browne. There isn't a chance we can get to the *Rhode Island* this wild night. We'll drift about for a time, hoping we can find more of your mates. The odds are against it, but we can't leave a swimming man to die out there if we can help it."

They made a drag of the boat's mast to hold her bow on in the storming seas and began to drift to leeward almost in the same direction where the *Monitor* had vanished forever.

An hour drifted past, and there was no sign of men or of the *Monitor*, and the *Rhode Island* had vanished too.

Browne stood up again. "We'll have to row, men," he said, "hauling to the north and westward. If we don't, the strong offshore current will sweep us far out beyond the coastal ship track. If we keep moving, we'll be bound to see a ship by dawn."

They formed pulling crews, and the men who were off dropped to the bottom of the boat for sleep. Dick rowed the port bow oar, pulling easily as tired as he was, for the night was cold and wet, and the effort seemed to warm him a little. Now and then, the thought of his lost ship came to him, and the faces of his lost shipmates too.

His brother, Ben, was in the boat, as well as Jonas Barklew, while old Lobscouse slept curled up in the bow just behind Dick. Maybe most of them had been taken to the *Rhode Island*. But Spec had vanished, and Dick somehow knew the boy had been lost. He hadn't realized until then how much he had thought of his spectacled shipmate.

The cold light of dawn crept up in the eastern sky so slowly that Dick found it hard to believe it was coming at long last. Cheered as he was by the coming of daylight, there was still a leaden lump of sadness in his heart. He looked out across the heaving waves. The seas had abated during the night, and the cutter had a good chance to survive. The United States Navy had its cutters built well, and they were top sea boats. But the seas were cold-looking and dangerous, and somewhere beneath those lead-colored waves were many men of the *Monitor* and the brave little ship herself, undefeated by enemy guns but defeated by the sea itself.

"Sail ho!" cried out a seaman in a cracked voice. "Sail ho! There she is, mates!"

A slim slice of canvas showed now and then across the heaving wastes. "She's heading away from us," said Acting Master's Mate Browne.

In a little time, the faint triangular shape of the sail had vanished. Browne cracked open the emergency stores, hard ship's biscuits, and several containers of salt meat. The men munched steadily, their eyes scanning the horizon.

"Sail ho!" yelled Lobscouse.

"Where away?" asked Browne.

"Two points on the starboard bow, sir!"

They all stared in the direction indicated. There was the faintest suggestion of smoke and above it the barest sight of canvas on a tall mast. The ship was moving fast, in the opposite direction, and in a little while, she too had vanished.

Dick finished his dry meal and looked at Ben. "What are the chances, Ben?" he asked.

His brother grinned. "We ain't licked yet, as the man says, young'un."

"What man?" demanded Lobscouse sourly. "The only man who has any say out here is Davy Jones, and it looks to me like we're aheadin' for his locker."

"Stop that kind of talk!" snapped Browne. "You talk like a lubber!"

Lobscouse reddened and looked away.

Browne shoved back his cap. "We have a mast and some rigging, but the sail was lost overside last night. We can make a jury rig with our pea jackets and whatever else we can find."

"There's a hunk of tarpaulin up forward here," said Jonas Barklew.

"Good! Pass it aft!"

Dick reached for the canvas. There was something under it, and as he hauled on the canvas, it seemed to stick to something. He braced himself and hauled at it, but it was still stubborn, so he kicked at it.

"Urrrk!" a voice said from beneath the tarpaulin.

"What's that?" demanded Jonas. He tugged at the canvas and started back in surprise as a pale, bespectacled face peered out at him and Dick. "Good morning, mates," said Spec Simpson. "Time for breakfast, I take it?"

"I'll be blowed!" said Jonas.

"Time for breakfast, he says," roared Lobscouse. "Where was he last night when we was all tuggin' our hearts out on these oars making an ash breeze?"

Dick grinned. He hauled Spec out. "Well," he said, "I heard that when the whaler Essex was rammed by a bowhead whale and sunk, the small boats started clear across the Pacific for South America, and the only way one boat crew got there was by drawing lots to see who'd eat who. Maybe we can start with Spec here."

"Who would eat whom," corrected Spec as he sat up.

"Not much meat on him," said a whiskered seaman. "But bones make broth, mates."

Lobscouse spat over the side. "Jonah's bones," he said.

They raised the mast and stayed it, then fashioned a crude but serviceable sail of the tarpaulin and the pea jackets, buttoned and tied together. The stiff breeze began to fill it, and the cutter slogged along steadily. Cape Hatteras, of ill fame, was somewhere ahead of them. The Union forces had occupied the area, so there wasn't much danger of being captured by the Confederates, but the Diamond Shoals could be a great deal more dangerous than the rebels.

The sun was well up when they sighted a schooner, and in an hour, she picked them up. She was the A. Colby, out of Bucksport, Maine, bound for Fernandina with a load of brick for government use. Her skipper agreed to land the men at Beaufort, now a U.S. naval base in the Carolinas.

Dick Morgan sat on the foredeck of the schooner, grateful for the sun that warmed his back. Most of the cutter crew were asleep on the deck. But the *Monitor* men sat together, and none of them could sleep. There were too many memories to keep them awake.

"Well," said Ben Morgan at last, "she's gone, but there are more to come. It isn't as though she was the only one of her breed. Ericsson contracted to build others. The Passaic, which was with us at the start of the voyage, was one of them. But the old *Monitor* was first, mates."

Lobscouse grunted. "What do they plan to call these new ships?"

Ben smiled. "Monitors," he said. "Can you think of a better name for them?"

Jonas shook his head. "Well, I wonder where we'll end up now?"

"They'll need crews for those new monitors, Jonas,"

said Spec quietly. "Who can be of more use on one of them than we *Monitor* Boys?"

"Hawww!" said Lobscouse. "Listen to him! Not for me, mates. Old Lobscouse is going back to stick-and-string sailorin.' None of this half-submerged iron tank business for me."

Jonas nodded. "Aye, Lobscouse! Give me a good bow pivot rifle on the Hartford or the Sabine or the old Wabash."

Dick looked at Ben. Ben scratched his bristly jaws. "Well, they might be right," he said. "We did our share on a strictly experimental type of ship. It's over now. Back to a heaving deck, sails, and the sound of the wind through tight rigging, eh, mates?"

Dick nodded. He remembered all too well that horrible, eerie feeling of being below the surface of the water in the *Monitor*; and his memories of that damp, cold, water-filled berth deck, as he saw it for the last time, would be too much to let him go back into one of the monitor type.

Spec closed his eyes. "Well, I'll go back if they'll have me," he said.

"Jonah!" snorted Lobscouse.

Spec stood up and placed his thin hands on his thin hips, "Listen Lobscouse," he said quietly. "There's war in this country, and they need monitors and monitor men. You go back to your stick-and-string sailoring, Old Stormalong, and waggle your chin whiskers at the mermaids. It takes a real modern type of seaman and engineer aboard a monitor! Another thing! Don't call me a Jonah! If there ever was a Jonah that shipped aboard a ship, it was you, Silas Jones! Crying all the time about omens and superstitions and bad luck aboard the *Monitor*. Well, maybe you brought it on her. She did the job for which she was intended, didn't she? They sure nicknamed you right, Jones. Lobscouse is a hash and baked mixture of sea biscuit, chopped salt meat, potatoes, and onions.

You're a hash, all right! Now you let me alone, and you let the *Monitor* alone! She was as good a little ship as ever went to sea, and don't you ever forget it!" The boy's voice broke as he walked away.

Lobscouse's face was red, and his whiskers waggled a little. "I never heard the like o' that," he said.

"Maybe he was right," said Jonas darkly.

"Aye," said Ben.

Dick got up to follow Spec.

Lobscouse swallowed. "Well, I been rough on the boy. He ain't no sailor, that's for sartin, but he's a man, that lad. Strike me with a harpoon if I ever say different!"

Ben nodded. "You know, Lobscouse, you might just go and tell him that."

Lobscouse jumped to his feet and smiled. "Aye, mate, that I will! That I will!"

By the time they raised the shore line and the inlet for which their course had been shaped, a great many thoughts had raced through Dick Morgan's mind. The war was still young, and from all indications, it would go on for quite some time. The Navy was expanding like a gigantic net along the coast line to blockade the Southern seaports. There was hard fighting along the Mississippi and the Tennessee Rivers by ironclads and other ships working hand in glove with the Army. Rumors were rife that the rebels were building fast commerce-destroyer ships in England and other foreign countries, and fast, seagoing ships of the United States Navy would have to track them down and fight them. That would be fine service.

Dick stood at the rail looking toward the shore, but his thoughts were elsewhere. He, too, wanted to go back to the orthodox type of ship, such as the Sabine, or the fine Hartford, to fight on for the rest of the war. But Spec's words came back to him as though borne on the offshore breeze. *"They'll need crews for those new monitors. Who can be of more use on one of them than we Monitor Boys?"*

CHAPTER ELEVEN

"They call this a *Navy?*" growled Lobscouse. He looked into the water below the rickety wharf. "Lookit them things they call *ships!*" He waved a hand to encompass the anchorage at Beaufort and the myriad types of vessels that were moored there.

Dick Morgan couldn't help smiling. The news hadn't been all bad at Beaufort, for the *Rhode Island* had come in several days after the arrival of the *A. Colby,* carrying the rest of the survivors of the *Monitor.* Forty-seven officers and men had been saved for further service, while twelve men and four officers had been lost. Now the crew of the *Monitor* was more or less "on the beach" waiting for orders. And it looked as if those orders might place all of them on some of the very ships that Lobscouse viewed with such disgust.

Secretary of the Navy Gideon Welles had the difficult task of enforcing the President's formal naval blockade of the Southern coast. The 3,549 statute miles and 189 navigable harbors and inlets had to be blockaded by a navy that at the start of the war numbered but 64 commissioned vessels. But Old Gideon was a driving man and a doer. He had recalled ships from foreign stations and had recommissioned ships that had not been to sea in many years. In the first nine months of the war, the Navy had jumped to almost 300 ships.

Seamen had increased in number from 7,600 to 22,000. Welles had purchased river steamers, and coastal steamers, New York ferryboats, hardly fitted for sea service, and double-ended paddle-wheel steamers that didn't have to turn around in the shallow, narrow tidal rivers but could travel either way. There were cut-down sailing ships, armed tugboats, and excursion vessels — in short, anything and everything that had a bottom, propulsion, and enough strength to stand the recoil shock of heavy guns in action.

The handful of *Monitor* Boys sat along the rickety wharf gloomily, studying the patchwork squadron resting at anchor in front of them. All Dick's closest shipmates were there — his brother, Ben, Lobscouse, Jonas Barklew, Hank Bascomb, Jimmy Fox, Mike Reilly, and of course, the ever-talking Spec Simpson.

As a special concession for their hard service aboard the *Monitor*, the officer in charge of assignments had been ordered to let them select the ship they wished to serve on. There was one catch. It had to be in the Beaufort area.

But the Beaufort area didn't have any of the tall, white-winged sailing ships they all missed. There were a few sail and steam ships, converted merchantmen, but somehow it was not quite the same thing. The seven of them were all that were left of the *Monitor* Boys still on the beach, and they had been told sharply they would have one more day to make up their minds.

"We can always ask to be transferred to the Army," said Jonas.

"Or the Marines," said Hank.

A clerk from the naval office came out on the wharf. "You *Monitor* men," he called out importantly. "I have a ship that needs gunners and such like. The Commodore Worthington."

"Don't sound bad," said Hank. "Where is she, mate?"

"Out there. The one moored to that end buoy."

They all stared at the craft.

"Blow me for a lubber," said Lobscouse. "What is it?"

"Garbage scow with guns on it," said Jonas.

"It can't be real," said Ben.

The Commodore Worthington was a small, double-ended ferryboat that had seen far, far better days. She was low in the water, needed paint, and had been so badly hogged that they had strung heavy wire cables from bow to stern over the ugly-looking superstructure to hold up her ends.

The clerk grinned wickedly. "It's either her or the *Montauk,*" he said. "But then you boys don't like monitors, from what I hear."

They all looked at one another.

"Well," continued the clerk, studying his fingernails, "they need men of your ratings aboard the *Montauk.* It's her or the Commodore Worthington."

Lobscouse squinted at the dilapidated ferryboat. "If ye close yere eyes and look the other way, she don't look so bad, mates. Besides, we might not have to stay on her forever."

Jonas Barklew nodded. "I think I'm going to get sick, mates."

Hank held his head in his hands. "And I joined the 'Navy,'" he groaned.

"Which one?" prompted the clerk.

"Where's the Montauk?" asked Dick.

"Down South somewhere off Charleston with Admiral Du Pont's squadron. They say there's going to be a lot of action down there."

"I ain't bitin' on that slum," said Lobscouse.

"Then it's the *Commodore Worthington?*" demanded the clerk impatiently.

They all looked at one another again. "At least we'll be on *top* of the water," said Jonas.

"Yeh, but for how long?" asked Hank.

"Well?" called out the clerk.

"Make it the *Commodore Worthington*," said Ben quietly.

Spec stood up. "Not for me," he said. "I still feel the same way. I'll take the *Montauk* if they'll take me."

The clerk's face broke into a smirk. "Oh, I'm sure Captain Worden will be more than pleased to have you aboard."

Ben jumped to his feet. "Did you say, *Captain Worden?*"

"I did."

"Captain John L. Worden? The old commander of the *Monitor?*"

"Yes, that's him, but you said you wanted duty on the *Commodore Worthington*."

The *Monitor* Boys walked toward the startled little clerk. "You tell your commanding officer we'll be more than pleased to serve on the *Montauk*," said Ben.

"You said you'd go on the *Commodore Worthington!* I can make it hard for you men, you know."

Jonas smiled gently and leaned forward, his face close to the man. "Mate," he said in a kindly tone, "can you swim?"

"Yes, but..."

Jonas placed a huge hand flat on the man's chest and shoved just a little. He placed a hand to his ear and smiled again. "I could have sworn I heard someone cry 'help,' mates."

Mike Reilly grinned. "No, Jonas. Tis likely only a fish splashin' around down there. 'Tis a known fact that some fishes can sound like a man splutterin' for the breath av life."

They all linked arms and walked toward the naval office, and anyone who saw them coming got out of the way in a hurry, for Army, Navy, and Marines had had some little trouble with the *Monitor* Boys in the past few days, and they wanted no more of it.

———

IT WAS late in January when the *Rhode Island*, on one of her periodic supply trips to the vessels of the blockading squadrons, dropped the seven *Monitor* men at their destination off Charleston, the new *Montauk*. One after the other, they stepped onto the flat iron deck and saluted the quarterdeck—if one could call it that—where the Stars and Stripes rippled in the cold offshore breeze.

The *Monitor* men looked about. "She's bigger," said Jonas Barklew.

"Look," said Hank Bascomb, "they've placed her pilothouse atop the turret."

Ben Morgan peered into the open ports. "Two guns," he said. "Dahlgren's. One 11-incher and a 15-incher! I wish we had had 15-inchers with full charges aboard the old *Monitor*! We'd have blown the *Merrimac* out of the water."

Jimmy Fox looked about. "Bigger and better built, mates," he said.

"Report below, men," ordered an officer from atop the turret. "The captain wants to see you in the wardroom."

They went below out of the cold, searching wind into the familiar warmth of the berth deck. Seamen looked curiously at them as they walked forward. "Fresh fish," one of them said. "Stick-and-string boys, by the looks of them. Just when we need monitor men!"

The new draft dropped their sea bags near the door of the wardroom, removed their flat hats, and filed into the brightly lighted room. An officer stood there with a wide smile on his bearded face. It was Captain Worden, all right, but he didn't look quite the same. His eyes were different, and his face was still blackened as a result of the terrible wounding he had received on the *Monitor*.

"Welcome aboard, men," said Captain Worden. "It seems like an awfully long time since we served together on the *Monitor*."

"Not too long, sir, beggin' yere pardon," said Lobscouse, "for we never forgot ye, Captain Worden."

The officer smiled again. "I can use you, men, aboard the *Montauk*. I am glad you all volunteered, as you did for service aboard the *Monitor*."

Jonas Barklew swallowed hard.

"I heard that some of the old *Monitor* Boys requested duty on any other type of ship but a monitor," said Worden, "but I knew this group could hardly wait to serve aboard one."

"Oh, yes, sir," said Hank Bascomb. "We could hardly wait, all right, sir."

"Yes, sorr," said Mike Reilly. "We turned down service in a foine ship, the Commodore Worthington, to serve with ye again, sorr. That we did!"

Worden nodded. "You'll find the *Montauk* much improved over the *Monitor*. The engines are more powerful, and we have more speed. You have seen where the new pilothouse is located—a vast improvement over the little iron-log hut of the *Monitor*. We have cold water pipes to improve the ventilation, better bolting and jointing, and more powerful bilge pumps, with strainers in them."

"Thank the good Lord for that," said Lobscouse.

"You've arrived just in time," said Worden. "We leave in the morning for the Georgia coast, off the Ogeechee River. Admiral Du Pont is anxious to give us a preliminary trial before attempting to attack Charleston and Fort Sumter with his squadron. The enemy has constructed a powerful fort down there, Fort McAllister, and we are going to see how strong it is."

"It didn't take us long," said Jimmy Fox under his breath.

Worden held out his hand to shake the hand of each one of his old crewmen. "Welcome aboard," he said.

"Glad to be aboard, sir," each of them responded.

They knew he meant it; they were not quite sure just yet if each of them meant it.

———

THE DAY OF JANUARY 27, 1863, dawned bright and clear off the wide mouth of the Ogeechee River. The Montau moved slowly up the river, followed by the gunboats Seneca and Wissahickon on, the steamer Dawn, and the mortar-schooner C. P. Williams. The rebels had placed obstructions in the river opposite Fort McAllister. There were also torpedoes in the river—not the deadly, swift-moving tin fish of later wars, but rather metal containers filled with explosives that could be set off either by hull contact or electrical charges from the shore.

The *Montauk* did not have company for long. The four escort vessels could not stand up to the pounding the heavy guns of the fort could give them. They anchored a mile from the fort while Captain Worden conned his ship closer and closer to the quiet fort that seemed to crouch on the low riverbank, waiting to erupt into flames and smoke and to sink the audacious Monitor that was coolly challenging them on their own ground.

The enemy's gun-ranging marks and buoys had already been removed before daylight by a daring small boat party led by Lieutenant Commander Davis of the Wissahickon. Now the enemy gunners would have to estimate the range of the *Montauk* and waste time getting her under close fire.

Closer and closer moved the Monitor until she was only about one hundred and fifty yards below the obstructions. Then the anchor plunged down its well, and the chain ran out with a thunderous roar. The Monitor moved sideways in the current and rode easily at her anchor.

The gun crews were ready at their guns, stripped to the waist despite the cold morning air. It would soon be hot enough in the turret. The officer in charge was listening at the voice tube. He nodded and hung it up. "Trice up port stoppers!" he commanded. "Run out! Fire at will! Target the fort!"

The port stoppers creaked up, and the guns were run out. A gunner grinned at the *Monitor* men who were serving on both crews. "Maybe yell learn something about monitors now," he said with a sly grin.

The 11-inch Dahlgren cracked and then smashed back in recoil. "Sponge! Load! Run out! Stand clear!" The old familiar commands rang out as the two big guns settled to their work.

A huge spout of water arose close beside the *Montauk* and deluged the deck. A moment later, something struck on the far side of the ship.

"They've straddled us," said the officer. "Next shot will be a hit."

The grinning gunner eyed Dick. "Ye'll see something now, mate. Wait until they get a hit on the turret. Scares ye a bit, it does." He stepped back and rested a shoulder against the inside wall of the turret. "Nothing to be afraid of," he said loftily. "Ye get used to it."

Something slammed with terrifying force against the turret, causing the whole ship to shudder. The gunner was hurled clear across the turret to come to rest over the scuttle hatch. Blood ran from his nose, and there was a dazed look in his eyes.

"Suspend firing until the smoke clears," said the officer in charge. "How are you, Sanders?"

The gunner shook his head. "I ain't sure, sir."

Mike Reilly rubbed his jaws. "Fresh fish," he said. "Stick-and-string boys, by the looks av them. Just when we need monitor men!"

"Maybe we'll learn something about monitors now," said Jimmy Fox.

"Ye'll see something now, mate," said Dick dryly.

"Wait until they get a hit on the turret. Scares ye a bit, it does."

"Nothing to be afraid of," Jonas Barklew said softly. "Ye get used to it."

Ben Morgan helped the dazed man to his feet. "Never lean against the inside wall of a monitor turret when she's under fire, mate. A man can get killed that way."

"Aye, I can see that! But where did ye lads learn that?" the gunner asked.

Ben smiled a little. "On the *Monitor*, matie. You see, all of us served on her from the day she was commissioned until she was lost off Hatteras. We learned quite a bit in that parlor party with the *Merrimac*."

The gunner flushed. "Sorry, mates. This is my first experience on one of these tin cans."

"They'll take care of you if you take care of them," said Hank Bascomb.

"Commence firing!" came the crisp command.

And so it was for four mortal hours. The *Montauk* hammered at the fort, and the fort hammered at the *Montauk* until the Monitor was out of ammunition, and the fort still sat there shrouded in smoke, practically undamaged. But that could be said for both sides, for the Monitor had been hit repeatedly, with hardly a mark to show for it.

They dropped down the river out of range of Fort McAllister, and even as they did so, they could see small boats putting out from the shore to replace the ranging marks and buoys that had been removed by the men of the *Wissahickon*.

But the Montauk did not go far. It was anchored at the mouth of the river, ready for another trial of strength with stubborn Fort McAllister. The crew left the steaming heat of the turret and the lower decks to examine their ship. Here and there were marks upon deck and turret but no damage whatsoever.

"Stout little barge," said Jonas Barklew. He wiped the

sweat from his face. "On the other hand, Fort McAllister is no pushover."

"Good gunners in that fort," said Hank Bascomb. "I'd say we was no further than six hundred yards from 'em, and they were hitting us regular."

A seaman nodded. "They say there are at least twenty-four guns at McAllister. Some of them are columbiads, 8-inch, forty-eight pounders."

"They can't hurt us then," said Ben Morgan. "The *Monitor* was taking hits from bigger guns than that at Hampton Roads and later at Drewry's Bluff."

"What's up this muddy river anyways?" asked Lobscouse. "Don't hardly look worthwhile foolin' with it."

"Confederates," said Spec Simpson dryly. "There are blockade runners and privateers, itching to get out to sea."

"That's right," said the seaman. "They think the rebel commerce-destroyer Nashville is up there somewheres, waiting for a chance to get to sea. If she does get past us, we don't have a ship out here fast enough to catch her."

————

THE *MONTAUK* TRIED AGAIN on the first day of February, but this time the tide was against her, and she could not get close enough to the fort for a real trial of strength. But the big 11-inch and 15-inch shot and shell of the Monitor played havoc with the earthen ramparts of the fort, tossing great clouds of earth and dust high into the air to mingle with the thick smoke of the enemy guns. This time the rebels had thought of another annoyance. The riverbank was thick with sharpshooters who peppered away for hours trying to get slugs through the eye slits of the pilothouse or into the turrets through the great ports when the stoppers were triced up. Three men were wounded by the Minie balls of the sharpshooters, and the Monitor sustained forty-six direct hits before she retired down the river for the second time.

There was no question of letting up on the blockade. The Union ships would stay out there in Warsaw and Ossabaw Sounds waiting for rebel blockade runners. The Nashville was said to be ready for sea, but there was no sign of her. It became the old cat and mouse game that the *Monitor* had played at Hampton Roads while waiting for the *Merrimac* to reappear. It was a chance for Captain Worden to train his crew to top efficiency, and as long as they knew they could creep up the Ogeechee to fight it out with Fort McAllister now and then, to test her strength and the accuracy of her guns, it was not so bad.

Dick Morgan was happy enough. He had been *promoted.* Now, instead of being the lowest rating on the gun crew, that of powder monkey, he had become a rated gunner and worked as a tackle man. Not much of a promotion, it was true, but it was better than being a powder monkey.

The crew kept busy with gun drills, small-arms drills, cutlass exercises, pulling the small boats, and all the other training needed aboard a man-of-war. But all the time the men drilled, they thought of the *Nashville* and hoped she'd try to make a break for the sea. Just let her try!

CHAPTER TWELVE

The offshore wind swept a spit of chilly rain against the faces of the men standing on the afterdeck of the *Montauk*. A cutter was being lowered into the choppy waters of the sound. Captain Worden watched the men as they unhooked the fall tackles and clambered into the boat. Boatswain's Mate Ben Morgan looked up at his commanding officer. "Are there any final orders, sir?" he asked.

Worden shook his head. "You know what to do, Morgan. The *Nashville* has been seen above Fort McAllister. She's obviously getting ready to make a dash for the open sea. But every time she sees us, she scoots upriver again. In the morning, we're going to attempt to get close to the obstructions of the fort and see if we can't reach the Nashville with our 15-inch gun before she gets out of range."

"Yes, sir."

"You may shove off then, Morgan. Now, remember that you are only to remove the range markers and buoys. You are not, under any circumstances, to make a landing. Is that clear?"

"Aye, aye, sir."

"The best of luck to you then, men."

"Shove off forward! Stand by to give way together! Give way together!" came the commands from Ben Morgan.

The cutter swung away from the low side of the Monitor and moved toward the river mouth. In a little time, the Monitor had vanished in the darkness. Dick Morgan pulled steadily at port bow oar, seated beside Spec Simpson, who pulled starboard bow oar. The rest of the *Monitor* Boys were there too, plus four other seamen from the *Montauk*, Neilson, Sanders, Sutter, and Duff, all good men and crack oarsmen. Jimmy Fox was up forward, peering into the rainy darkness, for he had the best eyesight of any of them.

The twelve *Montauk* men were well armed with cutlasses, Navy Colts, and Sharps carbines. They had boarding axes and other tools to help in removing the range markers and buoys. It was getting to be quite a game. The rebels would place the markers during the early morning if they were not under fire from Yankee ships before they got them put in, and if they succeeded in placing them, the Yankees would sneak out at any hour of darkness and cut them loose.

Spec leaned toward Dick. "Supposing those Johnny rebs happen to be there when we get there?"

Dick laughed. "We can trade 'em Yankee coffee for a bale or two of cotton."

"More likely lead for lead and steel for steel," growled Lobscouse, who was pulling an oar in front of Dick.

"Silence in the boat!" snapped Ben Morgan from his steering position. "Those Georgia sharpshooters can part your hair with a Minie ball at two hundred yards, and they can shoot by sound too, mates."

The rowlocks had been muffled, and the oars dipped quietly into dark waters. It seemed to Dick Morgan that they had rowed completely from the earth and were moving softly through some great void. There was no sight of shore or ship, but somewhere up ahead of them was the Ogeechee River, and on the left bank was humped and dangerous Fort McAllister, with shotted guns aimed at the broad reach of the river, while sharp-eyed and sharp-eared Georgia marksmen prowled along the shore line waiting for nosy Yankees to come up the Ogeechee.

It was a wonder to Dick that Jimmy Fox could see at all through the wet darkness. But the little seaman stood up in the bows, guiding Ben Morgan by pointing to port or starboard.

The water pulled back from the cutwater and lapped along the sides of the deeply laden cutter, and quiet as it was, it sounded like Niagara Falls after a heavy rainfall.

They were in the river now, for every time they stopped to listen, Dick could hear the water lapping against the low shores. Slowly and carefully, they ascended the river until, at last, the very wind seemed to warn them that they were getting close to the piles and obstructions placed in the river.

Ben Morgan let the cutter drift while Jimmy Fox peered through the darkness, trying to find the marker buoys. Every man in the cutter was straining his ears and eyes too. The softest sound they made might carry hundreds of yards to that grim fort on the south shore.

A dark form drifted by the cutter, and Dick's heart leaped lumpily into his throat. A torpedo! He was sure of it, but what was to be to do? If he touched it, it might explode. If he didn't find it off, it might hit the boat and explode. But he couldn't cry out, for that would bring instant retaliation from the shore. He stared at the horrible thing until Lobscouse casually reached over the side of the boat and shoved it away. "Blasted log," he said. "River seems filled with 'em."

"Buoy," said Jimmy softly.

They came up alongside of it, and Jimmy felt carefully around it to make sure it did not have a trip line on it attached to a torpedo. Then he cut the anchor line and let the buoy drift downriver. Slowly and quietly, they moved about on the surface of the river until they had cut loose three more markers.

The rain pattered down steadily now, and the sound of it dulled the noises the men and the cutter made. A dog barked sharply from the shore. The men in the boat felt that it was no more than fifty yards away from them, although that couldn't be so, for they were on the northern side of the river, and the sound came from the southern side.

They drifted quietly. Dick was thinking that the Nashville, had she chosen such a night to go downriver, with a competent pilot aboard, might have been able to reach Ossabaw Sound and get past the blockers when the dog barked hoarsely again.

"That dog ain't on shore," said Hank Bascomb.

"He can't swim and bark too," said Jonas Barklew.

"Quiet!" hissed Lobscouse. He turned and peered into the darkness.

Then they heard the soft creaking of oars not fifty feet from them. Dick's eyes watered as he stared directly at the point where he had heard the noise of the oars. He saw a dim shape. A big rowboat filled with men wearing slouch hats!

None of the Montau\ men so much as moved a fraction, except to breathe as noiselessly as possible. There were, but twelve Yankees in the cutter, and they were not ready or willing to open fire until absolutely necessary, for two reasons: one being that it would bring a hornets' nest of fighting mad rebels down on them; the second being that they had not yet finished their mission.

The wind had shifted and was blowing across the enemy boat toward the *Montauk* cutter. If that wind shifted again and the dog in the rebel patrol boat winded them, those Georgia sharpshooters who filled the patrol boat would almost blast the cutter out of the water.

"You sure you heard a boat out heah, Norris?" said a man in the stern of the patrol boat.

"Positive, suh!"

"You must have been hearin' things."

"The ol' dawg theah, he heard somethin,' too, suh."

"That's right. But he isn't barkin' now."

The patrol boat moved on a little. "Range markah missin,' Suh," said a man in the bow of the boat.

"Cain't see that othah one either, suh," said another man.

"Them Yankee thieves out heah, all right," said a deep-voiced man.

The two boats were hardly fifty yards apart. The rain drove down hard now, pattering steadily on the surface of the Ogeechee.

"Back water," said Ben Morgan softly.

They lowered their oars and began to back water ever so delicately, moving downriver now with the current.

"Oars," said Ben Morgan.

The dripping blades were raised parallel with the water, and the current began to turn the bow of the boat slowly.

Every man stared over his shoulder, and Ben Morgan hunched forward as though trying to pierce the veil of darkness and rain. "Hold water port. Pull easy starboard," he said. Now they were almost pointing downriver, and every man began to breathe easier.

Then the dog barked sharply and steadily, like a boy slowly dragging a stick along a picket fence. The rebel boat's oars struck the water hard and fast, and she came down toward the Yankee boat.

There was no time to fool now. "Pull hard together!" snapped Ben Morgan.

The blades dug in, and the heavy cutter began to

surge forward. Once the cutter was beyond point-blank range, there was no doubt in the minds of the *Montauk* men that they could out pull any rebel boat on that river, but they could not outspeed a .58-caliber Minie ball looking for a home in soft flesh.

"Give her ten!" cried out Ben. He bent low in the stern as the cutter surged on, driven by trained oarsmen putting their all into ten hard strokes to gain impetus.

A ripple of orange-red light came from the patrol boat, followed by the heavy crash of musketry. Ben Morgan staggered and fell into the bottom of the boat. Neilson, pulling port second stroke behind Sutter, fell forward, and his oar caught a crab and was driven back against Sutter's oar, forcing it up so that the handle struck the big stroke oarsman under the chin, lifting him from his seat and dropping him over against Duff, who was starboard stroke. From a well-trained rowing crew driving a heavy cutter with speed and precision through the rainy darkness, the boat became a tangle of oars and yelling men. She wallowed up and down as men thrashed about, and because there was now no one at the helm, she yawed toward the southern shore.

Dick stared toward the hunched shape of his brother, not knowing whether Ben was alive or dead, but there was no going to him, for the iron discipline of men-o-war's men of the United States Navy held him on his thwart.

Jonas Barklew worked his way aft and took the tiller, dragging Neilson from underfoot as he did so. "Oars!" he directed. "Stand by to give way! Give way together!"

The rebels were still firing, and now and then, a bullet struck the cutter. There were only eight men at the oars in the cutter, but Jimmy Fox left his post in the bow and worked his way aft, stepping between the hard-pulling men, until he reached Barklew's seat and got his oar into the water to pick up the racing stroke.

"Cease firin'!" yelled the rebel officer. "We'll take them prisoners, men!"

"Fat chance!" jeered Jonas Barklew.

"Ye'll have to learn to pull an oar, ye lubbers!" yelled Lobscouse.

But the rebels had gained in the chaotic interval that the cutter had lost way, and now they were but a few yards astern and gaining steadily.

"There's something dead ahead!" cried out Jonas.

Spec Simpson turned and stood up. "Torpedo!" he screamed. He gripped his oar to fend it off, but the oar caught and twisted in his hands and lifted him swiftly over the side. Dick got to his feet and took his oar, pointing it toward the dark shape on the river. Something flashed and exploded alongside the boat, and a blast of gas and displaced air struck him and blew him over the side into the cold waters of the Ogeechee.

He went down deep and came slowly upward with fear in his heart that he would be run down by the cutter or the following patrol boat.

The rain was like icy needles when he surfaced. There was nothing to see, but he could hear men yelling and screaming in the water. He knew in his heart that the cutter crew was in the water and that the *Montauk* men could either be killed, drowned, or captured within a matter of minutes.

He unbuckled his broad waist belt as he trod water and let his Colt and cutlass sink. He had been barefoot when he had left the *Montauk* and had been wearing blouse, bell-bottomed trousers, and flat hat. Now the flat hat was floating down the Ogeechee.

He was a strong swimmer, so there was no fear in him of keeping afloat unless he caught a cramp from the cold water. Everything seemed the same out on that wide, dark river, as though he was drifting about in an aqueous world with no land anywhere within miles. He didn't want to drift out into Ossabaw Sound, and he certainly didn't want to land on the rebel-haunted southern shore of the Ogeechee. But the northern shore was nothing more than salt marsh with a thin crust upon it through which a man could easily break and be mired to the knees. From what Dick had seen of it, there wasn't much cover for a fugitive Yankee bluejacket on the northern bank.

Now and then, he heard voices carrying through the darkness, and once he saw a gleam of yellow light as a bull's-eye lamp was briefly unshuttered. There had been such a lamp in the cutter, but it was probably at the bottom of the river by now.

He swam slowly, using a breast stroke, pausing every few strokes to look and listen, feeling the tug of the current against his left side so that he was sure he was swimming toward the northern bank. Every so often, he let his feet down but felt no bottom. Something drifted past him, and he thought it was a log. He put out a hand to fend it off, and his fingers touched the cold face of a drowned man floating toward the sound. Before he could make out who it was, the body drifted beyond sight on its journey to a seaman's unmarked grave.

An icy panic welled up in Dick, and the sheer horror of the night, the pursuit by the rebels, the wounding or killing of his brother, the loss of the cutter—added to the horrible experience he had just gone through—almost unnerved him. Just when he knew he could stand no more, his feet struck the soft bottom, and he waded ashore with his hands outstretched until he was on the marshy ground. He fell across a low hummock and lay there a long time with his face hidden in his cold, wet hands.

At last, he forced himself to get to his feet, and he looked about, shivering in the cold wind and the rain, which now seemed to drift noiselessly down upon the wide mud marsh. Across the river, he saw lights moving about upon the far shore, and the faint sound of voices came to him when the wind shifted. He knew whose voices they would be.

He started plodding along, keeping the river on his right so that he would be heading easterly toward the sound. By daylight, he should be somewhere near the shore, and he might be able to hail or signal one of the blockading ships. But the going got progressively worse as he struggled along. At times he broke through the thin-crusted surface and became mired knee-deep in the semifluid mud beneath it. The rain was now a steady drizzle that chilled him to the bone. It didn't help either when he stepped from a hummock into waist-deep water and fell face forward into it. He came spluttering to the surface and realized he had walked into the river.

He turned away from the river and within minutes found himself wading up to his waist again. There was no way to orient himself in that liquid darkness, and now he could see no lights upon the southern shore. There was nothing to do but keep on. He knew if he spent a night on those marshes, he might die there by drowning or from the cold. He plunged on through water and mud, sometimes falling, sometimes swimming, until he wasn't sure whether he was walking east, west, north, or south.

At last, he had to stop and rest, and as he did so, he thought he saw something looming up in the darkness ahead of him. It looked like a small craft of some kind, but if it was, it was quite a distance from the river. Come to think of it, decided Dick grimly, craft of a certain size could probably move about quite a bit on the half land and half water around the Ogeechee. He got wearily to his feet and plodded toward it. There were no lights, and it looked as though the vessel was ashore rather than anchored or moored. He came up close and saw that it was a scabrous, peeling hulk of a small steamer, probably a river tug, that had seen far better days. He walked around the starboard side and noticed a dark area which, upon inspection, proved to be a great gaping hole in the side, as though it had been rammed or hit by a big-caliber shell.

The thing was abandoned, he was sure. He clambered up the side and stood upon the warped deck. At least it would be a place to stay out of the wind and rain until daylight came and he could see where he was. He tried a door into the wheelhouse, and it opened easily. He stepped in and looked around. The wheel was still in place, but the windows had been smashed, and the wind blew steadily through them. There was a small companionway at the after end of the wheelhouse, and he felt his way down it into the hull. His questing hands touched the engine. He turned and walked forward, finding another door. He opened it and entered what appeared to be quarters of some sort, for his left hand struck two bunks, one atop the other, and there were musty-smelling, straw-filled mattresses in them.

Rain leaked through cracks in the decking above his head and pattered down on the deck beneath his feet. The compartment he stood in seemed rather large, or at least he sensed that it was, and strangely enough, the mingled odors of wood fires, greasy food, and musty cloth still hung in it, although it must have been abandoned for some time.

He shivered violently and then set out to find some dry clothing or anything that would take the chill out of his bones. He felt his way about, passing his hands across a table and touching a lamp that stood on it. He picked up the lamp, and it smelled as though it had been used not too long ago. Maybe fishermen used the craft as a shelter in bad weather.

There were bunks on the far side of the compartment too, and he felt first in the upper one, but it was empty even of a mattress. The lower bunk yielded better results. It was filled with blankets, and pieces of canvas humped over something. He prodded at it, and his blood ran cold as he felt a body. He jumped back and struck the table.

He sensed, rather than saw, something moving about in the bunk, and then it rose and faced him, draped in blankets. There was no time to waste on formality. Dick lowered his head and charged, catching whatever or whoever it was in the midriff. The figure fell back into the bunk with a strangled cry that was somehow familiar to Dick. "*Urrk!*" it said in a gasping tone.

Dick stared at the jumbled mass of blankets. "Spec?" he said.

The figure moved from side to side like a robed snake charmer playing on a pipe and swaying in time with a hooded cobra. "Dick?" it said weakly.

"How'd you get here? "

"Swam. I thought you got lost when the cutter was blown up by that torpedo."

Dick shook his head. "I was blown overboard and swam ashore. I thought if I followed the riverbank to the east, I'd reach the sound and hail one of our ships."

"Dick, I had the same idea, but in the night, everything looked alike, and I found this wreck here. It must either be the Mayflower or Henry Hudson's Half Moon."

"Too far south," chattered Dick. "More likely a Spanish galleon or Blackbeard's Queen Anne's Revenge. Give me some of those blankets!"

They sat side by side, swathed in the moldy-smelling blankets. Spec had scoured the boat for every scrap of covering he could find, and although the odors trapped in the material were more than strong, it was better than freezing to death on the shores of the Ogeechee.

"What do we do now, Dick?" asked Spec gloomily.

"Sit tight until morning to see where we are, then try to get back aboard one of our ships." Dick looked away. "We'll have to report the loss of the cutter and most of the crew and that we didn't remove all of the range markers."

Spec nodded. "Do you think they're all lost?" he said

quietly. "Your brother and Jonas, Hank Bascomb and Lobscouse? All the others? *All* of them, Dick?"

Dick clambered into the top bunk and stretched out. "I don't know, Spec. I hope not." He lay still for a long time staring up into the darkness, listening to the steady pattering of the rain on the decks. Finally, he fell asleep.

CHAPTER THIRTEEN

Dick Morgan opened his eyes and wrinkled his
nose; the accumulated odors of the blankets,
warmed by his body, hung about him like a
miasma. Dim light filtered through the dirty glass of the
portholes and through cracks and splits in the ancient
woodwork of the wrecked craft. A gentle snoring sound
reminded him that at least Spec Simpson had survived
the tragedy of the night before.

Dick climbed out of the bunk. His clothing was still
damp, but at least he was warm now. He walked to a
porthole and peered through the filthy glass, but all he
saw was an opaque grayness that seemed to shift and
move even as he watched it. A damp, salty smell hung
about the craft. They must be close to the sound.

He padded across the tilted deck to the door and let
himself into the engine room, walked past the pile of
rusting metal that had been the engine, and climbed up
the ladder to the wheelhouse. Gray mist swirled in
through the open windows. He rested his hands on a sill
and peered out into the whitish-gray world. Dick shook
his head. They had slept all night, hoping that they could
orient themselves by daylight, but the mist and fog that

hung over the area was almost as bad as the rainy darkness of the night before.

He walked out onto the deck and let himself over the side.

Going toward the bow of the vessel, he suddenly found himself in ankle-deep water. He knelt and tried to peer through the mist. He could see a broad, calm water surface stretching away to be lost in the mist. He tasted the water and found it fresh enough, with a slightly brackish taste. Dick stood up, a puzzled look on his face. If they had reached the shores of the sound during the night, the water would have been salty. Yet with the ebb and flow of tides, perhaps the sound water was mostly water from the Ogeechee, mingled with the salt water.

He went back to the vessel and climbed to the deck, noting the name on the bows of the abandoned craft. Ogeechee Prince. He climbed aboard and walked out on the foredeck. There had been a gun mounted on the battered planking at one time. He could see broken tackle and metal set into the deck to prevent the wear and tear of recoil and the pounding of the gun. Then he remembered the big hole in her side. Maybe she had been a patrol craft. One of Gideon Welles's Crackerbox fleet sent down South to enforce the Federal blockade. Maybe the gunners at Fort McAllister had slammed a 48-pounder solid shot through her thin planking.

He went into the wheelhouse again and peered through the mist. It was thinning a little. A faint sound came to him — a bugle crying out brassily. Tilting his head to one side, he could have sworn he heard faint voices. It was a characteristic of fog and mist. Many a time when aboard the Sabine, or the *Monitor*, with thick grayness about the ships, the men on deck could hear voices carrying from great distances.

He shrugged. All they could do was wait. The wind had picked up a little and was feeling its way through the veil, ready to tatter it and drive it away.

He stood there for a long time and suddenly realized that he could see many yards out into the mist. The water was calm enough, hardly like Ossabaw Sound. Still, they could be within the mouth of the Ogeechee. Bluejacket patrol boats nosed about on those waters. It wasn't rebel territory as far as their crews were concerned. They poked into every tidal stream and into every cove and inlet, landing at times to raid small rebel installations or to seek information.

Now he could see across the body of water to a low shoreline, but he could not identify it. He looked right and left but saw no landmarks. Vague doubts began to chase themselves through his mind and to haunt him. By now, he should have been able to orient himself. If he had gone downriver last night, the river would have been on his right, but a number of times during that miserable night, he had waded into deep water and had never been quite sure which way he had been heading. The land had hardly been land at all — more like water and land mixed together in a witch's brew.

He idly watched a piece of driftwood floating slowly past from left to right. Then he stared at it. If he was on the northern bank of the Ogeechee, facing the river, the flow would have been from right to left, toward the sea. How could this be? Could he possibly have landed on the southern shore, then kept the river on his right, and walked west in the direction of Fort McAllister? Yet, he had walked several hours at least. He closed his eyes. If he had walked that far, he would have stumbled onto the fort. He began to go over his actions of the night. He opened his eyes again. The tug of the current had been against his left side during that tiring swim to shore. The river flowed west to east, in general, for it was a winding skein of a thing in its course to the sea. So he had made the northern shore. But now the current was running from left to right, or to the west! He grinned weakly. The tide was coming in! Certainly, the current would be reversed until it ebbed again!

He looked to his left, downriver, but even though the mist was clearing rapidly now, he still could not see the broader waters of the sound. He could detect nothing but low shoreline mantled with scrub trees, scraggy brush, and whitened driftwood. That was the odd part of the whole thing.

He heard Spec stirring down below, grunting and yawning. In a little while, as long as the tatters of mist held out, they could walk to the east toward the sound. Vague noises drifted again to him through the opaqueness that was thicker upriver. They were vaguely familiar noises. The rattling of chains. The slapping of bare feet on a hard surface. The muted sound of men's voices. He raised his head and suddenly caught the smell of smoke, and it wasn't the bittersweet of wood smoke or the gaseous odor of soft-coal smoke. It was the tang of good anthracite! That meant one thing to Dick Morgan: the rebels had little access to hard coal in the Confederacy, so their steamers burned soft coal. The Federals had the anthracite mines of the North and burned it in their fireboxes. There had to be a Union vessel out there, for the sounds were unmistakable to a young man who had spent a good part of his life around water and ships.

A feeling of relief flooded through Dick. As soon as the sun drove off the mist, they would see the ship out there. They would hail her, and a cutter would put out for them. It might even be the *Montauk*!

He heard the faint, strident sound of squealing blocks and tackles and the thumping of something heavy at intervals. To Dick, it sounded like something that was either being unloaded from the mysterious and unseen ship, or else it was being loaded; the squealing noises would indicate that the cargo was being raised or lowered, and the thumping sound would be that of the cargo striking the deck.

Then he saw the indistinct shape of a vessel to the right, not more than several hundred yards away. It was a two-masted vessel, about the size of a small steam sloop. Smoke drifted from her tall funnel to mingle with the mist. She didn't look familiar to Dick, but vessels came and went on blockading duty, some relieving others that moved on to different duties or else to be refitted after a hard term of blockading.

Spec came slowly up the ladder, grumbling. "Even Navy coffee would taste good now, mate."

He stopped behind Dick. "Where are we, Dick?"

"On the north bank of the Ogeechee."

"I agree. But where on the north bank of the Ogeechee?"

Dick shrugged. "There's a vessel loading or unloading something out there. One of ours, no doubt. There wouldn't be any rebel vessels loading or unloading cargo below Fort McAllister."

"No." Spec polished his glasses and peered at the vessel. "Side-wheeler, ain't she?"

"Yes. But I can't place her, Spec."

"Hmm..." Spec peered downriver, then quickly turned to stare at the vessel. "Oh, my," he said in a strange voice.

"What is it, Spec?"

"Did you say below Fort McAllister?"

"Yes."

Spec swallowed hard. "You'd better look again, mate, for if that conglomeration of humps and bumps across the river isn't Fort McAllister, we're on some other river than the Ogeechee."

Dick turned slowly and stared in the direction in which Spec pointed. Through the drifting whorls of mist, he saw a too-familiar sight, the high brown earthen ramparts of Fort McAllister and the huge humped shapes of the bomb-proofs and magazines within the ramparts. They were upriver of the fort! "Oh, my," said Dick faintly.

They looked at each other and then at that strange vessel.

Dick squinted his eyes and saw the flag at her peak. The wind raised it and fluttered it. There wasn't any doubt that she was rebel, all right.

"The *Nashville*!" they said instantaneously.

"Why would she be working at cargo this time of day?" said Spec.

Dick eyed the vessel. She had had an interesting career as blockade-runner and a commerce destroyer. She had burned a big Yankee ship, the Harvey Birch, in the English Channel late in 1861. The Harvey Birch had been laden with tea; ship and cargo were worth half a million dollars. In June 1862, she had tried to run through the Federal blockade off Charleston and had been forced to turn back and head to sea, hotly pursued by three Union ships, and she had easily outrun two of them, while the big and fast Keystone State, the fleetest of the block-aders, had been unable to catch her after a three-hundred-mile sea chase.

"Seems odd," said Spec. "Workin! on cargo."

There were lighters beside the ship, and as the boys watched, they saw the sling and whip tackles raise bales high over the runner's bulwarks and lower them into a lighter.

Dick half-closed his eyes, then suddenly he wet the middle finger of his right hand, as he had often seen Lobscouse do, laid it on the palm of his left hand, then smacked his left palm smartly with his right fist. "She's aground, Spec!" he cried. "This is what we've been waiting for!"

The mist was rising and fading away, but the air still had its vague and uncertain look. Spec eyed the Nash-ville. "You sure, Dick?" he asked dubiously.

"Positive! Listen! She came down the river during the night under cover of the darkness and the rain, figuring on fog and mist this morning. She might have made it too; the fog was so thick, but she went aground, and now they're trying to lighten her before us Yankees find out she's there and reach her with 15-inch Dahlgren shells!"

Spec's face widened into a grin, and then it slumped into a sad look. "Sure! Sure! We two Yankees know she's stuck in the mud there, but the rest of the Yankees don't know that. So here we sit on the luxurious Ogeechee Prince, within spitting distance of the Nashville, and we can't even shoot a blank cartridge at her! Dick, your head is on backward."

Dick gripped the boy by his thin arm and drew him close, thrusting a scowling face close to Specs. "Listen, dumb block! The river curves in a big bend east of us. Our ship can't get past those obstructions below Fort McAllister. I grant you that. But the *Montauk* can fire across this half-sunken bend of land, can't she?"

"Aye, mate."

Dick grinned. "So, we figure the range from about where we sat the other day and traded shot with Fort McAllister to about where the Nashville is stuck and pass it on to Captain Worden."

"Just like that! We get our instruments, which we don't have, and sight them on the Nashville, then figure the range from her to the obstructions. From the gallant Ogeechee Prince, we take a boat, which isn't aboard her, and row easily down the river, passing Fort McAllister, which isn't there, through the obstructions, which aren't there, calmly board the *Montauk*, which doesn't happen to be there either, give Captain Worden our figures, and sit back and watch the show. Don't call me a dumb block, you big dumb block!"

Dick grinned wickedly. "If we have to fight this war with lubbers like you, Spencer Simpson, the Second, I wonder how we've managed to last so long. If those rebels ever find out about dumb blocks like you!"

Spec leaned close to Dick. "All right, *powder monkey*, you tell me how we're going to do it."

"Rated gunner, you grease wiper. Listen!" Dick raised his head. Somewhere down the river, a gun had roared. "Smooth-bore that," he said quickly.

They eyed Fort McAllister and saw a puff of smoke drifting from one of her embrasures. A cloud of brown pelicans rose from the water and flapped quickly off. Farther down the river and hardly visible to the boys was an odd but familiar sight, a big tin can on a shingle. It was the *Montauk*, all right! She was right where she had anchored the first day she had fought her inconclusive duel with the columbiads of Fort McAllister. The fort was firing regularly now, raising spouts of water about the ugly little fighter while the *Montauk* nonchalantly squatted there on the clay-colored water, ignoring the cannonading.

"She's opening her ports!" said Spec.

The twin gun muzzles were thrust out, and one of the guns blasted flame and smoke. The report was flatter-sounding and much more distinct than that of the fort's guns.

The shell whistled over the Ogeechee Prince and burst far short of the Nashville, whose upper masts and upper works would be just about visible to the Yankee gunners. Five more rounds burst at varying ranges as the gunners felt about for the grounded ship.

Dick slapped a first down on his palm. "It's the fog patches that make it difficult to estimate range," he said.

Spec nodded. First, he looked at the stranded Nashville and then at the anchored Montauk. Gunsmoke was mingling with the fog and mist now — smoke from the fort's growling guns and from the *Montauk*'s crackling Dahlgren's.

"They've got a pivot gun forward on the Nashville," said Dick. "Looks like a Brooke rifle to me."

Spec glanced again at the two ships and down at his gangling legs. "Dick," he said quietly, "I think I could easily pace off a measured yard or two with these skinny legs of mine."

Dick looked quickly at his shipmate. The same thing had occurred to him. "Sure," he said, "but we'd have to leave the gallant Ogeechee Prince and walk toward the Nashville and turn and pace off toward the *Montauk* across this mud marsh of land, wearing blue uniforms, and every gunner in Fort McAllister will know what we are doing. It won't take long before they'll try the range on us with some of those columbiads they have, and those boys in gray are good gunners—for artillerymen," he concluded loftily.

"Aye," said Spec. He slowly wiped his spectacles. "Maybe you've got another way to figure this thing? Anything, matie?"

"We haven't time, Spec."

"I thought you'd say that." The thin boy opened the door of the wheelhouse and stepped out onto the deck. In a minute, he had dropped over the side to the soft marsh. Dick followed him to the edge of the deck and looked down on Spec. "Where do you think you're going, Spencer?" he asked.

Spec waved a hand toward the Nashville. "It's a nice day for a walk, mate." He started off across the soggy ground toward the grounded rebel ship.

Dick placed a hand on the cap rail of the Ogeechee Prince and dropped to the ground. In a minute, he was close beside his shipmate, heading toward the water's edge near the Nashville. The going was all right at first, for the ground was fairly firm, and they sank only a few inches into it. They could hear the faint whistling of a Dahlgren shell as it sped overhead to burst short of the Nashville. They could see the men still working on the stranded ship, lightening her. The guns of Fort McAllister still roared and flamed, but they might just as well have been throwing mud balls at the calm little Monitor anchored within fair range of the rebel columbiads.

"If they lighten her enough," said Dick, "the tide will help her off that mud bank, and with her power, she'll get upriver again."

Spec nodded. They passed through a low grove of straggling palmettos and were within fifty yards of the low shore. A man aboard the Nashville was watching them curiously. He turned and spoke to another man, and the two of them eyed the muddy figures walking slowly to the water's edge.

"She's quartering the channel," said Dick out of the side of his mouth. "How far from shore do you think she is?"

"A hundred yards?"

"More likely one hundred and fifty," said Dick.

"One hundred!"

"Hundred and fifty, you dumb block!"

They stood now at the very edge of the water. Then both of them turned and began deliberately to walk with measured strides across the soft ground, and neither of them dared look back, for they heard a man shout at them. "Hey, theah! Who are yuh? What're yuh doin' theah! Halt or we fire!"

They were halfway through the palmettos before they dared to glance back. Three men stood at the railing with poised rifles in their hands.

"Don't run," said Dick. "We'll lose count."

Spec rolled his eyes upward. "Who was going to run?"

"Me," said Dick dryly. He looked back again. A rifle spat flame and smoke, and the ball smacked against a palmetto. The marksman was too good to suit Dick. The men on the Nashville were now dumping everything they could get their hands on over the side. Smoke gushed from her stack, and her great paddle wheels were threshing in reverse.

"Fog coming in again," said Spec as they reached the far edge of the palmettos.

They were almost to the Ogeechee Prince when a

rushing sound came through the damp air, and something struck the marsh far behind them.

"Well, anyway, they didn't shoot that one at the *Montauk*," said Dick.

"Oh, happy thought!"

Suddenly they heard a flat cracking sound, and both of them turned involuntarily to see smoke issuing from the muzzle of the Brooke rifled gun on the foredeck of the *Nashville*. The calm surface of the Ogeechee was dotted with flotsam and jetsam from the ship. Cotton bales drifted and bobbed in the current. Her other guns opened up as she tried to cover herself with clouds of smoke, for she probably knew she could not hit that little *Monitor* at that range or hurt her if she did.

Then something struck the Ogeechee Prince and smashed through her rotting timbers. Spec staggered a little in his measured stride.

"You all right, mate?" asked Dick.

The boy turned a little, still counting his stride, and nodded.

Once again, the Ogeechee Prince was hit, and splinters flew through the air. Both boys fell to the ground. Dick looked back toward the *Nashville*. "Three hundred yards from here to the shoreline, Spec, and one hundred and fifty from shoreline to the *Nashville*. Any argument?"

Spec shook his head. His face seemed whiter than usual.

Dick got up. They were still quite a distance from the *Montauk*, at least two-thirds of the way from her to the *Nashville*, and the way was wide open. Nothing but mud. No trees, brush, nothing but flat ground, broken by winding little rivulets of clay-colored water. Easy going, thought Dick. Easy going if those boys in Fort McAllister didn't slip a 48-pounder solid shot or shell down his neck while he wasn't looking.

They passed the shattered hulk of the Ogeechee Prince. Fog and smoke swirled about them as they kept on. Dick was tiring, but Spec even more so, for the thin lad fell behind now and then and had to struggle to keep up.

"Six hundred?" said Dick.

"Aye, mate."

Minutes ticked past as they forded a morass of a stream and waded waist deep through mud and water to stagger out on the more open ground.

"Eight hundred and fifty," gasped Spec.

"Close," said Dick. "I have eight hundred and forty."

They hung on to each other. The air was filled with whirring noise as though huge invisible partridges had taken wing and were flying at full speed. But those were cast-iron partridges shot from columbiads, Dahlgren's, and a Brooke rifle.

There was a sudden crash behind them, and gas and smoke swirled about them as they hit the ground. Dick looked back over his shoulder. There was a smoking hole in the marsh right where they had been walking only moments ago. He felt a little sick, and his legs were like rubber.

"Nine hundred and eighty," said Spec in a strange, faraway voice.

They could plainly see the obstructions in the river, placed below Fort McAllister, and the few range markers that were still on the water. The *Montauk* looked like some strange mechanical monster squatting on the water, almost awash. Nothing human could be seen about her, and despite their peril, a great feeling of admiration for John Ericsson and his Yankee Notion came over Dick. As he watched, the *Montauk* turret would turn a little. The port stoppers would swing back mysteriously, and gun muzzles would be thrust out to peer like great myopic eyes at the distant upper works of the *Nashville*. One of them would roar angrily, driving rings of smoke ahead of the muzzle, followed by the flare of light and the sharp detonating crash of the shell. A wisp of bluish smoke in the air came far short of the grounded ship. Then the number-two gun would crash, and almost instantly, the guns would withdraw into their iron carapaces, like twin turtle heads, and the port stoppers would drop. At intervals, a solid shot from Fort McAllister would strike the turret without any effect. And in all that time, never a sight was seen of the men who served that phlegmatic iron ship so well. It was uncanny, unreal, and magnificently effective.

They reached the soggy shore in line with the anchored *Monitor.* Dick looked at Spec. "One thousand yards, mate?"

"Close enough. What do we do now, mate?"

Dick was startled. It had never occurred to him that there would be anything else to do once they had reached the shore opposite their ship. But Spec's words were coldly disconcerting. No one would be watching two mud-splattered, soaked boys in blue uniforms. The gunners would be reloading, and they could hardly see much more than a flat area of iron deck and the surface of the Ogeechee beyond that for a few yards, the whole wreathed in thick powder smoke from the discharge of the two guns. The conning tower, or pilothouse atop the turret, had small eye slits for vision, and they would be used only to look toward the distant *Nashville* to call downrange and training directions to the gunnery officer in the turret. The men below decks could see nothing at all beyond the interior of their ship.

"Drop!" snapped Spec.

They hit the ground as a shell from the fort crashed to their right, throwing up a mingled geyser of water and mud that covered the two boys like a thick, cold blanket. A solid shot glanced from the turret of the *Montauk,* shot upward and then downward to hit the water fifty feet from shore. Dick closed his eyes. He had an incredibly naked feeling and wanted to burrow deep into that chilling mud. But they had to reach that ship!

"We'll have to swim," said Dick quietly.

Spec stared at Dick through splattered glasses. "Not me, mate," he said faintly. "You go on. Leave me here, Dick."

Dick crept closer to his friend. "You hit, Spec?"

The boy nodded. "Splinter from the Ogeechee Prince," he said. He shivered. "My right side."

Dick pulled up Spec's blouse and winced at what he saw. A jagged fragment of half-rotten wood from the wreck had been driven into Spec's side, and the swollen flesh had an angry, purplish-red look about it. The splinter had to come out. Dick looked toward the *Montauk*, but there was no chance of getting help.

"Go on without me, Dick," said Spec faintly.

"Not on your life, mate!"

The boy smiled a little. "It's not that serious, Dick."

Dick looked out toward the *Montauk* again. It wasn't too far for a fair swimmer, but he was tired and cold, and trying to tow along a wounded shipmate might make the distance far too much. He looked down the shoreline. There was some driftwood there, enough to make some sort of raft.

Spec groaned in agony. Dick took his courage in his hands. He gripped the splinter, set his teeth, and yanked it out. "Ahhh!" gasped Spec. He fainted dead away. There was no time to waste. Dick ran to the driftwood and tore his trousers off to use for lashings. The cannonading never ceased as he worked.

CHAPTER FOURTEEN

Dick waded along the shore, pulling his raft behind him. He reached the unconscious Spec and rolled him onto the crude little craft. It sank beneath his weight. Dick waded out into the cold waters, pulling the raft by a twisted painter formed from part of a trouser leg. His feet stuck in the bottom, and he pulled them free and began to swim toward the *Montauk*. There had been no firing for some minutes now, for it took about seven minutes' time to reload the big turret guns.

But twelve guns of Fort McAllister's twenty-four could bear on the *Monitor*, and the busy gunners were slamming everything they had at the *Montauk*, which didn't hurt her a bit. The waters of the Ogeechee were thrashed into spume and spray by the firing, and the shells landed between the *Montauk* and the northern shore of the river. In that channel of peril swam Dick Morgan, towing his shipmate. Every so often, they were deluged by the clay-colored water thrown up by shot and shell. The tiny raft bobbed perilously, and water washed at times across Spec's thin, pale face. Dick Morgan wondered even at that time what magic power the boy possessed to keep those spectacles on his nose and ears.

Dick's head sank under the water several times, but always he came up, and he knew now that if he hadn't the slight buoyancy of the raft to hold him up as well as Spec, he wouldn't have a chance to reach his ship.

When, incredibly, he was right beside the low deck of the ship, he hung on, reaching for a pad eye set into the deck and gripped it. He turned and grasped hold of Spec with his free hand and managed to get a leg up onto the deck. As he rolled over flat onto the deck and began to haul Spec aboard, the big 15-inch Dahlgren crashed. The deck shuddered beneath Dick, and he felt as though every rib had been broken. Stinking smoke blew back about him. He rolled Spec over and looked desperately toward the conning tower atop the smoke-shrouded turret.

He heard a grating noise as the port stoppers went down after the second gun fired. There was another grating sound. The deck hatch was being opened, and a seaman, stripped to the waist, came across the deck toward Dick. Dick looked up and yelled. The figure looked vague and unreal through the smoke as it came toward him. Its face was set and pale. Fear that Dick had never known during his adventures after falling overboard from the cutter overwhelmed him. It was the face of his dead brother, Ben, he saw, and he fainted.

———

THE SMELLING SALTS brought Dick around, and he opened his eyes to see a familiar sight, the underdeck structure of a monitor, while the old mingled odors of grease, oil, coal smoke, food, and gun smoke followed the sharp odor of the smelling salts in his nostrils. He looked up into the face of the ship's surgeon. "How is Spec, sir?" he asked.

"He'll be all right, Morgan. How do you feel?"

"All right, sir. It was seeing the ghost of my brother that frightened me."

The surgeon stared at him. "Ghost? What do you mean?"

Dick quickly explained.

The surgeon smiled. "You'll be happy to know that the cutter was slightly damaged when the torpedo blew up. The torpedo hit the rebel picket boat. Our cutter got back safely enough. Your brother was only creased by a Minie ball. Neilson was badly wounded, but he'll recover. We onboard thought that you and your shipmate Simpson had been drowned or captured. Your brother was in the turret when you were seen towing Simpson to the side of the ship. Captain Worden stopped firing and gave your brother permission to get you."

The *Montauk* shook with the concussion of one of her guns. Dick sat up. "How long have I been unconscious, sir?"

"Just a few minutes."

"Have we hit the *Nashville* yet?"

"No, and it doesn't seem likely."

The second gun thundered.

Dick got out of the sickbay bunk. "I've got information for Captain Worden," he said.

"You stay here, young man!"

"Mutiny, sir, for I'm going."

"You are not! I'll call the master-at-arms!"

"I happen to know almost the exact range to the yard of the Nashville, sir."

"In that case, why are you standing there?"

Dick saw Spec lying in a bunk, and the boy's eyes were open. "Thanks, mate," he said.

Dick passed a hand across Spec's brow. "I'm going to give the captain our information."

"I wish I could see the results. Buried down here, I won't know anything."

The surgeon smiled. "You'll know soon enough, Simpson."

Dick was allowed to enter the turret as the guns were being reloaded, and they all cheered him. Ben Morgan, Jonas Barklew, Hank Bascomb, Jimmy Fox, Mike Reilly, Lobscouse, Sanders, Sutter, Duff, and all the others.

He stood in front of Captain Worden and saluted him. Worden smiled and gripped Dick's shoulder. "That was a brave thing you did, Morgan."

Dick swiftly gave his report about the range to the *Nashville*.

The guns had been reloaded, and the gunners awaited the word to fire as the shells from Fort McAllister smashed against the iron skin of the *Montauk* or geysered the waters of the Ogeechee.

"One hundred yards from the *Nashville* to the shore, you say?" said Worden thoughtfully.

"Yes, sir. Then about nine hundred yards across land to the shoreline opposite the *Montauk*. I figured about two hundred to the *Montauk* from the shoreline, sir."

"Twelve hundred yards approximately. We'll try it, Morgan." Worden spoke into the voice tube. "Mister Wallace," he said crisply, "we are firing short, probably due to the refraction of light from the smoke and fog. Young Morgan here paced off the distance and estimates it at twelve hundred yards. A long shot for the 11-inch gun, but fine for the 15-inch. Load with shell, as usual, cut with seven-second fuse, and try a ranging shot."

Worden peered through an eye slit.

"Begging the captain's pardon, sir," said Dick, "but I'd like to serve on my gun, Captain Worden."

"No," said Worden.

Dick flushed.

The officer turned. "You stand right beside me at an eye slit, young man, and see the results of your fine work!"

Dick Morgan stood there as the big gun blasted flame

and smoke, and in seconds a 150-pounder shell shattered neatly amidst the upper deck works of the Nashville.

"On target," said Worden. He picked up the voice tube. "Mister Wallace, you're right on top of her now, sir. Load with shell, both guns, same range, seven-second fuses, and keep on firing until I order you to cease firing."

As a thick wraith of fog crept across the broad waters of the Ogeechee, a shell set the Nashville aflame. Through the drifting fog and smoke, the flames could be seen leaping and dancing.

"Fire at intervals through the fog, Mister Wallace," commanded Captain Worden.

The big guns thudded steadily at about ten-minute intervals, and although the *Nashville* herself could not be seen, the men on the *Montauk* saw the flames and smoke of her destruction through smoke and fog.

When the fog lifted, the guns fired more accurately, round after round, until suddenly there was a great gush of flame, gas, and smoke, followed by a shattering explosion. Debris was hurtled upward in a great fan shape.

Captain Worden nodded in satisfaction. He took up the turret voice tube. "You may cease firing, Mister Wallace. That sound was the death explosion of the *Nashville*. Secure your guns, sir." He picked up another tube that led to the engine room and ordered the engines readied. The anchor was heaved up, and as the *Montauk* got underway, Fort McAllister let go with the twelve great guns that bore on her, with no effect whatsoever, for this time, they did not even touch the *Monitor*.

Dick was all smiles as he looked through a rear eye slit toward smoking Fort McAllister. He was still eying the now-distant scene when a dull, thudding noise came from beneath the *Montauk,* and she seemed to rise a little and then settle.

Captain Worden snatched up the engine room voice tube. "What was that?" he demanded. He listened, and a frown came over his bearded and blackened face. "Is the damage serious? No? Well, we'll beach her just the same. We'll be safe enough. We're almost out of the river mouth, and we Yankees own Ossabaw Sound these days."

"What happened, sir?" asked the quartermaster at the wheel.

Worden shrugged. "We hit one of their infernal torpedoes. They couldn't hit us with most of their shots, and the few that did hit us didn't hurt us. Now we run onto one of their torpedoes. Luckily, it did not happen back there, or it might have meant the death of the *Montauk* rather than the *Nashville,* Quartermaster. Fortunes of war! It is our day rather than theirs."

Dick smiled. "It means that the *Montauk* and the other monitors are needed to finish the war for the Union, sir."

The officer turned quickly and looked intently at Dick. "That's what I was thinking, Morgan. A foresight, perhaps? Such things happen, you know."

Dick nodded. "Yes, sir. It is a foresight, and I know I am right." He glanced through an after-eye slit and saw the smoke-stained and tattered Stars and Stripes fluttering in the fresh morning breeze as though agreeing with them.

———

ON A BRIGHT DAY IN 1898, the battleship *U.S.S. Iowa* steamed slowly out of the Brooklyn Navy Yard bound for Cuban waters. Commander Richard Morgan, Executive Officer of the Iowa, stood on her bridge, but he wasn't looking forward on the big one-year-old battleship to which he had been assigned after thirty-seven years' service in the United States Navy. His eyes were set on a rather odd-looking craft moored beside a little-used pier in the yard. She looked utterly out of place beside the 11,000-ton fighting ship that was slowly passing her, making her wallow in the waves.

A young ensign, fresh from the United States Naval Academy at Annapolis, eyed the strange-looking little craft. "What is that thing, sir?" he asked Commander Morgan. "A floating water tank?"

"No, Mister Downey. You can see she is armed."

The young officer smiled. "Those are two gun muzzles sticking out of that water tank?"

Dick Morgan nodded. "Seems as though they are getting ready to commission her again."

"May I ask for what, sir?"

"Harbor defense perhaps, in case the Spaniards take it into their heads to raid New York harbor."

"If we let them get this far, that thing won't stop them. It looks like a Civil War relic."

"It is, Downey. It's a monitor."

The young officer shook his head. "Does the commander mean that the United States Navy actually sent men to sea in a thing like that?"

Dick Morgan was still looking at the bobbing little ship, turning his head farther and farther aft to keep her in view. "She was pretty small even in those days, Downey, as compared to ships like the Iowa and her 11,346-ton displacement."

"As compared to a monitor's 776 tons," said a dry, precise voice.

Dick glanced over his shoulder and saw the thin face of Lieutenant Commander Spencer Simpson, the Second, Navigating Officer of the *Iowa*. "The comparison of length and beam might be rather interesting too, Mister Downey. The Iowa is 360 feet long and has a beam of 72 feet."

"A monitor was 172 feet long and had a beam of 41 feet," echoed Lieutenant Commander Simpson.

"She had two guns, one 11-inch Dahlgren and one 15-inch Dahlgren," said Dick.

"As compared to the armament of the *Iowa*," said

Spencer Simpson. "Four 12-inch, eight 8-inch, and ten 4-inch guns."

"But those beat-up Dahlgren's were muzzle-loaders using black powder," said Downey. "I often wonder how they ever did any damage with them."

Dick smiled. "Oh, they did all right, didn't they, Mister Simpson?"

"Some," admitted Mister Simpson.

Dick kept looking at the little fighting ship. After the *Montauk* had fought at the Ogeechee and had destroyed the *Nashville*, she had been ordered to Charleston, South Carolina, and had participated in Du Pont's attack in April of 1863, being struck fourteen times with little material damage to herself. From July 18 to September 8, 1863, she had fought the batteries of Forts Sumter, Moultrie, Wagner, and Gregg, and the batteries on Morris and Sullivan's Islands a total of fifteen times, more than any of the other monitors engaged, and had been struck 154 times, mostly by solid shot from 10-inch guns, sustaining only superficial damage.

Spec Simpson adjusted his glasses. "So they're recommissioning her, Dick."

Dick nodded. "After thirty-six years' service, they still need her. John Ericsson would be proud of that, Spec."

"Both of you seem to know what ship she is," said Downey. "What's her name, Commander Morgan?"

Dick smiled a little. "The U.S.S. *Montauk*, Mr. Downey."

Spec Simpson removed his pince-nez glasses and hastily blew on them before wiping them. His eyes were suspiciously bright. "Well," he said briskly, "We're bound for Cuban waters, gentlemen! We'll join Admiral Sampson's North Atlantic Squadron there. The *Indiana, New York, Oregon, Brooklyn, and Texas.* Blockading duty again, eh, Dick?"

Dick nodded. "After all these years."

"You suppose there will be any action, sir?" asked the young ensign.

"Yes," said Dick. He looked forward across the great turret just below the bridge. "There *will* be action, Mr. Downey."

"I hope so, sir!"

Spec Simpson smiled. "There will be, Mr. Downey. When Commander Morgan talks and looks like that, you can be sure there will be action. He has had these foresights before."

Dick Morgan was right again, for Admiral Sampson's squadron had a date with destiny off a place called Santiago de Cuba. There the United States ships would meet and defeat the Spanish *Infanta Maria Teresa, Vizcaya, Cristobal Colon, Almirante Oquendo,* the *Furor,* and the *Pluton,* destroying every one of them, taking 1,300 prisoners and killing 600 of the enemy, while the United States would not lose one ship, and only suffer casualties of one killed and one wounded. One of the little ships assigned to Sampson's squadron was the little torpedo boat, *Ericsson.*

The *Montauk* was out of sight now, and the Iowa moved majestically toward the open sea. Spec Simpson polished his glasses again. "Our course will take us clear to Cape Hatteras, Dick," he said.

"Cape Hatteras, sir?" said Ensign Downey. "Isn't that where the original *Monitor* went down?"

"Yes," said Spec Simpson. He looked quickly at Dick.

Commander Dick Morgan, U.S.N., raised his head. "Give me an approximate position of the wreck, Spec. I want the colors dipped when we pass over the *Tin Can on a Shingle.*"

AUTHOR'S NOTE

Dick Morgan, his brother, Ben, Silas Jones, Spencer "Spec" Simpson, the Second, Jonas Barklew, Hank Bascomb, Jimmy Fox, Mike Reilly, Gunner Sanders, Neilson, Sutter, Duff, Norris, and Ensign Downey are all fictional characters in this story. The ships mentioned by name are all actual vessels that participated in the War Between the States, with the exceptions of the *Commodore Worthington* and the *Ogeechee Prince*. The scene in which the U.S.S. *Iowa* passes the U.S.S. *Montauk* is fictional, as are, of course, the presence of Dick Morgan, Spencer Simpson, and Ensign Downey aboard the *Iowa*. It is a historical fact that some of the original Ericsson monitors were still in service in 1898.

The story closely follows the actual historical chronology and events. Certain literary license has been taken in the interests of a better story, but the basic tale of the gallant little *Monitor* hardly needed any embellishments.

The author, at one time, during the latter part of World War Two, was stationed at Hampton Roads Port of Embarkation and crossed the James River many times in the area where the historic battle between the *Monitor* and *Merrimac* took place. The thought came to him that although he had read many accounts of that famous battle, he had never been able to find much material on the actual experiences of the men aboard the *Monitor*. A few years ago, a Marine skin diver claimed to have walked on the deck of the sunken *Monitor* off Cape Hatteras, and this event triggered the eventual writing of POWDER BOY OF THE *Monitor*.

BIBLIOGRAPHY

Battles and Leaders of the Civil War (Century 1887).

Thomas Yoseloff Reprint Edition, 1957. Volumes 1, 2, and 4.

Photographic History of the Civil War, 1910.

Thomas Yoseloff Reprint Edition, 1957. Volumes 1, 3, 5, 6, and 8.

The United States Navy (From the Revolution to Date).

P. F. Collier & Son, 1917. A Sailor's Treasury, Frank Shay and Edward A. Wilson.

W. W. Norton & Company, Inc., 1951.

Official Records of the Union and Confederate Navies in the War of the Rebellion.

Tin Can on a Shingle, William Chapman White, and Ruth White. E. P. Dutton & Co., Inc., 1957.

Mr. Lincoln's Navy, Richard S. West, Jr. Longmans, Green & Co. Inc., 1957.

Blockade, Robert Carse. Rinehart & Company, Inc., 1958.

The Union Reader, edited by Richard B. Harwell.

Longmans, Green & Co., Inc., 1958.

The American Navy. George M. Hill Company, 1898.

BIBLIOGRAPHY

TAKE A LOOK AT ACTION FRONT! AND THE GRAY SEA RAIDERS:

Two Full-Length Historical Novels of the American Civil War

Gordon D. Shirreffs, master of the Western action novel, turns his keen wit and skill toward two distinctly captivating tales of the American Civil War, told through the eyes of the young men who were duty bound to serve their country.

In *Action Front!*: At Gettysburg, on the hot and heavy first day of battle, Battery B—known as "Crispin's Bulldogs"—faces not only the fierce rebel lines but disastrous panic in a huge wheel horse on one of its own gun teams.

When Confederate metal finds its target, three figures in ill-fitting blue step from the war-shocked air to help serve the stricken gun. One underage, the second with a limp, and the third a half-pint, Ben Buell, Seth Pomeroy, and Zack Pascoe are the only members of their scattered company of Pennsylvania Volunteer Militia to answer at last the thrilling, terrible command of "Action front!" Allowed to remain with the gruff and grateful Bulldogs, little Zack becomes an assistant cook, Seth a gunnery corporal, and Ben, reunited with the horse that had been his pet back on the family farm, is made a wheel team driver.

In *The Gray Sea Raiders*, Shirreffs tells the tales of the daring men of the Confederate States Navy who were determined to harass, burn, or capture ships of the opposing Northern fleet as they plied the waterways of the Atlantic.

Overcoming numerous obstacles, including foul disease, Union retaliation, and ammunition problems, the crew of the vessel, *Florida* carried out its orders with great success and made young Clint Wallace a hero among his peers.

"Written by the hand of a master!" —*The New York Times*

ABOUT THE AUTHOR

Gordon D. Shirreffs published more than 80 western novels, 20 of them juvenile books, and John Wayne bought his book title, Rio Bravo, during the 1950s for a motion picture, which Shirreffs said constituted *"the most money I ever earned for two words."* Four of his novels were adapted to motion pictures, and he wrote a Playhouse 90 and the Boots and Saddles TV series pilot in 1957.

A former pulp magazine writer, he survived the transition to western novels without undue trauma, earning the admiration of his peers along the way. The novelist saw life a bit cynically from the edge of his funny bone and described himself as looking like a slightly parboiled owl. Despite his multifarious quips, he was dead serious about the writing profession.

Gordon D. Shirreffs was the 1995 recipient of the Owen Wister Award, given by the Western Writers of America for "a living individual who has made an outstanding contribution to the American West."

He passed in 1996.